W9-AAB-240

Anthologies

AN ENCHANTED SEASON
(with Maggie Shayne, Erin McCarthy, and Jean Johnson)

THE MAGICAL CHRISTMAS CAT
(with Lora Leigh, Erin McCarthy, and Linda Winstead Jones)

MUST LOVE HELLHOUNDS
(with Charlaine Harris, Ilona Andrews, and Meljean Brook)

BURNING UP
(with Angela Knight, Virginia Kantra, and Meljean Brook)

ANGELS OF DARKNESS
(with Ilona Andrews, Meljean Brook, and Sharon Shinn)

ANGELS' FLIGHT

WILD INVITATION

NIGHT SHIFT
(with Ilona Andrews, Lisa Shearin, and Milla Vane)

WILD EMBRACE

Specials

ANGELS' PAWN

ANGELS' DANCE

TEXTURE OF INTIMACY

DECLARATION OF COURTSHIP

WHISPER OF SIN

SECRETS AT MIDNIGHT

Alpha Night

A PSY-CHANGELING TRINITY NOVEL

NALINI SINGH

JOVE
New York

A JOVE BOOK
Published by Berkley
An imprint of Penguin Random House LLC
penguinrandomhouse.com

ISBN: 9781984803641

Berkley hardcover edition / June 2020
Jove mass-market edition / January 2021

Printed in the United States of America
1   3   5   7   9   10   8   6   4   2

Cover design by Rita Frangie

For Kay

Alpha Night

Graveyard of Secrets

THE YEAR IS 2083, and after one hundred years of an endless emotionless night, the Psy have emerged into a painful dawn. Love and elation, hate and envy, joy and anguish, sorrow and amusement, all this and more, the psychic race can now feel without fear of a brainwipe that leaves them hollow automatons.

Foreseers, telekinetics, empaths, telepaths, psychometrics, all are free to exist.

But one hundred years leaves a scar.

For some, life is an eternal midnight of the soul.

The dawnlight cuts, shattered glass in the eyes.

These are the lost, the unknown, the hidden. For one hundred years is also time enough to conceal truths upon truths, heap lies upon lies . . . and erase those who once shone luminous as stars.

The PsyNet is a graveyard of secrets.

Chapter 1

The subject displays obsessive tendencies that can be utilized to your advantage. If you manage to turn his loyalty toward you, he will never betray you.

—Intake report: Psych, on subject Ethan Night, age six, for Councilor Ming LeBon (2061)

SELENKA BLAMED THE bears.

If Valentin hadn't gone and mated Silver Mercant, the rest of them wouldn't be standing around at this giant target of a symposium. It might as well be flashing the words "Here We Are! Come Attack Us!"

As if he'd felt her burning gaze, the bear changeling alpha turned from where he was talking to one of his senior people and waved, accompanying it with a big grin. She glared at him, in no mood for bear charm.

"You don't like bears?" asked a clear male voice, his Russian unaccented and his words toneless.

Selenka had sensed his approach—she wasn't alpha of the most powerful wolf pack in Russia because people could sneak up on her. Not that she had to worry much about sneaking when it came to the other major pack in the area. Bears could sneak about as well as ten-thousand-pound elephants.

This man, however, he was *quiet*. He also smelled like a crisp winter wind around a flame so hot it was blue, with none of that cold metallic smell changelings had learned to look out for among Psy. Those of the psychic race who had that smell were so far gone into the emotionless protocol they called Silence that there was usually no coming back.

"Yesterday, I had to bail three normally well-behaved

wolves out of jail," she said without looking at the male who stood next to her, his height maybe an inch above her five eleven. "Do you know why?"

"Bears?"

"Bears." A grim confirmation. "*Nice* bears who talked my wolves into going for a 'friendly' drink. So friendly that half the bar ended up in a brawl." The bears had found it hilarious, had still been grinning when she bailed out her three sheepish wolves.

Selenka did *not* find it amusing.

Her wolves were disciplined predators; they didn't go around starting bar brawls. Especially not bar brawls where one of them ended up stinking of raspberry daiquiri, his blond hair pink as a result of the enormous cocktail that had been poured over him. The three would be working off the bar's repair bill into next year.

Her wolves weren't disciplined simply because she was a hard-ass; it had to do with the different temperaments of their animals. Bears could be brutal hunters, but generally, they were laid-back unless provoked. You could poke a changeling bear multiple times before it rumbled a growl and swiped out with a paw.

Wolves could be pushed to violence far faster. A bear might laugh off an insult that would send a wolf into cold anger. Because bears took not much seriously, while many wolves had an innate and deadly intensity.

Each had pros and cons. The laid-back ursine nature could lead to laziness and had done so in a previous alpha— the reason Selenka's pack had been able to take over a chunk of bear territory. But her wolves' primal instincts could lead to rash actions and bloodshed.

Discipline was key to a strong wolf pack.

"But the relationship must be cordial," the stranger said, with no alteration in his flat tone, and yet his voice, it was hauntingly beautiful in its clarity and pitch. "If the two groups are drinking together?"

"'Cordial' isn't quite how I'd put it." The BlackEdge wolves and the StoneWater bears had a teeth-gritted truce. Mostly because they were each as dangerous as the other. After a few skirmishes, the two groups had grudgingly come to the same conclusion: a war would decimate them both and leave Moscow and its surrounds open for takeover by another changeling pack.

These days, they satisfied themselves by growling or glaring at each other over the border—or blowing kisses across rooms. That last was nearly always a bear move. Selenka knew Valentin's bears did it to get a rise out of her wolves—which was why she'd told her wolves to respond with fluttered lashes and obviously fake smiles.

Selenka wasn't proud of it, but the damn bears could drive a saint to murder. And wolf and bear were both predators. It was either play this game of mutual annoyance, or tear each other to pieces. Right now, however, Valentin's bears were a peripheral concern at best. She was far more interested in the cool, dangerous presence next to her.

Had to be an Arrow.

No one else would be suicidal enough to walk up to a wolf alpha who was so clearly in a bad mood.

She shifted on her heel to face him and her gaze slammed into eyes of the palest brown she had ever seen. The color was beyond hazel, beyond topaz, and into a crystalline purity that was the faintest wash of color.

Only the jet black of his pupils broke the startling paleness.

The effect was even more striking against the honey brown of his skin. Chiseled cheekbones pushed against that skin, and his hair was a shaggy black, the same shade as the scruff that darkened his jaw. His eyes had the faintest upward tilt. It was impossible to pinpoint his ethnicity. Not surprising, since the Psy apparently had a way of mixing and mingling genes to increase the chances of powerful psychic offspring.

To the psychic race that shared the world with humans and changelings, looks were secondary to psychic power, but this Arrow was a hell of a good-looking man by any estimation. Add in the sense of lethal strength that clung to him, and, no, Selenka wouldn't kick him out of her bed. The scruff, too, was interesting. Arrows tended to be clean-shaven as a rule. But what had both parts of her—wolf and woman—giving him a second look was the unwavering focus with which he watched her.

Rare non-changelings *could* hold an alpha changeling's gaze, but usually only for a second or two. They'd start to sweat at that point, their hearts pounding as their primal core recognized the threat in front of them. The only ones who could maintain the contact full stop were alphas in their own right, even if humans or the Psy didn't think in terms of changeling hierarchy.

This man wasn't an alpha.

The knowledge was pure instinct, born of her wolf.

He wore the black combat uniform of an Arrow, with its high collar and pants cuffed into boots, and he gave off an effect similar to those deadly telekinetics, telepaths, and assorted other Psy who—according to Selenka's intel—had once been assassins for the now-defunct Psy Council. He even had a gleaming black gauntlet clipped over his left forearm, which her tech specialist had informed her was a new form of field-suitable mobile comm the Arrows were trialing.

Yet this man didn't come across the same way as other members of the squad.

He also continued to hold her gaze with zero appearance of discomfort. Her wolf could've read that as a challenge, but instead, dark red embers glowed to life in her belly. It had been too long since she'd shared intimate skin privileges with anyone; why not an Arrow dangerous and pretty . . . and not quite as he should be.

Selenka narrowed her eyes—just because he made her blood heat didn't mean she'd taken leave of her senses. Her grandparents hadn't raised an *idiotka*. "What are you?" The blunt question would've earned her a disappointed look from her polite and gentle and loving babushka, but the Arrow showed no reaction at all.

"A Gradient 7.9 Tk," he said in that clear voice that was music to her changeling hearing. Even toneless, it sang and made things inside her shiver in awareness.

"A telekinetic?" Drinking in the sound without being a slave to it, Selenka folded her arms and set her feet apart. "There's something else there—it's making my wolf's fur stand up." An odd resonance she couldn't explain. But it was nothing that repelled. No, there was nothing at all disturbing about the Arrow with the pale eyes—it was her strong physical response that was peculiar. Then again, her body was starved and he was pretty and dangerous with a voice straight out of a certain alpha's fantasies.

No wonder her wolf wanted to take a bite out of him.

The Arrow didn't respond to her challenge with aggression or cold retreat. "I am permanently damaged in ways that affect my psychic balance," he said. "You're likely sensing that—I haven't previously been in close contact with changelings, so I don't know if that is part of your natural skill set."

Selenka raised an eyebrow, her fascination with him unabated. Ivy Jane Zen, president of the Empathic Collective, had exhaustively briefed each and every person involved with the symposium, and one thing she'd made clear was that they'd be coming into contact with Es at all stages of post-Silence recovery.

"Silence," the small and curvy and fiercely protective woman had said, "was about eliminating emotion from our race. That made empaths a liability—but the PsyNet can't survive without Es in the mix. As a result, Designation E was erased from the books and our minds suffocated, our abilities crushed under shielding so brutal that scars are inevitable."

No one, however, had warned Selenka about an Arrow who spoke about psychic damage as if it were a simple scratch—even when that damage was so profound that it registered on changeling senses. Unless it wasn't about damage at all. More likely, he was giving her a pat answer in order to conceal some secret Arrow ability.

People who belonged to clandestine black ops squads didn't usually go around—as her dedushka would put it—spilling water out of their buckets. Selenka had a sneaking suspicion her grandfather had made up that proverb, but since he'd infected the whole pack with it, it was now set in cement.

As for the Arrow, well, alpha wolves didn't spill water out of their buckets, either.

Even as she parted her lips to reply, his attention jerked to over her head. His pupils flared, a sea of darkness that eclipsed the translucent brown.

"Close your eyes," he said, the words clipped and cold.

Selenka didn't take orders from anyone, including potential playmates.

But he slammed into her before she could respond, arms locking tight around her body. He had one hand on the back of her head, shoving her face into the hard muscle of his shoulder, the other clamped around her waist.

Claws slicing out as a snarl filled her chest, she went to thrust the sharp points into his gut . . . and that was when she heard the quiet.

Pristine.

Piercing.

Painful.

No murmur from the more than three hundred people scattered through the massive symposium hall. No faint echoes of comm calls taken or sent. No click of heels or boots on the floor. Blood chilling, she pricked the Arrow with her claws instead of eviscerating him. "Let go unless you want immediate abdominal surgery." It came out a growl.

Unlocking from around her, he took a step backward, palms held up.

As if that meant anything. You could break every bone in a Psy body and they could still take you out with their mental abilities.

Especially when that Psy was an Arrow.

The hairs on her nape prickling, she continued to monitor him with her peripheral vision as she scanned as much of the hall as she could. *Bozhe moi!* Everyone was down. *Everyone.* She couldn't see Valentin or Silver, so they must've left the hall before whatever it was that had happened, but two of her lieutenants as well as two of Valentin's were on the floor, along with every single Arrow in her line of sight.

"It was the fastest way to neutralize the threat."

She snapped her gaze back to the *very* dangerous man who spoke without inflection or emotion—and had a voice that continued to purr against her ears. "What threat?" It came out harsh, but her wolf wasn't ready to go for blood, its instincts tempered by an unknown *something* nagging at her.

"The E in the green velvet jacket." He nodded toward the center of the room.

Selenka could see nothing unusual about the woman from this distance. "Stay ahead of me," she said. "No sudden movements."

Making no effort to use his telekinetic powers against Selenka, he walked with deadly grace to where the small brunette lay on her front. Hunkering down beside her after a glance at Selenka, he motioned that he'd like to turn the brunette woman over.

Selenka flexed her hands, claws still out. "Slow and easy."

The Arrow performed the action with an ease that spoke of honed strength, a stealthy hunter who didn't need to flash his power.

The empath's jacket was unbuttoned. It fell open to reveal a device Selenka recognized at once as a gas bomb. That Selenka was still standing meant the Arrow had taken down the woman before she could activate the bomb. "She's breathing." A soft rise and fall of her chest.

"She—and the others—are just unconscious," the Arrow said. "A few sore heads and the odd broken bone if they fell wrong, but it's better than death." Not an explanation but a statement.

Selenka had to agree. Chance the gas was harmless was around the same as a bear being on good behavior for more than ten minutes: a big fat zero. "Good call." Slicing her claws back into her body, she held out a hand before recalling that, Es aside, many of the psychic race tended to eschew contact.

A warm, rough hand slid against hers.

The contact shocked, an electric jolt straight to her core.

There you are, whispered a primal part of her psyche.

She was trying to breathe past the rush of noise in her brain when she caught motion in her peripheral vision. It could've been an innocent walking back into the hall, but her wolf smelled the faintest hint of old sweat—acrid and bitter, *afraid*. She reacted without thought, slamming her body into the Arrow's and taking him to the ground.

The projectile bullet that would've slammed into him scraped across her upper back. Hissing out a breath as the bullet penetrated the soft blue leather of her favorite jacket as well as the fine cotton of her T-shirt to dig a furrow in her skin, before smashing into the wall to their left, she went to twist to go for the shooter.

But the Arrow held out a hand and said, "Eyes," in that cold and uninflected tone.

She shut them this time.

She still "saw" the flash, a dazzling glow beneath her eyelids, a luminous beauty.

When she lifted her lashes, it was to tiny lights dancing in front of her. The assailant was down. Selenka recognized the brown-skinned woman from earlier that morning. Another E.

They were in trouble.

Chapter 2

ETHAN LOOKED UP at the fine jawline of the woman who
had her body on his, her pink-and-purple-streaked black
braid hanging over one shoulder, and thought, *This wasn't in
the plan.* He'd been meant to save everyone from the attack,
gain her trust, and then . . .

And then . . .

Despite the beliefs of his "handler," Ethan hadn't decided
on his next action. He'd agreed to the plan not because of any
political leanings, but because he'd wanted to see if the idea
of being a traitor would ignite anything in him. It hadn't. The
world had remained a distant blur, his body and mind disconnected from every other living being around him.

Another dead end . . . until his target had put her body in
the line of fire to *protect him.* Too well trained not to react
with instinctive speed, he'd locked his arms around her as
they fell, and the smell of burned flesh was yet in his nose
when she twisted out of his hold with changeling strength
and bounded toward the empath who'd aimed at Ethan.

That was when he saw the seared red of Selenka's back,
the flesh raw and bleeding.

No more gray, the world hemorrhaging with color and noise, his pulse in his throat.

Rising on that violent rush, he ran after her. He couldn't catch her. She was a wolf alpha and not even an Arrow could match a powerful wolf at full lope. But she wasn't going far and he reached the second assailant only a moment or two behind her.

This second attack wasn't meant to take place. Either someone had screwed up, or his handler didn't trust Ethan and had decided on a backup option that involved removing him from the chessboard. He was right not to trust Ethan, but that the gambit had harmed the wolf who'd saved Ethan's life? *Unacceptable*.

Selenka disarmed the assailant. "How long does the unconsciousness last?"

"I used less power this time, so unless she hit her head, she'll come around with everyone else—about three more minutes." It was a guess; while *everyone* went down when he used his ability, recovery time fluctuated. A few would be groggy ten minutes in, while others would be up within the next two.

"Can't see an obvious head wound," Selenka said after a careful look. "Good, that—"

A sound at the doors before the big bear alpha ran in. Valentin Nikolaev's dark eyes went directly to Ethan, the only unknown in this situation. But Selenka immediately stood, putting herself in front of Ethan. "He's not the threat."

Ethan didn't hear the deep murmur of the other alpha's response. He was staring at the back of Selenka's head, and lower, to her wound. He'd been hurt far worse by his Arrow trainers and by Ming LeBon himself. But Selenka was bleeding because she'd put herself in the line of fire for *him*.

Breath tight in his lungs and skin hot, he broke away to head for the nearest first-aid kit. There were multiple in the hall because a number of the newly trained Es had a tendency to overload and collapse. It took him only a short time to grab it, but several more people had entered the hall by the time he got back to Selenka.

"Your back," he said, the red of her blood pulsing in his vision.

She shot him an irritated look but shrugged off her ruined jacket, then stripped off her T-shirt. The purple-edged black sports bra she wore underneath was damaged as a result of the strike but had enough structural integrity left to hold against the cool white of her skin. Opening the first-aid kit while she continued to talk to Valentin Nikolaev and Silver Mercant, he took out the disinfectant spray. "This will sting."

A curt nod was her only response.

Acknowledgment or not, she hissed out a breath while shooting him a golden-eyed look when he began to spray on the disinfectant. Those eyes had been dark brown when they'd first spoken.

He held the wolf's snarling gaze, caught by the primal brilliance—he'd never been near anyone this vividly alive. However, he wasn't about to back down. She was his priority. "I did warn you."

Another instant of contact that shimmered with untamed power before she returned to her discussion with the others. He ignored that discussion, focused on the damage done to her. A heavy, dark sensation gripped his lungs with stone hands. An emotional reaction? Ethan didn't know; he had no barometer against which to judge his response.

Silence may have fallen, his race free to feel, but none of it'd had any impact on the cold gray place in which he lived. Until today.

Ethan did not find Selenka's wound in any way permissible.

She was bleeding because she'd put her body between Ethan and danger.

His brain kept repeating that in a dazed loop, while his blood pounded in his ears. Even when his trainers had beaten him as a child, he hadn't felt this thundering avalanche inside his head. He'd already been living in the cold place by then, the place from which he saw the world without being a part of it.

He used to analyze the strength of their blows, calculate how far they'd go, then strategize his response. Every so often, he'd managed to hurt them back enough that they'd become even more vicious. Yet he hadn't stopped, the distant rationality in him warning that to surrender was to die in a way that went beyond the body.

His cool calculation should've equaled perfect scores on the Silence tests, but his results had always come back with the words PATHOLOGICALLY DETACHED stamped on them. He'd noted the paradoxical nature of such a conclusion in a race determined to condition emotion out of themselves, then continued on existing in the icy grayness that permitted him to be a functional individual—and a lethal Arrow.

Ming LeBon certainly hadn't cared about the results of the psych evaluations.

The former Psy Councilor then in charge of the squad had cared only that Ethan do as he was told, kill when he was told to kill, wound when he was told to wound. Ethan had never verbally refused to follow orders—he'd stopped talking to his trainers and Ming the first time Ming ordered him to commit murder.

Eight-year-old Ethan had simply stopped cooperating. In anything.

His recalcitrance had resulted in physical and psychic punishments so severe that long parts of his childhood were blank, his mind erasing that which would break him. Those punishments had stopped when Ming worked out that such things had zero effect on a child who lived in the cold gray place.

But the cold was gone now, the gray obliterated. Ethan's veins pumped fire as he stared at Selenka's wound. Changelings healed fast, but a wound this deep would take time even for an alpha wolf, and it had to hurt. "Is your healer nearby?" he asked, interrupting the conversation with no care whatsoever.

"No." A scowl aimed at him, her eyes that luminous gold, fascinating and dangerous. "I'll have him look at it later. Just slather that goop in there on it."

He knew she was referring to a numbing gel that would also protect the injured area. Gloving up before he retrieved the tube, he took care to be gentle as he spread the gel over the wound.

The heat of her body pulsed against him, almost as if the predator that lived under her skin was testing his mettle. The BlackEdge wolves weren't exactly known for being sweet or compliant. He'd looked them up in the squad's files and found the notation: *Dangerous if provoked. Do not underestimate.*

Despite the odd itch in his palm from when she'd offered him her hand, he kept his touch businesslike. It took effort. That initial contact had shoved sensation through him in a savage punch his brain hadn't been able to process. Perhaps because that had been the closest he'd been to another person for a long, long time.

After realizing physical torture had no effect on Ethan, Ming had relied on vicious mental chains and on the pitch black of a room without light. Ethan had lived alone in the dark for a long time, so long that he'd forgotten the sun. It had seared his eyes when he'd seen it again after an eternity.

He'd also forgotten what it was to have skin-to-skin contact with another living being, forgotten that people burned hot . . . and he had never known that a woman's skin could be so soft. Even when the woman was more dangerous than an Arrow. Selenka's claws weren't for show. She could've gutted him before he could react.

Ending his contact with her caused a physical reaction, his power crackling in his veins and his muscles tensing, but her wound was now coated with the gel. It looked no less red, but the pain should've already begun to dull. The thought did nothing for the strain knotting his body—because she was still hurt. And he had helped cause that hurt.

Ethan's jaw clenched as he forced himself to move away from her.

Changeling soldiers had taken both assailants from the hall while he'd been doing first aid, and medics called in from a nearby hospital were checking on the collapsed. Aden had also appeared in the hall, no doubt alerted by one of the Arrows who'd been outside during Ethan's blast.

Ethan? The mental signature of the current leader of the squad was cool and controlled.

It was also a voice to which Ethan would respond; he'd made that decision when he first saw Aden and realized the other man was close to him in age. Logic alone told him there was no way Aden Kai could've ever been one of Ming's pet torturers.

Aden had told Ethan other relevant facts about the changes in the squad, but Ethan had wanted only one thing: the names of the men and women who'd come inside that pitch-dark room and tried to break a boy who wouldn't speak. Even in the gray, that knowledge had had meaning to him.

As did the fact that Aden had kept his promise and found Ethan the data.

From the list of seven names, only Ming LeBon remained alive. As squad intel had confirmed the former Councilor was being stealthily hunted by an American pack of wolves who appeared to want to crush his empire before they tore him to pieces, Ethan had laid down his blades for the time being.

That Ming LeBon, a man used to power, would lose it all before he died, that had struck him as ice-cold justice. Should the wolves fail in their quest, however, Ethan would be waiting in the shadows with a blade of light that would cut the former Councilor to tiny pieces that Ethan would then feed to feral hogs.

The ferocity and specificity of the thought caught him unawares but only for an instant. He embraced the black fire of it, deciding vengeance was better with emotion as he replied to Aden, *I saw the threat. I neutralized it.* Going down on one knee, he put his used glove in a biohazard destruction bag, then riffled through the rest of the first-aid kit. *No fatal harm.*

Report understood. Aden's voice held a depth Ethan had never before felt but that suddenly made him certain he was missing the full meaning of that outwardly straightforward statement. *What is your status?*

Abilities at fifty percent charge.

No, Ethan. Aden waited until Ethan glanced up; the squad leader's dark eyes met his across the room. *Are you injured?*

Ethan realized that was tactical information, too. *No.* Ming's silent weapon remained as functional as it had ever been—not whole, Ethan hadn't been that since he was six years old, but functional. *Do you need me to neutralize another threat?*

No. I just wanted to make sure you hadn't been hurt. More foreign depth in Aden's words, tones Ethan couldn't comprehend. *We're family, Ethan. And family looks after one another.*

Ethan didn't reply.

Rising with an antiseptic seal in hand, he opened it out with care; the seal would protect Selenka's wound from infection until she could get to her healer. Well aware by now that she was conscious of every action in her vicinity, he offered no verbal warning.

She didn't stiffen when he began to press the transparent seal into place around the wound, so the numbing gel had to be working. Once the wound was sealed, he picked up her torn T-shirt but realized at once that she couldn't put it back on without stretching and possibly exacerbating her wound. Picking up the jacket instead, he held it out. She slipped one arm, then the other into it without looking back.

The sound of her doing up the zipper was fast and crisp.

"The numbing effect will fade within the hour," he said. "You should get to your healer by then."

Both Selenka and the bear alpha stared at him.

Selenka raised an eyebrow. "You always interrupt big, scary changelings who could eat you in one bite, *zaichik*?"

Ethan was fluent in Russian, but he still wasn't sure if he was translating the last word correctly. Because he thought it meant "little rabbit." Possibly, it was a predator-to-assumed-to-be-prey interaction.

Shrugging that aside, he said, "If necessary." Ethan knew fear was an emotion, but it wasn't one with which he had any familiarity. "I believe, given my muscle mass, I'd be fairly unappetizing in any case."

The bear laughed, big and loud and with a warmth that crashed against Ethan like a wave in a near-physical way, but Selenka narrowed her eyes.

"You should watch this one, Selenka," the bear said, before he turned to go to where his lieutenants were stirring awake.

"Should I watch you?" Selenka's question held a wolf's growl . . . alongside a glint in the eye that didn't appear to be aggressive at all. "Are you a threat?"

"Yes." Lying to the only person in his entire life who had

saved him was out of the question. "We should talk after this."

Selenka closed her fingers around his chin, the contact light even as she sliced out her claws. The glint was gone, to be replaced by a deadly ruthlessness. "If you are a true threat to me or mine, I will tear out your throat and walk away with your blood on my claws—and in my mouth." She brushed one claw over his lips. "But if you're not . . . well, *zaichik*, then we'll play."

Inside him, the dark heat coalesced into an ignition point that flared to searing brightness, its tendrils spreading in a wave of color and heat and pain. The door to the cold place didn't slam shut. No, it was obliterated from within by the tendrils that wove out around the frame, as liquid gold as Selenka's eyes. He watched her with unyielding focus even as shards of white-hot agony thrust into his brain.

Ethan had chosen.

The Architect

Scarab Syndrome: Sudden increase in psychic abilities paired with erratic behavior, possible violent outbursts, hallucinations, and/or memory loss. Refer all possible cases immediately to Dr. Maia Ndiaye at PsyMed SF Echo.

If subject is already violent and out of control, utilize the emergency codes listed below to request urgent teleport assistance.

—Code Red medical alert sent by PsyMed Central to medical facilities worldwide (April 25, 2083)

THE ARCHITECT OF the Consortium considered the achievements and failures of her brainchild to date. She had formed the Consortium to destabilize the world, so that she and those she had handpicked and positioned with tactical precision could then take advantage of the lack of stability.

It had been a good plan, and she had achieved a measure of success.

However, in the overall scheme of things, she had to accept that she had failed. The formation of the Trinity Accord, the cooperation agreement signed by major elements of all three races, had made it far more difficult to sow discord that led to fragmentation. People talked to one another now, or called up a bigger player to do the talking on their behalf.

Not all, but enough.

The problems in the PsyNet had made the situation even more challenging. She couldn't risk further destabilizing the psychic fabric on which the entire Psy race relied for survival—without the biofeedback provided by the PsyNet, even she would die in a matter of minutes.

It was a fundamental of psychic biology.

She had to back off on anything that threatened the psychic network—at least until she had a solution in place that would mean the survival of a large percentage of Psy. Genocide wasn't good for business, wasn't good for power.

The odd massacre could help maintain control, but she saw no value in ruling over a decimated world. She wanted to rule a powerful, operational world. Only then would it mean anything. Ultimate control had been the endgame all along, the others in the Consortium pawns to get her to the throne.

The Architect leaned back in her chair and looked out the window of the retreat where she came to think and plan, but she saw nothing of the idyllic landscape beyond, her gaze turned inward. It was time for a new plan, a new strategy. Those who survived and thrived didn't cling to failures; they cut off those failures like diseased limbs.

First, she took stock of her resources.

She still had a number of strong pieces in play, people in positions of power hidden in pockets no one expected. It was a gift she had, pinpointing those who could be twisted and turned and used.

As for active Consortium operations, she'd permit a critical few to play out, see what they yielded. Most, however, she'd mothball—along with many of those running the ops. Not all her surviving pawns would be happy with the Consortium's change in direction, but that could be handled.

A dull throb pulsed in her left temple as she returned her attention to her desk and the datapad on which she'd been making notes. She ignored the throb; it was a minor irritation and she had work to do if she was going to salvage her brainchild. The first thing was to reconsider her goals.

Did she still want to rule?

Yes.

Being a powerful civilian was not her natural state.

Who did she want to rule?

Now, that, she thought, leaning back in her chair again, was an interesting question. Dominion over one race was far different from dominion over all three. The latter had never been achieved in the history of the world.

It was a goal worthy enough for the Architect. She had

been stuck in old ways of thinking before, had only gone for the small, shiny goal. But all great leaders and visionaries had to grow into their path. The Consortium idea had been a worthy stepping-stone to prepare her for what was to come: she would gain control of the world . . . then she would re-shape it to be her greatest legacy.

No one would ever forget her name.

Chapter 3

Tracker successfully deactivated.

(Personal note: You make the decisions, Aden, but are you sure about this? The patient's psychological profile gives me cause for concern.)

—Dr. Edgard Bashir to Aden Kai (March 2083)

THE ARROW HADN'T stopped watching Selenka since they last spoke.

It should've been irritating, but turned out she didn't object to the scrutiny. The man made both woman and wolf ravenous. Especially as he continued to watch her that way after she'd shown him her claws—he either felt no fear or was a lunatic with zero self-preservation skills.

Because Selenka *would* gut him if it came down to it.

A desire to eat him up like the rabbit she called him didn't mean he was safe from retaliation should he prove to be a snake in the nest. Though, yes, she would be disappointed. It had been a long time since she'd reacted so viscerally to a male. Like most changelings, she wasn't shy about intimate skin privileges—such contact was a part of life, and in her case, necessary to control her wolf's aggressive instincts.

Alpha wolves weren't exactly shy, retiring types.

Her wolf snorted at the idea of it.

For the past six months, however, that wolf had turned away from even close friends who'd offered to assuage her need. It didn't want just the physical, and neither did the human side of her. Inside her was a need that was an ache.

"Ah, *cucciola*, such a hole you have inside you. It will swallow you up if you are not careful."

Words spoken by a fairground fortune-teller when she'd been a teenager.

The angry girl she'd been had laughed it off, but the woman she'd become often wondered if the "human" fortune-teller, draped in her scarves and skirts, had been an F-Psy who'd escaped the watchful eyes of the PsyNet. Because Madame Zostra with her heavy Italian accent and flamboyant sparkling rings had been right.

Selenka wanted *more*. What her grandparents had. What she saw between her lieutenants Alia and Artem. Gods protect her, she even envied Valentin. The bear had found a mate of whom any alpha would be proud.

This primal attraction she felt for the Arrow was a far more raw thing—but it had wakened the slumbering need in her with a vengeance, reminding her that she wasn't only an alpha wolf.

She was an alpha wolf who liked men.

Hot, sweaty skin privileges with this deadly stranger sounded perfect.

Especially if he continued to give her that baffled look when she called him *zaichik*.

Her lips quirked, but it wasn't amusement or primal sexual attraction at the top of her mind. It was the seasoned consideration of a woman who'd been the leader of her pack since her twenty-fifth birthday. Why would he tell her he was a threat? A clever ploy to set up a double cross? It made little sense when he'd already begun to win her trust by saving her life.

Setting that question aside for later, she walked over to join Valentin, Silver, and Aden Kai. Together, the four of them were the security committee for this cursed event, though Aden often delegated to two of his senior Arrows—Cristabel Rodriguez and Axl Rye.

The impetus for the delegation was the same reason Kaleb Krychek had stayed away from anything to do with the symposium aside from offering the Es this hall. "My priority is the PsyNet," he'd told Selenka and Valentin when the three of them met to discuss the proposed gathering. "I have to control any major ruptures before they turn into breaks."

Thanks to information shared with the signatories of the Trinity Accord, Selenka knew that, except for a small number of defectors, all Psy needed the PsyNet to survive. It had to do with some type of psychic feedback. But the massive network was failing. Two weeks earlier, twenty-five people in a rural region of Laos had dropped dead where they stood when the Net failed in their area with such suddenness that even Kaleb couldn't repair it in time.

Now Selenka saw faint lines of tiredness on Aden's face, knew the disintegration was accelerating. The leader of the Arrows was also Kaleb's partner in sealing up the breaches in the PsyNet. "How are things in the Net?" she asked this man who was the quietest alpha in the room, but no less deadly for it.

Aden just shook his head in response.

Ivy Jane Zen reached them a second later. The sun-brushed cream of her skin taut over the bones of her face and her pupils dilated against the copper of her irises, the president of the Empathic Collective said, "We've identified the assailants as members of the Collective. Neither's particularly active in the group, but each appeared stable."

The shorter, curvier woman thrust a hand through her hair, disordering the soft black curls. "My designation is not meant to be violent." A shaken tone. "I don't understand this."

"That is not quite correct," Silver replied in that crisp, businesslike way of hers, her cool blonde hair a sheet of light down her back, not a strand out of place—and her confidence in her own power an unassailable truth.

Selenka had always liked Silver, back from when the other woman had been Kaleb's aide. How the extremely sane and pragmatic telepath who had efficiency down to a science was mated to a bear, Selenka would never understand. She'd drunk five vodka shots in a row when she'd heard the news.

"According to my information," Silver continued, "empaths can be violent in self-defense and in defense of those for whom they care."

Selenka scowled. "Who would either E think they were

protecting here?" Folding her arms, she fought not to look over her shoulder and pin the pale-eyed Arrow with her gaze. Because from the way her nape prickled, he was definitely still staring at her. If the man wasn't careful, her wolf *would* start to take his attention as a threat.

Her sheathed claws pricked at her fingertips, her wolf sliding against her inner skin.

Paradoxically, that same wild heart found his refusal to back down attractive as all hell. This was not a man who'd flinch when faced with the primal reality of her. She would not see fear in his eyes if she let go. Dark embers glowing hotter in her stomach, she added, "That gas bomb would've killed everyone in the hall—assuming it's lethal?"

"Still being tested," Valentin rumbled, his bear in his voice even if his eyes had stayed human. "Aden's people are probably going to be the fastest at getting back a result, but I've sent a sample to my own team, too."

The damn bear might be one of the most aggravating people in Selenka's existence, the sure source of the rogue gray hair she'd found the other day, but he understood certain things. One of those was that Selenka wasn't yet at a level of comfort with Aden Kai that would permit her to take his report at face value; yes, the Arrow had created the Trinity Accord, but he remained a stranger to her. A stranger from a psychic race that had done her pack a lot of damage over the years.

Excruciating as it was to admit, she trusted Valentin on matters like this. One thing you could say about bears: they didn't do manipulation or subtle game playing. It was all out in the open, and once they agreed to any kind of alliance, they'd be loyal to it unless the other side broke their faith.

Selenka could work with people like that. Even if they drove her insane.

Because wolves didn't break promises, either. *Selenka* didn't break promises.

"I don't have any answers." Ivy Jane shook her head, the vivid orange of her fine wool sweater a pop of sunshine in the cloud that hung over the hall but her voice holding confused pain. "The symposium is a *good* thing for Es. It's the first time we've been able to meet as a large group. The sessions and talks are about sharing knowledge, discussing breakthroughs, and making friendships beyond our local groups."

Selenka was caught between the urge to snuggle Ivy until the E felt better and the instinct to growl at her. Empaths were often as idealistic as pups, stars in their eyes and a belief in the innate goodness of people. Many had no self-protective instincts. It was enough to push an alpha into adopting the whole lot of them just to keep them safe.

Just as well the Arrows had already done that. Probably for the same reason.

"It's a good thing that Ethan was here." Ivy Jane swallowed. "I don't think anyone else could've stopped a massacre with almost no harm."

Ethan.

Tasting the name, Selenka couldn't decide if it fit or not. "He's one of yours," she said to Aden, more to see if she could get any further information on the Arrow than because she had any doubts about his status as a member of Aden's squad.

"Yes." Aden's tone made it clear no other information would be forthcoming.

Selenka had to respect him for that; an alpha protected their people.

Stirrings around them, as more and more of the fallen began to wake. Separating without further conversation—there was nothing to discuss until they could interview the two assailants—the five of them moved to help where they could. The paramedics had already carried out the attendees with broken bones or who'd taken knocks to the head.

She'd just crouched down to help up a dazed E when the hairs on her nape stirred, her nostrils flaring as she caught a brightly cold scent. Brutal sexual attraction or not, there was something about Ethan . . . something that didn't fit, an intensity that was a scrape of claws against her skin, a resonance that made her want to haul him close and just *listen* until she figured him out.

"Two broken wrists and a wrenched shoulder," he said on reaching her. "No major head injuries." He sounded as if he was reciting a grocery list, but inside her, her wolf lay down with its head on its paws and closed its eyes. And regardless of her awareness that he wasn't quite right in a way she couldn't pinpoint, her mind painted a vivid picture of her lying naked and sated in bed just listening to him talk.

She wasn't the only one who noticed him, either. The other changelings nearby who'd caught his voice had all looked up, heads cocked and expressions appreciative—especially after they caught a glimpse of the speaker.

Selenka smiled at them.

The smart ones became interested in other things. Two bears tried to stare her down, but she was expecting that and held their gazes without blinking until the man and woman both dropped their heads with low, complaining grumbles.

Her wolf was very clear: Ethan was hers to play with—or to punish.

That wolf's fur brushed against the inside of her skin again as it stretched luxuriantly, happy now that it had marked its territory, made its claim clear. It wanted a closer sniff of this Arrow who had labeled himself a threat and described himself as damaged.

We're all damaged in one way or another, Selenushka.

It was BlackEdge's senior healer, Oleg, who'd spoken those words to a distraught fourteen-year-old Selenka. She'd been a wounded child then, was a grown woman now, but Oleg's words remained apt. Damage meant nothing except that the person had lived life and taken a few knocks along the way.

After dusting off the empath she'd been helping, she sent him on his way and turned to Ethan. Pale eyes locked onto her own with a focused intent that had her wolf growling softly in her chest. "Careful, *zaichik*," she whispered, touching clawed fingers to Ethan's chest. "I'm not an E. I bite. Hard. And you've told me that you're a threat."

The Arrow took a step closer, allowing her claws to prick him through his uniform.

No fear. No hesitation.

Her breasts tightened, her thighs clenched, but Selenka was no green pup. "Skin privileges with you might be delicious, but this attraction won't protect you if you're a danger to those I've sworn to protect." She dug her claws in deeper. "Will you come as sweetly if I'm about to rip out your throat?"

Eyes not moving from hers, the Arrow angled his head.

Selenka's wolf lunged to the surface.

Chapter 4

Discipline, Selenushka. *Discipline.* You're already too
powerful a wolf to strike out or react without thought.
Today, you almost took off a packmate's arm in a fit of
anger. Tomorrow, you may claw out someone's throat. With
discipline, you are an asset to the pack. Without it, you are
a liability.

—Alpha Yevgeni Durev to his granddaughter, Selenka (12)

SELENKA LEANED HARD on the self-control it had taken her
years to develop. Passion and emotion were her greatest
strength and greatest weakness—as alpha, her pack adored
her for loving them so ferociously, but the flip side to that
was a stormy temperament that had turned her into a brawler
as a teen.

Blin! She couldn't believe her wolf had nearly lost control
that way. She had to be more touch deprived than she'd realized. Well, she'd take care of that with this Arrow who offered his throat to an alpha wolf without fear—but she'd do
so *after* she'd figured out whether he was a foe under the
skin, and handled her responsibilities to the symposium.

Stepping away from Ethan, she caught an E who'd staggered to his feet but was none too steady. The empath, his
eyes huge and guileless as a pup's, dropped his head against
her shoulder while wrapping his arms around her. Selenka
didn't hesitate to put her own around the heavily built male,
stroking his trembling back. Empaths aroused the same protective instincts in her that she felt around submissive members of the pack. They were so damn helpless.

"You're fine," she said in a firm and reassuring tone.

He cuddled harder into her. Wolf sighing, she hugged him

tight and nuzzled his hair—and narrowed her eyes at Ethan when he stirred as if to haul the E away. He'd get a swipe of claws across his pretty face if he tried. But he had brains, this Arrow, enough brains to stay in position until the E in her arms finally calmed enough to wander away to join a knot of other Es.

"You're an alpha wolf." Ethan's voice wrapped around her. "Why did you permit such encroachment into your space?"

"We don't usually eat helpless Es." It'd be like kicking pups. "A good alpha knows when to hug and when to dole out a dressing-down."

Ethan's expression gave nothing away, but he said, "Why am I compelled to you?" He didn't sound disturbed by the compulsion. "I want to put my hands on your skin, want to taste you."

Another man may have come across as flirtatious or trying his luck with those words. With Ethan . . . it was cold, factual, unvarnished. The man wanted to strip her bare and put his mouth on her and he didn't understand why.

But those unembellished words, in that voice . . .

Her wolf strained against her skin. If she hadn't been aware Psy couldn't influence changeling minds in such a way, she might've suspected telepathic coercion. "I have no answers for you except that sometimes, the body wants what it wants."

Eyes hot with a need that burned dark and deadly, he said, "Would you like to have our discussion now? So you can decide whether to kill me or . . . allow me to indulge this compulsion."

Selenka's eyes went to his throat again, a strong column against the black of his uniform collar. That raised collar wouldn't protect him from wolf teeth—especially when he didn't want to be protected. "No. We'll do that in private." There were far too many big changeling ears here, and whatever Ethan had to tell her was specific to her—or he would've told her while she was with Valentin.

A growl built in the back of her chest as her wolf fought her in a way it had never before done. It *wanted* Ethan, and logic and reason be damned. Wrenching it under control with teeth-gritted will, she took another look at the Arrow across from her. He was watching her like he wanted to hunt her down—but she felt no sense of threat.

Because the cold Arrow looked as feral as she currently felt.

Whatever this was, it wasn't an attempt at psychic manipulation. It was chemistry so violent that it had laid waste to both an Arrow's and an alpha's control. "Talk about something else," she ordered, her voice harsh. "Tell me about your telekinesis. In as much technical detail as possible."

"The theory is that I move and reshape available light."

"Does that mean you don't have the ability in a lightless room?"

A stillness fell over him. And she knew. *Knew*. He had survived a room without light . . . and he hadn't put himself there. Because how better to control a man whose power was linked to light than to deny him fuel for that power?

Blood boiling, she sliced out a hand. "Never mind." She would not expose Ethan here, in this place where others might overhear; some wounds were private, to be shown only to those you chose. "I see another E who looks lost."

The woman all but burrowed into her. Ethan, meanwhile, stopped to assist a fallen empath to his feet. Selenka had met the teenage cardinal earlier that day, after he walked over and asked her about the colors in her hair. His own was cut close to his skull, the curls tight.

"I saw a boy with stripes shaved into his hair," he'd said afterward. "I'm considering it. Ivy is my guardian at present, and she authorized it but said I had to be sure since my hair will take time to recover."

Now the teenager blinked at Ethan. "I can't see you." His voice shook, his ebony skin devoid of its usual glow.

"I'll call a paramedic to check your vision."

"No." The teenager grabbed his arm. "I can see you, but I can't *see* you . . . No, wait." A deep frown. "You're not gone. You're . . . lost. Don't fade. Don't throw away the broken shards. You just need glue."

Releasing a motionless Ethan, the E patted him on the arm before weaving his way over to Ivy Jane Zen, who enfolded his taller form against her and pressed a kiss to his temple.

Selenka knew the boy had likely been rambling and confused, but his words had raised the tiny hairs on her body. Especially since she knew the young cardinal was training directly under Sascha Duncan, the most experienced E in the world. The teen was a *power*.

Ethan stayed silent, his expression glacial . . . and his eyes never moving off her. Then she was alone again, and he was walking toward her.

Don't throw away the broken shards.

Her wolf took advantage of her absorption in the mystery of Ethan and, desperate in a way that made no rational sense, lunged so powerfully inside her that she slammed up against him, one hand on his chest and their gazes locked as the air punched out of both of them.

He clasped her hips with strong hands, holding her close. The primal heart of her reached out for the shattered heart of him and a cold, brilliant, paradoxically light-fractured darkness exploded into her mind.

His eyes went black in front of her, his fingers digging into her.

But he didn't attempt to shove her out.

And her wolf, possessive and unbending, staked its claim, was claimed in turn.

Heart thundering and breath shallow, she stared at Ethan. His skin was dotted with perspiration, and she could see his pulse thudding in his neck, the rhythm erratic. Inside her moved a cold light that tasted of the night, chilling her veins and whispering of wrongness. Too jagged, too broken, the bond filled with static.

"This isn't supposed to happen." Harsh words that scraped her throat.

"What?" His eyes were pure black. "Why can I—" A shake of his head. "There is a presence inside me."

"Do you want it out?" If he did, this was an even worse disaster than she'd believed.

"I don't know." The words were flat. "What is it?"

Conscious of her packmates having gone predator-still around the hall, Selenka battled to modulate her face and voice.

"Me," she rasped, her vocal cords raw from a cry she'd

never uttered. "That presence is me. We've . . ." She bit back a growl. "It's like we've mated, but the bond doesn't feel right." A heavy fog lay between them, murky and thick and littered with jagged edges that made her wolf snarl. "I can't sense you in the way a mate should."

Ethan didn't move, didn't blink.

Selenka stepped back, breaking the physical link between them. "Don't ask me to explain it. This isn't how the mating bond is supposed to come into effect—we're meant to dance, to court each other, to *know* each other."

Ethan was a stranger to her . . . a stranger who didn't *fit* inside her. She'd been around enough mated pairs to know this bond was catastrophically wrong. Rather than fitting her like a lost half, Ethan was serrated darkness inside her, raising her wolf's hackles.

And yet, the wolf gripped on to him with teeth and claws, its possessive need dark in Selenka's veins. She wanted to mark him, wanted to *take* him.

"You burn," Ethan ground out, closing the distance between them until they were separated by a bare inch. "Fire scalding my veins. I want more."

Sucking in a breath at the naked want of him, her own need a craving unlike any she'd ever before experienced, Selenka looked around. Margo was the one who caught her eye, the shock in the senior lieutenant's eyes a spread of amber against pupils of jet black. Selenka's closest friend was ready to intercede, ready to go for Ethan and draw blood.

Selenka gave a tiny shake of her head, and—after a taut pause—the lieutenant turned away. Other packmates would follow Margo's example. Only BlackEdge's most senior people here would've even realized what had actually happened. And none of them could help Selenka navigate this bond that shouldn't exist.

"Whatever has occurred, it wasn't because of psychic coercion," Ethan said, his eyes still obsidian and his body a wall of muscled heat right up against her. "Such coercion isn't possible with changelings."

Selenka clenched her hand, released it with conscious care. "This isn't a Psy thing." Even with the light-fractured night of him, the bond was too primal, too much a thing of teeth and claws. "We'll talk about it later—I can't think right now."

Caught between snarl and satisfaction, need and reason, she focused on the mate she'd gained without warning. "How are you doing?" The sudden intimate connection had to be even worse for an Arrow.

"I'm still in the PsyNet."

It took a minute for his meaning to penetrate her fuzzy brain. "Good," she said, the cold starlight of him brilliant and broken inside her. "Are you stable?"

"No." Jerked breaths, out of time and out of sync. "I need—" He stared at her, and she could almost see him fighting for the words to describe that need.

He didn't have the vocabulary, but she did.

"Govno!" Grabbing his hand, she hauled him out of the closest door and strode down the hall until she found a small unused room. She walked in, kicked the door shut behind them both, then turned and pushed him up against the door. "This is what you need."

Gripping the hair at his nape in a fist, she pulled down his head to her own.

The kiss was all lips and wetness and the slick slide of tongue against tongue, her breasts pressed up hard against his chest, and his arms locked around her. This had nothing to do with technique or finesse. It was a kiss that sought to momentarily assuage the skin starvation that had kicked into high gear in both of them.

When his bristles prickled her skin, she snarled and tightened her grip in his hair for an even deeper kiss. Widening his stance, he just leaned into it, his arms bands of titanium around her.

They were both breathless when she ended the kiss.

Hair falling across his forehead and eyes black, he said, "More."

"No." She wasn't some hormone-crazed juvenile; she was Selenka Durev, Alpha of BlackEdge, and she had a job to do.

Snapping out of Ethan's hold using a technique she'd learned from her trainers back when she was a junior soldier, she wiped the back of her hand over her mouth. "I have to get back in there and do what I promised. Can you maintain?"

Ethan took one long breath, then another. "I know how to compartmentalize." In front of her, his eyes began to fade from black to that stunning pale shade. Shutters came down, the lines of tension wiped from his face.

Inside her, the cold fractures of light intensified.

Her wolf snarled, wanting to rip that strange broken fog aside, because behind it lay her mate. Unlike Ethan, she couldn't just wipe things away. Her wolf rode close to her skin, her eyes the animal's. Everything was more acute with the predator's vision, her senses jacked up.

But feral as she must look, Ethan watched her with banked—but not conquered—desire, even as he moved aside so she could open the door. The two of them walked back into the symposium hall in silence, and though Selenka knew the changelings in particular would've noted their absence, the scene was much the same.

They hadn't been gone for more than a minute, two at most.

But it had been long enough to pacify the wolf, get its possessive instincts to the point where she was no longer in danger of violence. Want for Ethan still surged inside her like a wild thing. It wasn't normal. *Nothing* about this was normal. Mating at first sight was the kind of thing they showcased in the daytime soap operas to which Margo was addicted. It was the stuff of fantasy and romance novels.

It was not real life.

Except the truth sang a cold song in Selenka's blood.

"Your skin is very soft." Toneless words from Ethan, his eyes fixated on her neck, but they raised every tiny hair on her body.

Sucking in a breath as she realized he was fighting the same compulsion to touch, she bared her teeth. "Not until we're alone." As for his confession of being a threat to her, their strange mating had thrown a spanner in those works.

Mates didn't betray each other. It was a truth set in stone.

Yet her mate was an absolute stranger.

Another primal surge against her, the sense of a massive wave rising just out of eyesight, a thing of cold and blue fire, death and light. She sucked in a breath, realizing she was catching the backwash of *his* emotions. "You're no natural-born Arrow. There's too much violent energy inside you." A hungry, deadly energy that was oddly primal.

His breath brushed her face as he spoke, they stood so close to each other though she had no awareness of moving. "I was a child barely through level one of Silence when an event triggered my ability to use light as a weapon."

Silence.

The secretive program the Psy race had used to condition emotion out of their young, until the world began to believe the Psy were born without emotions. Only after the fall of Silence had the psychic race begun to talk about it—and even now, most hesitated.

"What was being done to you at the time?" she asked, her voice a low growl, knowing it had to be terror that had driven a child to strike out.

"Fingers in my brain," he said, tone distant. "Attempting to make my mind behave. I kept failing my Silence evaluations and the family was not pleased."

Chest rumbling, Selenka found her hand was once more in his hair. "You didn't fail anything. Your family failed you." It was an alpha's job to protect a pup, not allow that pup's mind to be violated. "I'll tear them to pieces for what they did to you—then I'll eat their hearts." It was a deliberate provocation, that last, an attempt to incite anger or disgust. *Anything* that would push them away from one another and allow her to think.

But her mate said, "How much longer?" his breath rough, and his eyes beginning to bleed black at the edges.

Chapter 5

The child shows signs of severe psychological trauma. His sanity may not be salvageable—at best, he may only ever be a blunt weapon that must be kept contained until use.
   —Report by Dr. Johannes Marr, senior Arrow medic,
     to Councilor Ming LeBon (2062)

ETHAN DIDN'T KNOW what was happening, didn't understand the alien heat in his veins. It *hurt* but the pain was one in which he gloried. As he did in the primal being that was a shadow in his mind, its teeth and claws bared. Should anyone try to get between him and Selenka, he'd use his power without compunction.

She was his now. That was how mating worked.

"Maintain." It was a growled order from his mate. "Or you'll push my wolf to violence."

Ethan didn't want to stifle the heat that scalded him, but even in the fog, he'd learned things. He'd watched Aden with Zaira, Vasic with Ivy Jane, Abbot with Jaya. He understood that mates backed one another—they didn't smash foundations but built them. Ethan's mate was an alpha wolf and right now, she was in the middle of an operation.

He leaned into the brutal training he'd undergone as a child and used it to assist his mate by slowly, methodically rebuilding the control mechanisms in his mind. The deep red flame that was his compulsion toward Selenka continued to burn in his gut, potent and visceral and unlike anything he'd ever before felt, but he could think again.

"I'm stabilizing," he told her, though—at the deepest level—it was a lie. His core hadn't been stable for a long time. But for today, for this time, he was functional again.

Selenka's eyes were half-gold, half-brown as she examined him. "I can feel it, the ice crawling over the fire." An edge of a growl in her tone. "Can most Arrows do that? Just shut down emotion after such a vicious shock?"

He hadn't shut anything down; he had it barely caged behind a construction of chill control. "I'm not normal," he told her, because he would not lie to his mate. "I don't know how another Arrow would respond."

Selenka's jaw tightened, the words that emerged from her lips harsh. "Is that what your family taught you? That you're not normal?"

Ethan *knew* he wasn't normal; he'd always known, but now the truth was unavoidable. There was something deeply wrong with his brain. "I was a disappointment as the eldest son of the Night family." He felt nothing as he spoke of his dead family, the memories a permanent numbness that even the searing flame that was Selenka couldn't eradicate.

He wondered if that fire would burn him to cinders.

Ethan didn't flinch; he would rather die scalded by her heat than alone in the cold dark. "I think if they could have put me down like an unwanted animal, they would have. But by the time my problems became obvious, I was too old to conveniently disappear. So they tried to break my mind and make me into another Ethan."

The words that came from Selenka's lips were profane. Then she pressed her lips to his in a contact that short-circuited his brain and threatened to erase what control he'd managed. Stepping back in the aftermath, her chest heaving, she said, "I shouldn't have done that—but I'm not sorry." Anger coated each word, but it wasn't directed at him. "Do your work and I'll do mine and when that's done, we'll talk about your family's chances of survival."

Skin electric and light rimming his fingertips, he nodded. And didn't speak again for ten more minutes, till after they'd helped clear the hall.

Then he told Selenka the rest of it. "My family isn't alive." A flash of light behind his eyelids, the memory of a scream cut off almost before it began. "I murdered my father, mother, grandfather, and uncle when I was six years old. All the adults involved in my upbringing. I also killed the telepath who was digging inside my brain."

Ethan tried to think of who he'd been before that moment when his power struck out in a desperate attempt to protect his mind, couldn't remember. The numbness had begun then, erasing all that had once existed. "That was when I was damaged." Part of his psyche destroyed.

Selenka shrugged. "Good. They should've known better than to harm a pup." The light caught on her cheekbone as she shifted to look at someone.

Ethan's fingers curled into his palms, his skin tight. The lips she'd claimed burned. He killed with light but she lived in it, and until he went slowly, inexorably insane, he'd chance the brilliance with her.

"I have to disappear for a while." An edge of gold in her eyes once more, her next words a promise—or a threat. "I'll find you afterward."

"I'll be waiting." Ethan had made his choice, picked his loyalty.

SELENKA strode in the direction Valentin had indicated.

It didn't matter if her mind was a place of howling wolves, her body clawing with craving; the safety of her pack came first. The symposium attacks had happened in *her* city—that made the situation her problem to handle.

Being alpha is more than a position. It is more than a responsibility. It is a joy and a weight and it is who you are.

Her grandfather's words were still ringing in her brain when she ran into Margo in the otherwise empty external corridor—her best friend bounced off her, Selenka was moving so fast. Realizing she was far more shaken than she'd consciously accepted, she gave herself half a minute to bend over, put her hands on her knees, and exhale hard.

Her head rang, her veins kissed by cold night.

Margo, of medium height, with large breasts Selenka had envied as a teen, sleek muscle, and the thickest, silkiest blonde hair in the universe, said, "Whoa."

"Yes," Selenka agreed. "Whoa."

"Have you met Mr. Tall, Dangerous, and Smoldering before?" Margo put a hand on Selenka's shoulder, the contact instinctive between packmates. "It's a serious breach of the girlfriend code to hide snacks like that."

Listening to her, you'd never know Margo was Selenka's security specialist and so lethal even the bears didn't pick fights with her. The pushy, often aggressive creatures gave her a wide berth—and constantly sent drinks and hopeful looks her way when she went out for a night. The last time it had happened, Margo had deigned to dance with the six-foot-tall bear soldier who'd sent her a cocktail.

The other woman had looked scared but delighted.

Ethan wasn't scared of Selenka. Not even for a second.

Rising to her full height on a wave of primal satisfaction, the wolf smug in its choice of a mate, Selenka shook her head. "I'd barely spoken to him before it happened." Though physical attraction had never been in question. The embers glowed, hot and dark, deep in her belly, ready to engulf her at the slightest encouragement.

Getting naked with her mate was not going to be an issue.

Margo's eyes widened, her hands flying to her mouth. "*O Bozhe!* You're just like Chantelle and Ridge from *Hourglass Lives!*"

Selenka groaned. "Stop it."

But her tough-as-granite security specialist was all but dancing on her work-booted feet, her blue eyes bright. "I can't! A real-life mating at first sight?! All my fan-forum buddies will just *die!*"

Narrowing her eyes, Selenka pointed a finger at her best friend and only then remembered little Zhanna had decorated her nails with tiny stickers of big-eyed cartoon cats. "This goes nowhere near the forum."

"Fine, spoilsport." Margo's smile didn't dim in wattage. "Do you feel different?"

"Yes. He lives in me now." What she couldn't explain to Margo was the sense of wrongness tied to the mating, the static she couldn't hear but could feel—as if the bond was skewed slightly out of time. "We'll talk more later. I have to go deal with the assailants."

Margo transformed from soap opera addict to ruthless

security specialist in the blink of an eye. "I made sure that area is secure. We've also checked everyone for weapons and verified that the only ones with them are part of the security team. Hall and surrounds are secure."

"You have enough people to escort the Es to their hotels?"

"With the bears"—a roll of her eyes—"the Arrows, and that team of Krychek's, we'll be fine. I'll handle all peripherals while you deal with the major issue."

"Thanks, Margo." Selenka deliberately brushed against her friend as they passed; she needed the touch of pack.

Margo waited till she was halfway down the corridor before whispering at a volume only Selenka's wolf ears would pick up, "I'm going to speak to your Ridge."

Since sending Margo a glare would only increase her friend's determination, Selenka just wished Ethan good luck. Margo could pry tears out of a stone. It'd be interesting to see what she'd get out of Selenka's Arrow. Because however their mating had come into being, and regardless of the fog or static or whatever it was that was messing it up, he was hers now.

Damaged. Not normal.

Her hand locked into a hard fist, and she had to force it open. She had no sympathy for anyone who would treat a child with such brutality that the child had to kill in self-defense. And now that child was a dangerous, beautiful man who spoke of himself as if he were a cracked object, broken and of questionable—if any—value.

Selenka bit back a growl as she turned the corner.

Valentin, who'd apparently paused when he heard her coming, lifted both eyebrows. "I pity your mate, if that's your mood," he said. "What did he do?"

Blin! Of course another alpha would've picked up what had happened. "Do not say a *word* to anyone until I have a chance to tell my pack," she growled.

"What do you think I am?" Valentin grumbled back. "I can keep secrets. Except from Silver." He grinned, utterly delighted with himself for having the director of EmNet as his mate.

Selenka would find it insufferable if her wolf wasn't posturing back as hard. "My mate is an Arrow."

"Silver could take him."

"In your dreams."

They reached the right area of the sprawling symposium center together. The two assailants had been put into different meeting rooms. Both rooms were internal, with no windows to the outside, and only a single door. Each door was guarded by a pair: an Arrow and a changeling.

Might seem like overkill, but Psy were their minds—this way, while the Arrow member of the team fought off any psychic attack, a changeling's powerful mental shield meant they could get in the room and physically incapacitate the threat.

Aden, Silver, and Ivy were already in place outside the rooms.

Aden was the first to speak. "We'll need to interrogate the two in teams."

"An E and one other," Ivy said at once. "I've had a close look at Emilie's and Natalia's records—while both seemed outwardly stable, the Collective's internal psych team did note a latent element of psychological fragility. As if they stood on shaky foundations.

"No one was unduly concerned, because that's not unusual with waking empaths—it can take an E time to find their feet," she added. "The Collective offered them extra counseling, but of course the decision was theirs. It seems neither took up the offer." She squared her shoulders and all at once, she wasn't a gentle, warmhearted E; she was Ivy Jane Zen, president of the Empathic Collective.

An alpha willing to fight for her people.

In this case, however, she didn't have to flex her muscles; the Arrows had thrown their weight behind the empaths and Aden said, "You're the expert here."

Taking a deep breath, Ivy looked around. When her gaze settled, it was firmly on Selenka. "You come in with me. Aden, you take Natalia—I've contacted Jaya to partner you."

"What's wrong with me?" Valentin folded his arms across his chest, face set in a grumpy scowl. "Your Es like me. I cuddled at least ten of them just before."

"Your size might intimidate in a smaller space," Ivy said in a tone designed to calm an irritable bear. "I'll leave on a phone relay so you and Silver won't miss anything."

"If you need to know what types of questions to ask," Silver said, "I have a strategic brain."

That was putting it mildly. Selenka was fairly certain Kaleb's former aide could take over the world should she be in the mood. Kaleb's choice of aide had, in fact, been an important reason Selenka had chosen to work with him; the man respected strength rather than being intimidated by it.

It was just as well Silver had decided to run the worldwide Emergency Response Network instead of turning megalomaniacal, or they'd all be in trouble. Of course, she'd also chosen to mate with a bear, so maybe there was a little crazy mixed in with the intelligence.

Though, Valentin's courtship of her *had* been the best reality show on the planet as far as changelings were concerned—so much so that Selenka hadn't even bothered to warn off the bear alpha for constantly coming into the wolf half of Moscow, where Silver had then lived. Margo and the rest of Selenka's nosy pack would've never forgiven her for ending their entertainment.

But now, Selenka realized with a sinking stomach, *she* was going to be the reality show. Valentin was being all polite now, but he'd probably fall to the floor laughing when he was alone. Selenka wouldn't blame him. What non–soap opera alpha mated to a man she'd only just met? A man about whom she knew next to nothing?

Govno! She'd done an even more impulsive thing than a *bear*.

She would never live it down.

"Telepath me if you think of anything that could help," Ivy said to Silver, deep purple shadows already forming under her eyes. "I'm hoping that being an E will give me an advantage, but this isn't a normal situation."

Silver's icy blonde hair shone in the light as she nodded. "I won't interrupt unless absolutely necessary."

Ivy called Valentin's phone, then put her own in her pocket once he'd answered; the little rose-gold device would pick up all conversation in the room. "Her full name is Emilie Onruang," Ivy told Selenka as they moved toward the door on the left. "A Gradient 6.3 E who chose to work totally outside her designation after completing her training. She's in the Honeycomb but otherwise doesn't use her empathy."

Selenka couldn't imagine having a gift and not utilizing it; it'd be like a wolf not using their claws. "That usual?"

"No. But it's not unknown—about five percent of Es choose not to use their empathic abilities." Ivy blew out a breath. "We also believe there're a large number of undiscovered Es. My feeling is some are hiding consciously—maybe out of fear, maybe because after a lifetime of Silence the idea of dealing with emotion is terrifying."

Selenka's changeling brain couldn't comprehend the latter—emotion was the lifeblood of a changeling pack . . . and of the primal bond that was at the heart of the entire pack structure. A bond that now burned a jagged and cold blue flame inside Selenka. She was mated. And her mate was an Arrow, trained and honed, who had reacted to the influx of emotion with an obsessive hunger that fed her own.

He appeared to have no mental block against it, unlike so many Psy.

I'm not normal.

Angry as those words made her, they held a critical truth: her mate did not respond in ways she could predict.

Ethan was a total unknown.

Chapter 6

An alpha's greatest strength is their heart. Trust yours,
Selenushka.

—Yevgeni Durev to Selenka Durev (2077)

HAVING REACHED THE door of the makeshift holding
room, Selenka slipped inside ahead of Ivy Jane. The other
woman might be an empathic alpha, but her default mode
was compassion, and the person inside this room had already
shown an inclination toward violence.

Then Selenka laid eyes on the captive. She knew then and
there that whatever had driven Emilie Onruang, it was gone.
A woman with the sleek build of a swimmer, she sat with her
shoulders slumped as tears streaked down the pallid brown
of her face, her hands bunched on the table. Her eyes were
swollen, the whites bloodshot. She looked up at Ivy with an
utterly lost expression on her face, a pup who'd done a bad
thing and didn't know what to do now.

Selenka had already clocked everything about Emilie,
so she permitted Ivy to go around to her while ensuring
she was close enough to intervene in a split second should
Emilie make any hostile moves. She wasn't concerned about
a psychic assault—the Arrows would've tracked her down
on the PsyNet by now, would react immediately to any
threat.

Emilie was unlikely to survive any such intervention.

"Emilie." Gentle voice, a face full of worry and sadness
as Ivy wrapped the sobbing woman in a tender embrace and
rocked her.

Emilie's sobs intensified until the wolf inside Selenka strained at her skin. This woman wasn't pack, had tried to *kill* Selenka, but part of what made Selenka a dominant wolf was an overriding desire to care for those who were weaker or hurt. Emilie's anguish was nails on a chalkboard to her instincts.

It took a long time, but Ivy finally managed to bring the other E to a semblance of calm. Never dropping her guard, Selenka moved a chair so that Ivy could sit directly in front of Emilie. After a quick glance of thanks, Ivy took the other woman's hands in her own, her gaze locked with Emilie's puffy eyes. "Talk to me." It wasn't a command, but a request. "You can feel my emotions; you know I'm confused and sad, not angry."

Emilie nodded in a staccato movement before turning to the cup of tea that Silver had brought into the room toward the end of the crying jag. One hand locked bloodlessly tight around Ivy's, she picked up the insulated cup with her other and hugged the tea close before whispering, "It hurts."

"What, sweetheart?"

"Living." A broken sound brushed by a soft accent unlike Ivy's own. "It *hurts*."

Ivy smoothed Emilie's hair back from her face, gently tugging away the strands stuck to her cheeks as a result of her tears. "Being outside Silence?"

Emilie began to rock back and forth just slightly. "I hurt before, too. Like my head was going to explode."

"That was Silence crushing your empathic abilities." Ivy continued to hold Emilie's hand, and even though she wasn't focusing her empathic power on Selenka, it was impossible to be this close to her and not feel the embrace of warm acceptance.

Healers. Selenka's wolf shook its head in affectionate non-surprise. This was why, even in battle, changeling alphas never tried to stop their healers from helping enemy wounded. It'd be like asking a leopard to change its spots: an impossibility.

"What hurts now?" Ivy asked. "The emotions of others?"

"Yes. And my own." Emilie squeezed her eyes shut. "I don't feel good. *Ever.*"

Selenka's protective instincts snarled again at the young woman's despair. This was it; she'd had enough. She closed the distance between her and Emilie on that thought, ready to stop the instant the empath showed any fear. But Emilie's eyes just filled with water when Selenka placed her hand on her shoulder.

"I'm sorry." Shaky, whispery words. "I just wanted everyone to stop hurting. The gas wouldn't have caused anyone pain."

Selenka's brain was going a hundred miles an hour, but she spoke with conscious kindness. "What was it?"

Emilie looked up, gaze guileless. "Gas?" A rising intonation, a question that asked Selenka to confirm. "It'd have put us all to sleep forever."

"Sleeping gas?" Selenka asked.

"Yes." A big smile. "Sleeping gas."

Selenka nodded, as if satisfied by the vague answer. "Did you make it?"

"Make it? No, I can't—" Emilie sucked in a gulp of air, teeth sinking into her lower lip. "Yes, I made it. I did."

"Emilie." Ivy's tone was chiding, though she changed nothing about the warmth and forgiveness she was projecting at her fellow empath. "I can sense your emotions. Your shielding has fallen."

Emilie looked down on a hiccupping breath, the tea still clutched to her chest. When she didn't say another word, Selenka squeezed her shoulder again. "You're safe. You didn't hurt anyone." Emilie might be psychologically unstable, but it was blindingly obvious that violence didn't come naturally to her.

As Selenka's dedushka would say, this E wasn't hanging noodles on her ears. Her pain was true, as was her shock, and desire to help others by ending what she believed must be their own pain.

Not that Selenka would trust the E anywhere near her pack. Emilie needed intensive therapy and constant supervision until multiple specialists were certain she was no longer suicidal. For now, she remained a threat to both herself and others. "Tell me." This time, Selenka put an alpha push into her voice.

Emilie crumpled. "It was a man I met on the PsyNet." Her head fell, her hair crescent wedges against her cheeks. "He was so kind. We talked a lot and I told him how I hurt and he . . . After a while, he understood. He said I could make the pain end for myself and for others, that it would be the kindest thing to do."

Selenka's claws pricked the insides of her skin at the same time that Ivy Jane's pupils flared outward, white lines bracketing her mouth. Someone had taken a hurt, broken E and, rather than helping her, had groomed her to be an assassin. Tempering her anger because Emilie might be functional enough to feel it, Selenka petted the other woman's hair, the strands slick and thick under her touch.

Looking up with wet eyes and quivering lips, the empath made a small movement.

The instant Selenka closed the small gap between them, Emilie leaned up against her while continuing to maintain a death grip on Ivy's hand. Having no anger inside her for this healer who had been abused by a person she trusted, Selenka murmured words of comfort she'd use with a submissive packmate in a similar situation.

Only once the E had stopped trembling, her eyes heavy but dry, did Selenka nod at Ivy and say, "Emilie, it's time to go."

Having put her tea aside by then, Emilie rose without hesitation, her eyes huge as she looked first to Ivy, then to Selenka, for approval. Ivy murmured, "That's good, Emilie, you're doing really well," while Selenka pressed a kiss to the empath's temple.

For a wolf, touch said more than any words.

Outside the room waited a blue-eyed Arrow with black hair.

"Abbot." Ivy's tone was soft, her hand holding Emilie's. "We're ready."

The Arrow teleported out with Ivy and Emilie a second later.

"Will she get help?" Valentin's square face held the same anger that bubbled inside Selenka, bear and wolf in perfect harmony on the ugliness of the violation of Emilie's trust.

"Yes. She's one of Ivy's people." As Ethan was now Selenka's. He should've been *more* hers than any other person in the world, but that silent static, it hung murky and disjointed between them.

Chapter 7

Loulou27: Mating at first sight is *so* fake.

RidgesGirl: I know, right? Like do the writers do any research?

MagsW: I think it's romantic. It's as if their souls are destined for one another.

Loulou27: Ugh, let's see what happens the first time he leaves towels on the floor.

MagsW: He's a billionaire wolf. Towel pickup is not a problem.

RidgesGirl: Mags has a point. But damn, now I'm imagining Ridge in a towel, water beading on his chest.

MagsW: Swoon.

—Forum: True Fans of *Hourglass Lives*

GOOD. THEY SHOULD'VE known better than to harm a pup.

Selenka's unforgiving words rang in Ethan's head as she strode away from him and toward the exit from the symposium hall. Her primal grace was hypnotic. She reminded him of fellow Arrow Zaira. Zaira was as confident, and as committed to protecting those who couldn't protect themselves. Damaged Arrows gravitated toward Zaira.

Most anyway.

Until today, Ethan hadn't gravitated toward anyone. Despite knowing that Aden had been a child like him when Ming's torturers sought to methodically destroy Ethan from the inside out, he hadn't been able to bring himself to trust the Arrow leader. It was nothing against Aden.

Ethan didn't trust anyone.

Except Selenka. She'd saved his life. He was now hers.

A part of him tried to argue that such obsessive devotion

wasn't a rational or healthy response to her actions, but Ethan hadn't considered himself sane for a long time. Rationality meant nothing to him. He would far rather live in this world of primal compulsion and need than in the numb gray where he'd felt nothing.

Deadly wolf gold was now the color of his existence.

The woman who walked into the mostly empty hall not long after Selenka disappeared carried the same edge of danger. Her hair was a mass of shiny blonde curls, her height five-six or so, her lips plump, and her body deceptively soft and curvy-looking. Deceptive because no one moved that smoothly without significant muscle on their bones—and intense martial training.

Threat assessment: red.

He noted all of that at the same time that he noted she was not human.

He didn't know how he knew that, but he knew. Ethan *always* knew.

Her eyes, a hazy blue, landed on him at that instant. Expression altering in a subtle fashion he couldn't name, she crossed the echoing space to face him. "I hear your name is Ethan."

Ethan didn't respond except with a slight nod.

"Margo Lucenko," she said, her shoulders relaxed and feet set slightly apart. "One of Selenka's senior lieutenants."

His attention sharpened. "Are you here to warn me off?" If so, she would fail. Ethan had chosen and he wasn't about to budge. Should Selenka decide against him, she could tear out his throat. That was the only way he'd leave her before his time ran out.

A tug of Margo's lips. "No one on the planet can warn mates off one another," she said, so much amusement in her voice that even he had no trouble recognizing it. "No, gorgeous. I'm here to discover what's so special about you that Selenka's wolf picked you out of millions of others."

Ethan had no answer for her.

Folding her arms, Margo tilted her head slightly to the side. "You have the body and the looks. And since you're an Arrow, you *might* be able to go head-to-head with an alpha wolf of Selenka's caliber and come out alive." Lifting her hand, she tapped a finger on her lower lip, her nail polished a glossy pink. "But the emotions . . . now, that's the interesting part."

Again, Ethan stayed silent, as inside him built an inexorable pressure that pushed him to find Selenka, make physical contact, ensure she *remembered* him. People liked to forget Ethan. Shut him up in pitch-dark rooms and ignore his existence. Mates didn't do that, he told himself, but the pressure didn't stop.

"Don't say much, do you. You're a total Ridge." Dropping her hands to her hips with that statement that didn't make sense in either English or Russian, Margo Lucenko continued to speak. "Look, I love Selenka. Given the whole mating-at-first-sight thing, if you don't know how to make her happy, ask me. I'd rather give you advice than warn you off."

It was the one thing Ethan hadn't been expecting, and his sudden acute attention snapped the crescendo inside his skull. "I appreciate the offer." A true statement. He was a novice in this arena, Selenka a prize he intended to clutch at with greedy hands.

No, not a prize.

She was an alpha wolf, not an object or a being who could be owned or possessed. To keep her, he'd have to make her want to be with him. His only advantage was the mating bond—even a mating bond that was so badly damaged by his mental state that it didn't appear in the PsyNet.

Look into the network and Ethan was connected to no one, a black star alone in the darkness. Even the empathic Honeycomb didn't reach him. Aden had repeatedly told him how important it was that he link himself to an empath even if the link was thin and threadbare, that the connection would help protect his mind from the ravages of the disintegrating PsyNet, but Ethan hadn't wanted to be connected to anyone.

Until an alpha wolf crashed into him, saving his life and driving an anvil through the dull nothingness that had kept him distant and separate from the world. He still didn't want to be linked to anyone else. Just her. His mate.

In front of him, Margo narrowed her eyes. "You're hard to read, but I can usually get a handle on dominance regardless. With you . . ."

"I can't assist. I'm not changeling."

"Hmm." Frown creasing her forehead, Margo glanced at her timepiece. "I have to pick up a couple of juveniles from a mechanical class in town. Better head off—we'll talk more later."

"What is Ridge?" Ethan asked before she could turn around.

Her smile was suddenly . . . sparkly. "I'm so glad you asked." She pressed her hands together. "Ridge is a man." The last word was a drawn-out sigh. "I'll introduce you two the next time you have a spare hour or three. Or, if you can't wait, check out *Hourglass Lives*. Season two will be especially interesting for you—that's where the mating-at-first-sight story line begins."

She snapped her fingers. "And you know what? You should read a few special editions of *Wild Woman*. I'll message you a list." The lieutenant wiggled her fingers in goodbye as she left, but he saw her stop halfway through to talk to Nerida. The telekinetic and Margo appeared to know each other well, and Nerida was pointing at Margo's eyes. Possibly to ask about the shiny particles that had dusted her eyelids.

Ethan had seen color on Selenka's eyelids, too, a faint purple that just caught the light. Her fingernails had also been painted—and decorated with images of cats with very large eyes. Ethan had been pondering those cats for some time and decided he would ask Selenka about them when they met.

"Final security sweep complete," Axl announced three minutes later, his big body in the center of the room and his light brown hair clipped so short to his skull that it had no movement.

Ethan's spine tensed, the searing glow of shadowlight coating his fingertips. He had to use conscious effort of will to curl those fingers inward. Because forty-three-year-old Axl was the only current member of the squad whom Ethan had seen *before* he escaped Ming. It had been on the comm screen, a conversation between Ming and the senior Arrow while Ethan sat out of view of the camera.

"Axl is mine," Aden had said when Ethan tried to kill Axl; the squad leader's cheekbones had cut sharply against his olive-hued skin, his breathing rough from the effort it had taken to bring Ethan down without harm or a psychic strike. "He has always been mine—I needed eyes and ears in Ming's camp. But, Ethan, he didn't know about you."

The squad leader had stared into Ethan's eyes, as if boring that knowledge into his brain. "As far as we've been able to determine, by the time Axl was old and senior enough to be invited into Ming's inner circle, Ming had isolated all knowledge of you to only four Arrows and two medics."

Ethan had killed the senior medic and two of the Arrows. Aden's people had taken out two more when those two attempted to breach Arrow HQ months after the leadership coup. The sixth—Dr. Johannes Marr's second-in-command, Dr. Rebekah Patel—had just been found dead, her throat ripped out as if by a large wild animal. Ming was now without a single long-term sycophant.

Axl's deep blue eyes met Ethan's, and in them was the knowledge of Ethan's murderous rage. Ethan knew Aden wasn't lying—Axl had never been near the child Ethan, had never laid a hand on him, and Ming had been careful never to expose Ethan to the comm—but Axl's face was linked to the bunker that had been his prison and Ethan wanted to raze all signs of that bunker to the ground.

Instead of breaking contact, Axl walked to stand directly opposite him. "I should've seen you," he said in a voice deep but quiet. "I am fifteen years older than you, and from the time I became an adult, I vowed to do everything I could to protect the children brought into the squad. I didn't keep that promise with you."

Ethan stared at the other man, seeing the fine lines at the corners of Axl's eyes and noting the delicate red cut that bisected the left side of his jaw. Abbot had told Ethan that the squad's civilian tech specialist, Tamar, had thrown a balled-up piece of paper at Axl and it was a paper cut. But Ethan had also heard Cristabel and Aden talking, and Cris thought Axl had walked into a door while he was distracted arguing with Tamar. Amin, meanwhile, was of the opinion that Axl had slipped on one of Tamar's fluffy slippers and fallen—thus explaining his bad temper.

Ethan had absorbed that data without it altering anything of his rage toward Axl. But today . . . Axl's expression was as open as an Arrow of his generation's would ever get, and it held a scar of regret. The emotion cut at Ethan, his senses no longer numb and blind but sharp and bright and savagely potent.

Absorbing the shadowlight back into himself, he said, "I saw you in that place. You will always be linked to it." The words came out gritty, hard. "I can't alter that." Not today, not tomorrow, or the day after that. If it was to happen, it'd take a lot of tomorrows—more than Ethan had.

Axl didn't argue with him, just said, "No matter what else lies between us, know that I am part of your family. If you need me, I'll be there."

Ethan couldn't speak any longer, the intensity of . . . everything too much. He took his leave of Axl with a curt nod, joining the flow of Arrows who weren't on watch overnight. He stayed silent, making no effort to join in the conversations in progress. His squadmates would find nothing unusual in that.

A tendency toward aloneness was expected of Arrows long in Silence. That Ethan was only twenty-eight didn't change that. He'd been brutalized by his trainers, then kept isolated from those who would've been his squadmates. Ethan had bonded with no one, the only people around him adults who hurt or caged him.

It hadn't only been because he was erratic and uncooperative, but because of the chaotic nature of his abilities. Ming had needed him close as he wove walls of containment around his mind. Perhaps the plan had been to introduce Ethan to others of his age once he was in charge of his own shields and no longer in danger of accidentally killing them, but by then, Ming had known Ethan wasn't fully sane.

He was too unpredictable to let off the leash.

Of course, Ming—a combat telepath skilled at slicing through psychic protections—had plenty of ways to force a badly damaged child to do what he wanted.

Ethan had been all but an automaton at that point, a marionette controlled by Ming.

When he began to emerge from his near-catatonic state at last, not quite normal but aware enough to fight being made a murderer over and over . . .

His hand twitched, wanting to rise to the part of his chest where Ming's favorite medic had placed the tag. Dr. Johannes Marr had been Ethan's first conscious kill. He'd made the decision coldly, clinically—the trainers had been hammering cost-benefit ratios and cold calculation into his mind for years, in an effort to turn him into a robotic killing machine. They'd succeeded . . . except that Ethan had chosen his own targets.

Placing a death device inside a child's chest could have no benefit to the child. And though Ethan hadn't seen another child for a decade or more by that point, he'd had the vague sense that if the doctor succeeded with Ethan, he'd implant the tag in other small bodies.

That made the doctor a threat to be neutralized. So Ethan had watched and waited—with such patient quietness that Ming and Ethan's trainers had begun to believe they'd finally broken him to their leash.

All he'd needed was one moment of inattention by his guards . . . and he'd snapped Dr. Marr's neck. Simply because Ethan didn't cooperate with his trainers didn't mean he hadn't learned every lethal skill they had forced on him. He'd ended the doctor's life in such efficient silence that the guards hadn't even noticed until the doctor's heavy body toppled on top of his tray of medical instruments.

Ming had stopped the calculation training after that. "You're a rabid dog," he'd said after Ethan was knocked out and put in a sensory deprivation tank, his world devoid of light or sound or touch or anything else that told him he was alive.

"I will let you off the leash only when I have a use for you," the former leader of the squad had added. "According to Marr's last psych report, you'll become totally insane without mental stimulation, so you'll get access to study materials after your punishment period, but I see no world in which you'll walk free and be able to use that knowledge."

A feral kind of heat bloomed in Ethan's gut as he walked freely out the door of the hall. Because he was mated to an alpha wolf who wanted to touch him, kiss him, even knowing he was critically damaged and not at all normal—while Ming was currently fighting for survival, his power slipping out of his grasp.

Aden had made a point of telling Ethan of Ming's downfall. "He made an enemy of a wolf alpha," he'd said. "Wolves hunt prey to ground with relentless focus, and the alpha has marked him as his kill. We don't have to be concerned about Ming any longer."

The wolf inside Ethan stirred, the sensation alien but welcome. He would tell Selenka about the stealthy hunt that was destroying Ming's life—he was near certain it would amuse her. As for the Marr tag, Dr. Edgard Bashir had deactivated it three months earlier.

"It's too embedded to be removed," the physician had said. "But I can break critical connections so it can never again be activated."

Because Dr. Marr's death *had* ended the nascent tag program, both Dr. Bashir and Aden believed the tag had been nothing but a tracking device. Ethan had never told them that it was a tool of torture that could be ratcheted up to kill. Nor had he shared that Ming had activated the nerve-pain generator multiple times as he wrote off the bunker after Aden took over the squad.

Having already lost control of Ethan's mind six months earlier, he'd only managed to keep Ethan down by the use of heavy drugs. Too far gone or too harried to use his telepathic abilities to kill his rabid dog, Ming had tried to do it via the tag instead. But it turned out that if you used such a tool against a person enough, he built up an immunity.

It also turned out that it caused a reaction in his body that counteracted the drugs. He'd been a creature of pain but fully conscious when an impatient Ming sent the last two remaining Arrows in the bunker to finish Ethan off. They had opened the door . . . and forgotten to turn off the light in the corridor.

Chapter 8

A: Card game tonight?
E: I don't know how to play cards.
A: I can teach you.
—Message stream between Abbot Storm and
Ethan Night (twenty-seven days ago)

"ETHAN."

He turned his head to the left, in the direction of the Arrow who'd spoken. "Nerida."

The telekinetic was small of stature and build—five-four in her combat boots, with a weight that was likely under a hundred pounds. Her skin was a hue that reminded Ethan of the milk-infused coffee that some of the squad had taken to drinking, and her large eyes a penetrating greenish hazel.

The short, feathered cap of her black hair was new—she'd worn it in a braid until two weeks ago, when she'd gone out with Ivy Jane Zen. She'd returned sans most of her hair, the change causing a buzz through Arrow HQ.

Ethan hadn't paid too much attention at the time, but now he saw that the cut emphasized both her eyes and the fine bones of her face. Her cheekbones were too sharp against her skin as a result of recent weight loss, but her face was no longer pinched with the tension that had dug lines into it after a major injury to another Arrow. And for the first time, Ethan understood why Nerida might've responded that way.

He'd seen her with taller, older Yuri, but the import of the way they'd interacted had escaped him until today—because he liked to stand too close to Selenka, just like Nerida did with Yuri. "How is Yuri?" he asked, wondering what else he had missed or not understood.

"Light duty." Nerida's jaw tightened. "Mostly at the empathic compound in DarkRiver/SnowDancer territory, but he's scheduled to start here tomorrow—this was meant to be light duty, too."

"Is he handing off to another member of the squad?"

"No. He has medical clearance and insists he's fully capable."

"Yuri is highly experienced and if he has medical clearance, then it may be time," Ethan said, because that was a normal, unobjectionable response to the information she'd shared. He'd long ago learned to mimic normal human behavior even when he stood distant from it.

Of course, that brought up the question of *whom* he'd learned it from.

Ivy Jane Zen, aware of Ethan's history because of her mating with Vasic and resulting deep connection to the squad, was one of the few people who'd perceived what he was doing. Though Ethan didn't talk much in comparison to his squadmates, it had taken the president of the Empathic Collective a very short time to pick up on how good he was at echoing what people wanted to hear.

"I'd call it a survival mechanism, but I have the strong feeling you didn't ever tell Ming what he wanted to hear," Ivy had murmured the last time they'd spoken, her brow furrowed and gaze intent. "There's something about you, Ethan . . ."

He'd stayed silent, but he knew what she must've sensed: the vein of madness that whispered in the quiet at the back of his mind. Ivy was an empath, a very strong empath. It was no surprise she'd picked that up in spite of the heavy shields he'd erected to hide the truth until it could no longer be hidden.

Ordinary people wouldn't have known what to do with him, but the squad was a brotherhood. That brotherhood had breached the secret bunker that was Ethan's prison minutes after Ethan killed Ming's two stalwarts and walked out of his cell—only to come face-to-face with a blue-eyed Arrow armed with heavy weaponry.

"Identify," had been the clipped order.

Ethan, pain yet ratcheting through his nerves, had considered just killing the other man . . . but a small, operational part of his brain had processed the fact that Abbot was young. In his twenties. In the time since he'd been held in the bunker, Ethan had seen only Arrows who were at least a decade and a half his senior. Abbot was the first peer he'd ever met.

So he'd said, "Ethan Night, Arrow, serial number Tk493b."

"A telekinetic?" Abbot had never moved the gun off him, but his tone had shifted. "Why don't I know you? I know all of us in the squad."

Us.

It had been the first time ever that Ethan had been included in a group. Perhaps that was why he'd told the pure truth. "Because this place is a cage, and I'm the animal it was built to contain."

Abbot had taken him to Aden, and whatever Aden had found in Ming's secret files, it'd led the new leader of the squad to welcome Ethan as one of his own. Then Abbot, Vasic, Nerida, and all the other telekinetics in the squad had shifted and made room for him at their virtual table even though he was strange and didn't speak for hours at a time and wasn't a Tk who could move objects or teleport.

Now Nerida said, "I was hoping you could take my shift tomorrow." She resettled her shoulders with a wince. "I trust you to have a cool head in any situation, especially around all these Es. Many of the newly trained tend to leak emotion."

Ethan thought of Selenka, of the scalding burn of her in his veins, but said, "I can do that." No alpha wolf was going to be anything but busy—better that he occupy his free hours or he would surrender to his obsession to stalk her every move, watch her with hot eyes and hotter need.

He didn't have to be an expert in predatory changelings to know such behavior would be acid on the bond between him and his mate; Selenka Durev was no one's prey, not even her Arrow mate's. "You have another engagement?"

"No." Nerida touched her shoulder with a hand built on bones so fine that no one looking at her would expect her to be able to throw around assailants three times her size. "Old injury acting up. Medic wants me to go in for treatment and with this situation contained and the world calmer than it's been for a while . . ."

"Yes, the timing is perfect." Of late, the Consortium had eased up on its violent attacks and assassination attempts. The gradual fade had some believing the power-hungry group was on the verge of disintegration.

Ethan was not one of those people.

"Thank you. I knew I could rely on you."

Curiosity stabbed, a glittery spiked ball in his gut. "Why do you and the others accept me?" It was a question he'd never asked.

"Because we were all lonely, dangerous children once." Nerida checked a message on the mobile comm wrapped around her left forearm. "All an Arrow expects from another Arrow is loyalty—and you have been loyal to us." She was gone a heartbeat later, her teleport abilities strong.

You have been loyal to us.

A truth. Even when he'd accepted the offer of his would be handler, he'd had no intention of betraying the squad.

Outside, the air was cool against him, the summer sun not yet at full strength. The colors of Moscow under the sunshine slapped into him at the same time as the mingled scents and the noises of people and birds.

Ethan sucked in a breath, throttling his sensory intake in instinctive self-defense. It still took five long minutes of intense focus to fight his way out of the howl of sensation and realize his shields hadn't failed—no, it was that he'd lived so long in the gray that he wasn't used to a world in full color.

There was so much he hadn't seen, didn't know. Such as how to satisfy his alpha wolf mate so she would want to be with him. Changelings were tactile by nature . . . yet Ethan hadn't touched another living being with any kind of intimacy until Selenka hauled his head down for a kiss.

He had no weapons with which to fight for her.

The thought had him reaching out to Abbot, the action an impulsive one. *Are you in Moscow?*

Yes. Do you need a lift back to HQ?

No, I have a question.

Where are you? We could talk in person.

Ethan gave him the location, and Abbot walked around the corner two minutes later. The first thing Ethan noticed was the pink mark on the collar of his uniform jacket.

Catching his gaze, Abbot looked down and his face softened a fraction. "Jaya's lipstick."

Selenka wasn't wearing color on her lips today, but Ethan wouldn't mind it if she did and got it on his collar. He *wanted* her mark on him, wanted to be like Abbot and have that satisfied, possessive look on his face.

Stretching out his body by doing a partial torso twist, Abbot said, "What did you want to ask?"

"What makes a woman happy?"

Abbot put his hands on his hips, his head angled down a little. When he looked up, his brilliant eyes held a sense of warmth Ethan could almost feel. "I asked the same question once. Only I asked Jaya."

Ethan paid close attention; an answer straight from the source could be invaluable. "What did she say?"

"That every woman is different—the key is to listen. She'll tell you what she wants if you pay attention."

Ethan thought of the madness in his head when he got close to Selenka, the way he turned into a devouring beast who had little of reason in him. Even now, his pulse accelerated and his body grew hard and tense at the thought of her lips slick and wet, her teeth taking bites out of him. "I'm not sure I can be that rational around her."

"Don't worry. There's a manual—it began with information about intimate physical interaction, but now has a growing section on emotional connection and how to nurture it." Abbot tapped his gauntlet. "I'm making a note to send it to you. I store it in my personal electronic vault."

Ethan stared at his fellow Arrow. "Who created the manual?"

"Another Arrow—but all of us add to it as we learn." Abbot held Ethan's gaze. "When I first met Jaya, I knew nothing of courtship, just that I would do anything to keep her safe. None of us are experts, Ethan. We all stumble."

That he wasn't the only one out there trying to find his feet on shaky ground, it meant more than he'd realized. "I owe you." For far more than this conversation; only now, the fog torn apart by wolf claws, did he see all the times Abbot had tried to reach out to him.

Waving away Ethan's statement, Abbot said, "There's no

debt in friendship." He paused. "I have to go do a pickup. We'll talk later."

Ethan was still digesting the other Arrow's words ten minutes later when he felt a ping against his mind, a request for PsyNet contact.

His "handler."

Ethan took his time responding, using the pause to consider his line of attack. The Consortium clearly had information that had led them to approach him in the first place. If Ethan had to guess, he'd say that the last of Ming's surviving coterie of loyalists had had a loose tongue prior to her violent death.

No doubt the Consortium had seen him as ripe for manipulation. Too late, his handler had realized they'd put their hand out to a vicious dog. So they had arranged the surprise second assailant—but their attempt to eliminate him had put Selenka in the line of fire.

Selenka had *never* been meant to take physical damage.

Black ice crawled across his senses, so cold it would burn anyone in its path. In harming the strong, beautiful, dangerous woman who was his mate, the Consortium had made an enemy of Ethan Night, and Ethan never forgave or forgot.

"Yes," he said at last, after stepping into the private psychic vault he and Operative C used for such meetings. He'd never met his Consortium handler in real life, but the mind that faced his was crystalline with power. A high Gradient but not a trained hand at subterfuge, he'd given away enough that he wasn't as anonymous as he believed.

"Did it go according to plan?" the other man asked, his gender one of the things he'd allowed to slip.

"There was a second assailant—one who was aiming at me."

"We decided to add her to ensure no suspicion fell on you."

"She was shooting to kill."

"We had faith in your reflexes—and she is an E. Not the best shot."

Ethan felt a growl inside him, born of the shadow wolf that was his mate's faint static-broken presence. Did the Consortium believe him mentally incapable as well as gullible?

"Does the alpha trust you?" Operative C asked.

"It's too early for that. But we've made a connection." A connection that meant Ethan would run this double cross until he could end Operative C, taking another chunk out of the Consortium.

The group would learn to never again look to an Arrow for collusion.

"I'll work it as we discussed." He had to utilize serious effort to sound as neutral as always because the wolf inside him was snarling. "Do not interfere."

"Keep us updated."

"When I can." He dropped out of the PsyNet before he could surrender to the urge to strike out at that mind that thought it could control him and that had been involved in the wounding of his mate. Operative C was simply a symptom of a larger malignancy and might serve as a conduit to the core.

Regardless of reason and logic, however, the black ice continued to grow.

When he attempted to step back into the cold place simply to see if he could, he found it gone, obliterated from existence. Where it had been glowed tendrils of red flame that burned in furrows formed by claws.

Madness, his brain misfiring . . . but it was a beautiful madness.

Beyond the madness, his shields held firm, holding back the far more deadly force within.

Settling back against the outer wall of the symposium hall, he took in the area around him. Trees and gardens shimmered green in the sunlight and dappled shade onto the footpaths as people moved here and there, going about their lives in a way Ethan had never experienced.

"Woof."

Ethan looked down at the dog with ragged fur that had wandered up to him, its body so thin that its rib cage pressed stripes against its skin. "I have no food."

Tail wagging and tongue out as it huffed, the stray sat down beside Ethan. He resolved to ignore it, but his eyes kept being drawn to the creature's ribs. Ethan had been that skinny during the worst periods of torture. The black ice cracked, riven with dark red embers.

"Stay here," he told the dog, and went back into the symposium center.

It followed him to the door, then dropped its head when he went inside. Ethan didn't think the creature would be there when he returned, but it was lying on the ground, tail flat—only to bound up in noisy excitement the instant it sensed Ethan.

"Down." Ethan waited until the animal settled before giving it the food he'd gathered from the supplies inside.

There was no reason for it to starve when Ethan had access to food.

As the stray ate, Ethan leaned back against the wall and thought of Selenka, of her kiss, of her hands on his body and her claws against his nape, of how she scorched him with her primal intensity. Ethan wanted to be burned. It was the first time in his adult life he could remember wanting anything—but he *wanted* Selenka.

The stab of pain that lanced through his temples was accompanied by a head butting against his leg. The dog, wanting his attention. Used to the pain, he glanced down at the mangy creature. "Don't look to be saved by me," he warned. "I kill. I don't protect."

He was a monster, trained and raised. But he was now Selenka's monster.

Chapter 9

Suspected cases of Scarab Syndrome logged to date: 32
    Confirmed cases: 3
    Excluded cases: 18
    Tests in progress to ascertain status of the remainder of the group. Referrals speeding up, so the likelihood of further confirmed cases is certain. Patient Zero and Memory Aven-Rose, primary empath attached to this team, are assisting.
    —Report to the Psy Ruling Coalition from Dr. Maia Ndiaye, PsyMed SF Echo

EZRA PUT HIS satchel down on the lounge sofa and screwed his eyes shut. The faint headache that had been plaguing him all day continued to linger like an unwelcome odor, but at least it hadn't grown in strength.

The odd thing was, his telepathic powers felt stronger and sharper in an intense way. As if he'd gone up three or four Gradients in the space of a single day and could now telepath across continents.

Halos surrounded the objects around him, color refractions of light.

Groaning, he went to see if he had any medication on hand. At the same time, he reminded himself that he was a teacher of physics with an exam paper to write. He didn't need to be distracted by migraine-induced delusions of grandeur and impossible spikes in his Gradient level.

He was also a respectable Gradient 6.9 telepath with a good job and excellent feedback ratings from his students, both Psy and otherwise. Not only that; he was partway through the post-Silence recovery program run by his new community PsyMed facility and was learning to recognize and deal with emotions. It appeared he was naturally inclined toward muted emotions, but he was definitely beginning to experience them.

Today, he'd spent a half hour longer than necessary in the facility library simply because he'd wanted to spend more time with another faculty member. His possible new friend hadn't seemed averse to his presence, either.

Life was good.

Chapter 10

Ethan would be the perfect man to add to my team. His abilities allow for a non-damaging way to push out-of-control individuals into sleep.

He's not ready. He barely communicates with us—to Ethan, we're no more his people than any other strangers. I failed him, Vasic.

You were a child when he was brought in. Not even Axl knew of his existence and he was the closest operative we had to Ming.

The logic of it doesn't matter. I see a broken Arrow and I feel him slipping away from the family we're trying to build. Ethan is alone in a way I can't comprehend.

—Conversation between Vasic Zen and Aden Kai
(three months ago)

"HOW DID IT go with Natalia?" Selenka asked Valentin after Ivy Jane and Emilie teleported out with the blue-eyed Arrow.

Aden stepped out of the other room before the bear alpha could reply. "I recalled Nerida and had her teleport Jaya and Natalia straight to a mental health clinic for assessment—she was aggressive to the point of verbal and physical eruptions, with no sense of guilt or sorrow."

Silver tapped one high-heel-clad foot, her sleek gray skirt suit spotless despite the events of the day. "That doesn't seem a very empathic way to act."

The other woman would know. Silver's brother was an empath. The only reason Selenka had clued in to that well-hidden fact was because a month back, Enforcement had arrested Arwen Mercant alongside bears who'd been having too good a time—and the damn bears had managed to pull three of her wolves into the mess.

To his credit, Valentin had reamed his bears on that occasion. "There is fun," he'd rumbled, "and there is anarchy. You're *all* restricted to Denhome until I say otherwise. With no beer."

As gasps of horror filled the cell where the miscreants had been sitting, Selenka had found herself watching the one person in the cell who wasn't a bear or a wolf—and who aroused the same protective instincts in her alpha heart as healers. She'd ID'd him as Silver's brother and figured he must be a medic. Then she'd come to this symposium, met all these Es, and realized the truth.

As for what the polished and sophisticated male had been doing in that cell, he apparently had terrible taste in men. So terrible that he hadn't even seemed to care that his designer shirt was torn and his stylishly cut hair mussed. No, he'd been sitting there with a dreamy smile on his face, his head pillowed on the shoulder of one of the most troublemaking bears in Valentin's clan.

As her dedushka had said to Selenka on the occasion of her first unrequited crush: *Love is cruel—you could fall for a goat. Imagine having half-goat children. They'd baaaowl instead of howl.*

The poor Mercants apparently had a habit of falling for bears. She'd said a prayer for their clan before leaving her drunk packmates in jail to sleep it off. Surviving a night in a small area resonant with bear snores had made all three vow to never again trust a bear who promised to show them a fun time.

Now she leaned one shoulder against the wall and folded her arms. "I'm with Silver. Empaths tend to flinch if they accidentally step on an insect. Killing other sentient beings is a whole level up."

Aden echoed her position on the other side of the corridor, but with a martial tension to him that reminded her of her mate. Cold night and jagged pieces and *hers*. Gripped by a sudden possessive fury that had her eyes semi-shifting, she almost missed Aden's reply. "Natalia didn't read as unstable to my senses, but I'm no specialist. It does appear that she suffered extreme physical abuse under Silence."

Selenka's lip curled. Abused submissives in a wolf pack didn't often strike out, but when they did, the results tended to be catastrophic. In a healthy pack, any sign of abuse was picked up long before it got to that point. But the PsyNet hadn't been a healthy place for empaths for over a century. "She's angry."

"In a way I've never before seen in any empath. While her Empathic Collective psychological profile did note an anger issue for which counseling was strongly suggested, no one had reason to be concerned about violence."

"We think we know empaths," Silver said, "but they may as well be a new designation, so much information has been lost. We have a single expert in Alice Eldridge and we can't expect her to know each and every facet of an entire designation."

Aden nodded. "Ivy's planning to speak to Alice, see if she does have any insights into Natalia's behavior."

"Seems simple enough to me." Selenka shrugged. "A creature with its paw caught in a trap will gnaw off that paw to escape—and a wounded animal maddened by pain will bite any hand that comes near."

Valentin's face was thunderous, but the words he spoke were calm. "Odd that two of them decided to strike at the same time." He leaned into Silver's body when the telepath aligned herself against his side. "I can see targeting the symposium to make a big splash, but two at once? Not coincidence."

"I agree," Aden said. "However, the two don't appear to have any kind of a connection. Natalia seemed genuinely confused when we asked her about Emilie—her only goal was to make the shot."

Selenka's wolf prowled against the inside of her skin. "She was aiming at Ethan," she said. "Why? Did he hurt her?" Even asking that question made her stomach roil and her mouth bloom with the taste of betrayal.

Aden shook his head. "She's never met him, but she heard through a trusted source—a source she refuses to identify—that he was guilty of similar actions against other victims across a period of years."

Selenka's claws pushed so hard at the insides of her skin

that she had to clench her teeth to keep them from slicing out and gouging into her own body. There was no fucking way she could ask the next logical question.

It was Valentin who broke the silence. "Chance Natalia's information is correct?"

"Less than zero."

"I know you trust your man." Silver's clear tone, with her razor-sharp ability to cut through bullshit like a knife. "But you can't guarantee where he was twenty-four hours of the day for years."

Aden hesitated for a second before saying, "Actually, I can."

Selenka's wolf bared its teeth, her vision acute and predatory. "Did you have him tagged?" Like an animal in a pen, its freedom only an illusion.

"I don't believe in tagging individuals as if they're cattle." Aden's voice never rose, his tone steady, but his anger was a cold wind against her. "Ming LeBon had different ideas."

"What about the rumored drug leash?" Silver asked, as Valentin wrapped an arm around her waist and held her possessively against his chest.

To those who didn't understand changeling bears, didn't know Valentin, that would've appeared to be nothing but a male asserting his right over a woman. Selenka knew the truth was far more complicated—Valentin was really, really angry at the idea of a man being leashed in such a way, and was cuddling up to his mate in an effort to take the edge off his temper.

Bears rarely lost it, but—so long as it had nothing to do with a territorial skirmish—Selenka had made sure her wolves knew to give the ursine changelings a wide berth should it ever happen. It'd take three wolves to take down an enraged bear of Valentin's size in a sudden fight—and they'd all come out with broken bones and shattered teeth.

Wolf rage was a quieter, harder, deadlier thing. Wolves didn't smash up rooms and swipe out heedlessly. Wolves planned. *Selenka* planned. If she wanted to attack Valentin, she'd think out every step ahead of time—and when she closed her jaws over his throat, it'd be precisely over his jugular and carotid.

That cold rage sharpened her senses now, had her hearing a distant door closing as Aden said, "The drug leash wasn't foolproof. In particular, there was no way to know its effect on those with incredibly rare abilities. There is no one like Ethan. Ming wouldn't have risked ruining him."

Ruin, Selenka thought, could have different meanings.

I am permanently damaged in ways that affect my psychic balance.

"What I'm about to share is highly confidential," Aden said, white lines bracketing his mouth. "I'm only doing so because you can't have any doubts about Ethan. This information cannot be shared with any others."

"As long as it isn't relevant to the safety of others, we have no reason to share it."

Aden waited until Valentin and Selenka both nodded agreement to Silver's statement before he continued. "Ming tagged Ethan. Dr. Edgard Bashir deactivated that tag three months ago once he'd worked out a way to do it without damaging Ethan's organs." Flat, hard words. "The device was placed inside him when he was a child and it grew tendrils around his heart in the time since. It can't be removed, but it's dead."

Selenka's growl echoed against the walls. The idea of being watched that way, until nothing you did was private, it would've driven her insane. That Ethan wasn't locked up in an institution was an indication of his strength, another piece of the dangerous enigma that was her mate.

"I was able to confirm that, at the times concerned, Ethan was in lockdown deep inside a bunker Ming used as a secret satellite base."

Selenka's claws thrust out of her fingers as, inside her, the cold night that was Ethan twisted with broken shards. She didn't even flinch as those claws sliced holes in her jacket, woman and wolf both hungry for vengeance. "Did you tell the E who shot at him?"

A nod. "She's too tied into the delusion of righteous vengeance to see reason."

"What I find interesting," Silver murmured while placing her hand over her mate's where he had it splayed against her abdomen, "is how someone managed to manipulate two empaths into an attack. I can't understand the motive. If the empaths fall, so does the Honeycomb—and by default the PsyNet. Even the Consortium can't have any wish to see the PsyNet fail."

"None of it makes any sense." Aden glanced at the sleek black comm device on his wrist. "Both Natalia and Emilie are under medical review and inaccessible to further questioning for the time being. However, I'll set my people to tracking those of their communications that took place via non-telepathic channels."

Meeting over, Selenka tracked Ethan, his scent a shining thread to her wolf. Her beautiful, dangerous stranger of a mate was leaning against the external wall beside the main door, a stray at his feet, its tail wagging.

Pale eyes locked with her own.

"You need to see your healer," he said with no indication that he felt any sense of intimidation in her presence. Arousal licked through her—but her stubborn mate wasn't finished. "The numbing agent in the gel will have long worn off."

Her wolf curled its upper lip at the demand in his tone but grudgingly accepted he was right. Her back hurt. "Yes. I messaged him just before. He's already at the pack's city HQ, so we'll meet him there." She looked at the dog—now quivering, but staying staunchly at Ethan's side. "That your dog?"

Ethan looked down at the hopeful, scared, loyal animal. "It appears we are equally damaged." He didn't try to shoo the creature away as it walked with them . . . its body trembling the entire time.

Impressed by its courage, she caught the animal's eyes. It froze. She didn't crouch—that would just confuse it. She just bent and patted its head. "I'm not going to eat you." The dog knew it stood next to a wolf, a predator that could rip it to shreds.

Ethan said nothing after she drew back, but his new pet wagged its tail like a metronome. She found her gaze drawn to Ethan's throat again, to the strength of the cords, to the steady beat of his pulse against the warmth of his skin . . . and had her teeth sunk into his flesh before she realized she'd moved.

A growl filled her chest, the scent of him in her blood.

And the deadly Arrow she'd just bitten didn't lift a finger to defend himself. He just placed his hand on her hip, holding her close to the muscled strength of his body.

Growl turning into a low rumble, she released her bite, then licked her tongue over the indentation in his skin—she'd been careful even in her lack of control, hadn't broken skin.

His breathing altered. The sharp intake of it had her jerking away.

What the hell was she doing? She'd just *bitten* a man she'd only met hours earlier . . . and she was very, very satisfied to see she'd marked him. Even now, she couldn't help but brush her fingers over the mark. "This isn't normal." It came out husky.

Ethan looked at her with unflinching intensity. "I've never been normal. But you're my mate now and I'm not going to give that up."

Selenka had no idea who this man was—but that he was her mate was unquestionable. The bond, jagged and cold and subtly out of tune, hummed in her blood, her wolf craving skin privileges. But the dissonance in their bond sharpened her instincts and gave her the clarity to say, "Tell me about why you're a threat."

Ethan's pupils spread outward, until his irises were a sweep of obsidian.

Patient Zero

Your current psychic readings are a cause for concern.
—Dr. Maia Ndiaye, PsyMed SF Echo, to Pax Marshall,
CEO, Marshall Group

PATIENT ZERO.

That's what Dr. Ndiaye and the others on the Scarab team called him.

It was to maintain his anonymity, but also because it was true. He was the first known case of Scarab Syndrome in the post-Silence world, a powerful man anchored to sanity by two slender threads.

Sporadic contact with an empath as unique as he was a patient.

And a bond with his twin that not even Silence had been able to break. She worried about him despite the fact that he'd let her down in so many ways.

"You have that look in your eye," Theo said now, leaning in the doorway of the suite that was her own in this sprawling apartment that consumed an entire floor of the building.

For so long, Pax had protected her by making her irrelevant. Those days were done. He was now the head of the family and he protected her by making it clear she was *never* to be prey in the vicious game of politics and power that was their family—anyone who came after her would be putting themselves front and center in his crosshairs.

And Pax was not a man known for mercy.

Yet with Scarab in his head, he'd also planned for the future. Whatever happened to him, his twin would never again be without protection. Money could buy a lot of things—including the safety of a sibling who had always been the better half of their broken pair.

"What look?" He turned, hands in his pockets and suit jacket unbuttoned. "You couldn't even see my eyes from where you're standing."

"I feel it." Quiet, intense words. "The power calls to you."

It did and always would, whispering a siren song beyond all he'd ever known. "It's madness," he said. "I wouldn't exchange my sanity for power."

She looked at him with those sky-blue eyes for a long time before retreating back into her suite and shutting the door. The last thing he saw was the sunlight glinting off the golden strands of her hair. She was his twin, but they hadn't been truly bonded for a long time. Still, she wouldn't let him fall.

Patient Zero could not be permitted to terrorize the world.

No matter how sweetly the sirens sang.

Chapter 11

A sharp blade
Thrust deep
Bloody droplets in the snow
　　—"Love Song" by Adina Mercant, poet (b. 1832, d. 1901)

ETHAN KNEW THAT he was about to put his life and his mating with Selenka on the line. The temptation to lie and lessen his complicity in the plan whispered at the back of his mind, but the claws that raked his insides were a warning—to lie would be to poison their bond in its very infancy.

He had to speak the truth—and if his mate chose to rip out his throat for it, so be it. "The gas attack was a setup," he said, and saw the wolf come into her eyes. "I was meant to save you."

The growl that filled the air was a thing of withheld fury that made the dog at his side freeze. "Why?"

"So you would then be more inclined to trust me and I could work my way deeper into your confidence. Their aim was to control you through me."

Selenka's reaction was not what he expected. After staring at him with golden eyes for a long moment, she bared her teeth in a feral smile. "What *mudak* thought this up?"

"He calls himself Operative C and he's part of the Consortium." Off-balance and unsure of the meaning of her reaction, Ethan stuck doggedly to the truth. "I've managed to track down part of his identity—he's in computronic distribution—but I don't have his name yet."

Selenka gripped his chin. "Why did you decide to betray

all that the Arrows stand for and align yourself with a man who would use traumatized empaths for his own gain?"

Once more, Ethan fought the urge to diminish his role in this. "I felt nothing when he came to me, was trapped behind a gray fog where nothing penetrated. I wondered if being a traitor would incite a spark in me." Such a strange, inexplicable decision, and yet it had made sense in that time and place. "I will say one thing in my defense."

Selenka raised an eyebrow.

"I didn't know that he'd be using empaths." Never would he have agreed to anything that meant another sentient being was twisted and used. "I believed empaths couldn't be pushed to violence, and it'd be a member of the security team with Consortium sympathies who'd be the assailant."

Grip tightening, Selenka growled again. "What if we hadn't mated? Would you have gone through with it?"

"The entire operation was off the instant they drew blood." Ethan shoved back the dark power that bulged against his shields, fed by his cold rage. "I was clear on that—no blood was to be spilled." He'd been forced to be a murderer most of his life; if he killed again, it would be by choice and not because he'd been manipulated into it.

Selenka was caught between twin urges: to bite her mate for taking such a traitorous step, and to hold him close—because the amount of hurt that would cause a child to create a "gray fog" between himself and the world that lasted into adulthood was a thing of horror.

Incendiary rage might've still burned them both to a cinder—except that he was standing here, laying out all of it and making no attempt to hide his involvement. "You realize it wouldn't have worked?" Trust so deep that it began to affect an alpha's decisions took a long time to grow.

"I didn't care," Ethan said bluntly. "I had zero investment in the scheme itself. The only thing I wanted out of it was to know if it would erase the numbness." Midnight eyes awash in darkness. "I set up a time-release communication to go to Aden should I be killed by Operative C. I didn't stop the clock in the aftermath, so Aden will receive the information in the next minute."

Truly, her mate was an enigma. "I'll have to share the

possible gambit with others in Trinity." Though she would conceal Ethan's identity—he was her mate now, hers to protect . . . or to destroy if he was a monster. That was the brutal reality that came with a mating between dominants.

Some couldn't do it even if their mate turned to evil or became a bloodthirsty rogue who forgot their human self. In that case, it was the alpha who took care of the problem. But when you were an alpha, the responsibility for your mate was wholly in your hands. Selenka would not delegate it to anyone else.

If Ethan proved monstrous, she would be the one to end him—even if it tore her wolf apart.

"You should know that Operative C appears to be running this as a test," Ethan said. "Its spectacular failure should halt any further attempts."

Because instead of Ethan infiltrating BlackEdge, BlackEdge had stolen Ethan. Wolf still smug about that despite everything, Selenka released his chin just as Aden exited the symposium hall to make a beeline to them.

Ethan's dog growled at the leader of the squad until Ethan said a firm, "No."

What followed was an interaction Selenka found fascinating, there was so little outward emotion in it—yet a cadre of heavy, dark elements moved beneath. "If Operative C isn't aware of your defection, don't alert him," the leader of the squad said. "We may be able to use him to get to bigger players in the Consortium."

Ethan inclined his head, his eyes having faded back to their pale hue. "You have my apology, Aden. I didn't think of the impact on the squad when I did this. It was never my intention to cause you disrepute."

Aden Kai looked down at the ground for a long second before glancing up. "I failed you, Ethan. We all failed you. That you wished for vengeance is understandable."

Selenka felt Ethan's confusion even through their muddled bond. "He didn't want revenge," she told Aden. "Trust me on this."

Aden's responding glance quickly turned into a frown as he looked from her to Ethan . . . and seemed to focus on the bite mark on Ethan's neck. "I see," he said. "In that case, may I request that you not mention an Arrow connection when you share this Consortium play with other alphas? Distrust between changelings and Arrows will cause far more harm than good."

Selenka had already come to that same conclusion. "Don't worry. I'm not about to give the Consortium what they want." Division, distrust, fragmentation, that was the Consortium's goal. "Especially over such a stupid plan." As if alpha changelings were children, to be maneuvered and swayed by a single person when they carried their entire pack on their shoulders.

"You may disavow me if you wish," Ethan said to Aden.

Aden's response was absolute. "Never. You're one of us, Ethan, and you always will be."

"Will you not always distrust me?"

"If Selenka hasn't torn out your throat, then you've told us the truth," the Arrow leader said quietly. "A mate can scent betrayal."

Selenka's smile was feral. Because Aden was right. Even the static in her bond with Ethan couldn't hide the truth of him from her—her mate was intense, dangerous, and honest as a blade. "Other than alerting the others to a possible plan to gain their trust via miraculous rescues and other such," she said, "this is now a private matter between Ethan and me."

"Accepted." Aden stepped back . . . but didn't leave. "Just remember this, Ethan—you're an Arrow. We may have let you down for too many years, but we will never again do so. Call us and we will come."

Selenka kept her silence till after the squad leader had returned inside the building. Then she gripped Ethan's jaw and pulled him down for a kiss that was all tongue and possession. He was breathing heavily in the aftermath, his lips wet and a touch swollen from the ferocity of her kiss. "Will you ever betray me or mine?" she asked.

The answer was a storm of devotion so violent that it came through despite the interference and jagged edges of their bond. "No," he said while her head rang from the strength of his response. "I am yours in every way. You own me."

Selenka's wolf growled in exultation, but the human half of her struggled. Not because he'd given her his allegiance—the mating bond was a powerful force—but because of the lack of boundaries in it. "I'm a stranger to you," she said, the taste of him yet in her mouth. "Aren't you afraid I'll use you to spill blood?"

"For you, I will." No hesitation, no blink.

Ethan had chosen and if the mate he'd chosen wanted to use him until he broke, he'd permit that to happen. He knew no other way to be, had no fail-safes except for the gray fog—and never would he return to that.

Selenka's response was a growl and another kiss that scalded him. "I have no idea what I'm going to do with you." It was a snarl.

"Do it later," Ethan said, unable to contain the words any longer. "Your back wound needs attention." He'd been fighting the urge to push at her about that wound since he began telling her about Operative C. "You can tear out my throat later if you wish." He angled his head to the side to show her that vulnerability, make it clear he wouldn't fight her.

Another growl lifted into the air, the brush of hot breath against his skin as she licked over the mark. "We're going to have to share skin privileges soon, or my wolf is going to strip you naked on the street."

"After you see the healer," Ethan insisted.

Selenka's laughter was edgy. "Come then, mate, let's go do this."

She used the short walk to calm down some, get her head in the right space. The compulsion for skin privileges, however, wouldn't die. Her wolf was *insistent* that she deepen her physical connection with her mate, its insistence so frantic that it was making it difficult to think.

Growling low in her throat as they passed a narrow alleyway swathed in shadows and devoid of any watchful eyes, whether real or computronic, she pushed Ethan up against the wall. "Skin privileges, yes or no?"

"Does that mean skin contact with you?" His eyes were going black in front of her as he spoke, his breathing speeding up.

"Yes."

"Yes," he answered so quickly that it tumbled over her response. *"Yes."* Raw, unadorned need.

He reached for her as she slid her hand around his nape,

the kiss that followed so primal that she made a deep sound that came from her wolf. Instead of backing off, he moved his hand to her hair and held on as she deepened the kiss . . . before echoing her moves. The Arrow was a quick learner.

The thought fired up another in her brain.

Tearing her lips from his, she said, "Are you a virgin?" Psy under Silence hadn't indulged in skin privileges—a little fact that wasn't common knowledge but was right there to see if you looked at the available information.

A society based on eliminating emotion from their people wouldn't be big on sexual contact—it was damn hard to stay detached while you were tangled up with a lover, even if that emotion was sensual pleasure untouched by any other emotion.

"Yes," Ethan said, and kissed her again.

Selenka groaned and bit down on his lower lip, but the Arrow didn't retreat. Her hands went to his jacket, and she had the front fastening open before she'd consciously thought about it. Snarling when she discovered he was wearing something underneath, she used her claws to tear it . . . and flattened her palms on hot skin over taut muscle.

Ethan made a deep sound in his chest and pushed into her touch, both his hands now tangled in her hair and his arousal rigid against her. Breaking the kiss, she ran her mouth over his throat, licking over the bite mark in the process. He shuddered, his powerful frame a slave to her touch.

It was erotic as hell.

Unzipping her jacket, she took one of his hands and put it on her breast. Even through the bra, the contact had her arching her spine. Then her Arrow bent his head and kissed the plump upper curve, all tongue and wetness, and she wanted to push him to the ground and ride him until they both came so hard they saw stars.

But beneath the feral need was a potent tenderness.

They both needed to let off a little of the steam, but she wouldn't have his first time be a frantic coupling in a Moscow alley. The possessive tenderness was enough to temper even her wolf's strangely violent need; that tenderness should've felt wrong being directed at a man who was part of a squad of deadly assassins, but in this, he was a novice.

So even as she pulled his head back up for another kiss,

she was stroking her hand down his chest in a gentling caress. Nuzzling his throat when they broke the kiss to catch a breath, she said, "We'll finish this later, when we can properly taste each other."

His hand was on her waist, skin to skin, and it tightened for a moment before he released her. "Consent is key," he said, as if repeating a rote statement.

Selenka ran her nails down his chest. "That's true. Who taught you?"

"An empath who gives the squad lessons in how to interact socially." Rough words, his breathing erratic. "But I knew the one about consent before her lesson."

Because the right to give or refuse consent had been stolen from him over and over again.

Biting back her snarl, she pressed a gentle kiss to his chest before stepping back and zipping up her jacket—she was aware of his hot eyes on her skin as it was covered inch by inch, and if she hadn't been so determined to properly introduce him to pleasure, she'd have jumped him then and there.

"Sorry about the tee," she said, seeing the mess she'd made of the black fabric.

He looked down. "I have more. I would rather you touch me than protect my clothing."

Overcome by a wave of wolfish affection, Selenka pulled the sides of his jacket together and began to seal it up the front, hiding the torn tee. He stayed still under her touch. "What I did, will it poison us?"

Need no longer clouding her mind, Selenka looked into those pale eyes that had gone acute with concentration . . . and made a decision. "You chose to participate in a Consortium plan before you met me. Our relationship began from the point we first spoke, and you've said you won't betray me or mine now."

"I won't." Agreement so positive it was a punch through the mating bond.

You own me.

Still disturbed by that statement, Selenka also saw it for the absolute commitment to her that it was. "Some choices are unforgiveable, no matter how far back in the past."

Finishing with his jacket, she took a step back. "But some choices are missteps that we can correct if given the chance. This is your chance to be better than what others would make of you, Ethan. A better man, a better friend to your squadmates, and a man I would be proud to call my own." He was her mate now, and she could do nothing but fight for him—especially against his own demons.

"You are not proud now?"

Selenka thought of her wolf's smugness, placed it against the darkness of Ethan's past, and knew he needed both sides of the truth. "The most primal part of me is proud of your strength and that you're deadly." She was a dominant wolf and such things mattered to her. "But to the rest of me, you're a stranger. I don't yet know the heart of you—and the heart is what turns a bond into a true mating."

Ethan's pale eyes drank her in with an intense possessiveness that might've terrified another woman. "My heart is unlikely to be normal, either."

Gut cold with anger all over again for how his view of himself had been twisted, Selenka ran her claws over his jaw. "Then show me your jagged edges and your fractured pieces, your obsession and your need. Show me you."

Chapter 12

Since you will not respect your father's advice, consider this an edict from your alpha. Your pup will now live with Lada and me.

—Alpha Yevgeni Durev to Kiev Durev (2062)

OLEG'S VEHICLE WAS parked out front of BlackEdge's city HQ, the white-haired senior healer hovering right by the front door. He pounced on her the instant she appeared. "What happened to you?" he demanded, spinning her around as if she was the child he'd helped birth and not the most dominant wolf in the pack.

Sixty years old, his skin dark as teak and his eyes a soft brown, Oleg had been a healer for longer than Selenka had been alpha. A gentle wolf by nature, he went crazy when one of his people was hurt. Selenka had learned to let him get it out of his system, her wolf's affection for the healer a smile in her blood; Oleg would calm once he'd seen her injury and worked out the steps to deal with it.

She'd sensed Ethan's sudden deadly motionlessness when the older man first reached for her, had immediately caught his eyes and scowled in warning. *No one* touched a healer in violence. Tension continued to hum in the air, the ice inside her cracked with fire, but Ethan didn't attempt to get in Oleg's way.

Ruffled fur settled.

A part of her had been braced for another reaction, even though nothing Ethan had said or done had indicated a lack of respect for women in power. That was her own shit to deal with, her own open wound.

"Inside, Selya." Oleg pulled her in, using the version of her name most often used by packmates; Selenka's mother hadn't chosen a traditionally Russian name for her daughter, instead going for the name of a favorite singer, but that had proved no barrier when it came to the tradition of using diminutives in everyday life.

To her mother, she'd been Selenochka as a babe. To her packmates and friends, she was Selya. To her grandparents—and often to Oleg—she was Selenushka. And to the pups who were still learning to speak, she was whatever combination of syllables they could put together.

"You can come, too," Oleg said to Ethan, "but the dog stays just inside the door until he's had a bath."

"Stay." Ethan's tone was absolute.

The stray sat down as Selenka followed Oleg into the small infirmary inside the HQ.

After taking off her jacket with a withheld wince—because now that she was no longer hopped up on primal sexual attraction, the injury fucking *hurt*—she jumped up onto the examining table and sat with her legs hanging over the edge while Oleg went behind her to uncover, then examine the wound.

Ethan, having followed them in, took a watchful position next to the doorway.

His pale eyes found hers.

And her wolf lunged at her skin, wanting out, wanting him.

Oleg's hands hesitated against her skin for a second before the healer carried on in his work. That was the trouble with being changeling—her packmates could smell all kinds of things. That Oleg had scented her sharp, sensual response to the man who stood silently by the doorway meant that response was even more potent than she'd thought.

Not that Oleg would do anything but be nosy. Arousal and skin privileges weren't a thing of shame, but a joyful part of life. Even Selenka, with her constant awareness of the lack of discipline that might be in her blood, had never seen uninhibited skin privileges as a negative. Her problem had always been in finding someone to whom she was attracted and whom she wouldn't break.

But now she had an Arrow for a mate. Though he was a stranger in many ways, she did know several critical facts about him. One of which was that beyond his Arrow skin, he was a protector with the capacity to feel empathy for those who were weaker. Ethan might not see it that way, but the man had just adopted a flea-bitten stray.

Her lips curved slightly.

Yes, she wanted this complex stranger in her bed, was looking forward to introducing him to pleasure that was slower and deeper than what they'd already shared. She'd keep her instincts in check and debauch him later.

"Did you take any injury?" Oleg asked Ethan even as he continued to work on Selenka. "I can't smell blood on you, but not all wounds cause blood loss."

"I am uninjured." Flat, toneless, with no attempt to ingratiate or appear friendly.

Oleg, however, had wrangled too many snarly dominants to be that easily shut down. "One of our pack who's helping out with security came in muttering about lights that had him seeing stars. Apparently that was you?"

Selenka wondered what her mate would or would not reveal.

"I am a telekinetic who can't move objects. My power lies with photons—light particles." Ethan's eyes were on Selenka, not Oleg, the force of concentration in the paleness a sensual challenge that said her mate didn't appreciate her reserve. "As far as anyone knows, I either manipulate or focus those particles. Akin to how a pane of glass focuses light."

"Hmm," Oleg said. "I've never thought of light as deadly, but of course what's a laser but a blade of light?"

Selenka stilled at the realization of why Ethan was so many jagged shards inside her. She'd thought she'd understood but hadn't grasped the full scope of it. He saw himself as a *weapon*. One who'd been forced by his trainers to kill and kill again. What did that do to a child already traumatized by a self-defensive strike that had left him an orphan?

Her mate had shattered into broken shards long ago, each shard edged with blood.

"I don't have an official subdesignation." Ethan continued

to look at Selenka, his compulsion toward her unhidden. "I'm listed as an atypical Tk on the squad's roll, though Aden has told me that I appear to work on the same micro-levels as Tks who can move the cells in a body."

Selenka's phone chimed with an alert as she went to reply. Recognizing that pattern as the one she'd assigned Gregori, she pulled the phone out of her pocket and read the message. "Graffiti on Nat's shop." Her eyes narrowed. "Gregori caught the scent of one of Blaise's wolves in the same spot."

Oleg tut-tutted, his hands warm and gentle against her. "Those young wolves are too strong and dangerous to be outside of a pack—and Blaise might be a dominant wolf himself, but he's no alpha. Neither is that lieutenant of his. What's her name? Nomani, that's it. Neither one of them dominant enough to lead."

"Hmm." The problematic and potentially risky setup was part of the reason why Selenka had agreed to her lieutenant Emanuel's passionate plea that Haven's Disciples be allowed to set up shop at the edge of her territory.

Emanuel had once been a wayward youth, but: "I had a pack that cared behind me. These youths don't have that if they've hooked up with a charismatic charlatan. We have to help them before it's too late and they're forever twisted by their association with that *mudak*."

To say that her lieutenant had strong feelings about Blaise was a vast understatement. Selenka agreed the Disciples' "spiritual leader" was a slimy bastard who'd charmed the four nineteen- to twenty-one-year-old wolves into leaving their packs to become part of his congregation.

The four were strong and getting stronger. At that level of dominance, they only had two options: become loners or be part of a pack. To roam together in a group *without* a hier-archical pack structure would lead only to bloodshed. Both among themselves and against others unfortunate enough to cross their path.

As Oleg had pointed out, Blaise wasn't strong enough to control them for much longer. Of course, they weren't BlackEdge wolves and Selenka was within her rights to have denied Emanuel's request, but that would've just dumped the problem on another pack—likely one not as strong as

BlackEdge, and therefore not as capable of ensuring those four wolves didn't cause mayhem. Because without the correct oversight, they could do irreparable damage to changeling relationships with humans and Psy.

A single vicious attack by an out-of-control wolf was all it would take.

Blaise also had a cohort of humans, nonpredatory changelings, and Psy in his fold. As with the wolves, they were in thrall to him. Which was why Selenka hadn't invited the four wolves to join BlackEdge—she had no desire to invite resentful spies into their midst. If one of the four wished to defect, he or she would have to run a gauntlet more difficult than those navigated by loners who wished to reintegrate into a pack.

Blaise had promised to ensure his "flock" behaved with "utmost care" in Selenka's territory. That promise was falling short even faster than Selenka had expected. "Poor Emanuel," she muttered. "He'll be so disappoin—" A howling pain, the wrench inside her so vicious that she couldn't form words. But she was already moving, though the agony reverberated through every cell in her body.

Oleg, connected to her by a blood bond, staggered at the same time.

"What is the threat?" Ethan's eyes obsidian, the ice inside her a frigid inferno.

Selenka hauled on her ruined jacket over nothing but her damaged sports bra as she ran out the door. "One of my people is hurt." The alpha-lieutenant bond with Emanuel had severed with bloody ferocity, but she couldn't accept the finality of the loss until she'd seen his body.

Oleg was the last person to make it to the vehicle, but she waited for him because they'd need a healer. Ethan's dog jumped into the back a second before the healer. Not saying another word, Selenka hit the accelerator, going at speeds no human could ever match. She didn't know the exact location where Emanuel had gone down, but she'd felt enough in that shocking moment of loss to point her vehicle toward the pack's intensely guarded green heart.

Her phone rang minutes into the drive, the tone the one she'd assigned her father. She had no time for his drama today, but something made her answer using the car's system. "What?" It was a growl, her wolf so close to her skin she could barely form words.

"Emanuel, he's hurt." Her father's voice was frantic. "There's so much blood."

Selenka leaned into Ethan's ice. "Coordinates." It took Kiev Durev two attempts to convey the exact location.

Even though Selenka knew it was too late, she still drove with unalloyed fury. Skidding the vehicle to a stop as far into the thick green of the pack's forest home as she could, she then got out and ran. An alpha could often hold on to even a very badly wounded member of the pack if she got to him fast enough.

Oleg would track her by scent.

As for Ethan, she was abandoning him in unfamiliar territory, but the man was an Arrow and bonded to her deeper than her lieutenants.

He'd find her.

Her alpha heart drove her on as pain echoed through her veins, the anguish of a lost limb throbbing in her psyche. But though she ran with a speed that turned the world into a blur, Emanuel was gone by the time she reached him. He lay slumped on the ground in the lap of another member of her pack who had blood all over his tailored shirt and pants.

"I ran as fast as I could when I smelled blood," her father said, the pointed vee of his goatee quivering with the extent of his trembling. "I tried to help." His Adam's apple bobbed. "But I couldn't hold him."

Selenka knew he'd had no hope of doing that; Emanuel had died in an instant, likely a heartbeat after taking what looked to be a point-blank shot to the heart. Else she would've felt *some* warning through her link with her lieutenant. Dropping to her knees beside his bloody body regardless, she gathered him to her and tried to will life back into him. But even an alpha's power couldn't bring the dead back to life.

Anguish ripped her in two.

With sandy blond hair and playful green eyes, Emanuel had been only forty-four, a wolf in the prime of his life. He hadn't yet found a mate but had been courting a sweet, submissive wolf who blushed shyly each time he approached her. A gentler kind of dominant, one who'd laugh as easily as growl, he was beloved by his packmates—and deeply valued by his alpha.

Selenka had expected to have his calm, amused presence with her as she aged and settled into her role in the pack. Emanuel—never Manny or any other shortening of a name that honored his adored *grand-père*—was meant to be an honorary uncle to her future children, a friend to her till they were both "grumpy old graybeards." But she didn't cry. An alpha couldn't. Not until her work was done.

"Did you see or scent anything?" she asked her father; right now, all she could scent was Emanuel's blood, her every breath filled with cold iron.

"I think I heard a vehicle—maybe a jetcycle." He shoved a trembling hand through the neatly cut strands of his light brown hair. "To be honest, I didn't pay much attention. I was more worried about Emanuel. I thought he might still be alive."

As that had been Selenka's first reaction regardless of the way the bond had broken, she just cradled her friend and lieutenant's body closer to her and nodded.

"I found a weapon, too." Kiev held up that weapon before putting it on the blood-soaked ground. "I know I shouldn't have picked it up, that I'll have contaminated the evidence, but I wasn't thinking straight." Sitting back on the forest floor, he stared at the dried blood on his palms. "I thought maybe someone would be coming back."

Selenka wasn't worried about evidence while she held Emanuel's already cooling body in her arms. Her wolf anguished, she threw back her head on a howl that reverberated throughout their territory. Wolf after wolf took up the mourning cry, and the sadness spread. Soon, the entire pack would know that they'd lost one of their own.

Oleg arrived on the heels of that howl, in his wolf form, his medical kit strapped to his body.

Ethan, she thought. Ethan must've done up the straps.

The healer keened with her.

Soon came another sound in the trees, her mate having tracked her. Her father's head jerked up at the same time, his eyes wolf gold and rimmed with red. Kiev Durev might bemoan the changeling way of life as "primitive" and "uncivilized," but he was a wolf, too, and not exactly a weak one.

Selenka kicked the weapon away from his hand before he could reach for it.

His jaw hardened, his eyes glittering. But Selenka was used to both her father's bitter anger and his lack of discipline in concealing it. Shrugging it off with the ease of long practice, she stroked Emanuel's hair back from his face and pressed a kiss to his cheek. "You were one of the best of us," she murmured. "I will remember you always."

BlackEdge had been lucky, so lucky since she came to power. There'd been losses, yes, but most through the natural effect of time or in accidents. None of her people had died in this kind of violence. She carried each and every lost member inside her heart.

But Emanuel . . . His absence would leave a hole in that heart.

Coming down on his knees next to her, Ethan placed one hand on her nape. The black ice of her mate, the churning blue fire caged within, held her steady in the storm of howls and pain; the feel of him was an icy calmness, a night without stars. As if he knew she needed the cold, needed the ice. Else her anger and grief would swallow her whole.

Someone had come into her territory and harmed one of her own. Selenka would not stop until that someone was brought to account. She would hunt them to the ends of the earth, leave them bloody and broken.

Chapter 13

A strong pack is built on a core of family, of loyalty.
—Excerpt from a school essay by Ilarion Chernyshevsky (18),
BlackEdge pack

ETHAN STAYED WITH Selenka through all that followed. When he'd first appeared out of the trees behind her, all he'd seen was blood. Light had coated his fingertips, his lethal instincts zeroing in on the man who sat across from her. A second later his brain had noted the familiar eyes in that masculine face and recognized that Selenka held the body that was the source of all the blood.

Her grief was stabbing knives inside him, an emotion that triggered memories of a small boy surrounded by death. Slamming that door shut, for that way lay madness, he'd made skin contact in an attempt to give comfort in the way he knew was a changeling thing. She hadn't leaned back into him, but neither had she shaken off his touch.

It took several minutes before more wolves poured out of the trees around them—some in human form, some in wolf.

Placing her dead packmate gently on the ground, she rose to her feet. "Gregori, Ivo," she said, speaking to a big man with a full blond beard against golden skin, and a slender black male who appeared several years younger than the one with the beard. "Take Emanuel home."

Faces carved with lines of loss, the two came forward. The one she'd called Gregori acknowledged Ethan's presence with a nod, before he and the younger man bent down to pick up their fallen packmate's body.

Ethan didn't point out that from a forensic point of view, they should've left the body where it was. This was a changeling space and these were changeling rules. He knew they had other ways of tracking prey.

"The rest of you except for Margo and Kostya stay in place. We're going to try and track the person who did this to Emanuel." She angled her head at Ethan. "I want those Arrow eyes looking for any clues."

He followed her as she began to slowly circle the area. Margo Lucenko and a changeling wolf broke away in different directions at the same time—but all three wolves eventually came to the same point and began to walk in the same direction. They didn't get far before reaching a disturbed patch of earth that, to Ethan's eyes, was clear evidence that a jetcycle had been parked there. It had taken off in a hurry, spraying the forest debris around them.

He crouched down. "No clear tire prints." No way to track the specific make of the vehicle.

The four of them followed the trail until it disappeared onto a proper pathway that led out of the forest.

"I'll talk to the surveillance team when I get back." Margo's voice held none of the joy it had earlier that day, her eyes hard. "See if our cameras picked up anything."

Ethan considered the location. "Do you have access to a surveillance satellite?"

Three pairs of wolf eyes landed on him, but it was Selenka who spoke. "We're in the process of buying a satellite, but we don't have one yet."

"It's possible another satellite might've caught a useful image. I can ask Arrow techs to have a look." Ethan never asked for help, but for Selenka, he'd do whatever it took.

"Ask." Selenka's voice held a low growl. "We have agreements with everyone in this region that they won't spy on us and we won't spy on them when we have our satellites, but if anyone has footage, I want to know."

Even as Ethan sent through a priority request using his mobile comm, she fisted her hand, her shoulders rigid. "I need to go look after my pack. Margo, Kostya."

"We'll stay on this," Margo promised, while the wolf

brushed its body against Selenka's leg in a silent statement of intent.

The madness in Ethan whispered that he had to remain with Selenka, that she needed him. It was an arrogant thing to think about a wolf alpha, but still the compulsion would not fade.

It was by pure accident that his eyes met Margo's. She mouthed, *Look after her.*

Ethan had no need of the direction but inclined his head slightly nonetheless. Margo had made it clear her loyalty was Selenka's, and for that alone, Ethan was predisposed to listen to her.

Returning to the clearing with his mate, he saw it now held what looked to be a forensics team. One of whom was bagging the weapon. Another stood impassive and silent while the man who must be Selenka's father shrugged off his bloody clothing and handed it over. "It's Emanuel's blood," he growled, his voice clipped and furious. "What did you expect me to do but hold him?"

"Forensics needs to check the evidence," Selenka said, her own tone curt. "There might be evidence on your clothing that could lead us to the killer."

"I'm your father and a tenured professor. I deserve respect."

"I don't have time for this," Selenka replied shortly. "A man smart enough to have a PhD should be smart enough to understand the necessity for forensics."

A flash of fire in the older man's eyes that had Ethan categorizing him as a future threat. The male didn't treat his daughter as an alpha wolf should be treated. Selenka was permitting him to buck the hierarchy, likely because of their familial bond, but Ethan had no such bond. He would watch the man . . . and he would end him if he proved a threat to Selenka.

He had never liked being a murderer but discovered at that instant that he had no trouble with killing to protect.

He moved to stand by Margo, the security specialist having returned to the area without the wolf Selenka had called Kostya. "Why do you allow him to speak to her that way?"

Margo's tone held an edge that wasn't human when she said, "Kiev's her father. We can't touch him even if we'd like to wring his neck."

"The familial bond trumps the hierarchy?" Ethan needed data, needed to know what was and wasn't acceptable.

"In certain situations," Margo muttered before crossing her arms across her chest. "Fact is, it usually never comes up—not many fathers would treat their alpha daughter like this. Kiev's a Grade A *mudak*."

A growl sounded in the clearing at that moment, and it came from Selenka's throat. *"Enough,"* she said, her tone a punch of power.

Ethan felt it, but it went through him rather than wrapping around him. But *all* the other wolves in the clearing flinched. Her anger, however, was concentrated on her father. "I don't have time for your grandstanding when we've lost one of our own. Act like a damn elder and not a spoiled infant."

Her father's face chilled, but he shut his mouth and bent down to undo his boots without further argument.

Ethan closed his fingers into his palm to contain the urge to do violence, checking on his disintegrating shields at the same time. The stretching in his mind, it continued to push outward at those shields, beguiling him with promises of vast power. He silenced the seductive words with another level of shielding because the instant he listened and allowed it free, he began his descent into madness.

Scarab Syndrome had no cure.

Chapter 14

An alpha's word is law
An alpha's heart is pack
An alpha's tears are unseen
Alpha mine, my life is yours
                    —From the poem "Alpha" by Anonymous

SELENKA WAS PAST the first fury of anger and rage by the time she left the clearing. Leaving Margo and a group of senior soldiers to guard the forensic team, and aware Gregori would've already increased patrols around their borders, she glanced at Ethan.

The almost disturbing intensity of his devotion was a clawed beast inside her.

This Arrow would do anything for her. She couldn't, however, guarantee the safety of anyone who hurt her. She'd felt ice coat her veins, crackle through her skin, when her father was mouthing off. She and Ethan, they'd have to talk about why he couldn't go around zapping anyone who went up against her.

Her wolf kind of shrugged inside her; the animal part of her had long ago given up expecting anything from Kiev Durev and wasn't sure it'd care if Ethan did decide to erase Kiev from the board.

Her mate fell in step with her as she moved away from the site. His dog, which had sat quivering at the edge of the site on Ethan's orders, waited until Ethan gave it the command to follow before it got up and padded after them. She wondered if Ethan realized what it said about him that the dog had so quickly accepted him as alpha to it—it was the same reason her packmates had given him second and third looks.

This close to her and Ethan, it was obvious to her wolves that their alpha had mated. What took longer was the realization of Ethan's dominance . . . because it was a hushed thing. A stiletto in the dark rather than a snarling growl. Deadly enough to raise the hair on the back of your neck without any apparent reason.

"Emanuel was important to your pack?" Ethan asked about twenty minutes later. "To you?"

"Every member of my pack is important to me." It came out sharp, the words serrated.

But Ethan didn't flinch. "Some people always hold more value in any group," he responded quietly. "I am on the periphery of the squad. My loss wouldn't cripple Aden. If he lost Vasic, however, the impact would be significant and long-term."

Selenka snapped.

Hauling his head close with a hand fisted in his hair, she slammed her mouth over his. The kiss was on the edge of violence, but he didn't draw back. No, he wrapped his arms around her and held her in a way she'd permit no one else.

Everyone else in her pack needed her to be strong right now, needed her to be their rock. She couldn't be Emanuel's grieving friend, acid on her heart. Even now, she fought the need to break, afraid that once she allowed the grief a voice, she'd never be able to silence it. Her emotions were too big, had always been too big.

Ah, my Selenushka, so strong and wild. Her grandmother's soft voice, even softer hands on her face. *You carry a storm inside. Be careful that it does not savage you with its fury.*

It had certainly not been anything Kiev Durev could handle.

"If you don't release it now, this rage I feel inside you," Ethan said, "it'll explode out of you without warning."

"How do you know?" He was right, but damn if she didn't want him to be wrong.

"Your wolf howls inside me."

Selenka dug her nails into his back, struck by the visceral power of his words.

No Arrow should be so good at describing emotion. But

then, most Arrows weren't hauled into a mating bond without warning. And as Ethan had told her more than once, he wasn't a usual type of Arrow. Her mate had turbulent depths beneath the light-cracked ice of his surface, a massive surge she could just sense.

"Emanuel *was* special," she admitted, her voice husky with the scream he could hear and she couldn't bring herself to voice. "He could make even Gregori laugh—I used to joke he should have his own comedy show. I'll miss him." The words weren't anywhere near adequate for the depth of loss tearing her to pieces, but they were all she had.

Ethan bent his head so his chin rested on her hair, his arms steel around her. "I think, to be missed is a gift. To be remembered an even bigger one."

"I'll remember him. We'll all remember him." After allowing herself one more moment in the strange comfort of his arms, she broke the embrace and looked Ethan in the eye. "No more hugs, no more affection, no more comfort. Not until after I've done what I can for my pack. From now on, I'm Alpha Durev and though I'll never be that to you, I need you to help me maintain that part of me." Because he was inside her now, an icy night, calm as a frozen lake.

The calm might only be on the surface, but it was enough to chill the fire of her rage, give her the ability to think with reason.

"Use me in any way you wish," said the Arrow who was hers.

Selenka sucked in her stomach at the potent power of his words. Even if Fate, that bitch, was laughing at her by tying her to a mate who was a stranger, she'd also sent him to her at the hardest time in her life.

Her wolves did a double then triple take when she appeared with Ethan by her side, but no one challenged him— he was with their alpha. That was good enough for everyone in her pack except her father. Those who picked up the scent bond that shouted their status as mates shot her confused and stunned looks, but even they were too grief stricken to comment on how she'd appeared with a mate after leaving the den that morning without even a lover.

Their den had multiple levels and was built under a hill,

with extensions into the surrounding land. It had been constructed year after year from the dawn of their time as a pack and had the look of a home put together in pieces, but the pieces flowed, corridors going this way and that, up and down.

Some wit long ago had compared it to a rabbit warren and so now the deadliest pack of wolves in Russia lived in a place called the Warren. Its walls and floors were relatively simple, carved out of smooth gray stone, with floors that glittered with minerals. But plants thrived everywhere, wild splashes of green and red and yellow.

The lighting inside the Warren had cost them a bundle, but it was worth it.

Hawke, the alpha of the pack that had invented the artificial sunlight and moonlight technology, was a tough bastard, but he hadn't tried to gouge her. And now BlackEdge's den shone bright with sunlight even as the wolves within grieved.

She hugged those she saw, but most got out of her way, aware others had a deeper claim on her. She went straight to Emanuel's parents' quarters. Ethan took a watch position by the door without her having to say a word, his dog at his feet.

Heart tight, she stepped in to find not just the two older wolves within but also Emanuel's brother Vadem, and Dia, the sweet young submissive Emanuel had been courting. While Vadem, an aggressive dominant, paced, his rage straining his skin, Dia sat between Emanuel's mother and father, their arms around her.

That was the well of love and kindness from which their son had come. Vadem was the same when he wasn't so angry.

All four looked to her with huge eyes devastated by pain.

Closing the door behind her, she went first to Vadem, took his hand. "This won't destroy who you are. I won't permit it and neither would Emanuel."

Swallowing hard, he nodded; then, together, they went to his parents and Dia . . , and just held them. Held a family as they grieved, their hearts forever broken.

ETHAN kept watch outside the room into which Selenka had disappeared, the dog sitting silently by his side. Inside his mind, the tendrils of fire continued to stretch out, and with each increment of gain, he felt himself open up, his insides raw. Like sandpaper rubbing against his brain, against his senses.

Wanting to forestall the inevitable, he began to patch up the increasingly thin sections in his internal shields, the ones holding back the wave of Scarab power. It was a losing battle, but it was a battle he'd fight to the end. If he permitted his mind to expand as it was attempting to do, if he allowed the massive wave of power to explode out of his shields, it was all over. Scarab Syndrome had no cure, though Aden had told him one particular E might be able to help him manage it when the time came.

Memory Aven-Rose.

The leader of the squad had shared that data with him after Ethan was forced to ask for a medical checkup as the pressure in his brain grew and grew. Even deep in the gray fog, he'd known his already unusual brain was starting to show signs of severe abnormalities.

The diagnosis had been: "Strong indication of Scarab Syndrome." But the squad hadn't turned him in to Dr. Maia Ndiaye's team. "I won't take this choice from you." Aden's face had been set in unyielding lines as he spoke, his eyes brilliant with what Ethan now recognized as angry sadness. "You've had enough choices stolen from you. But I need a promise: you'll come to me when things are critical."

Because Ethan would then be in danger of spilling innocent blood. As Yuri's blood had been spilled—because it was Patient Zero who'd caused the senior Arrow's critical injuries. Since even in the fog, Ethan had no desire to be a mindless beast with no control over his actions, he'd made the promise.

Command over his mind and his body was everything to him.

Aden had also briefed him extensively on Patient Zero. Zero, according to Aden, had been in a far worse state than Ethan was now, but Memory Aven-Rose had stabilized him. It'd be a thing of luminous hope if not for the twist in the story: Patient Zero had a twin who was sane.

Ethan had no twin. No one to leach off part of the pressure building in his brain.

It was time to ask Aden for the favor he'd promised.

He stepped out into the sprawling psychic space of the PsyNet. Faint lightning strikes lingered and flickered against the night sky of the Net, each mind a bright star. A number of the strikes were strong, most weak, others all but faded. He'd seen such lightning strikes all his life—mostly during the times when he was permitted a strictly controlled look into the PsyNet.

Ming had allowed him those "furloughs" because the psychologists had made the recommendation. Ethan had read the psych report after Aden took over, seen the relevant paragraphs: *The boy's mental state is precarious. Total isolation from the PsyNet may pitch him over into a condition where he will be of no use as a weapon.*

We recommend supervised visits. The vastness of the Net will help temper his psychological distress at being kept underground and alone the great majority of the time, and he is not a flight risk. He cannot escape the walls you've constructed around his mind.

The glimpses hadn't had the intended effect. Instead of soothing the maddened beast, they had only enraged him in the deep, cold place where he'd existed. The only things he'd enjoyed during his visits had been the mind-stars that went on forever in a glittering carpet—and the flashes of lightning. But it was only recently that those strikes had become more than faint echoes.

It was even more recently that he'd realized others didn't see them. Something had *always* been very wrong with his brain. No one had noticed because he was so isolated, and trapped in Ming's shields. The secret would die with him, but until then, he'd stand in a starry night riven with silver strikes.

Aden didn't respond to his attempt to make contact. From the faint ripples Ethan could see in the PsyNet, the other man had to be busy sealing another rupture in its failing psychic fabric. Aden and Kaleb Krychek took it in turns, so that one of them was always at full strength in case of a major rupture.

Dropping out of the Net, he used the comm function of the gauntlet on his left forearm to send a message: *I would like to meet Memory Aven-Rose.—Ethan*

In the time since he'd first taken up position by this room, multiple wolves had passed through the corridor. All made eye contact and all had slumped shoulders or wet faces, but only one approached him: a tall woman older than Ethan with an angular face and a sense of tranquility to her.

"I'm Ivina, one of the healers," she said, purple shadows under her eyes. "Your dog needs a bath and inoculations." She bent to pet the dog and when the animal didn't shy, Ethan nodded. "I appreciate the assistance."

Smile sad, Ivina patted her thigh, but the dog didn't follow her until Ethan said, "Go."

Then he stood alone . . . until a small girl walked over to stare at him. She was perhaps four, though he had no confidence in his assessment. He wasn't much good at gauging age in non-adults.

Her silky black hair was cut in blunt bangs above her up-tilted dark brown eyes, her brown-skinned face round with the impression of cheekbones that might or might not sharpen as she aged. She wore a blue dress with a scalloped edge that came to her knees, along with shining shoes of black buckled over white socks with ruffled edges. In her arms, she clutched an item he recognized as a doll. That doll looked like the child, and it wore an identical dress in miniature.

"Hello," he said, when no adult appeared with her. "Are you lost?"

She shook her head.

Figuring another wolf would come by for her soon enough, he returned to his vigil. But it proved startlingly difficult to ignore a child staring at him with big brown eyes. Her stare scrubbed the sandpaper over his brain even harder.

Chapter 15

I can't give you a definitive diagnosis. We have no real diagnostic tools yet, but from all that you've disclosed, especially the sense of their powers expanding, I am ninety percent certain that this individual is showing the first indications of Scarab Syndrome. That sense of power, of expansion, appears to be a uniting factor across the confirmed cases.

As it seems the individual on whose behalf you're inquiring is currently rational and able to think logically about what's happening in their brain, I would urge they get in direct contact with me. Their assistance could be invaluable in helping us understand the Syndrome, and such clarity of thought does not last long once the Syndrome takes full effect—this individual may, at best, have only a week or two of clear thought.

It's possible a specialist empath could help the affected individual maintain rational thought for longer, but that is not guaranteed—it appears dependent on the individual. At present, there is no cure. I am sorry.
—Dr. Maia Ndiaye's reply to an anonymous and untrackable communication sent directly to her private inbox

"DO YOU NEED something?" Ethan asked in desperation, as that was why people mostly requested his presence.

A jagged nod, silky black hair gleaming in the light. "What?"

In answer, the child closed the distance between them, so close that he had to bend his head to see her. She stood right by his leg, staring up at him, as if expecting him to know what to do. As he didn't, he told her so.

A wrinkling in her brow, before her lips parted at last. "You smell Lenka," she said, and the way she formed the words told him he'd overestimated her age.

"I am bonded to your alpha. I may carry her scent." The idea made the madness in him rise and rise, a smashing anvil against his shields.

Gritting his teeth, he held back the attack as the child gestured for him to bend down. As he saw no threats that required him to stay upright, he obeyed, crouching down so they were eye-to-eye.

"I sad," she said. "Pack sad."

"Yes." The numbness shredded, he could feel their sorrow as black rain against his senses.

His priority right now, however, was the little wolf child. He'd undergone "child management lessons" alongside all other adult Arrows—the new squad would care for their children as no one had cared for them.

At the time, he'd sat through the classes robotically. Today, he realized that he'd been wrong to believe such lessons had no value to him, that he didn't care. He *would* care if something or someone hurt the Arrow children—because as with this child, they were innocents who'd done nothing to deserve pain or scorn.

No child had ever caused him harm.

No child had ever looked at him and seen a monster to be put to the leash.

No child had ever called him broken or aberrant.

Dredging up the lessons he hadn't thought about since he attended them, he said, "Do you know why everyone is sad?"

"Yes," the child said, her lower lip quivering. "Ema gone." A tear rolled down her cheek. "No come back."

Ethan looked around for help but the corridor was empty of all other life. Remembering what Zaira often said about defaulting to kindness if lost in how to deal with a child, and since this child was changeling, he awkwardly opened one arm. It was as if she'd been waiting for that the entire time. Burying her face into his shoulder, she didn't argue when he wrapped both arms around her. He rose to his feet with her held close, a ferocious kind of protectiveness stealing his breath.

He would kill to protect her and all children. His desire not to be a murderer wasn't as strong as his need to protect. That need had him raising one hand to stroke the child's hair, the silk of it cool water.

She sniffled against his shoulder, the doll pressed between their bodies.

An adult wolf entered the corridor at last. Seeing Ethan with the girl, he said, "Our little Zhanusya. She's very attached to Selya—she probably escaped her parents and followed Selya's scent trail to you."

A pat on the child's back, before the other man was gone. But Ethan was no longer lost. He knew the child in his arms was content to be there. Even as he held her, he worked on his shields. It was difficult. Things kept cracking and breaking, his mind feeling as if it were bleeding from the constant barrage.

"I no cry now." Sitting up against his arm, Zhanusya—an affectionate diminutive for Zhanna if he had it correct—rubbed at her eyes. "Vika sad, too." Holding up the doll.

The doll wasn't sentient, but Ethan could see that to Zhanna, her invisible wounds mattered. "Yes," he said, because it wasn't hard to know what to say to a child—Zhanna was wide open in a way that only heightened his protective urges. "You should wipe her tears."

After doing so with soft little fingers while murmuring soothing words, Zhanna cuddled her doll close. "Lenka man?" A pointed look at him.

"Yes." Pride was a roaring lion inside him. "I'm hers."

Smiling, the child leaned her head against his shoulder.

"Nice dress," she whispered a moment later, as if telling him a secret. "Don't dirty. Party." Her face fell. "Don't wanna party. Pack sad."

Ethan cradled her distressed body against him again, rocking gently in a way that seemed to soothe her. Whatever plans this pack'd had for today, they lay in ashes. It was a time of pain and sorrow—and though the weight of those emotions in the air was exacerbating his lack of control and the rising Scarab power, he wouldn't leave the den.

He wouldn't leave Selenka.

Not until he had no choice.

Not until he lost the battle against Scarab.

His telepathy wasn't strong enough to reach outside Russia, but it was more than strong enough to touch base with Axl. Even with what had happened earlier, his acceptance that Axl wasn't a villain, the engagement caused him intense discomfort. Scars didn't fade overnight.

The senior Arrow responded at once, his own voice crystalline—Axl was a Gradient 9.7 telepath. *Ethan, what is it?*

I'd like to request time off for the foreseeable future. It was the first time since his escape from Ming that he'd made a request for leave. *I also promised to cover Nerida's shift tomorrow.*

I'll take care of it, Axl said. *Is there a problem?*

No. This is a personal request. Words he'd never thought he'd utter. *I'll speak to Aden about the long term.* Though it wouldn't be necessary; Aden would know some of it at least the instant he saw Ethan's request to meet Memory Aven-Rose.

Understood. Leave actioned.

Thank you.

"Itchy head," Zhanna said, screwing up her nose.

"Your head is itchy?"

"No, *you* itchy head."

Ethan realized belatedly that she must've sensed something while he telepathed. He'd never come across that before, but he didn't exactly have a wide social circle. "Perhaps you have a Psy ancestor."

Zhanna smiled. "You funny talk, Lenka man."

The door opened on those words and Selenka walked out. When Zhanna lunged for her, she brought up her arms to gather the child close. "I should've known I'd find you here," she said with a nip of Zhanna's nose that, from the way the child burrowed into her, didn't seem to cause any pain.

Eyes rimmed with red met his. "My Zhannochka is trouble." A kiss pressed to the top of Zhanna's head, love in the arms that held her.

Ethan had never comprehended love, but today, it was as bright and glowing a knowledge as his awareness of Axl's sincerity and Aden's dedication to his squad—including

Ethan. This, how Selenka held Zhanna, how Zhanna petted her alpha's cheek with a soft hand, it was love.

"Let's go talk to my senior people."

"Anything you want." *Always.*

Selenka found a word or a touch for every grieving packmate they passed.

Ethan stayed by her side but a step back; this was her time to be alpha and his to be her support. And though he had an excellent spatial sense, even he had to concentrate to remember the route after they'd turned several times.

"Here's your stop." Selenka snuggled Zhanna close for another long moment before handing her over to a woman with the same hair and eyes who stood in the doorway to what must be a family apartment.

The child went without argument, a wolf heeding her alpha's decision. "Bye, Lenka." She made her doll wave, too. "Bye, Lenka man."

Selenka's lips twitched slightly as they left, a ray of light piercing the heavy darkness. "How do you like being Lenka's man?"

"It is the truth."

A wolfish moment of eye contact. "Be careful what you give of yourself, Ethan. My wolf can be a possessive beast."

"I am yours."

Her pupils flared and inside him the scalding heat of her was a dangerous kiss.

Ethan walked into the burn.

Gold in her eyes, Selenka cupped his jaw. "So much passion, so much emotion." A husky murmur. "Are you sure you're an Arrow?" Not waiting for an answer, she tugged him close for a kiss that was soft and slow and deep and lava in his veins.

The Scarab power shoved against his shields for freedom, and he was caught between the craving to press his body to her own and never let go—and the need to take a step back so he could strengthen his shields. But Selenka was an alpha with a grieving pack. And a small moment was all she'd allow herself.

They continued on, eventually entering a large room that appeared to be a meeting area. Seven people stood within, all of whom bristled with power. The bearded male with tattooed arms—Gregori—was there, along with the one Selenka had called Ivo. Ethan also recognized Margo Lucenko and Artem Güvenc from the security team at the symposium, but that was all he had time for before the world blazed at the edges.

He halted in the doorway, slammed by a massive wave of energy that had no form he could identify. It hit him with the force of a punch to the solar plexus and he might've doubled over if he hadn't suffered far worse in Arrow training.

As it was, Selenka swung around to look at him, her hair streaks of color in the air. He kept his expression calm though his heart pounded and perspiration threatened to break out over his skin. He couldn't permit the latter—the wolves would scent it, and his job was to be Selenka's shield and sword, not divide her already strained attention.

His mate's eyes narrowed slightly, but she continued on to her lieutenants without calling him on what was happening. "Ethan, you know Margo."

Artem, fine boned with pale skin and piercing hazel eyes, his height around the same as Ethan's, raised his hand. "We met at the symposium."

With a nod, Selenka introduced the others. "Alia." A tall woman with generous curves fluid with muscle, her skin a soft brown, her eyes a deeper shade of the same hue, and her hair black curls pulled back into a loose bun.

She smiled at Ethan, her welcome open despite the sadness in her eyes.

The woman next to her, on the other hand, her skin ebony and her eyes strikingly, unexpectedly electric blue, the tight coils of her hair cropped close to her skull and body small and sleek, gave Ethan a short nod when Selenka introduced her as Dinara. It should've felt like suspicion, but Ethan was dead certain Dinara was barely holding back a scream within. He wouldn't know what she actually thought of him until after she came out from under the weight of grief and anger.

"You saw Gregori and Ivo earlier."

Both greeted him aloud, Gregori's voice deeper than Ivo's more lyrical one.

"Kostya was in wolf form at the time." She indicated a man of medium height with a compact body and slate-colored eyes against skin that barely held the sun's touch, his hair a deep brown.

"Skin contact okay?" He held out a hand but didn't push it forward until Ethan nodded. His skin was warm and rough, his handclasp firm without being crushing. A man confident in his skin, and with a sense of contentment to him that came through despite the sorrow that had carved grooves in his cheeks.

"My lieutenants," Selenka said, before taking position in the circle created by her people, her legs in a wide stance and her arms folded.

Ethan would've stood at her back, except Artem shifted to make a space next to Selenka, and so Ethan stood by his mate's side.

"Tell me what you have," she said.

"Forensic team confirmed the presence of the jetcycle." Kostya's steady voice. "Nothing on it after we lose the trail as it heads out of the territory."

"Weapon?"

Margo stirred. "Standard piece you can buy off the street if you know the right people. Markings filed off, but there's no doubt it was the murder weapon."

A strange element of hesitation that Ethan perceived even through his overloaded senses.

"Spit it out." Selenka's voice was a growl. "You don't have Emanuel anymore. None of us do. We have to learn how to have the hard conversations without him."

Dinara folded her arms, her voice edged with razor wire as she said, "Kiev was meant to be teaching a class to our senior trainees at the den. He was already twenty minutes late when Emanuel was shot—what the fuck was he doing at that location?"

Chapter 16

Son, your pup is a gift, strong and courageous and beloved
by her packmates. She's young yet, but already, I see signs
of the adult wolf she'll become. Cherish her, be the one to
whom she can turn in the years to come. Do not allow this
seed of bitterness to fester in you, or it will destroy what
matters most.

—Alpha Yevgeni Durev to Kiev Durev (2059)

"BLYA." SELENKA SHOVED a hand through her hair, her
shoulders falling for an instant before she squared them
again. "We all know my father does things like this for no
reason except that it's Wednesday and he's feeling pissy.

"It probably means nothing, but you follow up on it." She
nodded at the lieutenant who'd spoken. "I know I let too
much slide with him, but not this. You get his explanation for
why he was in that area."

Dinara nodded, but her face was pinched. "Selya." It
came out husky, nearly broken. "I shouldn't ha—"

"It's all right." Selenka walked close enough to hug the
petite woman close.

Wrapping her arms around Selenka, Dinara just held on.

"This isn't on you," Selenka added after dropping a kiss
on her packmate's hair. "It's on him."

"If it was anyone else," Gregori said, the tattoos on his
arm standing out in sharp relief as he fisted his hand, "I
swear, I'd take him out. The way he talks to you—it's not
how a wolf should address his alpha."

Ethan was in full agreement with the male and from the
looks on the faces around him, so were the rest of Selenka's
lieutenants. Alia was the most difficult to read, her serene

expression a mask, but Ethan had no doubts about her loyalties. There was something about the statuesque lieutenant . . .

Releasing Dinara but staying beside her, Selenka put her hands on her hips and addressed her entire team. "Treat my father like any other senior packmate who's out of line—and that's an order from your alpha. Any problems, you come to me. One of our own is dead; *no one* gets to slide on anything that could lead to his murderer."

The lieutenants all nodded, and despite the feral energy that kept scraping against Ethan, doing damage to his shields that he couldn't seem to fix, his senses were crystal clear and one thing he knew—each and every person in this room would die for Selenka. For that reason, Ethan would do everything in his power to protect them.

Gregori, Margo, Alia, Artem, Dinara, Kostya, and Ivo would act as her defense after he was gone. Because he *would* go. Scarab Syndrome could be held at bay in certain circumstances, but as Dr. Ndiaye had made clear, the end result was inevitable: madness leading to death. His only hope for even a short reprieve lay with Memory Aven-Rose.

"What else?" Selenka looked around the circle of dominant wolves. "Tell me we have something."

"No defensive wounds," Margo said, her jaw held so tight that her skin was white over bone. "Emanuel was taken by surprise. No other way to explain it, not as fast as he was."

"He'd have heard the cycle unless the attacker was already there, lying in wait," Ivo said, his own anger a sense of intense tightness of the body, as if he held back a hurricane. "The question of it all is why."

Ethan might be a less than optimal Arrow, but he was an Arrow. "A mistake," he said.

Eight pairs of eyes turned to him, with Margo the one who said, "Explain."

"Was your packmate on a routine patrol?"

A shake of the head from Artem. "I saw him before he left—he was just going for a run. Planned to be back in a few hours, had a date and wanted to dress up."

Another punch of wild energy against Ethan's senses, clawed and angry and unforgiving. Not Psy in any way. It had to be an artefact of the mating bond—Selenka was attuned to the emotional tone of the room as a result of her connection with her lieutenants, and Ethan was getting the overflow.

That it was so significant despite the fragmented nature of their bond gave him hope that the bond would find a way around the roadblocks presented by his abnormal psyche and he'd get to be with his mate in the deepest sense, without static or broken shards or wisps of lingering fog.

Riding out the painful blast, he said, "My theory is that your packmate stumbled into something he wasn't supposed to see." Ethan's mind kept on moving the available pieces, and this was the only scenario that fit. "It's possible your father may have escaped death by a very fine margin. Had he been the first to arrive, Emanuel could've found him instead."

He looked at Selenka, his loyalty to her making him hesitate on voicing the other option. But her lips tightened. "It's possible that what Emanuel saw," she said, "was my father doing something he shouldn't."

Margo sucked in a breath. "Forensics tested his hands. No signs he shot the weapon."

That, Ethan knew, didn't equal a lack of involvement.

Selenka's expression made it clear she was well aware of the same. "Debrief my father personally," she ordered Margo. "Don't accuse him, but push *hard*." She flexed, then tightened her hand just as Ethan's gauntlet vibrated gently against his skin—a discreet indication that he'd received a message.

He glanced at it as Selenka said, "Ivo, what did our surveillance pick up?"

"Nothing." The black male ran a hand over the smoothness of his scalp, the angles and lines of his features such that he'd be considered handsome by all three races.

The dangerous predator that lived under the aesthetically pleasing appearance was apparent only in the low growl that accompanied his words as he added, "The cameras at the entrance used by the jetcycle were disabled remotely minutes before the shooting."

"An inside job?" Selenka's tone had gone beyond growls and into frigid control.

"Not necessarily—could've been done by the shooter themselves." Ivo's skin tightened over his cheekbones. "It's older tech that we've been replacing as the cameras die. Didn't seem to be any urgency when we have regular patrols in those areas."

"Guilt will make you useless to Selenka in this situation," Ethan said without thought. "The better question is where were those patrols and why didn't they stop the intrusion into your territory?"

The affected wolf glared at Ethan, while Selenka said, "Ethan's right. We decided as a group that the cameras weren't a priority upgrade. Where *were* the patrols?"

"Diverted." Alia's soft voice caught at Ethan, made him wonder about her all over again. "Someone called in an emergency—child missing one sector over. Everyone moved, but it was a false alert."

"I'm trying to trace the source of the alert." Ivo indicated a small tablet he'd been holding at his side. "It came through our own systems, which is why it was trusted."

"Hacked?" Selenka asked. "Or do we have a traitor?" The last word was unsheathed claws, that of a wolf who would offer no mercy, not for this crime.

"I can't confirm yet, but it's likely to be the latter." Ivo worked his tablet. "We're pretty much hackproof on that level—systems are rock solid after all those years of trying to keep out Psy spies." The last words were muttered, his attention on his tablet.

"Ethan," Selenka said, "any word on the satellite image search?"

"I just got a response—techs can't find anything, even using less-than-legal tactics. It appears all parties are sticking to your agreement not to surveil each other's territory."

A curt nod, her muscles remaining rigid. "It was a long shot anyway."

Dinara threw a glance Ethan's way. "Your grandfather met him yet?" No antagonism in the question, even a hint of amusement below the grief.

"We're not discussing my grandfather," Selenka muttered, but Dinara's words seemed to release a little of the tension in the room.

A few others smirked, and Gregori glanced at Margo. The look they exchanged was intimate . . . but not romantic. Ethan was suddenly sure the two were siblings. A sign of Scarab madness or another indication he was picking up emotional information via the mating bond? Because he was equally certain that Alia and Artem were romantically involved. Deeply so. Once more, his attention went to Alia.

Her responding smile was gentle, her eyes soft.

"*Govno.*"

The muttered expletive had everyone looking back at Ivo. Mouth set in a flat line, he said, "Alert was sent, using the pack ID code belonging to Elder Bykov."

Snarls filled the room. "The elder spends his days sunning his bones and hasn't used a comm for a decade or more," Artem told Ethan, a starburst of amber around his pupils that hadn't previously existed.

"Are the codes confidential?"

It was Kostya who answered. "The senior members of the pack have secure IDs, but we don't throw our general IDs around, either." He shook his head, causing the slightly overlong strands of his hair to slide against each other. "Wouldn't have been hard to get the elder's ID, though. He'd probably give it to you if asked, then forget all about it."

"He's a hundred and thirty-two and says he has too many memories to worry about remembering frip-fraps," Alia said with an affectionate shake of her head.

"Talk to him anyway, Alia," Selenka said. "He's the least grumpy with you."

"That's because she pets and coddles him as if he's a pup." Artem's grumble was so patently false that Ethan wondered why he'd said anything at all.

Alia ran her fingernails down Artem's nape. "Tyoma, why do you lie so? I saw you bring the elder his favorite snack just hours ago, then sit down and massage his aching paw."

A ripple of laughter around the room as Artem pretended to bite a smiling Alia, but the spark of joy faded almost before it had come to life. Face falling, Alia leaned her head against Artem's shoulder. "I can't believe we'll never again hear Emanuel's laughter."

"Or wait for the punch line to one of his bad jokes," Kostya said roughly. "I'm going to miss him grinning while I groan at him to stop."

"Is that all we have?" Selenka asked, her own grief so closely held that it was a clawing wolf inside Ethan. "No other leads?" When her lieutenants remained silent, she muttered words low and dark under her breath. "We work on the theory that we have a traitor. Look at *everyone* who might be involved with a critical eye."

After getting their agreement, she rubbed a hand over her face, her head bowed for a moment before she lifted it. "I've spoken to Emanuel's parents about his funeral arrangements."

The weight returned to the room. Ethan felt the crushing power of it on his shoulders, could barely breathe past it. His brain was clearly having difficulty processing the emotional overflow from his mate. Unwilling to let her down, however, he patched up the fractures in his shields and held.

"They want it to be tonight, as soon as Oleg's finished his examination of the body." Selenka's wolf glowed in her eyes. "He told his parents once that he planned to be buried under the stars, in that field where he used to go to read his science fiction novels."

"I'll take care of it," Gregori said, the words gritty. "You know the entire pack will want to come?"

"His parents are more than okay with that. They just want a little time alone with him first. I'll organize that with Oleg." She exhaled on a shudder. "Tonight is for Emanuel. His parents want a celebration of his life and he deserves every moment of it. After that, we go hunting." Rage was a conflagration in that last word, the fury of an alpha who would not stop until she'd brought down her prey.

The Architect

We are united in our goals. Only with an adherence to a
policy of cooperation and loyalty can we succeed.
—The Architect of the Consortium to its upper-echelon
membership (2082)

THE ARCHITECT MADE contact with one of her senior operatives via an anonymizing comm device that hid both her face and her trail. That was how the Consortium had been set up, with various layers of anonymity. She, of course, knew the name, location, and relevant details of every single member.

She was the Architect and this was her creation.

"Explain the operation," she said, while staring out the large glass window of her office. "You say you have an Arrow on the leash?" That could prove problematic in the extreme—the Arrow squad was adept at playing black ops games, and Operative Cray could've inadvertently created a massive hole in the Consortium's defenses.

As she intended to utilize the useful elements of the Consortium as the foundation for her new power, she did not want it destroyed. "How do you control him?"

"He is mentally unstable," Cray replied. "He was also abused by those in charge of the squad and has no loyalty to them."

Idiot. If the Arrow had been abused, it would've been under Ming LeBon's regime. Aden Kai was too young to have done anything to another adult Arrow. "You still haven't explained your plan." Any operations involving major parties were meant to be run by her before being put into action—and each and every Arrow counted as a major party.

"The intention was for the Arrow to gain the trust of an alpha, so he could then begin to influence her in our favor," Cray said. "I gave him the initial in by having him save her life. Also, I have another operative in play who I intend to use to solidify his status with her."

The Architect rubbed at her temple as her vision blurred for a split second, and made a mental note to get herself scanned by medics for any emergent health problems. "Tell me about the other operative."

After listening to Cray's explanation, she considered the value of this op. Having a compromised pack could come in useful in the long term, and Cray's plan didn't threaten to destabilize the PsyNet. It was all focused on a single pack in Russia—but that pack was one of the two biggest in that region.

Having Selenka Durev as an unwitting accomplice to the Architect's stealthy rise to power could be useful. Especially if she could be nudged to restart hostilities with the bears. As history had shown, when two dominant packs were focused on each other, they didn't pay attention to what was happening with the rest of the world.

The changelings' animal and clannish nature was both their greatest strength and their greatest weakness.

"Continue," she said at last. "Eliminate all contact the instant you can no longer control the Arrow." Better to leave an operation half-complete than to open a portal into the Consortium's inner core.

Though, should Cray's gambit work, it would prove a useful template for how to manipulate changeling alphas. In that case, she'd reward him with power. Should the operation fail, however, she would sacrifice him without a qualm.

To gain the throne of the world required a mind without mercy.

The Architect had been training for this all her life.

Chapter 17

Changelings mourn our dead as we live our lives. Openly, with love, and in the wild.
— "An Essay on Death and Life" by Keelie Schaeffer, PhD, *Journal of Psychology* (2067)

ETHAN HAD NO place in BlackEdge's hierarchy except as an adjunct of Selenka —and Selenka's priority in the lead-up to the funeral was to ease her people's pain. His was to do whatever she needed.

He wasn't, however, expecting her to turn to him and say, "Will you help in the nursery?"

But all he said was, "Yes."

Guessing she'd assigned him the task because he had the training to protect the children, he deferred to Alia, the lieutenant having volunteered for the same task. "I'm ready to do whatever you require," he told her once he reached the nursery —after checking on his dog and discovering the stray bathed and fed, and fast asleep in a pile of blankets.

The tall woman with gentle eyes gave him a funny look. "I can't quite work out what you are," she murmured. "You're obviously extremely dangerous, but I'm a submissive, and my wolf is comfortable in your presence in a way it shouldn't be with a strange dominant."

"Likely because I'm mated to Selenka," Ethan said absently, far more fascinated by the rest of her statement. "How can you be a submissive and a lieutenant?"

"Selenka." Lush lips forming a tranquil smile. "She finds my advice useful and is of the opinion that dominance alone shouldn't keep the pack from recognizing my value to her. So I am a lieutenant."

Alia's advice had to be far more than useful for Selenka to take such a step; she must consider the woman a key member of her team. "How do the dominants who aren't lieutenants deal with it? Is there resentment?"

"No, they treat me the same as they would a healer." Alia continued to examine him with a piercing attention that should've seemed aggressive, but wasn't, not with her.

"There is precedent in changeling history of high-ranking submissives, so I'm not unique," she added. "We're sometimes called gamma wolves in the history books. It helps that the senior lieutenants accepted me from day one—to those who came after, I've always held the position, so they never think about it."

Alia might not know it, but her psychic presence had a lot to do with her packmates' response to her. She was the most serene being Ethan had ever met, and that included Ivy Jane. "Were you born this way?" he asked, unable to resist the compulsion. "So . . . balanced."

A tilt of her head. "I've always felt the rhythms of the universe. We are but motes in the slipstream." Her smile deepened. "Ethan, I *like* you." A statement laced with joy. "We will be friends, you and I."

Oddly enough, Ethan agreed with her. "Is Artem your mate?"

Bright wolf eyes. "Yes, and how funny that you didn't say lover or boyfriend. Did you pick up anything else?"

"Margo and Gregori are siblings."

"Exactly nine months between them. Who is the older?"

"Margo," he said without having to think about it.

"Ethan, oh, Ethan," Alia whispered. "Who are you?"

Ethan went to reply when a sense of movement made him glance down.

Now dressed in soft blue fleece pants and a matching long-sleeved top decorated with a rainbow, Zhanna was petting him on the calf in an effort to get his attention.

"Did you escape again?"

Solemnly shaking her head, she raised her arms. He bent, picked her up. "Last I saw her, she was with her parents."

"Her father is a senior soldier, her mother a florist," Alia told him. "All the pups in the nursery tonight belong to wolves who're helping with the preparations. That's my little Inja there."

Ethan followed her gaze to a tiny wolf pup who was using her nose to roll a ball to another small wolf, who'd then roll it back.

When Alia began to move around the room, Ethan copied her example.

The children seemed at ease with him. Probably because he smelled like Selenka. Understanding the value of that trust, he helped with their projects and—after Zhanna scrambled down—held any that wished it.

All the while, the rogue Scarab power shoved at the walls he'd built to contain it.

The clock was counting down faster than he'd expected. If Memory Aven-Rose couldn't help him . . .

Ethan. Aden's telepathic signature, accompanied by a sense of tiredness Ethan had never before intuited from this type of contact.

Was there a Net rupture? he asked.

Yes. I've contained it. No fatalities. I'm back in Moscow to see Kaleb, and I've also spoken to Memory—she's happy to meet with you tomorrow.

Ethan considered what was happening in the pack, weighed it up against his degrading mental status. He wouldn't be any use to Selenka if he was insane or dead. *I'll be there.*

I'll forward you her comm details so you can settle on a time. Don't attempt telepathic, PsyNet, or physical contact without permission.

Understood. He would've ended the conversation there at any other time before Selenka and the shredding of the gray numbness. Today, he said, *I thank you for the help.*

Aden took a long time to reply. *I hope Memory can assist you. I would not lose you, Ethan.*

Hope alone wouldn't be enough. Not when the Scarab power was creating fissures in his shields faster than he could patch them up. It was gaining in strength, becoming a behemoth that would soon erase all evidence of an Arrow named Ethan Night.

• • •

SELENKA was ragged at the edges by the time the funeral drew near. Everything was in place, the only thing left being to ensure their young and vulnerable would be protected while the vast majority of her wolves attended Emanuel's farewell. She left the nursery to last, wasn't sure what to expect when she finally stepped into the doorway.

Others might question her decision to place Ethan in the nursery, but others didn't have his presence inside them. Cold and jagged he might be, but he was also devoted in a way that wasn't healthy, wasn't normal. That obsessive devotion meant she could trust her stranger of a mate without question.

Ethan was *hers*.

What she saw inside the nursery had her halting in the doorway. Most of the children were asleep on thick mattresses, their small bodies covered by fluffy blankets. More than a few were in wolf form, snuggled into the bodies of their playmates.

The few who remained awake were heavy eyed . . . and her black-clad Arrow had one of the littlest in his arms, the pup's face buried against Ethan's neck. Her wary heart opened a crack, and for the first time, their mating moved beyond a primal bond desired by the wolf and into a promise that beguiled the human side of her.

Because violence was easy. It was the rest that came hard.

She watched as Ethan got the pup to sleep before placing him on a bed beside two other pups in wolf form. The boy curled sleepily around his packmates.

Rising, Ethan turned and looked directly at her. And the dark embers in her gut sparked to full life, the craving even deeper and hotter than it had been before. She *needed* her mate on a bone-deep level, and it wasn't about intimate skin privileges. It was about having one person with whom she could drop her head and just fucking cry, give in to the emotions lodged like a stone on her chest.

"Not yet," she ordered herself, as he closed the distance between them.

His eyes pale and fathomless, the ice of him cracked with

ever-bigger fractures of light, he reached her at the same time as Alia. Kind and gentle Alia, with her way of seeing the world that was beyond the here and now. It was as if she'd been born wise.

No wonder her parents called her "owlet" to this day.

"Your relief's on the way," Selenka told the lieutenant, for the pack would need Alia's serenity at the funeral.

Dark eyes examined her before Alia walked into her arms on a wave of muted perfume. Taking comfort but giving more. A sneaky thing submissives had long perfected.

"Thank you for sending Ethan," the other woman said when she drew back. "The children adore him."

After Alia left to do one last check on the sleeping pups, Ethan moved closer to Selenka. His eyes devoured her, the air between them hot with need and something more—a hunger to smash through the fog in the bond, claw into each other's souls. But his voice was tempered when he said, "Do you want me to stand security while the funeral takes place?"

Selenka nodded. She'd spoken to each of her lieutenants privately, needing to know how her shock mating had affected them. Her pack was her heart; if they were uncomfortable with a Psy presence in the den, she'd find a way to deal. A good alpha didn't put her needs first, didn't focus on her own emotions.

But all her closest people had backed her.

"Mates don't betray one another," each had said in their own way, that fact as fundamental as that the sky was blue, and the grass green.

Margo had added, "Thanks for stealing an Arrow for the pack. SnowDancer's all smug about having that Tk who can lob missiles about. I can't wait to brag about *our* Arrow."

"Uh-huh." Dinara had nodded. "Also, now when the bears smirk at us because their alpha managed to court himself a kickass mate, we can smirk right back."

Kostya had bared his teeth at that. "Yeah, and Valentin had to climb her building to get access to Silver. *Our* alpha, meanwhile . . ." He'd bumped fists with Ivo, before they both said, "Boom."

Only her father had questioned Selenka's decision.

"That Psy might be your mate," he'd said with a condescension that was business as usual with him, "but have you considered whether he's controlling you psychically?"

Not only was the supposition ludicrous given the strength of natural changeling shields; it brought her instincts as alpha into question. So much of what she did, the decisions she made, ran on instinct. She wasn't Psy or a human CEO, to make a decision based on a step-by-step decision tree. She was a wolf.

And her gut knew Ethan was hers.

When he touched his palm to her cheek, she leaned into the warm strength of it. Her eyes began to flutter shut, body and mind giving in to the need to take just one moment. That was when she scented blood. Her eyelashes flew up at the same time that Ethan dropped his hand and reached into his pocket for a tissue. Even as he blotted up the drops at his nose, she took a step back, her claws shoving at the tips of her fingers.

"What the hell is going on?" With the fall of Silence had come whispers of information—so she knew that with Psy, simple nosebleeds weren't always so simple.

"A small pressure problem caused by shields," he said, and she knew it for a lie—but a slight movement of his head told her it was because Alia was drawing closer.

Fine, they'd talk about it later, after she'd survived this funeral. Seeing that the nursery volunteers had arrived, she asked Alia to brief them, then gestured for Ethan to come with her. "Gregori's running security tonight, with Artem in support, and he'll place you where he needs you." The two had loved Emanuel and it was a sacrifice for them to not attend the funeral, but someone needed to watch over their vulnerable.

Before she tracked them down, however, she detoured to a small kitchenette. "Eat." She thrust a filled roll into Ethan's hand; her wolf needed desperately to look after its mate.

Ethan gave the roll a dubious look but took a bite . . . then offered her a bite. Her heart kicked. This Arrow of hers, he kept on doing the unexpected, kept on catching her unawares. She accepted that bite, and together, the two of them took three minutes to fuel up before heading back out.

She tracked Artem and Gregori to near the den entrance,

two strong men who'd often had a laughing third to balance out their more solemn natures.

"You with us?" Gregori said to Ethan.

"Yes." Ethan took an at-ease stance, hands clasped behind his back. "I'm an efficient watcher, and I can cause injury at a distance using a blade of light."

Pride was a wolf's growl through her; her mate was dangerous and skilled and confident. "Don't forget he can also make tens of people unconscious in one go." Since Gregori hadn't been there at the time, she added, "He's the reason we caught the empathic terrorists at the symposium."

"I went down like a log." Artem's hazel eyes gave nothing away as he spoke—as was usual with the most self-contained of all her lieutenants. Before he'd had the good sense to fall madly in love with Alia, Artem had been on the way to turning lone wolf. As it was, he was now even more entwined with the pack than gregarious Ivo.

Being Alia's mate kind of allowed no other option.

"I still can't believe we're using those two words together," Gregori rumbled. "'Empathic terrorist' should be a fucking oxymoron."

Selenka had to leave the conversation at that point, her duties elsewhere tonight. She deliberately didn't make physical contact with Ethan as she left. She had to be Selenka Durev, alpha of BlackEdge, right now, not a woman grieving the loss of her friend.

A jagged stretching inside her as she walked away, a darkness cold and sweet, and she knew her Arrow had hugged her anyway.

Chapter 18

ETHAN STOOD ALONE under the darkness, the sky above a stunning spread of stars. There was little light pollution in changeling lands, and as a result, they had truly dark skies—places where the stars could shine bright without competing against created sources of light. It was silent, too, a silence that had nothing in common with the noxious emptiness that had been his only companion when Ming locked him up.

This silence held whispers of leaves, a faint breeze brushing the tree branches as it passed, and after he'd been motionless long enough, he heard the rustle of nocturnal creatures going about their business. The wolf that prowled out of the trees two hours into his vigil on the far left flank of BlackEdge territory made no sound at all—yet Ethan had known he was coming.

The wolf's coat was a deep reddish brown. Nothing about the animal stated his human identity, but Ethan knew this was Gregori the same way he'd known Margo and Gregori were siblings. "No problems to report."

Gregori had shared that this flank was vulnerable because it backed onto a road, instead of against bear land or an inhospitable geographic feature. That made Ethan the perfect sentry to place here tonight, while wolf sentries took areas with more uneven terrain. He had the capacity to run telepathic scans all the way out to the road.

After acknowledging his report with an incline of his head, Gregori began to turn away.

"Wait." Ethan put his hand on the wolf's nape, its fur unexpectedly soft.

Gregori paused, body motionless and eyes locked in the same direction from which Ethan had sensed a threat.

"Intruders to the left of the road entrance." Their minds were chaos in the silence, a burst of noise that shattered the quiet. "At least ten of them." He did another scan. "No, fifteen. Six I can't get a lock on except to know they're there— they must be changeling. Five are human. Four Psy."

Ethan could attempt to hit those minds, but he wasn't a powerful enough telepath to neutralize them in one go. "If we can get to them, I can push them into unconsciousness."

The wolf's jaw fell open in a smile full of a predator's teeth.

"Close your eyes when it's time."

Gregori angled his head and Ethan understood that he was to follow. The two of them made good time through the forest, with Ethan keeping a mental eye on the encroaching group.

Whoever this was, they were either very lost—or *very* stupid. Selenka's wolves weren't known to be nice to intruders. Should a lost tourist wander in, they'd get a good scare and an escort out, but anyone with hostile intent? There was a reason the bears had agreed to a truce with BlackEdge.

Selenka's wolves might be smaller in animal form, but they were lethal and relentless fighters who would not give up. Even the lower-than-usual number of border sentries wasn't any guarantee of safety.

"We're getting closer," he told the wolf when Gregori paused and looked at him.

The two of them moved with more stealth from that point . . . until Gregori snarled and snapped ahead without warning. Ethan ran full tilt after him. He didn't know why the lieutenant had revealed their presence until he reached the location and saw the red fuel containers.

A number were open and tipped out at the feet of trees.

These people had planned to start a fire that would've decimated part of Selenka's territory. Ethan's blood iced, his protective instincts ascendant. Not bothering to shout a warning since Gregori was facing away from him, he sliced out a wave of light. Six of the intruders dropped. The ones still on their feet had their backs to him and so the light hadn't hit their eyes. No one had worked out why he needed to hit the eyes, but that seemed to be the conduit to the necessary brain circuitry.

The only reason he'd been able to take down everyone at the symposium hall was because he'd used a massive blast of power that reflected back from the slick walls. As it was, he had no reason to waste power with Gregori as his partner.

The wolf male had taken down four already.

Ethan spun a throwing blade into the calf muscle of an intruder, the weapon one he'd learned to use during his imprisonment as part of Dr. Marr's attempts to "enrich" his environment. His jailors hadn't cared what he learned since he was scanned for smuggled blades before they ever allowed him out of his cell, but Ethan had practiced with resolute intent regardless. It had been preparation for a freedom he was determined to snatch.

Tonight the intruder crumpled to the ground with a loud cry, one hand clutching reflexively at his calf; he sliced his palm to shreds. Gregori took out another one even as Ethan's target screamed again; the wolf lieutenant had ripped out a chunk of thigh to leave the woman writhing on the forest floor as she bled out. Sandpaper scraped over Ethan's senses, hard enough to do severe damage to his shields, but his refusal to allow anyone to harm Selenka had him overriding the pain.

Forming his power into a blade, he sliced the back of a parked vehicle in half. All the runners froze where they were . . . then very slowly went down to their knees, hands locked behind their heads.

"Turn around," Ethan ordered in a voice colder than the Arctic.

Gregori accompanied that with a menacing growl.

Ethan murmured, "Eyes," to Gregori the instant the intruders were facing them, then flashed his power again.

Everyone went out—including the ones with chunks of missing flesh.

"Fuckers are from Blaise's church," Gregori said, his voice half growl even though he'd shifted into human form. "Youngest is nineteen. Old enough to be responsible for his actions." His snarl was deadly. "Can't let the idiots die, though."

Because Selenka was the only one with the authority to make that call. A truth so self-evident that Ethan didn't need to ask Gregori to explain. "I can cauterize their wounds so they don't bleed any further."

Ethan suited his actions to his words. It was a trick he hadn't often had a chance to use, but he'd practiced on his own skin to the point where he had fine control over the light blade. When young, he'd thought if he got good enough, Ming would see it as an asset and use him to save people sometimes, but the former leader of the squad had only ever seen him as a killer.

It took him two minutes to stop all the bleeding—his throwing blade had done serious damage and Gregori hadn't held back. Though the scent of burned flesh lingered in the air, it was overwhelmed by the pungent aroma of spilled fuel. With the intruders incapacitated, the two of them turned their attention to the fuel.

"Punks weren't playing," Gregori said, his eyes bright amber. "That amount of fuel could've started a serious blaze."

Recalling Selenka's mention of graffiti, Ethan said, "A retaliation because you confronted their church leader about petty vandalism? It seems ill thought out."

"They're not exactly geniuses—and it looks like there's no one older than twenty-three in this group. You said you picked up on Psy minds, too?"

"Yes." He pointed out the four.

The other man shoved a hand through his hair, his tattoos sinuous shadows in the starry darkness. "I don't want to pull sentries from other areas. Can you keep an eye on the entire group of fuckwits while I run back and see who I can gather up to deal with this?"

Reaching into a side pocket of his pants, Ethan pulled out a set of thin wires. "Cuffs," he said. "I shouldn't need to stun them again unless they become majorly disruptive."

"After seeing what you did to that car, I don't think any of these punks are going to be playing chicken with you." Grin feral, the other man slapped him on the shoulder, his strength reverberating through Ethan. "Trust Selya to find herself a mate who can cut people in half."

Ethan didn't respond, but all the times when he *had* cut people in half after Ming literally took control of his brain . . . they haunted him. Even worse were the memories of his family's screams as he sliced them to pieces.

But this, tonight, was different.

It was the first time he'd wounded and hurt in order to protect. The intruders had come to cause pain to Selenka and those under her care; they'd *made* themselves targets. He felt no guilt whatsoever, at peace with his actions in a way that would make Alia proud. This, he thought on a sudden, acute wave of understanding, was what he'd always been meant to be: a protector like Gregori, a weapon used to defend against evil.

A throb began at the back of his head as he started to handcuff the fallen intruders, each pulse deep and loud. Three minutes later, he was glad he was alone except for his unconscious captives. It gave him time to erase all evidence of his new nosebleed . . . a bleed that didn't stop for long minutes.

Scarab whispered in his head, so much power at his fingertips if he would only reach for it. Power enough to protect the entire world.

THE pack laid Emanuel to rest in a ceremony rich with song and laughter. It was what he would've wanted, this member of Selenka's pack who'd never been grim or hard. Emanuel had been smiles and amusement and silly practical jokes that drove his packmates crazy, but when it had mattered, he'd been there, solid as an oak. People had relied on him. *Selenka* had relied on him.

As was their way, her pack released their grief in a chorus of wolf song that echoed across the territory. It was a memorial more ephemeral than a stone carving, but to a wolf, what mattered were the memories. Emanuel would be kept alive in stories and in wolf song for generations to come.

Then they returned home under the starlight, to pick up the mantle of life again. Grief was a different process for each and every one of them. However, in one thing, BlackEdge was united—to bring up their pups in the world of the living and not of the dead.

It was a decision made during the start of her grandfather's reign as alpha, after the pack lost fifteen adult wolves at the same time. It had been a horrible accident, a small plane going down in flames after being caught in turbulent weather. The pack had been devastated and barely functional in the aftermath.

Her grandfather had lost a brother in the carnage, but he'd made his way beyond the grief to care for his heartbroken people. He'd made them remember the young, the babies who didn't understand what was happening and who were going small and silent under the weight of the grief that held the pack in thrall.

To raise a pup was a privilege and a gift. No wolf would do anything to destroy those vulnerable young hearts. And so Selenka's pack would laugh again in the days to come. They'd hold the birthday celebration for a small boy that had been canceled today. And they'd remember Emanuel at each celebration, in their hearts, or with a drink raised to the sky.

But, tonight, it was a time of mourning, a time to come to terms with the grief.

Only after her pack no longer needed her would she find her deadly, beautiful, and relentlessly devoted mate and lie with him skin to skin. Because no matter the violent abruptness of their mating, Ethan belonged to her in a way no one else had ever done or ever would do.

She was a wolf, had grown from girl to woman in the glow of her grandparents' loving union. But her parents' troubled relationship had already left scars on her heart by then, and even being aware of the damage hadn't changed the wariness deep inside her. She couldn't bring herself to trust anyone enough to allow them a glimpse of her heart.

Until a damaged Arrow said, "I am yours," and meant it with all that he was.

She was still thinking of Ethan when she spotted Gregori arriving at the den just as she returned from the funeral. She was the only one outside because the alpha was always the final one to leave a burial, the one who spoke the pack's last good-byes to their lost packmate. Others would go up there in the days to come, to speak their private thoughts, but for tonight, it was done.

Crouching down next to him, she fisted her hand in the fur at the back of his neck. "What's happened? Are you hurt?" The scent of fresh blood was pungent in her nose, the mingled scents telling her this involved more than just Gregori.

When he shook his head, she said, "Do I need to send healers?" That got her a nod. "Security?" Another nod. "Any of our own hurt?" The question was razors across her soul; she didn't know if BlackEdge could take another loss after Emanuel.

She only breathed easy after he shook his head again. She didn't ask about Ethan because the light-fractured night of him was jagged inside her. The static in their bond couldn't block that critical awareness.

Instead of running into the den and causing alarm, she used her phone to contact Margo and asked the other woman to put together a team of five—a glance at Gregori got her a nod on the number. Then she called the healers, asking for two with full medical kits.

Both groups responded quickly and discreetly, slipping out of the den one by one.

Once gathered, all of them melted back into the trees in Gregori's wake. They reached the site of the situation to find a group of people who were either lying silently on the ground with their eyes open, their arms handcuffed behind their backs, or in the same immobilized position but moaning in pain.

Ethan stood a deadly black sentinel over them.

"Who cauterized the wounds?" The scent of cooked flesh made her wolf curl its lip.

"I did." Ethan's voice, dark music to her ear.

"Nice little hidden gift there, mate of mine." His actions

had probably saved the lives of at least two of the injured, but they'd carry major scars unless they paid for reconstructive work. Because the pack certainly wasn't going to give them anything but basic first aid. Not when Selenka had scented petrol as she came in.

Seeing the red containers strewn on the ground was a match to a flame, her claws slicing out of her fingers and her growl silencing all chatter in the clearing.

Today was not the day to fuck with Selenka.

Chapter 19

Selenka Durev: BlackEdge Alpha, 5'11", brown-eyed, and sexy enough to fry your brains. Our sources tell us that she once went head-to-head with a bear in a bad temper and shredded the bear so badly that he's still growing back his fur. Is it any surprise that she's a badass who holds territory in an area that houses both a bear clan *and* Kaleb Krychek?

Our spies in BlackEdge also inform us that being one of Selenka's wolves is a badge they wear with pride. "Our alpha is our claws and she is our heart. She knows how to love with a ferociousness that encompasses us all—but she won't blink at tearing our enemies to bleeding, whimpering shreds. Don't mess with BlackEdge unless you want to end up missing a body part or five."

—From the "Scary but Sexy" column in the December 2082 issue of *Wild Woman* magazine: "Skin Privileges, Style & Primal Sophistication"

"WHICH ONE OF you is the leader?" Selenka asked the fallen. "Unless you're too much of a coward to identify yourself." That last was a deliberate piece of manipulation—the young tended to be easy to rile unless they'd learned discipline over their instincts and arrogance.

"Me."

As she'd expected, the answer came from one of the four dominant wolves in Blaise's congregation—and though the young male tried to square his shoulders and meet her gaze, he couldn't. Because Selenka wasn't Blaise, to coddle a wolf who should be acting like a fucking adult by now—and her wolf *definitely* wasn't feeling friendly.

Seeing that the changeling—Zivko was his name—had

lost a small chunk of his leg, she waited for a healer to confirm he was as well as he could be until he got reconstructive treatment. Then she asked Ethan and Margo to haul him up to his feet. His face contorted in pain but he didn't cry out. At least he had guts.

She locked her eyes with his the instant he was upright, her wolf in her own. He couldn't break the contact. The animal that was amber in his irises knew she was a predator with far stronger jaws. He had no choice but to look at her, no choice but to feel fear lock his body in place as perspiration broke out over his skin.

If Selenka wished, she could use nothing but the power of her dominance to force him to his knees, make him crawl. She didn't usually unleash the depth of her dominance in such an aggressive way, but Zivko had made himself a threat to her pack. He was changeling, was wolf. He'd known the consequences he was courting.

"Talk," she said on a growl.

He resisted for a split second, and a small part of her appreciated his grit. There was dominance there—the promise of real strength, if he ever got his head out of his ass.

But he was only an untrained and cocky boy against a honed alpha.

Shoulders slumping, he said, "We just wanted to mess with you." Heavily accented but fluent Russian. "For turning us in to Blaise for the graffiti."

Selenka took in the people on the ground. "How did you talk them into it?"

"They're friends. I told them you got a bunch of us into shit with Blaise."

Selenka wasn't buying it—she didn't think he was lying, but she also didn't think he was telling her the whole truth. Either that, or he'd been manipulated himself. "Who came up with the idea of fire?"

It was an ugly thing she wouldn't have predicted on the basis of the background checks Margo and Ivo had run on Blaise's Disciples. The two had uncovered a couple of juvenile offenses to do with boosting cars, the odd speeding ticket, and a disturbing-the-peace charge attached to a human who'd once been a drunk, but nothing beyond that.

"I don't know." Zivko frowned, his brown-skinned face thin in that way of youths who hadn't finished growing and filling out. "It just came up while we were talking. We figured since your pack protects this landscape, it'd hurt if you lost a couple of the big trees."

Selenka put her clawed hands on her hips to control the urge to slice his face to shreds. "I can't figure out if you're just brainless or a cold-blooded killer."

Zivko flinched with his whole body, but there was a withheld anger to him that was dangerous—Blaise had done Zivko no favors by allowing that anger to build. Dominant wolves who got that edgy did violence sooner rather than later.

"It was only trees," he retorted, his face flushed and muscles knotted. "It'd just have left an ugly empty patch in your land."

"It hasn't rained in this area for three weeks," Selenka said with a quietness none of her pack ever wanted to hear from her. "The trees are old and their roots draw from deep within the earth, but the land is dry. This territory is full of wolves, including the old and the very young, many of whom can't run faster than flame." Fire could spread like water across a territory. "Fire is classed as a deadly weapon among changelings. You're a would-be assassin."

Zivko had gone paler and paler as she spoke, the anger buried under a sudden horror. "We didn't want to kill anyone," he whispered, his face stark. "We just wanted to mess with you."

Selenka believed him—Zivko wasn't dominant enough to tell her bald-faced lies. However, *someone* had placed the idea of fire as a mechanism for revenge in their minds. Someone very clever. Either one of this young group was a psychopath, or they were being manipulated by an older individual.

"Why tonight?" she demanded. "Why here, at this location?"

Shattered by her quiet recitation of the possible consequences of his actions, Zivko didn't bother to fight his wolf's need to answer her. "It's a clear night and we heard that a ton of your pack would be in a far-off place, celebrating an event."

The growls that emerged from multiple throats had Zivko

freezing. Selenka barely kept her own wolf from ripping out the young male's throat. "Who told you?"

He swallowed hard. "What?"

"Who told you we'd be away from our den?"

"I—I don't know." A frown, natural intelligence pushing past the fear and anger and aggression. "I *should* know. But it was another thing that just kind of came up—and it was like a few of us had heard it."

"Is there anything else you think I should know?"

He swallowed again and, though he was drenched in sweat by now, found the strength to say, "We really didn't want to hurt anyone."

Selenka's wolf felt both anger at those who'd let this pup down—*and* anger that a wolf this dominant and intelligent hadn't stopped to think about exactly what he was about to do. "Intent doesn't matter when the consequences of your actions were foreseeable and could've been devastating—your punishment will reflect that."

Those who committed a crime on predatory changeling lands were subject to justice by those same predators. Human or Psy rules didn't apply here. "Furthermore, you came onto our land on a day when we are grieving one of our dead." The words were a hard slap. "You brought with you the specter of more death even as we buried a beloved packmate. We will not be merciful."

Zivko completely crumpled at this point, well aware that she was within her rights to execute him. But he raised his head enough to say, "I'm to blame." A rasp. "The others followed me."

Well, perhaps this one was salvageable. She would see. For now, she nodded at Margo and Ethan to haul him back to sit among his compatriots, all of whom had heard the conversation. Terror marked each and every face, a long-delayed awareness that they had fucked up beyond anything they could've imagined.

"I've got a goddamn headache," she muttered when Ethan, Margo, and Gregori came to talk to her in the aftermath. "I don't think Zivko's group came here with deadly intent, but someone else in that church does have such intent."

"No one else will dare anything like this if we summarily execute the intruders." Ethan's voice was black ice.

"I'm with Ethan," Gregori said, folding his arms across his chest; he'd pulled on a pair of pants the healers had brought down but was otherwise naked. The in-progress tattoo on the left side of his chest was angry and red—it took special DNA-bonded ink for a tattoo to remain on changeling bodies, and it wasn't exactly gentle on the skin.

"I'm happy to rip their heads off with my bare hands," he added.

Shooting her brother a long-suffering look, Margo stayed silent. But Selenka knew her security specialist was just as pissed as Gregori.

As for Ethan, it was becoming clear to her that he had very hard lines inside his head—and because her pack mattered to her, it now mattered to him. "Ethan," she said, squeezing the bridge of her nose between thumb and forefinger, "the two of us need to have a discussion about levels of punishment. Execution is reserved for the worst. In the interim, come to me for any such decisions."

"I would regardless," he said, as if that was self-evident. "It's an alpha's call."

"I think you're slightly crazy," Margo said to Ethan while Gregori rumbled disagreement. "But I like that about you." Hands on her hips, she curled her lip. "I want to kill them, too, but I can also see that they're idiot pups."

"Zivko isn't a child." Ethan's tone was flat. "I'd assassinated fourteen people by the time I was his age."

Rage burned hot against Selenka's eyes, and this time, she didn't fight it.

Thrusting her hand in the thickness of his hair, she fisted it tight and tugged him to her for a kiss. He kept his arms crossed throughout, and she had the feeling her once-emotionless Arrow was irritated with them all for not simply chopping off the intruders' heads. His protective drive was a powerful beast, a creature with serious teeth.

Maybe others would've worried about his homicidal tendencies, but as he'd proven more than once, he'd back Selenka's decisions even if he disagreed with them. The only exception, she knew without asking, was if it was her life at

risk. She couldn't really disagree with him on that point—
she'd rip out the throat of anyone who came after him, too.

Her lieutenants were grinning at her—and her mate—
when she broke the kiss, the unrepentant moment of joy an
unexpected light in the darkness. Yes, Ethan had fans for life
in Margo and Gregori, and the other lieutenants would follow their lead. "So," she said to all of them, "since execution
is out, what do you suggest as punishment?"

Gregori stirred, his features settling into a scowl. "For the
wolves, hand-to-hand combat against pack wolves of their
own age. We'll make sure our people know not to go lethal,
but these wolves will come out bruised and battered."

Selenka considered that. Physical punishment might not
work among the other races, but they were predatory changelings. Their wolves thought differently, viewed power and
redemption differently. "But we don't want it to be a humiliation."

The entire reason Emanuel had lobbied in favor of Haven's Disciples was because of worry for powerful lost
wolves. A humiliation would ruin them . . . and destroy what
her friend and lieutenant had sought to create. "Each bout
takes place one-on-one, with no audience—though one of us
will monitor it from where we can't be seen or scented."

"For the humans," Margo said with a twist of her lips,
"it'll have to be incarceration in the local jail network." Her
dour tone made it clear exactly how happy she was with that
option.

"No, they're not getting off that easy." Human and Psy
jails were far too comfortable as far as Selenka was concerned. "I want them doing hard labor on our land until I
decide they've done enough. Their wolf friends can join
them after they recover from their bouts."

"Yes, I like that much better." Margo's smile was all
teeth. "Ethan, any recommendations for the Psy? Aside from
execution since Selenka says we have to be civilized."

"Hard labor." Ethan's pale eyes were glimpses of light in
the dark. "But you also need to corral their minds so they
can't travel the PsyNet. I can handle that as all four are apt
to be anchored in the same general psychic area."

It was a good point and one Selenka might not have considered without Ethan. But she shook her head at his offer. "I don't want you wearing yourself out doing the monitoring on your own—especially as it's going to be a couple weeks at the least."

A change in Ethan she couldn't pinpoint, a savage twisting of the coldness inside her.

Clenching her gut on the promise she'd get to the bottom of whatever was happening, she said, "I'll talk to Kaleb, get us psychic backup from one of his private security teams." It was a considered political decision. "Having him in play will make it crystal clear what Psy risk when they decide to mess with this territory." *No one* in the psychic race wanted Kaleb's attention.

Selenka had gone toe-to-toe with the cardinal telekinetic more than once, but she appreciated him as another alpha. A deadly one. Peace held in Moscow because she stayed on her side of the line and he on his. Same with Valentin. All three predators keeping a respectful eye on each other—and cooperating on matters that affected more than one of them.

"But that's all for tomorrow." She waved over the senior healer in the team. "Will any of the intruders die if left to spend the night here?"

"No," Tana said at once, her husky voice even rougher after the emotional intensity of Emanuel's funeral. "The cauterization was incredibly precise. It sealed off the tiniest of blood vessels." She looked at Ethan with a definite glint in her eye. "You'd be handy to have in delicate operations."

Ethan stared at her as if she'd diagnosed him as having grown wings and horns. "My ability is a weapon."

Tana arched her eyebrows. "I can use a scalpel to stab you dead. Doesn't mean it's not also a tool of medicine."

Ethan's dubious expression didn't change but he said, "Feel free to call on me if you believe I can provide assistance."

Tana nodded before returning her attention to Selenka, her brown eyes tired and the usually glowing dark of her skin dull. "The injured will be fine, especially with the first aid we rendered and if we give them a blanket each."

She smoothed back curls that had escaped the tight bun she preferred to wear while working. "I hate to leave them out here when they're so scared, but a little hardship might knock sense into them." Tana's eyes flashed. "I've been telling them about burns and what they do to a body." That explained the renewed devastation and tears on more than one face. Nope, it wasn't a good idea to piss off a healer.

Selenka touched Tana on the cheek, alpha to distressed packmate, and the healer turned into her touch. Leaning in, Selenka nudged up her chin and gently pressed her lips to Tana's, giving the healer the strength of pack that ran in Selenka's veins. "This dark night is almost done, *lastochka*. Soon you can rest your healer's hands."

Only after Tana had taken a deep breath and nodded did Selenka walk over to the intruders. There was no gentleness in her now, nothing but tempered fury. "You'll be spending the night out here, under the trees you tried to destroy, with the ugly scent of fuel to keep you company."

Growls filled the clearing at the reminder of what the intruders had intended to do, the hell they'd nearly unleashed. "Don't try to escape unless you want to die under wolf claws and teeth." Selenka's wolf took grim pleasure in the acrid fear coming off the intruders' bodies. "Your punishments are to be as follows."

Only the six changelings—the four wolves and two nonpredatories—looked relieved after she stopped speaking. She decided to make the situation crystal clear to the others. "If I wished, I could claw you bloody, then throw your mauled bodies out on the road as a warning, and Enforcement wouldn't lift a finger to help you—because we *own* you now."

Chapter 20

It is agreed by all parties that the final treaty will formalize what is already accepted fact: that on lands held by predatory changeling groups, whether pack, clan, or family, it is that group's laws that hold sway. No interference by outside parties will be countenanced.

—Adrian Kenner, peace negotiator,
Territorial Wars (18th century)

HEADS JERKED UP, throats moving as the shocked Psy and humans *finally* realized the shit they were in. Wolf in her eyes, until she knew the reflective glow had to be eerie, Selenka pointed to the right. "Do you see that wolf? His name is Ilarion and he is only *eighteen* years old. A disciplined young male of my pack who'd die to protect those weaker than him.

"He would *never* think to go into the territory of another people and threaten their home and their vulnerable. You are all older than him. Yet I wouldn't trust any of you to watch so much as a kitten."

Shame suffused more than one face. Zivko's head fell forward, and the other wolves couldn't meet her gaze, either.

Leaving them to stew in their shame, she nodded at Ilarion and his fellow soldier trainee to begin passing out the blankets they'd brought down at Tana's request. The two strong young wolves were an asset to her pack, and she made sure they saw her pride in them.

That in progress, she turned to Gregori, Ethan and Margo having gone to help the healers pack up. "You okay to handle security here overnight?"

"No problem." From his tone he'd enjoy glowering at the intruders. "Cuffs on or off?"

"Go with your instincts." Blood hot, she pulled out her phone. "I'm going to talk to Blaise." Stepping into the trees, she didn't bother to introduce herself when the leader of Haven's Disciples answered at the other end. "Fifteen of your people aren't going to be coming home today. They are guests in BlackEdge territory."

A small silence before Blaise said, "How badly are they injured?"

Selenka told him. She also told him the extent of their attempted crime.

Blaise swore. "I'll punish them myself," he said. "And I won't go easy—you can count on it."

"I won't. They won't be coming home until they've completed their punishment." She had no faith in Blaise's ability to control his people. "We'll set up temporary accommodations for them here." It wouldn't be much more than tents and sanitary facilities, but the group was lucky she hadn't followed the approach taken by California's SnowDancer wolves: shoot first and ask questions of the corpses. Though that stance was looking more and more attractive.

"You can't do that," Blaise said, and for the first time since they'd met, there was a growl in his tone. There it was at last: a glimpse beyond Blaise's suave and civilized facade. He remained a wolf under the skin, and that wolf thought it could best an alpha of Selenka's strength.

A younger Selenka would've gone for his throat for the insult. Alpha Selenka Durev noted the slip and stored it for consideration. Blaise had just gone from a tolerated annoyance to a threat. Because what were the chances that a man who liked to control his flock would be unaware of their actions?

He *was* arrogant enough that things could be taking place under his nose, but the flip side was more likely to be true— that it was Blaise who'd manipulated Zivko and the others to an act that could've led to a catastrophic and heinous outcome.

Selenka was within her rights to order the Disciples out of the territory, but this wasn't about simple annoyance any longer. She wanted them in her sight so she could get proof that would mean the end of the Disciples once and for all—Blaise wouldn't be getting the chance to get his hands on other vulnerable wolves.

"Our laws are clear and your people broke them," she said on a growl of her own that shut him up. "Do not show your face anywhere near my territory, Blaise. You—or anyone you send—will end up without a throat."

She hung up without waiting for a response, then located Ethan. Seeing Gregori had the situation in hand and that Margo had decided to hang with her far grumpier younger brother, she said, "Walk with me." She could've ordered one of her people to bring down a vehicle earlier, but she'd known she'd need time in the forest to resettle her skin, be the alpha her grieving pack needed.

"I can return afterward to help Gregori," Ethan said fifteen minutes after they'd stepped into the dark embrace of the trees.

Halting, Selenka touched her fingers to his jaw. "No. I need you to stay with me." It was difficult for her to admit such need even to the man who was her mate, but Ethan's openness spoke to the wild girl she'd once been, the one who'd worn her heart on her sleeve and had it kicked for her trouble.

"For my pack," she told him, "I must be alpha. Yes, I can let down my hair with my lieutenants and my friends, but I can never be anything *but* their alpha. It is in my skin and it is who we are."

The light-fractured ice of him, jagged against her senses and riven with static, his pale eyes locked with hers. "The hierarchy always exists," he said, as if working through her words. "Whether or not you acknowledge it at any one time does not mean it's no longer there. I am outside the hierarchy, and thus, you don't have to be Alpha Durev with me, can be Selenka."

"If that was all it took," she said, continuing to stroke the bristled roughness of his jaw, stomach tight and wolf filled with pride, "all an alpha would have to do was make a close friend or two outside of the pack."

Ethan tilted his head slightly to the side, an action common amongst wolves. She wondered if he even realized he'd picked up the small motion. It fascinated her, how he was already integrating with her pack while remaining resolutely himself. No one would ever mistake Ethan for anything but an Arrow.

"It has to do with the bond between us," he said, pupils flaring. "Even with the interference, I can sense you within me, a primal wolf who . . . values me."

Selenka wanted to kill anyone who had ever hurt him and made him feel lesser. Closing her hand over his nape, she spoke with her lips against his. "Just know that you are the *one* person with whom I am not Alpha Durev. To you, I am and will always be Selenka. And you are and will always be *mine*." It was a growl, her wolf in agreement with the human part of her that this man was worth the risk to her heart. "You are mine first and you will always be mine first."

Making no effort to hide the embers that burned inside him, his hands possessive on her hips, her extraordinary, complex, deadly mate considered that for a long moment. "Am I your Zaira?"

It took her a second to place that name —Aden Kai's mate didn't court publicity. Like most of the Arrow squad, she preferred to live in the shadows. But her link with Aden meant she had a certain profile, especially among those who worked with the squad.

Selenka had seen Aden and Zaira together only once, but it had been enough for her to understand theirs was a mating. Maybe Psy didn't call it that, but it didn't change the fact the two were bonded to the core.

"Who is Zaira to Aden?" she asked, wondering how Ethan saw the relationship.

"Knight to his king." The starlight barely penetrated the canopy, yet what light there was seemed drawn to the angles of Ethan's face. "As I am the knight to your queen."

Selenka frowned. "I don't think Aden thinks of himself that way in relation to his mate, and I don't think of myself as queen over you." Mates were equals always. "You're my knight only in the sense that you're my permanent and for-ever backup."

Ethan deliberately broke eye contact with her for the first time that she could remember.

Her wolf came to attention. "We need to talk about something, don't we?"

"Yes. I have secrets you need to know." Full eye contact again, his beautiful voice solemn in the silence of the night. "I thought I could simply not tell you, but I can't lie to you, Selenka. Not even by omission."

Every time she thought about putting up a wall between them, he smashed it down with brutal openness. "Is it about the nosebleed?"

"Yes—and more."

Tension knotted her spine, a sense of dread in her gut. "After," she said, making a decision on the spot. "When we're alone." Whatever Ethan had to tell her, she already knew she'd be in no state to look after her pack if they got into it now.

"After." His kiss held an edge of desperation, his breathing ragged when they broke apart and his hair tumbled on his forehead.

Her own pulse wasn't any steadier, and her breasts ached. It would be so easy to surrender to this, to sink into intimate skin privileges, but she could no more ignore the grieving howls of her wolves than she could walk away from the mating bond. So she held out her hand.

Ethan slid his into it, and they covered the remaining distance side by side.

Once in the den, she took him to a space to the left of the entrance. The pack had been lucky with the large area they called the Terrace—though it was an internal space, it received direct sunlight courtesy of a number of natural holes in the stone of the mountain under which the den was located.

Over the years, over the generations, the Terrace had been turned into a wild garden. It even boasted a few small trees. There were tons of flowering bushes and vines that crawled up the walls, along with masses of soft grasses kept relatively short so even the smallest babies could play happily among it.

"This is the safe play area for our pups," she told Ethan. "They can roam and get the feel of being outdoors even when they're too small to cope with the rougher terrain outside."

Ethan took in the area with quiet intensity before touching his fingers to a slender tree. "We have an underground forest in Arrow HQ. The darkness, the psychologists said, cannot be endless or the people within will go insane."

What, she thought, had the darkness in which Ethan had been imprisoned done to him? But one thing she knew: "Whatever your scars," she told her mate, "your jagged and broken pieces, at your core is a place of light and cold reason. You're not damaged in the way you think."

Pale eyes searching hers. "Does the cold unsettle you?"

"No. I burn too hot at times, Ethan; my temper is my Achilles' heel." She'd been conscious of that since she was a teenager. "Your calm's helped me stay rational throughout this ugly day."

His hair fell across his forehead as he moved to touch another tree, and suddenly he looked so young that her heart threatened to break. She would show him a world beyond pain and murder and hurt, she vowed it.

There was a sound near the entrance to the Terrace at that moment, and when she looked that way, it was to meet the gaze of a stocky man with skin as pale as moonlight and eyes of deepest brown. Selenka just opened her arms.

SHELVING his words about how the scalding fire of her warmed him even as it burned, Ethan faded into the background. It was a skill he'd learned long ago . . . but it turned out fading was difficult among wolves.

A steady stream of Selenka's pack came into the Terrace in the hours that followed, and while most went directly to their alpha, a few came to Ethan. Some just stood shoulder to shoulder with him in silence. Others asked him questions about psychic power or the PsyNet. He had the sense they didn't actually care about his answers; the wolves simply wanted to hear his voice.

"It's so beautiful," a teenager told him at one point. "It makes my wolf less sad just to listen to the tones of it."

So Ethan spoke more than was his natural tendency.

He was, he realized an hour into it, the waiting room to Selenka. He found no insult in that. She might see being queen to his knight as referencing a power differential, but Ethan saw it another way. A knight belonged to his queen, as

Ethan belonged to Selenka. Sword or shield or babysitting pups in the nursery, whatever Selenka needed, Ethan would provide.

The shadow of night was fading into the dusty gray of very early morning by the time the Terrace emptied of wolves who needed their alpha. Taking his hand with a possessiveness that filed off the rough edges of the shards inside him, she led him through the empty corridors of the den.

When she did stop at a door and push it open, it proved to lead into a large bedroom.

Snick.

She locked the door behind them even as he was trying to absorb every nuance of this space that was Selenka's private haven. Strong, feminine arms wrapped around his waist from behind a moment later, Selenka pressing her cheek against his back.

Protective instincts kicking into high gear, he closed his hands over her own. "You're tired. Get in bed." He needed to take care of her, the drive even more visceral than the physical craving that smoldered in his veins.

"I need to take a shower first. I just . . . the sadness clings." She stepped back. "Shower with me."

Ethan's brain threatened to short-circuit.

She'd stripped down to her skin before he'd removed his boots, a tall and sleek woman whose hips flared out gently and whose breasts were small and taut and made his palms itch to touch them. But his eyes focused on her back first, the wound there, and he was pleased to see that the fresh seal Oleg had placed over the area was clean and unbroken. "Are you in pain?"

"No. Oleg worked on it right before I went to the funeral." After running her hands though her hair once, she arched her body, but there was a tiredness to her as she walked to the door at the far end of her private space.

Stopping at the entrance, she looked back at him with eyes aglow with the wolf. "Don't be long, *zaichik*."

Chapter 21

Only pack, mates, and lovers have skin privileges.
  —Lucas Hunter, Alpha, DarkRiver Leopards (2079)

ETHAN TORE OFF his clothes with Arrow speed, was with her only moments later. The entire bathing area was rock, with the showerhead set in the center of the ceiling, so the droplets fell like rain onto Selenka's head as she stepped underneath. As he watched, locked in place by the knowledge that this woman of strength and power was his, she lifted her face to the water, her hair a slick waterfall on her back.

Ethan wasn't aware of moving, but he found himself reaching into a niche in the wall to grab a bottle of shampoo. His mate's heart was aching and she needed tenderness beyond anything else. It was a knowing that went so deep it was beyond bone, beyond muscle.

After pouring a generous amount into his cupped palm, he set the bottle aside and stepped into the water with her. She sighed and leaned back into him as he worked the cleanser into the long strands of her hair from scalp to tip. Foamy suds dripped over both their bodies as the water washed the soft-smelling liquid from her hair.

Afterward, he worked her scalp with his fingers, content despite the need that clawed constantly at him. Being with Selenka, it filled an emptiness so deep inside him that it had no name. This was where he was meant to be. And she was the woman with whom he was meant to be.

Turning, Selenka dropped her forehead against his chest, her arms linked around his waist. Her tears were raw and unvarnished, broken pieces of her heart in every sound. Fueled by primal emotion, the rogue Scarab power shoved against his shields on a deep, rumbling roar. Because Silence had worked for some, for the broken who would otherwise be mad creatures without thought or reason.

Ethan punched back the power to wrap his arms around his mate and just held her as she cried not only for a packmate lost, but for a friend. Later, her sobs having turned her voice gritty, she told him about Emanuel. How he'd been a holdover lieutenant from her grandfather's days as alpha, the youngest of Yevgeni Durev's lieutenants by a large margin and the only one who hadn't chosen to voluntarily retire in the years after Yevgeni Durev stepped down in favor of his granddaughter.

"The others were older, ready to retire, and only stayed in their positions to ensure a smooth transition," Selenka said, her voice raw. "I knew I'd have them for five years at the most. But Emanuel was only in his thirties at the time and one of the strongest dominants in the pack—he *had* to be one of my lieutenants. Leaving him outside the power structure would've not only been a waste, it would've confused every wolf in the den."

A shuddering sigh. "I wasn't sure how we'd deal together—he was over a decade my senior and used to working with a much older alpha. But Emanuel was born of kindness and compassion and he was so confident in his own skin that he felt no envy or jealousy of the young wolf who'd risen past him in dominance."

Ethan promised himself that before his brain imploded, he'd ask her about her rise to alpha, about when she'd first known this responsibility would be hers to carry. He wanted to know everything about her, the need a hunger that could never be assuaged. "Emanuel sounds like a good man." A man who'd had Selenka's back; for that alone, Ethan would honor his memory.

"Yes, he was. Such a good man. I'll miss him." Quiet, potent words. "I'll miss his advice and his ability to make us all laugh, and most of all, I'll miss his smile." Inhaling deeply, she pushed her wet hair back from her face, then pressed a kiss to Ethan's chest. "Thank you."

He didn't know how to answer that, didn't understand how she could thank *him* when she'd hauled him out of the icy gray numbness and into the searing warmth of her, so he just reached out and switched off the water. She allowed him to wrap her in a towel and stood as he took another towel to her hair.

He didn't care that his own body was dripping wet. Selenka came first. He needed to take care of her, and even though no one had ever taken care of him, it wasn't a difficult matter to work out his mate's needs. Not when she made it so easy.

After he finished with her hair, she pointed to a jar on the countertop built into the stone wall closest to the bedroom. "It's conditioner that I leave in my hair."

Ethan worked it into the strands, and as he did so, he caught a hint of the rich green scent he associated with her. Below that, however, was the deeper, more integral scent of her. He might not be changeling, might not have a wolf's nose, but he would always know Selenka.

"Tell me," she said, and it was an order—but not from an alpha to a packmate. This was very private, very intimate, from mate to mate. "About the blood and about why you stiffen up every time I mention the future."

Ethan focused on her hair, on the scents in the air, on the lingering steam from the shower, but he couldn't hold back the cold, dark truth. "Have you heard of Scarab Syndrome? It only affects Psy, so you may not—"

"No." A frown he caught from his position slightly to her left. "I remember seeing those words on a medical alert I forwarded to Oleg. It has to do with rogue Psy abilities?"

"In a nutshell, Silence worked for a tiny minority of my race—it contained the most dangerous aspects of our abilities." Kept them from becoming monstrous and murderous. "The fall of Silence has led to the disintegration of those psychic chains. An unknown force is stretching inside me, a seductive vastness of power that can be only Scarab."

Grabbing another towel, Selenka turned and began to dry his hair. "What does that mean for you?"

Ethan stood unmoving under her careful motions—she was trying not to pull at his hair, he realized slowly, trying not to hurt him even that infinitesimal amount. The tenderness broke him. No one had ever seen Ethan Night as worthy of care. He wanted to just stand there in that impossible moment, but he had promised his mate the truth.

"There's no way to turn back the clock once the new powers become active—and these powers lead to insanity, violence, a lack of control." He could feel the madness whispering things to him, telling him he was capable of far more than he knew.

"There is one possible source of hope," he added when Selenka's eyes went gold. "An empath with the proven ability to leach off some of the Scarab power. I'm to meet her tomorrow . . . today."

"I'll come with you."

Ethan didn't say anything—because having her with him was never not acceptable. "The Consortium operative tried to make contact with me earlier tonight."

"What will you do?" she asked, no suspicion in her.

It broke bad things inside him, re-formed them into something better. "I've informed Aden of the contact, and offered to act as bait if necessary"—even though he didn't want to waste what time he had on that ugliness—"but he says the squad is on the verge of tracking the operative down using the dossier I provided yesterday."

"Good." Selenka turned to put away the towel she'd been using on his hair.

He wrapped his arms around her from behind, careful not to press against her wound, but needing her in a way he'd never needed anyone. Until her, need for a person hadn't even been a concept in his life. Light, air, those had been his deepest needs. Now she was his air and his light.

No one had ever just *accepted* him, and even though she was angry at him for hiding his physical and psychic status from her, her acceptance of him, of Ethan jagged and damaged, remained steadfast. "This is the closest I've ever been to another living being."

Turning in his embrace, Selenka ran her hands up his back as she pressed her lips to his right pectoral muscle. The contact made his body lock, the sensations that tore through him visceral.

"Does it hurt?" Wolf-gold eyes holding his in challenge. "Have you been in pain each time we kissed?"

He fought to find his feet so he could explain, fought to find his breath. "The majority of the squad underwent psychic training that included the embedding of a feedback loop that punished any deviation from Silence with increasing amounts of physical pain."

Selenka pricked his back with her claws. "Do you have that? Don't lie to me, mate of mine."

Drinking her in, drunk on her, he said, "My trainers had problems getting that part of the mental leash to stick. No one ever worked out why." Ethan exhaled, inhaled again because he could never get enough of her scent. "Ming told them to forget it—he already had me on a private leash."

Raising one hand, claws retracted but eyes yet wolf, Selenka ran her fingertips over the side of his bristled jaw. "Then why are your muscles like concrete, your breathing out of kilter?"

"Because I want to devour you." Like a ravaging beast. "Control is difficult."

A nip of his throat. "You sure you're not in pain?"

"No." Shuddering, he angled his neck for more. "But the sensory overload is significant, and I'm inexperienced. I don't know the next step."

Selenka's smile was different this time, a sensual and intimate thing that asked him to smile with her. "Figuring it out is part of the fun, *zaichik*."

He stiffened, jaw clenching. "I am not a rabbit. I am not prey." Ethan might not fully understand changeling ways, but he knew no alpha wolf would ever treat a prey creature as an equal intimate partner.

Selenka's laugh was wild and beautiful and it caused the hot tendrils inside him to strengthen and grow and grow. "That's why I call you *zaichik*," she growled with another nip of his throat. "Because you're the last thing from a fluffy little rabbit that I can imagine. I think it's funny, but I'll stop if you don't like it."

Ethan dared bite her shoulder, got a growl and a stroke

through his hair in response. Happy—truly *happy*—he said, "You can use it." Now that he understood the why behind it, the term was a secret joke between them. Others would hear her use it and be confused—because no one ever saw an Arrow as prey. But Ethan would know his wolf mate was playing with him and it would mean everything.

While on watch prior to the arrival of the intruders, he'd looked up the material to which Margo had directed him. While he hadn't been in a space conducive to consuming *Hourglass Lives* and Ridge remained a mystery to him, *Wild Woman* magazine had proved an excellent source of information. Several articles had reiterated that while wolves were serious with the world, they were playful, nosy, and deeply loyal with those they claimed.

Unable to resist tasting her smile, he took a kiss, deep and unskilled and voracious. Moaning and wrapping her arms around his neck, his mate flicked out her tongue to wet his lips and his brain blanked, the Scarab power pounding against his shields. Shoving it back with a violent push, Ethan sank into her, sank into sensation.

Selenka didn't deny him anything. Her lips were plush against his, her tongue wet, and body sleek and cool from the shower. Sliding his hands down her back, to just above the swell of her buttocks, he held her close as he indulged his senses as he'd never before done.

As she indulged him.

He felt spoiled by her, and he reveled in it, in being simply *given* what he wanted instead of having his need used to torture him.

When he broke the kiss to taste her throat, she arched her neck for him. And when he returned for another ravenous kiss, she gave it to him without hesitation. Inside, the shattered pieces of him continued to re-form into a whole, held by the glowing molten heat of her.

"What do you want?" Warm breath against his throat, Selenka's teeth closing over sensitive skin.

Ethan's engorged penis throbbed. "I've always understood the mechanics of sexual arousal." Had been taught those mechanics so he could then be taught how to crush it. "But I didn't *know*." That it'd be near pain, the *wanting* inside him, that he'd be breathless, his brain not fully functional.

Kisses on his throat, her nails scraping over his scalp in a caress that made the tiny hairs on his body rise. "We'll go slow." A sensual promise. "So you can ride each edge and be ready for the next." Another nip. "Even if I do want to eat you up and come back for seconds right now."

He kissed her again, certain beyond any doubt that kissing would always be one of his most favorite things. The taste of her, how her eyes looked into his at the moment of contact, before her lashes drifted shut, the way her breath brushed his skin. Having her so close to him, strong and dangerous yet willing to be soft in this time and place.

Making a rumbling sound in the back of her throat as he ran his hands over her back and down her arms before retracing his path with a stronger touch, Selenka broke the kiss to say, "For an ice-cold Arrow, you're very good at petting a wolf who needs exactly that today."

Eyes of wild gold examined him with wolfish suspicion. "Where did you learn that? To be clear, I'm jealous."

Blood languorous and heavy, Ethan continued his petting. He was never going to get enough of touching her. "I feel you inside me, and I know what you need."

Frown lines furrowed Selenka's brow, the tips of her breasts brushing his chest as she said, "I don't know if that's how mating works." A kiss to his chest. "How you're touching me, it's *precisely* what I need. It's too subtle and deep a read."

Ethan turned to stone. "I'm not reading your mind." He would *never* violate her in such a way.

It was her turn to "pet" him, the word she'd used perfect for what they were doing, this gentle caressing and learning. "I know, Ethan—that's not what I meant." Little kisses along his rigid jaw until he softened for her; she then slid her hand around to the back of his neck as she had a habit of doing.

According to *Wild Woman*, it was an act of "sneaky wolf possessiveness."

He'd never known that skin was so sensitive—or how much he'd love a possessive lover. Love how she touched him, how she saw him, how she smiled at him with wolf eyes. "I shouldn't be surprised you're figuring this out so quick—that brain of yours is sexy as hell."

Shudders rippled through his frame as she claimed his mouth in a deep, branding kind of a kiss after those caressing words. Wrapping her up in his arms, more than happy to be branded, he opened his mouth and licked at her tongue as she'd licked at his.

She growled, the rumble traveling from her body into his, and down to the heaviness of his erection. His penis had been rigid since first contact, but now, it throbbed so intensely it was a second heartbeat. He didn't know what to do with it, but as Selenka didn't seem to mind the aggressive heat shoving against the curve of her abdomen, he didn't move away, didn't attempt to give her space.

He didn't *want* to give her space.

All he wanted was to get closer and closer and closer.

He ran his nails down her back.

A hiss of sound and she broke the kiss to nip at his throat. The next bite was harder and at the point where his neck flowed into his shoulder. Hard enough that he knew while she hadn't broken skin, she would leave a mark. Blood molten, he also knew her bite wasn't a punishment.

She licked at the mark, her clawed fingers lightly scraping his shoulders.

Chapter 22

Aunt Rita pens a special column today on intimate skin privileges for virgins. All you experienced types can turn the page. The rest of you, listen up—because Aunt Rita knows. Aunt Rita has done the horizontal tango for longer than you've been alive. She's also done it vertically, diagonally, and upside down.

—From the February 2074 edition of *Wild Woman* magazine: "Skin Privileges, Style & Primal Sophistication"

"MINE." A GROWL of sound against Ethan as the wet silk of his mate's hair brushed over his body.

"Yours," he said without hesitation, then gripped the side of her neck. "You're mine, too."

The eyes that met his were somehow wilder, the gold glowing. And her kiss, it was feral, her hand fisted in his hair. "Yours," she said in a voice that was half-wolf, before she made a lithe movement that ended up with her legs hitched around his hips.

Ethan supported her with his hands under her buttocks, the strength of her thighs around him a delicious pressure, and the slick of musk in the air making his mind roar. He had no walls with Selenka, no boundaries. He kissed her back as raw and deep, his hands clenching on the curvy flesh in his palms.

The sounds she made encouraged him to open himself deeper, lower even more shields. Until the only ones left were those holding back his madness . . . and then the madness surged to smash against his shields with the force of a tidal wave, stabbing a sharp pain through his head.

Though he didn't make a sound, Selenka wrenched back. "Blood." It was a growled word.

Uncurling from around him, she dropped her feet to the floor, then twisted to grab a wad of tissues from the counter that held the sink. "You said you wouldn't lie, that this was safe for you." Her voice vibrated with fury.

"It is." Ethan wiped away the blood, but the bleeding wouldn't stop.

Tilting back his head, he squeezed the bridge of his nose. "I don't have a pain-feedback loop in my head. I want you with every cell in my body."

Selenka stalked out into her bedroom, and when she walked back in, she was angrily tying the belt on a robe the color of a dark stormy sky. "Let me see that." Taking the tissues from him, she dampened a clean part under the sink tap, then wiped away what appeared to be the last remnants.

They both waited, but the bleed appeared over.

"There's something very wrong in your head." Throwing the tissues in a small bin of obsidian green, Selenka thumped a fisted hand against her head. "I can feel you inside me, Ethan, and there are all these jagged points to you that don't feel right."

Ethan wrapped a towel around his hips, staggering under the agony spearing through his heart. "I told you I was damaged." Had believed she accepted him despite that, that she'd seen him and liked him as he was.

A growl of sound before she stalked over and gripped his jaw. "It's not about *you*. What I feel, it doesn't 'taste' like you to my wolf and it won't let my wolf in—I think it's causing the static in our bond, interfering with our connection." Dropping her hold, she folded her arms. "Ming LeBon put something in you that shouldn't be there."

Ethan wanted to believe that, but he knew what she didn't. "What you're sensing are incredibly powerful shields holding back the onset of Scarab Syndrome. It's the only good thing Ming ever did for me—teaching me how to build titanium shields. I'd be a nightmare otherwise." Not even for their bond would he drop those shields. "I can't let you in beyond those shields. I *won't*." If he hurt her, he'd be lost, a creature of insanity and violence.

Selenka put her hands on her hips. "I don't know if I'd go about believing Ming LeBon. Man just wanted to use and control you."

"I didn't." Exhaling and wishing he could turn back time so he was holding and kissing Selenka again, he shoved both hands through his hair. "When I felt the first stirrings of new power, I decided to ease up on my shields and see what lay beyond, see if Ming had crippled me on purpose. What emerged was madness." Howling screams that echoed and echoed.

"Recently, I saw an audiovisual ad for a human-made movie. The movie is set in a historical hospital for the criminally insane. The howls of the residents were like the ones inside my skull." A broken thing, shards of glass in the brain. "Something *isn't* right with me, Selenka." It was a truth he couldn't escape. "But it's *me*, not anything Ming put in me. I feel the Scarab power screaming now, shoving at my shields, trying to break free."

"I refuse to believe that." Selenka swept out a hand in a hard slice, a warrior queen in full flow. "My wolf would never mate me to a man caught in the grip of madness."

He would go to his knees, lower his head for her sword if she asked, but he couldn't give her this. "How do you know?"

The question quivered between them.

"I know." Selenka thumped her chest with a flat palm. "I *know*."

"What if you're wrong?" Ethan demanded on a wave of turbulent heat. "Who will I be to you then?" He had *never* been embraced as she'd embraced him, and he couldn't bear to lose that, couldn't bear to go back to being alone in the dark.

Yet even as he asked the question, his anger flatlined. Shaking his head, he said, "I can't be anything but a risk to you in madness. I'll remove myself from the equation long before that happens."

Selenka moved so fast that he had no hope of avoiding her. He slammed up against one of the rock walls, and though it was uneven, it wasn't sharp . . . and fury or not, she'd held back, so he was able to brace himself with his palms on either side of him. His mate knew his skills, had calibrated her movements with precision.

Looking after him even as she bared her teeth and hauled down his head with one hand in his hair. "Do not *ever*," she said, her voice no longer wholly human, "speak of ending yourself. You belong to me now."

It was the one thing Ethan couldn't—*wouldn't*—give her. "I won't allow myself to become a threat to you. I won't ever be an out-of-control mass murderer again."

Selenka was an alpha, used to going toe-to-toe with anyone and coming out satisfied by the outcome. But this? She *wasn't* fucking satisfied, yet she knew she had not a hope in hell of changing Ethan's mind.

Her Arrow mate had spoken quietly, in that voice so beautiful it was a song each time he opened his mouth, but that he was resolute was unmistakable. He would not bend in this, would not change his mind.

I am the knight to your queen.

She might not agree with his choice of description, but it was how he saw himself—and no knight would ever put his queen in danger, especially not danger that came from within.

Furious with him, and at the same time intensely proud to have a mate who could withstand her even at her angriest and most aggressive—she kissed him. Hard. "This conversation isn't over."

"What happens now?" A searing tautness to him.

Selenka's instinct was to protect, to shield, but Ethan didn't need protecting in this place that was their private den. As she'd pointed out, he was no *zaichik*, and she'd ruin them both if she forgot that. "Are you still in pain?"

"A faint throb at the back of my skull, but the sharp pain has passed." He watched her with eyes that gave nothing away . . . but she felt his need all the same, a contained explosion held so tightly that it was a touch away from ignition. "I am fully capable."

Selenka knew he hadn't meant that as a double entendre, but she decided to treat it as one anyway. Her mate had never played—but he was mated to an alpha wolf now, play an integral part of his life. "I know all about your capability," she murmured with a slow smile, as she reached down to brush the length of his cock through the towel.

Ethan turned to stone, his breathing going rough and shallow. Sweat beaded along his hairline, darkness spreading out from his pupils to eclipse the whites of his eyes. She'd witnessed the effect with other Psy and always found it eerie, but with Ethan, it was simply another indication of her mate's emotions.

"Should I stop?" she murmured huskily as she tugged off the towel.

The cords of his neck straining stark against his skin, he shook his head.

Her own pulse not exactly steady, she brushed her fingers over his naked length—and this time, he all but stopped breathing. Her breasts had been full and swollen, her core slick since they began, but his reaction squeezed everything inside her to breath-stealing tightness.

She'd intended to play, make his first time gentle and slow, but realized then and there her plan wouldn't work. It wasn't about her own trembling fingers or feral hunger. No, her wolf could keep it together if it was about making this a pleasurable experience for her mate—but Ethan wasn't yet at a place where he could ask for what he needed, or rush her when the play got too intense. This was torturous to him right now.

"Trust me?" she asked, running the nails of her free hand down his chest.

Those obsidian eyes held hers, and though she couldn't see his pupils in the sweep of black, she knew he was eye-to-eye with her. "With my throat. With my life."

A shudder raked her spine, her wolf shoving against her skin. Oh, but her Arrow knew just what to say to make her his—and the best thing of all was that he didn't calculate or analyze. He spoke as he felt and, in doing so, fractured all those walls she'd put up to protect her heart.

Ethan would never choose to leave her, would never choose to abandon her. She could trust him with herself and know the gift wouldn't be kicked back in her face. That she had to consciously think that even with her mate . . . yes,

Ethan wasn't the only one in this relationship who was damaged. And she'd tell him that. After.

Because this time was about the present, not the past. About pleasure, not pain.

"Let me show you pleasure." Overwhelmed with affection and the whispers of a deeper and far more dangerous emotion, she kissed him soft and sweet over his shoulders and chest until his muscles began to soften at last. "Let me ease your ache." She squeezed his cock.

"No, this is meant to be a mutual activity," her stubborn mate argued even as sweat broke out over his skin. "I read it in the manual Margo recommended. No one party should lie back and receive only."

Selenka blinked, momentarily distracted from the delicious heat and length of him in her grasp. "Manual?"

"The 'Skin Privileges & Satisfaction' and 'Aunt Rita' columns of *Wild Woman* magazine."

Wolf huffing inside with affectionate laughter—because *of course* Ethan had done his research—Selenka kissed him, her lips curved and her hand unmoving on his cock because this wasn't about teasing her mate. That would come later, after he knew how to tease her in return.

"The manual is correct," she said, "except in situations where one party wishes to give and finds deep pleasure in that."

Pressing a finger to his lips when he would've argued with her again, she said, "One day, you can do the same to me."

No more arguing, Ethan's features settling into lines of anticipation. So, her lover liked the idea of petting her to his heart's content. Lips curved, she removed her finger from his lips. "Yes?"

A small nod.

Releasing his cock, she pulled him into the bedroom and pushed him down onto his back on the bed. Then she climbed up over him. Staying on her knees as he lay below her, watching her with obsidian eyes that devoured her, she undid the belt of her robe and shrugged it off her shoulders.

Her feminine core clenched at the way he looked at her, all hot eyes and sensual craving. Ethan Night was going to wreck her when he got going. Throwing the robe aside on a wave of arousal, she dropped her mouth to his neck and licked over the mark she'd made, the mark that shouted to the world that he was hers. Only after she'd satisfied that primal urge did she begin to kiss her way down the hard, flat planes of his chest.

His hand jerked up to grip her hair. Releasing it almost at once, he said, "I'm sorry."

"Go ahead and hold on." A licking kiss pressed to his solar plexus. "Because I'm going for fast and hard today." Her mate didn't yet understand how to revel in taut sexual need—he was experiencing anticipation as pain, and that was unacceptable to either part of her.

He should know only pleasure in bed with her.

"If you want me to stop, just say 'stop.'" She'd also pay close attention to his nonverbal cues. It was a rule she'd put into effect after an illuminating—if mortifying—conversation with her grandmother as a teenager.

"You're an incredibly powerful wolf, Selenushka," her gentle and submissive babushka had murmured. "Your dominance is significant and might intimidate partners. You must *always* give them agency and power. And keep checking to see they're with you—we're wolves, not humans or Psy, and your dominance is *so* strong that not everyone will have the power to resist the compulsion to simply obey you."

A brush of a warm, soft hand over her hair. "I know my sweet Selenushka doesn't want obedience with a lover. It's not who you are. But you must take care that it doesn't happen by accident—because I know such a thing would devastate you."

She'd gone tomato red during that conversation, but she'd taken her grandmother's lesson to heart. Not that Ethan needed her to give him agency in that way. The man was lethal and fully capable of stopping her dead in her tracks anytime he wished. Or . . . maybe not.

She halted.

Ethan's devotion was a thing of stone, a thing that would not budge. While that devotion was an arrow straight to her heart, she had to be sure that he understood it didn't mean acceptance regardless of his own needs and wants and desires.

Raising her head, she caught his gaze and spoke with blunt honesty. "I can't enjoy myself if I'm worried you're not enjoying what I'm doing to you. So if you need something else, or if you've had enough, tell me. Otherwise, I'll feel like a *mudak* when I find out—because a mate will always know in the end."

Ethan wove his hand into her hair, his breathing uneven as he said, "I disagreed with you earlier. I promise to do so in bed, too."

Laughing because his stubbornness and unwillingness to budge on certain things *was* an annoying truth, she happily carried on in her path. Her thighs felt lusciously sensitive, her breasts plump and full, her core liquid honey. Ethan's skin was hot, the taste of him delicious to her.

Her mate already carried her scent on him, but she was determined to stamp it into his skin even harder and deeper. Yes, she was a possessive beast. Good thing he didn't seem to mind. Having reached the ridged lines of his abdomen, she licked and kissed, one hand on his hip and his erection an iron poker against her breasts.

Chapter 23

Lover mine
Kiss me
Murder me
A ruin in our bed
Pleasure in my veins
　　—"Pleasure" by Adina Mercant, poet (b. 1832, d. 1901)

ETHAN PULLED AT her hair, sharp enough that it stung a little, adding spice to the pleasure. "Selenka." It was a pained sound, his beautiful voice fragmenting. "I can't—"

She'd thought to show him heaven with her mouth, but realized now he didn't have the capacity to deal with the overload of sensation. But her hand didn't feel right, not for this, their first intimacy. Rising to straddle him once again, she ran her fingers over his lips, so lush in the bristled roughness of his unshaven face. "Will you let me lead this dance?"

Only after he'd jerked a nod, his hands gripping her hips, did she close her fingers around the base of his erection and begin to slide herself down on him. Quivers quaked through her, control threatening to slip from her grasp. Wrenching it back with gritted teeth because Ethan didn't need to be handling a wild wolf this first time, she focused on her beautiful, dangerous mate.

His head had fallen back, his neck arched and his fingers digging into her hips.

Along the mating bond, the jagged night that was Ethan shuddered with huge waves of light. And inside her, he was a thick heat that pushed at the walls of her core and claimed her even as she claimed him. She sank home with a shudder, her fingers clawed on his chest, and her inner muscles spasming.

Ethan's body jerked up without warning, a sudden wet heat inside her that made her muscles clench again as she watched Ethan's body get impossibly more taut, his shoulders so hard they could've been carved out of stone. Her wolf growled, her body moving rhythmically on his.

A small sound wrenched from his throat, his fingers clenching even tighter on her as the wet pulses inside her intensified. Just when she worried he might break from the strain he was putting on his body, he slumped to the bed, the obsidian eyes that met hers dazed, and his skin filmed with a fine layer of perspiration.

Squeezing him inside her because he was still hard despite the violence of his orgasm, she leaned in to lick at his throat before claiming a kiss, both of them breathless. "There," she said even as her heart beat like a drum, "that's taken the edge off." A small nip of his lower lip. "Shall we play now?"

Ethan raised his hand to her breast, cupping it with care. His hand made her moan, lean into the touch.

He parted his lips. "I feel . . ." A harsh exhale, a rough inhale.

"Me, too," she said, moving on him with sinuous fluidity because she couldn't stop. "You feel so good inside me." Already, she could feel him swelling to renewed readiness inside her. Her lover had a lot of pent-up sexual energy within.

"Show me what to do."

Selenka rose up with her hands braced on his chest. "Move with me."

He was an Arrow and a telekinetic, physical dexterity in his blood. He picked up the rhythm in a matter of seconds, and they rocked slow and deep together. Then she took his hand and showed him just how to touch her to make her break with pleasure as he'd broken—it was only fair.

Her moan a minute later had him repeating the circular motion he'd just tried. His skin dented under the tips of her claws, but when she sliced them back in, he gripped her wrist and said, "Don't hold back." Lifting her hand, he sucked one finger into his mouth, echoing the rhythmic sucking with the circles he was making over her clit.

"Manual?" she gasped.

Releasing her finger, he said, "No, I just wanted to do that." He flicked the nub of her clitoris. "That was in the manual."

Selenka barely heard him, the shock waves of molten heat rolling over her body. She came all over and around him, and when she looked at him in the aftermath, her hands braced on his chest, the look on his face was one of pure satisfaction. She couldn't help it; she leaned down and kissed him.

Arms wrapped around her, he kissed her deep and long and increasingly wild. "Can I do this between your legs?" he asked afterward.

She nipped him sharply on the lower lip. "Are you trying to kill me?"

No curve of his lips, but she could swear she felt a sunburst inside her. "Yes," she said, "you can kiss me anywhere you like." Squeezing his cock with her internal muscles, she sat back up.

The cords of his neck standing out in stark relief, and his hands at her waist, he rose up using nothing but the power of his abs—oh, how she liked that—and locked his mouth over her nipple. He didn't only suck; he tongued her as he might her mouth, taking the kissing lessons and putting them to good use.

"*Bozhe moi.*" She leaned into him, tumbling him to his back with her over him.

Unfazed, Ethan switched to her other breast.

The man was going to leave her limp and melted if he got that mouth anywhere between her legs. Moaning at the thought, Selenka pulled at his hair. He looked up . . . after one final suck. Oh, her mate was *definitely* going to be trouble in bed now that he was finding his feet.

Smile primal, she bit at his lower lip again and moved on him because she couldn't stay still. He sucked in a breath . . . then flipped them, so he was on top, all without disconnecting their intimately linked bodies. Hair falling over his forehead and eyes black ink, he braced himself on his arms above her.

"Is this acceptable?" A rough question.

Selenka scraped her claws over his shoulders. "Yes." She

wasn't the type of alpha who had to be on top always—what was the fun in that? Especially since her mate was a dominant, too.

The thought hitched, caught, felt wrong.

Then Ethan ran his hand down to her hip, squeezed and tried out a stroke, and the thought was torn in two by shocks of erotic pleasure. Raising her arms up above her head, she stretched luxuriantly as she wrapped her legs around his hips. His hands came down over her open palms, his fingers weaving with hers.

His first two strokes were experimental, his third one more confident. By the fourth, she was arching up her body to meet his, their bodies coming together in a soft clash of flesh, the liquid sound of her readiness, and his harsh breathing as he speeded up.

At one point, he tried to slow but she broke their hand-clasp to scratch her claws down his back and said, "Give me everything, Ethan," and he kissed her while never stopping his motions. It was fast and messy and they lost the rhythm at the end and she came so hard she saw stars—as she felt him pulse inside her again and again and again, his shoulders slick under her palms.

Chapter 24

Status on capture of Operative C: eighty percent certainty
the individual will be conclusively identified and within our
grasp in the next four hours.
                    —Abbot Storm, Strike Team Epsilon, to Aden Kai

OPERATIVE CRAY ATTEMPTED to contact Ethan Night multiple times and failed. The Arrow had his shields locked so
tight that nothing was getting in or out. That could simply
mean he was involved in an action that required concentration, or it could be problematic. Cray needed contact with
him to figure out the answer, but he was leaning toward problematic.

Despite what he'd told the Architect, Ethan Night was a
wild card.

Deciding to attempt contact again in another ten hours,
Cray considered his ace in the hole and decided to set up that
option. This contact had to be done via the comm and it was
successful at first attempt, though the screen remained blank.

Cray had connected with the anonymous individual who
called themselves Wolf Killer via a dark web chat room
dedicated to Cray's business as an arms dealer. Their conversations had been about explosives and guns for a long time,
until Wolf Killer indicated a base in Moscow. Taking a risk
based on the other person's user name, Cray had decided to
make a soft approach. And found fertile ground.

"Have you had any success in causing suspicion between
the StoneWater bears and the BlackEdge wolves?" An old
gambit that had failed in other quarters but was worth pursu-

ing here at least once, given the two packs' history of aggression toward one another.

"I had a plan in place, but it was compromised by the precipitous actions of others." The voice was robotic, fed through a cheap anonymizer that nonetheless did the task.

"We did, however, take advantage of an unexpected opportunity to kill one of Selenka Durev's lieutenants," the contact said. "I propose eliminating them all one by one. A weak BlackEdge won't be able to hold its territory and the entire area will destabilize as others attempt to move in, or the bears start flexing their muscle. You'll get what you want—just another way."

Cray could see the logic. "Wolves aren't easy to kill—you've done well." There was only one issue. "You called the alpha by her name. You're making this personal. It is not personal—it is about power."

"You're right—the recent failure got to me. But I'll focus on the success. BlackEdge will soon be broken." A hardness to Wolf Killer's tone that came through even the anonymizer. "Remember our deal—I get power in this area after I crush the wolves. The Consortium supports me; it doesn't interfere."

"The Consortium will have no reason to interfere with a loyal collaborator who does not get in our way." Cray signed off . . . and saw a motion out of the corner of his eye, on the balcony directly outside his apartment.

He hadn't closed the curtains.

And now it was too late. The teleporter who'd appeared there had seen him. Blue eyed and black haired, the male was in the room with Cray before Cray could send out a telepathic alert to warn the Architect that he'd been discovered.

The Arrow shot him point-blank in the chest.

Chapter 25

Capture complete. Target is stunned and in my custody.
    —Abbot Storm, Strike Team Epsilon, to Aden Kai

SELENKA WAS ALMOST asleep on top of her mate when she stirred herself. "We have to sleep clothed today." Just in case a packmate needed her.

And if she knew her people, someone would've already left a box of clothes for Ethan. Taken from their stores, it'd be nothing fancy, probably sweatpants and a tee, maybe a pair of jeans, new underwear.

Yawning, she lifted her head and took in his face. "You're not bleeding. Good."

Fingers weaving into her hair, hesitant, then sure when she laid her head back down instead of pulling away. "Even if I bled, I wouldn't miss this." A whisper of air against her temples. "If I'm to burn out before I get to live in the light, I would know you. I would go out with your wildness and loyalty and courage emblazoned on every neuron in my brain."

Claws slicing out, Selenka held him to her. Held this fascinating and complex man with the beautiful voice and the broken, jagged edges within. Edges that scraped her raw and made her wolf snarl. The animal kept insisting those edges shouldn't be there. But in those edges lived Ethan and so it accepted them without ever budging from its stance that there was something inside him that *shouldn't exist*.

Heart tight and angry, she kissed him long and hard before rising off him to pull on her robe, then checked outside the door.

She found a small box to the left of the doorway. The corridor was otherwise empty, the lighting dimmed for the late hour—or the very early hour, depending on your viewpoint.

Pulling the box inside, she put it on the desk at which she sometimes worked. It wasn't used much—she might not be as openly nosy as Margo, but she had a full measure of the pack gene. She liked being around her packmates, liked their interruptions and their gossip, and the way the pups would drop by simply to see her or show her their secret treasures.

Selenka's inability to open her heart might've made her a bad bet as a lover until Ethan slammed into her, but she was a good alpha and all those interruptions to her day were a welcome comment on that.

"Sweatpants." Pulling out the well-washed gray pair, she threw them at Ethan—who looked good enough to eat lying passion-wrecked in their bed.

Selenka was used to male bodies; changelings weren't prudes about nudity. They all came out of a shift naked, so it was pointless to get strange about it. Bodies were bodies. She was even used to extremely well-defined male bodies, with muscles carved as if into marble.

Her pack was full of dangerous, honed predators. A six-pack—even an eight-pack—wasn't an unusual sight. Neither were ripped biceps or taut thighs. But no one else was put together like Ethan. He was a cool drink of water, all sleek and strong and deadly. Not an ounce of anything else on him, just pure muscle and strength.

Frowning as he rose to pull on the sweatpants, she took her eyes off his body to go to the comm. Her intent had been to input a food order with the kitchen, but she saw she had a message waiting from Nodira and Maviya.

Fourteen and twelve, one with doll-like eyes and silky hair, the other leggy and with curls that wouldn't stay put. Both deeply attached to Selenka, their big sister who lived so far from them—but who would cut her veins to protect their fragile lives. Perhaps they would've had a different relationship had the girls been born while Selenka had still been an angry, abandoned teen, but she'd been eighteen at Nodira's birth, her response to the new arrival a storm of protective love.

After making a mental note to respond to the two tomorrow, she sent the order. She pretty much never used that privilege unless she was doing so for a packmate who needed an alpha's care. But her wolf needed to feed Ethan.

A return message popped up almost at once: *Selya, I already put something aside for you. I'll send it with one of my runners.*

Selenka should've known. Oksana might be only twenty-nine, but she mothered everyone, even her alpha: *Thank you. I know you must be tired.*

I'm baking the most enormous batch of cookies. Added some from the first lot to your tray.

Selenka smiled sadly. They all grieved—and cared for others—in different ways. *Spasibo*, Sana.

Ethan had put on his sweatpants and picked up her used towel by the time she turned around. As she watched, he went to the bathroom, returned without the towel. "You're neat," she drawled, finding intense pleasure in having him here, in her space.

"I just put the towel away."

"I like to drop them on the floor."

It was a running joke in a *Wild Woman* column she read regularly: stories of otherwise competent changelings who drove their lovers crazy because of their towel habits, and the cunning ways said lovers came up with to get revenge.

"Neatness was part of my training." No smile on Ethan's face, no teasing comeback about the makeup she'd left strewn on her vanity table, including her collection of vivid lipsticks.

A knock on the door.

Closer to it than Ethan, she opened it to see the round face of one of the sweetest juveniles in her pack. "Hello, Manya." The sixteen-year-old's blond hair was combed neatly, his shirt and pants equally precise in their tidiness, and his smile guileless.

"Hi." Manuil ducked his head shyly as he held out her tray. "Sana said this is for you."

"Thank you." She passed the tray back to Ethan, who'd come to her side the instant she opened the door. Then she took Manuil's face into her hands and pressed a gentle kiss to his forehead. "You did a great job."

Blushing, the boy looked over her shoulder with open curiosity. "Hi."

"Hello," Ethan responded. "Thank you for the food."

Manuil's eyes widened, his mouth falling open for a second. "Your voice is so pretty." A buzz had him glancing at his beloved sparkly purple wrist unit, which had been a combined gift from his year group on his sixteenth birthday. "I have to go. Sana needs me to do another job." He straightened his shoulders. "Sana says she can't do without me."

"She can't." Selenka released him with another kiss. "Off you go."

Ethan waited until she'd moved the box off her desk, then placed the tray there. "His brain is damaged?"

Selenka didn't like using that word to describe Manuil, who was so much more. But she knew, to Ethan, it wasn't pejorative. He'd used the same word to describe himself. "He was born that way. No one knows why and it didn't become apparent until he was a toddler, but mentally, he's about half his biological age."

"Your pack accepts him."

"Why wouldn't we?" Scowling at him, she suddenly thought about *who* had made that statement. "I've never seen a Psy child like Manya." Statistically, that was impossible. Even with all the medical advances in the world, nature occasionally took an unexpected turn, or a child had an accident or was harmed by someone evil and survived with lifelong injuries. No race was perfect. Except for the Psy.

"Genetic perfection," Ethan said, "was the gold standard under Silence."

Selenka's hand fisted at her side. "Children who were injured later in life or whose lack of 'perfection' became apparent after birth?"

"Since escaping, I've spent a lot of time just listening to the world." Ethan pulled a T-shirt from the box and tugged it over his head. It was white and just a touch too small, hugging his biceps. "I've heard rumors that some families protect their less-than-perfect members in secret enclaves, but aside from those who were forcibly brainwiped and institutionalized under the old regime, the only such person I've ever seen is an Arrow. Alejandro was damaged by an overdose of the drug Jax—Aden somehow managed to protect him while Ming was in charge."

Pale eyes the color of starlight on a winter's night held hers. "Those outside the squad have no Aden. Most don't have families who'll risk their own lives to protect them. They . . . disappear."

Blood cold and eyes hot, Selenka picked up a small object from her vanity and took it to Ethan. "Look."

Ethan examined the miniature plate that held a pile of equally miniature fruit. "A piece of art, constructed with attention to detail." He examined it from multiple angles. "The artist thought of the mix of colors, the design of the plate."

"It's Manya's work. He makes tiny sculptures for people he loves." Taking the precious gift back from Ethan, she returned it to her vanity. "He is a treasured member of the pack."

"I'm glad you accept your broken."

"That's just it, Ethan. Manya's not broken and neither are you." Never would she stop trying to teach him that. "You're you as Manya is Manya. Complete in yourself."

Ethan said nothing and she didn't push. The latter was difficult for her wolf, but she was learning that pushing Ethan got her nothing. He'd make his own decision—but Selenka could give him the information he needed to make it. Turning, she lifted the cover on the tray to reveal the dishes within. Small bowls of creamy pasta, a fruit salad, slices of cake, the promised cookies, and a couple of hot flaky rolls with a filling of spiced meat.

"Let's picnic on the bed."

Taking a seat across from her after bringing over the tray, Ethan examined the items on it with interest. "I've rarely eaten real food."

"My mission in life is to make you fat." Wolf and woman, neither part of her was joking; food was serious business to a wolf. "Just a little bit." So that he wasn't honed to the bone, so that she knew he had so much happiness in his life that he could afford to let go of the rigid control he maintained over himself.

"If you want, I can put on weight by eating twice my normal ration of nutrients."

"No, this is about fun. It's not the goal that matters but the journey." Picking up one of the rolls, she held it to his mouth.

He took a bite, chewed, swallowed. No reaction. But he took another bite and another. Until by the time he finally fell asleep, the two of them had cleared the tray, and he'd told her that he had "categorically" blown his nutritional quota for the day. Despite the loss and grief of the hours past, her wolf smiled as she fell into sleep . . . but she woke with a pounding heart.

How do you know?

Ethan's question reverberated in her head. She'd reacted out of instinct and passion when he'd asked it, but it wasn't only the single among changelings who went rogue. And being rogue was the worst kind of madness for a changeling— a rogue gave in to the animal and forgot their human self. They began to hunt those who'd once been pack, ravaging and tearing.

Rogues even killed their mates.

So, hard as it was to face, changelings weren't infallible in choosing mates.

Heart thumping so hard she could feel it against her rib cage just above where Ethan had his arm, she glanced behind her to see that he remained in a deep sleep. It startled her. She hadn't thought an Arrow would sleep that way . . . but he was her mate. He knew she'd never harm him. Affection had her stroking his forearm, but it didn't serve to soothe her skittering thoughts. She looked at the bedside table, saw her phone was within reach.

She didn't know what she was going to do with it until she found herself pulling up the medical alert on Scarab Syndrome. It began with a basic outline of the Syndrome, then gave a list of symptoms, followed by a closing paragraph:

Not every patient who exhibits these symptoms will have the Syndrome, but we urge you to be overcautious in this matter. The team would rather attend multiple false alerts than miss one real case. The earlier a patient is diagnosed, the higher the likelihood that individual can be given assistance to prolong their mental and psychic stability.

Selenka remembered seeing another mention of the Syndrome, though she couldn't remember where. Putting down her phone, she managed to pull over her organizer without waking Ethan—produced by a Psy manufacturer, the thin high-spec datapad was the best on the market. BlackEdge had been able to purchase fifty from the hotly contested first batch.

Psy usually favored Psy in such cases—Silence hadn't fallen long enough ago to change such habits, but BlackEdge and StoneWater'd had an in this time around. Silver Mercant had spoken to her well-connected family, and the Mercants had fronted the deal with the actual supplier to ensure the packs received fifty each.

That was the official word anyway—Selenka would bet the bears had received a few extra. Her spies told her Silver's icy-eyed grandmother was *the* Mercant, and she apparently liked Valentin.

Bears.

Still, it was a hell of a favor Silver had done BlackEdge, and Selenka wouldn't forget it.

Organizer in hand, she did a search in her private files, but "Scarab" brought up nothing. So she linked to the private server created for top-level Trinity Accord signatories. In no world was everyone equal, and Trinity couldn't continue to function unless it had some leadership. Changelings had no issue with that, hierarchy and dominance integral parts of their life. In this situation, that meant a number of senior alphas who spoke for multiple packs.

Lucas Hunter of the DarkRiver leopards represented the largest number, including the far bigger SnowDancer pack. And, by some strange stroke of cooperation—or madness— Selenka currently represented nearly all the packs in Russia— including the bears.

Valentin had volunteered her when the question had come up. "You're much more diplomatic than I am, Selya," he'd said, deliberately using the familiar term of address to rile her. "I'd just yell at everyone and get us thrown out of the Accord."

"Don't be too sad, Mishka," she'd said sweetly, using the *extra*-baby pet name his older sisters had a habit of using. "You can't help being a bear."

So now she was part of the Trinity leadership. As such,

she had direct access to this server. She'd made sure Valentin had all the passwords, too—he needed to be up to speed should anything happen to her. When she did a search for "Scarab" on the server, the information popped up at once.

Scarab was an experiment run in the early days of Silence. Data retrieved to date suggests it ran from 1999 to 2004, though a dedicated team is continuing to data mine in the hope of recovering more concrete information.

In short, the Silence Protocol worked for a small minority of Psy—it suppressed their violent and/or mentally unstable tendencies. However, that suppression came at a cost: a decrease in psychic power. Scarab posited that it was possible to modify Silence to ameliorate or fully annul that unintended effect.

Every individual enrolled in the project was either a very young child at the dawn of Silence, or was born in Silence—and thus considered part of the first wave of Silent "natives." Each subject was also physically and mentally fit, the best of the best.

At first, Scarab was a brilliant success, with the test subjects remaining Silent, but with full access to their—previously suppressed—abilities. However, that stability didn't last. Many of the subjects struck out violently at those around them, while others began to suffer from hallucinations, fugues, memory loss, screaming nightmares, and more. In the end, the entire set of subjects became a threat to those around them.

A number self-terminated when they realized Scarab could not be rolled back. Once open, their minds could not be returned to their stable pre-Scarab state. The destabilization continued for all—though we reiterate that there are gaps in the data, so it's possible that not all destabilized to the same extent.

We have no data on the long-term prognosis of Scarab subjects as the Psy Council of the time made the decision to terminate all living Scarab subjects in 2004.

The fall of Silence has brought with it a return of this "awakening" of suppressed power. For ease of reference, we have termed it Scarab Syndrome. At the time of the

writing of this briefing paper, only one Scarab subject*
has been definitively identified (to be referred to as Patient
Zero). Patient Zero has been stabilized by an empath
(Empath R) with very specific abilities. The Empathic
Collective is searching for other such Es, but so far, Em-
path R is the only one with this particular skill set.

Patient Zero is also unusual in another way that
means his results cannot be directly correlated to those
of others [information redacted for patient privacy]. At
this stage, with no other available data, our goal is to
identify those with Scarab Syndrome early, so that Empath R can work with them to foster such control as is
possible.

This paper will be updated as further information be-
comes available.

*Update 1: Scarab Syndrome diagnoses to date = 8.
Empath R able to assist only five of the eight. No data
available to explain the reason for the discrepancy.

Update 2: Do not approach or attempt to get through
to likely Scarab Syndrome sufferers. In the grip of the
Syndrome, they are not amenable to logic and may treat
everyone around them, including allies, as a threat.

Chapter 26

It is . . . a slow seduction. A promise of power so vast that it
is a song of sirens.
                    —Patient Zero to Dr. Maia Ndiaye, PsyMed SF Echo

SELENKA PUT DOWN the organizer. It wasn't much, but it
lined up with everything Ethan had said—and with the
broken shards she could feel within him, the uncontrolled
surges that were waves along the mating bond. A massive
energy was pushing and shoving inside Ethan.

"What is it?" Quiet music at her back.

When she turned on her side to look at him, she found
those pale eyes clear of sleep under mussed hair, his stubble
a day away from turning into a beard, and his skin aglow
with health.

He was beautiful.

She passed over the organizer because he deserved to
know. But he handed it back after a quick scan. "I've seen it.
Aden gave me a copy after it became clear I was exhibiting
signs of the Syndrome."

Selenka's respect for Aden Kai rose another notch—even
though Ethan had distanced himself from the squad, his alpha had continued to look out for him. "How did it become
clear?"

"Psychic breaches when I lowered my shields after I first
escaped Ming's control," he said, and if the eyes were the
windows to the soul, Ethan's were wide open to her.

It still took Selenka's breath away, the intensity of his
commitment.

"Those around me in the squad felt a psychic disturbance, and so did I—it made waves even in the cold fogbound place in which I existed then. I also did a test."

"That's when you heard the howls and screams."

"Yes. I described the symptoms to Aden; as he's maintained his medic credentials, we went through an exhaustive psychic testing routine and Scarab Syndrome is the only thing that fits."

He began to list those tests and the results.

Selenka's breath got tighter and tighter in her chest with each word he spoke because he was right: it all fit with what she'd just read about the Syndrome, especially the stretching inside his mind and the seductive sense that he could be a great power with access to so much more if he only let go.

"Selenka." Ethan cupped her cheek in that oddly tender way he had. "I'm sorry. If I could've stopped the mating—" He broke off. "No, that would be a lie. I wouldn't have stopped it even if I'd had warning, even if I saw this future. Being with you, it's the best thing I've ever had, the best *I've* ever been."

Selenka closed her hand over the solid strength of his wrist, hating that her mate's life had been barren and cold and ugly. "We're just getting started." Picking up his hand, she pressed a kiss to his palm.

Ethan shifted until he was braced on one forearm looking down at her, his hair tumbling onto his forehead. He was the one who initiated the kiss. It began slow and stayed slow, an intensely private exploration of touch and intimacy from a man used to training to be the best. She was breathless by the time they parted, and so was he. And he had a tiny pinprick hemorrhage in the white of his eye.

Claws slicing out on a wave of protective rage, Selenka wrapped both arms around him. He came down partially on top of her, a heavy weight of heat and muscle. They stayed that way as the lights of the den rose from dawn into day beyond the door of the bedroom.

The two of them had just risen and readied themselves for the day—with Ethan swapping out his sweatpants for a pair of jeans he found in the box—when Selenka received a message on her phone that made her heart bloom like a child's.

"My grandparents are back. They've been roaming in the most remote parts of our territory."

Ethan examined her face with the trademark intensity she was coming to expect from him. "They know I exist?"

"If I know my dedushka, he already has your entire background." She patted Ethan on the cheek, wondering if beneath that controlled exterior lay nerves; he had no need for them. Her grandfather would see him for what he was: a dangerous predator devoted to Selenka.

"He might've stepped down in my favor," she told Ethan, "but he will forever hold the respect of the entire pack. He's the one I go to for advice, for guidance. He and my babushka took an angry and confused teenager and taught her how to build herself up into a strong woman."

Ethan sealed his uniform jacket over his white T-shirt. "Was your father the cause of your confusion and anger?"

Scowling into the mirror where she was putting on a dusting of color over her eyelids, Selenka said, "My father is an acknowledged scholar. Because despite what the world thinks, predatory changelings don't only respect brawn." Her voice began to turn into a growl despite herself—talking of Kiev Durev did that to her.

Ethan's response was very Ethan. "I looked up Alia. She's a renowned scholar of literature."

Selenka bit out a laugh, then turned to nip him on the chin. He definitely knew how to handle his growly mate. "My father prefers to believe we look down on him because of his tendency and it's made him bitter."

"He resents you."

Again, it struck her, just *how* good Ethan was at picking up emotional cues. Then again, he'd made it clear his entire childhood had been unusual—he'd probably never been Silent in any way. And a child at the mercy of pitiless adults would've learned how to read people in pure self-defense.

Selenka's hand clenched on the eye shadow brush. She'd rather be holding a hunting knife and driving it into Ming's black heart, but she had to bring normality to her pack, and that meant many things—including a hint of makeup.

"Why do you wear colors on your skin?" Ethan watched her with open fascination.

His intrigued look served to bring her back to the here and now. "Why not? I've liked makeup since I was a teen and Margo and I were doing each other's faces in our rooms." She smiled at the memory of their fledgling efforts; thank goodness Alia, older by four years, had taken pity on them. "As for my father—for some reason, he thought he'd be alpha following my grandfather even though that's not how it works in a changeling pack." They weren't a monarchy, with rules of inheritance; they were *wolves*.

"Your dominance eclipsed his."

"Yes. He has a rather large chip on his shoulder because of that." Jaw rigid, she put down the mascara wand. "I just hope he hasn't allowed his bitterness to push him into becoming a traitor." Any involvement in Emanuel's death and it wouldn't be a matter of forgiveness between a father and daughter; it'd be a matter of pack and punishment.

Ethan cupped the back of her neck, squeezed. "Is your grandmother a dominant, too?"

There he went again, reading her emotional state and *handling* her. Selenka growled but didn't pull away. A mate was allowed those privileges, allowed to comfort and calm and handle.

"No, my babushka Lada is a shy submissive who was a source of constant hugs and affection during my childhood." The reminder made her spine soften, her lips curve. "You'll like her, Ethan, though she might take time to trust you near her." Selenka frowned. "I have the weirdest urge to take that back. My wolf thinks my reticent grandmother will be just fine with my deadly Arrow mate."

"We have you in common—that is a bond."

"Hmm." Not sold on that, she shifted on her heel to stroke her hand down the front of his black uniform jacket.

He stood silent and watchful as she fixed a collar that didn't need fixing, and she had the sense he was drinking in the contact . . . and the care. Fury threatened to erupt inside her all over again, but she stifled it on the wolfish promise that he'd never again starve for affection.

Hands on his shoulders, she took a kiss, possessive and hot. He was breathing shallowly by the time she drew back, color brushing his cheekbones and his eyes glittering. "Can we exchange skin privileges?" Hands on her hips, his mouth going to her throat.

Moaning at the unexpected shock of sensation, she dropped her hands to the waistband of his pants. "We'll have to be quick." Her mate's cock was thick and heavy and rigid in her hand when she released him.

Thighs clenching, she left him only long enough to tear off her leather pants, then her panties. Ethan, her telekinetic mate with his fast reflexes and physical dexterity, hitched her up on his hips. "We never finished this in the bathroom," he said in that beautiful voice that went straight to her clit this morning. "I want to."

Selenka pulled up his head from her throat, bit his lower lip. "Inside me. *Now*."

It took him a little maneuvering, but feeling the blunt end of his cock bump up against her soft, wet flesh wasn't exactly a hardship. Then he was pushing in, and she was sinking down and their mouths connected in a lick of tongues and hot breaths. One arm behind her back to protect her from the wall, Ethan pounded into her in a short, fast rhythm that made her clamp around him like a vice, the orgasm an erotic punch.

Falling against her, he came as her body spasmed around his cock.

ETHAN, flushed and content in a way he couldn't ever re-member being—and full of the taste of his mate even after their hurried cleanup—opened the door to step into the corridor . . . and almost tripped over the dog sleeping in front of it.

The canine bounded up on all four feet, tail wagging.

"You look clean," Ethan said, though he knew the creature couldn't understand him. Then because he knew the value of touch now, knew this dog had been as de-prived as him, he crouched to rub its bony head. "Will he have been fed?" he asked Selenka, because if he was to be responsible for this small life, he would not permit it to starve.

"Probably twice, but let me check." Allowing his pet to lean up against her leg, she made a quick call, got confirmation. "All good for now. Pack kitchens stock food suitable for pets, so just go by there when he needs feeding."

The dog padded alongside them as they walked on—through a place where Ethan was the recipient of smiles, and where people often stopped Selenka to exchange a hug or a piece of conversation. Sorrow continued to linger in the air—so rich and dark that he could almost taste it—but he also saw that sorrow had been consciously tempered so it wasn't a black cloud crushing the pack.

Eventually, they stepped out into an area different from the Terrace—while that had been enclosed but for the apertures that provided light, this was a part of the mountain that was exposed to the outside. A kind of curving ledge provided protection from the elements on one side but was open to the sky and the bright yellow sunshine on the other.

That sunshine fell on the tables set out under the morning light—at which sat groups of changelings eating breakfast. Small wolves padded here and there, and two made a beeline for Selenka and Ethan. Somehow knowing the pups wanted to be picked up and would be happy for him to be the one to do so, he went down on his haunches.

"Stay," he said to his excited pet.

Taking the two small pups into his arms, he held them with care as he rose to his full height. One curled up against him, while the other yawned and patted at his uniform jacket with clawed paws.

Selenka tapped those sharp tips with a finger and they retracted at once. "Good girl," she said, tugging gently at the pup's ears before taking her into her arms.

"Is that your dog?" a boy of maybe eight asked from a table.

At Ethan's nod, the boy said, "What's his name?"

Ethan looked down and thought, *The boy is right. Everyone should have a name.* "Loyal," he said without conscious forethought. "His name is Loyal."

The child scrambled over to pet the ecstatic dog. "Hi, Loyal! I'm a wolf. We like dogs. Wanna play?"

Seeing his pet was happy and in good hands, Ethan continued to cradle the warmth of the pup's body against his as Selenka led him to a table at the sunny edge. His view of the people seated there was blocked by the large group clustered around it—but that group disbanded with smiles upon seeing Selenka, revealing the man and woman who sat on the left side.

The man rose with a huge grin, his muscles solid and heavy, and his height on the short side for a male—five feet six if Ethan's estimation was correct. He had a shock of white hair and a white beard, his skin tanned leather, and his eyes a deep brown. And his voice a boom when he opened his arms and said, "Selenushka! Finally you remember your elders!"

Selenka walked into his embrace with a laugh, the pup she held happily enclosed between them. Ethan went to stand back when his gaze was caught by the petite woman who had to be Selenka's grandmother. Hair a rich dark brown sprinkled with fine threads of gold, and face unlined, she gave him a startled smile before getting up on a rush of swirling skirts to come to him.

"You're Selenka's." Soft fingers rising toward his face but not touching until he lowered his head.

Her touch was as delicate as a butterfly's wings . . . only to firm into warmth against his cheek.

"Hello, Babushka," he said.

Her pupils expanded, as did her smile. "You're the strangest dominant I've ever met, but I like you." Urging him farther down, she pressed warm, dry lips to his stubbled jaw. "You are a little scruffy, boy." Chiding words, but the pat on his cheek was kind.

"*Babulya!*" Selenka laughed. "I like his scruff."

Embracing her granddaughter, her grandmother said, "You would, my wild Selenushka."

Meanwhile, Ethan found himself the focus of eyes gone wolf amber. "You must be Ethan."

Shifting the pup to one arm, Ethan held out his hand, while maintaining the eye contact. "Sir."

Yevgeni Durev might not be alpha anymore, but power

prowled in him as it would in Selenka regardless of her age. That primal power shoved at Ethan, wanting him to back down—but Ethan had learned to hold his ground a long time ago, against far more hostile adversaries.

He didn't blink.

Chapter 27

Dear Aunt Rita,
   I mated a wolf. I'm about to meet her parents. All dominants (and, honestly, she's a bit growly so I'm expecting the same from her folks). Any advice?
   ~Besotted Human

Dear Besotted Human,
   If you can handle your growly mate, you can handle her parents. Stand your ground and you'll have a long and felicitous association. (Also, bring cake.)
   ~Aunt Rita
      —From the March 2082 issue of *Wild Woman* magazine:
         "Skin Privileges, Style & Primal Sophistication"

EXPLODING INTO A laugh, former alpha Durev ignored Ethan's outstretched hand to enfold him in a warm embrace. "I should've known my Selya would choose a tough-as-nails son of a bitch!"

"Yevgeni." It was a soft remonstration from Selenka's grandmother, but her eyes were smiling. "I swear he does have some manners." She touched her hand to Ethan's and he could do nothing but stand in place under the wave of maternal warmth. "And who's that asleep in your arms?"

Ethan glanced down. "I have no idea of his name."

The pup let out a snore.

Laughing, Selenka rubbed the little one's sleeping head. "Ethan has a soft spot for pups—I'll have to teach him to ignore their wiles or he'll constantly be carrying the babies."

Ethan had no idea what to say to that, so he said nothing

and took a seat at the breakfast table next to Selenka's grand-mother when the older woman invited him with a pat of the bench. "Shush now, you wolf-bear," she said to her mate when he grumbled about "seat-stealing pups." "I want to talk to our grandchild's mate."

Ethan had the sudden thought that he'd answer any question this woman asked. He'd never been near anyone so soft and warm and kind. Selenka took a seat across from him, beside her grandfather.

Food and drink appeared as if by magic, dropped off by smiling packmates—including a glass of nutrient drink placed directly by Ethan. Selenka's pack had no other Psy, so this must've been purchased specifically for him. And it had been purchased in the short time since he became her mate.

"Wait," he said to the youth who'd brought the drink. "Please thank whoever thought to supply this."

A bright-eyed nod. "Sure. Sana got a whole box, different flavors."

Turning back to the table, Ethan found himself being watched by Lada Durev. Selenka had just turned away with her grandfather to talk to an older woman at the table next to theirs, so he and her grandmother had relative privacy. "You two meet on equal ground," Babushka Lada murmured. "I can see it."

Ethan petted the pup's soft fur, its body hot underneath, when the child grumbled in its sleep. "I am knight to her queen."

A smile that surrounded him in warmth. Was this what it was like to have a mother who cared? Ethan thought that might be a wonderful thing.

"I am so happy she has you for a mate."

Ethan felt a dull pain in the region of his heart. "Yet you don't believe I'm right for her." A visceral knowledge.

"Oh, Ethan." Lada Durev brushed back his hair. "I think you're rather wonderful." A smile that softened the pain, made him listen to what she was trying to say. "I just . . . I'm sad she missed what comes before mating . . . Be tender with her, won't you? Spoil her. Adore her." A soft plea. "She's had so little of that in her life."

Ethan's answer was instinct. "I have no experience at

courting a woman, but I would court her." Before he left this planet, he'd make sure Selenka knew she was a gift beyond price. "Will you teach me how?"

A dazzling smile before Babushka Lada leaned in to kiss his cheek.

"Hey! Hey!" Yevgeni Durev thudded a fisted hand against the table. "What's this? A conspiracy?" He pinned Lada with a wolfish gaze. "I thought you were shy with strange dominants."

"Ethan is different," the petite woman said equably. "Now, stop being a bear and drink your coffee."

Across from Ethan, Selenka raised an eyebrow, her eyes sparkling.

The sleeping pup in his arms chose that moment to yawn awake and pop his head up over the top of the table. Seeing Yevgeni Durev, it yipped in excitement, paws scrabbling on the table. Ethan supported the pup gently with one hand, ensuring it wouldn't slip and fall to the floor.

The older man tapped the small wolf on the nose, but his eyes soon returned to Ethan. "You know what, pup? I like you, even if you are getting too cozy with my mate. Our Selenushka's found exactly the man she needs."

Ethan wanted to embrace those words, focus only on the happiness, but he knew the truth: even in the best-case scenario, he would one day abandon Selenka.

Scarab Syndrome had no cure.

The stark truth was still echoing in his head ten minutes later when he received a telepathic missive from Abbot: *We took Operative C into custody in the early hours. Cris is about to question him. Do you want to be there? I can do a pickup.*

Ethan looked down at the pup who was batting at Ethan's loosely fisted hand as if it were a ball, his mate's husky laughter flowing over him, while Yevgeni Durev's white hair glowed under the sun, and said, *No. I'd appreciate a briefing afterward, however.* This hour, he'd sit in the sun, in the laughter.

Because soon, he'd be meeting Memory Aven-Rose . . . and he'd find out if he had a future, even a broken one, or if these were his final days on the planet before Scarab ate away his mind, his personality, his heart.

Selenka looked across the table, her gaze acute . . . and her attention on his eyes. He knew from the tightening of her jawline that she'd spotted another pinprick hemorrhage. The clock, it was starting to speed up.

Chapter 28

Scarab invited a monster inside me, and now it devours me.
—From the diary of Subject JX, Operation Scarab (2003)

EZRA CAME TO consciousness disoriented, his elbow throbbing. Looking around, he tried to make sense of his location. He'd gone to sleep in his bed, but he was now in a narrow alleyway strewn with rubbish. A biodegradable food wrapper sat crumpled against his ankle, while his cheek pressed against a gritty and cold surface.

He was on the ground.

He went to push himself up into a sitting position, cried out when his left elbow screamed. His eyes filled with reflexive tears. Gritting his teeth against the pain, he tried again, this time using just his right arm. Only once he was sitting, his back to a wall, did he glance down at his injured arm. At first, he couldn't understand why he could see it—then realized he was wearing nothing on the top half of his body.

His elbow was grossly swollen and multiple scrapes and abrasions marked that side of his body. His hip hurt, too, his mouth was dry, and his head pounded as if he'd expended a massive amount of psychic power. Had he been in an altercation? Where *was* he? He had no phone on him, no timepiece, nothing with which to check his location.

The food wrapper made a whispery sound as he moved his leg and his eye fell on the black writing on the pale cream background. Picking it up, he smoothed it out. The language wasn't one he could read, but he recognized it as hangul, the neat script used for the Korean language.

That didn't mean anything. His city boasted many international shops and outlets.

After struggling to his feet, he began to look for other pieces of trash on which there might be a date or location. In the end, he found a discarded bottle that hadn't quite made it into the recycle bin a foot away, the torn printout of what may have been a shipping label, and a lost business card.

Two in hangul, one in the alphabet more familiar to him.

Having reached the end of the alleyway in his search, he looked beyond it into a busy square lit by billboards brilliant against the night . . . and he saw the sign with the name of the square. It was on a billboard advertising a timepiece manufacturer; the same advertisement also showed the time and date.

He was in Seoul, Korea.

In an alley he'd seen on a documentary about this square just before he went to sleep approximately three hours earlier.

In his bed in Dunedin, New Zealand.

Ezra swallowed. He looked behind him to check, and yes, there it was, the "hidden" and highly distinctive artwork that the host of the show had urged his viewers to find and visit. The perfect image for a teleport lock. Which meant that unless a rogue teleporter had attacked him and brought him here for reasons unknown . . . he'd teleported here.

Trembling, he slumped against the alley wall. He was a Gradient 5 telekinetic with highly limited teleport capabilities. He could barely teleport to the other side of the university, much less to a city half a world away.

What was happening to him?

Lights in his face, a shouted question in a language he couldn't comprehend. Heart punching into his rib cage, he backed away from the Enforcement officer.

But the man kept coming at him, and Ezra just wanted him to *stop*.

The officer's body flew back to smash into a billboard, creating cracks through its surface that broke the display model's face in half.

Ezra stared at his hands, frozen with fear. He just wanted to go home.

Chapter 29

Operative C (Cray Jitan) unable to provide any particulars
that could lead to the capture of the Architect, but he does
have knowledge of several sources of funding for the
Consortium. We can use that to critically wound the group.

He has also confessed to having a second contact in
Moscow; that contact killed a BlackEdge lieutenant and is
aiming to eliminate the others. We are working through all
of Cray's files in an attempt to identify the threat so the
wolves can neutralize it. Please advise Alpha Durev.

—Note from Cristabel Rodriguez to Ethan Night

ETHAN STOPPED A grim-faced Selenka from walking into
the pack's city HQ after they exited their vehicle. His meeting
with Memory Aven-Rose had initially been meant to take place
in a conference room at the symposium hall, but Selenka had
suggested they move it to the city HQ in order to ensure his
privacy.

Now he said, "I have something for you."

As she waited, head at a wolfish tilt, he reached inside his
pocket to retrieve a folded piece of paper. She watched curiously as he began to pull out the points so the paper object
was no longer flat.

"Oh!" Eyes golden, and cold anger forgotten for a heartbeat, she took the piece from his hand. "It's a howling wolf!"
She turned it this way and that. "How did you make this?"

A warmth inside him that felt like a small sun. "I can
teach you." It was an early trainer who'd taught him the dexterity exercise, and he'd continued it into adulthood. The precision folds and process fostered an intense calm inside him.

Holding the wolf carefully on the palm of her hand, Selenka

leaned in to press her lips to his jaw. "I love it. *Spasibo, zaichik.*"

Ethan absorbed the words, carefully storing them in the memory box in his mind as Selenka led him into the HQ. It included a large private courtyard around back that his mate had commandeered for this meeting. "You'll want the sky above you," she'd said, acute understanding in her tone.

Because Ethan's mind already felt like a cage.

When Selenka took him back for a quick look, the courtyard proved to be planted with flowers and trees, with benches hidden among the foliage. Reconnaissance complete, the two of them started to walk back to wait out front, halting only so Selenka could place the paper wolf on a shelf.

"Where he'll be safe." A glance at Ethan. "Do you have a reason for the gift?"

"I'm trying to court you."

No laughter, her smile a touch bemused. "We're already mated."

"I can court you if I want." The idea of courting her always was one that pleased him. "You can't stop me."

A spear of light through the primal rage incited by Cris's intel, a kiss on his jaw. "I think, Ethan, you're learning to play."

It made him wonder what else he could learn if he just had more time. Inside his mind, the power pulsed and surged again, so hard that Selenka hissed out a breath.

Memory Aven-Rose arrived on the heels of that pulse—in a vehicle driven by a male Ethan knew to be a wolf, though his eyes were human gray right now, his hair gilt even under the cloudy light.

Alexei Vasiliev Harte, lieutenant, SnowDancer wolves.

Permission to enter BlackEdge wolf territory granted because of his association with Memory.

"Does he have visiting privileges in your private pack lands?" he'd asked Selenka on the drive here, after she gave him that information.

"Most outside wolves wouldn't," she'd said, "but Lexie's a special case. His father came from a small Russian pack that BlackEdge absorbed twenty years ago when their alpha passed and they had no new alpha. Packs without an alpha inevitably crumble and they wanted to stay together, so they asked to join us."

"Then Alexei Harte has family in BlackEdge?"

"Some. Though he hasn't visited in a long time." A stillness to her. "This isn't a secret but it's private, you understand?" At his nod, she'd said, "His paternal line has spawned three rogues. He also lost his parents in childhood. It's all served to distance him from Russia."

A shadowed past, but the man who exited the four-wheeldrive vehicle had no sense of darkness to him. He went around to open his mate's door, then said something to her that made her scowl and push at his chest even as she pressed her lips together in a vain effort to fight a smile.

Ethan had seen Memory Aven-Rose from a distance in the symposium hall, but he was still struck by the sense of energy that clung to her. It was probably the wild curls of her hair, glossy and separated but in no type of order beyond that. The coils bounced against the warm brown of her face as the diminutive empath came to face him, her gaze wary.

She didn't make physical contact.

Her mate, in contrast, held out a hand toward Selenka. "Hawke sends his regards."

"I'm pretty sure that wolf didn't say anything so polite." Despite her suspicious words, Selenka shook Alexei's hand. "Tell him *zdravstvuyte* from me, too."

Alexei's expression held a primal watchfulness when he turned to Ethan, and Ethan knew the wolf lieutenant would tear out his throat should he do or say anything that made him appear a threat to Memory. He also knew Selenka would tear Alexei to pieces if he dared lay a hand on Ethan.

The knowledge of his worth to her shook him, would always shake him.

Ignoring the wolf's intense regard, Ethan directed his words to Memory Aven-Rose. "Thank you for agreeing to this." He couldn't keep from staring at her—she felt so oddly *familiar*. "I'm well aware you do critical work in the PsyNet."

The empath's forehead wrinkled, lines flaring out at the corners of her eyes as she stared back at him. Her nod was delayed, the wrinkles in her forehead deeper. "Do I know you? Have we met?"

"No," Ethan said. "Though I did glimpse you at the symposium from a long distance."

"Maybe that's it." She didn't sound convinced.

"I thought we'd do this in the back courtyard," Selenka said to Memory. "Unless you'd be more comfortable inside?"

"No." The empath broke the strange eye contact. "Outside is better."

None of them spoke as they walked to the courtyard, a subtle tension in the air.

He could sense that Memory was concerned about connecting with him on any level, and he didn't blame her. But he couldn't tell her it was all right, they didn't have to try. He needed to try, needed to fight to live so he could court Selenka with paper animals, so he could be the mate she deserved.

"How does this work?" he asked once they were in the cool light of the courtyard, shrugging aside his inexplicable reaction to the empath to focus on the critical. "Do we make a psychic link?"

"No. I just need physical contact." Taking a deep breath, she squared her shoulders and held out her hand.

He took it . . . and a violent surge of power slammed against his shields, hitting so hard that he had to grit his teeth to contain it, every muscle in his body taut to the breaking point. Memory's grip tightened, her frown getting deeper and deeper, until she dropped his hand with a shake of her head that sent her curls flying. "This isn't going to work."

"You have to try." Selenka's voice hummed with tension—but she kept her distance from Memory. "He's dying trying to keep this contained."

Ethan shook his head. "The surges are intensifying." That much violent energy might crush an empath. "If it's unsafe for Memory—"

"No," the empath interrupted, her features screwed into a look of utter frustration. Then, to his surprise, she gripped his hand once more, the polished ovals of her nails a vibrant magenta.

His power crashed against his shields, metal shavings drawn to a powerful magnet.

Memory's pupils expanded to nearly eclipse her irises. "There it is again," she whispered.

Ethan could feel energy pushing against him, a soft kind of power that didn't threaten but asked for permission. "Is that you?"

Memory twisted her mouth to one side. "I was trying to send you an emotion—happiness—to see what would happen, but I can't get through. Your shields must be phenomenal. Almost nothing blocks empathic power—and even though I'm a weird sort of empath, you should still feel *something*. Even Alexei senses it when I try to pet him with my empathy." She released his hand in a scowl. "I don't understand this."

Scanning his fractured internal landscape, Ethan saw no change. "You can't impact the Syndrome?" It was difficult to get the words out.

"Ethan, I don't think you *have* the Syndrome." Memory took his hand again, almost as if she couldn't help herself. "There's something wrong inside you . . . but you don't feel anything like the other confirmed cases of the Syndrome."

"Is it possible my case is a variation?"

"No." Memory's answer was absolute. "The psychic presence of Syndrome patients is disturbing to me on a fundamental level. As if there are fractures deep within them that I can paper over but can't fully heal. But with you . . ." Closing her eyes, she squeezed his hands, and once again, he felt that nonthreatening push of power against his senses.

More than willing to cooperate with this empath who worked with the broken, and who felt like a person he should know, he lowered his external shield just enough that she could get through. A wave of warmth whispering through him, a sensation he recognized as happiness because he'd felt it so often since being with Selenka.

"I feel it." He slammed up his shields an instant later, as the rogue power in him launched a sudden violent assault. His mind vibrated at the impact, the shock so powerful that it traveled through the mating bond and had Selenka growling.

Dropping Memory's hand as a bead of sweat trickled down his temple, he took a step back from her. "Something about you is exacerbating the Syndrome."

"No, Ethan. You don't *have* the Syndrome," Memory insisted, thrusting both hands through the electric curls of her hair. "I don't know what's happening with you, but you *do not* have that kind of fracture inside you."

Ethan shook his head. "I'm damaged."

Memory just stared at him before throwing back her head and laughing until tears ran down her face. "Ethan, honey," she said after sucking in a breath, "if you're damaged, I don't know what you'd call me. I was kept captive by a psychopath in an underground cell, my mind caged, for fifteen years."

Ethan's head rang, the words making no sense. "That's not in your squad file."

"That's because it's none of anyone's business," growled Alexei Harte. "Aden knows that. Who Memory chooses to tell is up to her." Eyes gone pale amber shot with gold locked on Ethan in open suspicion, the wolf clearly evaluating why its mate had judged Ethan worthy of the disclosure.

"Careful, Alexei." Selenka's husky voice. "You're a guest on my land and Ethan is my mate."

Even as Ethan struggled under a fury of pleasure at her open possessiveness, Memory waved a hand. "Shh," she said, clearly speaking to both wolves. "We're having a conversation here."

Scowling, Selenka folded her arms and glared at Alexei. "Great. You had to mate an empath. I can't even snarl at her without feeling guilty."

Alexei grinned without warning. "Shh. They're having a conversation."

Ethan barely heard the exchange, his attention locked on Memory. "How are you so sane?"

"Partially out of pure spite," she said cheerfully. "I wasn't about to let that bastard win by breaking me."

Ethan had never once considered spite a weapon. "I agree with your logic," he said slowly.

Memory pointed a finger at him. "Nurse that spite against those who harmed you, but instead of letting it poison you, use it to live your best life." She put her hands on her hips. "It also helped that I'm an empath. Theory is I was getting emotional feedback from the PsyNet even when I was blocked off from accessing it. The PsyNet likes Es. It protects us."

"Because you're critical to its survival." Ethan's head was

pounding from the constant power surges. "I'm not like you. I don't have a power that helps the Net. I kill."

Memory raised a hand as if to touch him, froze when he took a step back. "I thought I was a monster, too, but turns out we're all far more than one thing." Her dark eyes held haunting flickers of color, her voice drenched in passionate emotion. "Don't just accept the worst-case scenario, Ethan. What if you're wrong and I'm right? What if this *isn't* the Syndrome? What if you could have a life free of the specter of madness?"

Ethan felt Selenka's wolf rise to the surface of his own skin, its fur sliding against his insides. It should've been impossible, but the sensation—visceral and intense—couldn't be denied. The wolf was firmly on Memory's side. "The last time I lowered my shields, the howls and screams nearly caused my telekinetic energy to slip the leash and cut people in half."

At her confused look, he glanced at Selenka. Strained with holding back the surges, he didn't have the words to explain the darkness that lived in him. He needed his mate. She responded without hesitation, this alpha wolf for whom he was now a priority. Their mating might've been out of her control, but she chose to stay with him, *be* with him. With Ethan.

Interlocking her fingers with his, she laid out what he could do, then said, "Ethan's afraid he'll inadvertently kill under the pressure caused by the rogue power he's trying to hold back."

Memory frowned. "It can't be the same shield holding back both or you wouldn't be able to access your telekinetic abilities."

"No. But they're constructed on the same foundation. I had to build on what I had when the Scarab power woke."

Making a frustrated semigrowl sound that had Selenka giving the empath a second look, Memory didn't tell him again that he didn't have Scarab Syndrome. "There's one way to test this," she said instead. "You build two *totally* separate shields, with the one to contain your telekinetic power on an isolated base unconnected to the rogue power."

Ethan understood her logic, but—"I don't have the time."

That kind of highly individualized shield building took intense amounts of time to design and create.

As if to hammer home the point, the scent of iron filled his nose. He pulled a tissue from his pocket to stop the bleed, but both wolves in the courtyard were already growling. Gripping his jaw in one hand, Selenka turned his face to hers.

"Your eyes," she bit out. "You have multiple hemorrhages in the whites."

"It's from the pressure building in his brain." Memory's voice was taut, her hands fisted. "It goes on much longer, his brain will literally crush itself against his skull."

Chapter 30

I will pass on any and all information as retrieved or discovered. Please do the same. One of ours is now also yours. The squad wishes to assist you to eliminate this threat.

—Senior Arrow Cristabel Rodriguez in response to Alpha Selenka Durev

"ETHAN," MEMORY CONTINUED, "if you're willing to try, I know someone who can design those shields for you at speed. After it's done, you release the rogue power—and we see what comes out."

"I can't be a murderer again," Ethan whispered, speaking to his mate, her eyes the pure gold of her wolf. "I *won't* be a murderer again." He would not go to his grave with fresh blood on his hands.

Shifting her grip to his nape, Selenka dug her nails in. "We'll control the test," she said on a growl. "The den has plenty of rooms that can be made dark, without light. We can shut you inside one for the test."

Ethan knew without asking that it infuriated her to think of locking him in a room without light, but if that was what it would take for him to agree to Memory's test, she'd find a way to deal with it.

Pressing his forehead to hers, he said, "All right," to Memory. "But the shield builder will have to be very fast." Contact with Memory had supercharged the rogue power; the surges were coming once a minute now, each new surge causing another crack in his shields.

He was maintaining, but *just*.

Memory moved to speak to her mate, their heads nearly

touching. After a short conversation, Alexei Harte brushed his hand over her curls before turning to Selenka. "I need to make a call. If I get agreement, you'll have to permit one or two other predatory changelings into your territory."

"Do it."

Alone with Selenka when the other couple moved to the far end of the courtyard to make the call, Ethan slid his hand to her nape, under her hair. She tilted back her head to hold his gaze with her furious one, her hair catching the smudged sunlight. Pink and purple fire and obsidian silk, it slid over his hand.

"What if Memory is wrong and I lose myself when I allow the rogue power free?" It was the nightmare that haunted him. "What if I forget who I am and turn into the pitiless killer Ming trained me to be?"

"Then I'll execute you." His mate's hand went clawed against his chest, her words harsh, rough. "I will not allow you to become a murderer. It's a promise from your mate."

Ethan knew deep within that keeping the promise would break her in ways that would never heal. "No." He tightened his grip. "Not you. It can't be you."

When she stared at him without the least indication of changing her mind, he played dirty. "I won't allow the test unless you agree to delegate the task to the squad."

A hiss of air from between her teeth, her claws pressing in deeper. "This is *not* a negotiation." It was a growl.

"And you're not my alpha." He held those wolf eyes. "Agree or I call this off right now."

Cheekbones cutting against her skin, she said, "I won't forget this."

He waited.

"Fine." A word ground out between her teeth. "Stubborn *zaichik*."

Shuddering, he pressed his forehead to hers again. "Your *zaichik*."

That clawed hand fisted in his hair. "Yes. Don't you forget it." A sharp nip of his lower lip before she turned toward Alexei and Memory, who were walking back.

"Sascha's agreed to do it." Alexei slid away his phone, his next words directed at Ethan. "She needs a teleport to this

location, since she isn't in the PsyNet and can't access your
mind that way."

He could only be speaking about one Sascha. Sascha Duncan, cardinal empath, daughter of Councilor Nikita Duncan
and defector into the DarkRiver leopard pack. And, apparently, a shield builder. "I'll ask if a teleporter is free."

Aden's voice entered his mind at the same instant: *We
need you. Kaleb can lock onto your face if you're willing.*

Ethan's head throbbed with another surge, but he'd only
ever heard that kind of urgency in Aden's voice in severe
emergencies . . . though it had never before truly *registered.*
In the gray numbness in which he had lived, he'd cared about
nothing.

At times, he'd believed he was a stone-cold psychopath.

Today, he heard both the urgency and the exhaustion,
wanted only to help this man who'd fought for him when
Ethan couldn't fight for himself.

Five seconds. Grabbing Selenka's hand, he ran out of the
courtyard and through the HQ to arrive at the public front
entrance.

He had just enough time to say, "Critical emergency. Teleport pickup," before Kaleb Krychek appeared in front of him.
The cardinal telekinetic's eyes were pure black, as if to match
his black-on-black suit. His hair was unusually windblown,
his suit jacket unbuttoned.

When Ethan looked at Selenka, he saw the face of an alpha
who understood hard choices. "Go," she said and released his
hand. "I'll organize the rest."

Krychek teleported them.

And Ethan landed in a zone of madness. Screams rent the
air, people walking around in circles with their hands at their
temples as they keened. He had no idea of their number, but
it was large enough that the available assistance wasn't
enough. The keening walkers, however, were the calm ones.
Others rolled on the ground trying to gouge out their eyes, or
beat their foreheads bloody on the asphalt.

"I thought we had a solution to this," he said, having seen
images of such nightmarish scenes before the advent of the
empathic Honeycomb.

He didn't wait for Krychek to respond, just telepathed: *Close your eyes!* on a wide band.

The Arrows obeyed at once, as did Krychek, and Ethan released his light. He had to do it three more times, in quick succession, Krychek 'porting him to different areas of the street before he got all the affected—but it still only took seconds.

"Useful," Krychek murmured, staring at the bodies crumpled on the street. "We could've used you during the earlier incidents."

"I wasn't functional during those incidents." He'd been all but catatonic at the time, seeing the world through such a heavy gray veil that it had been a distant murmur. "Where is your empathic assistance?"

"Exhausted." A single flat word. "The Honeycomb is taking more and more of their energy to maintain we don't want to wipe them out when we need them so badly."

The deadly cardinal crouched down beside one of the fallen. "This isn't the same as the previous outbreaks—many of those individuals attacked others, but here, *all* the violence was self-directed. Not only that; they confined the violence to their heads, almost as if they were trying to tear an intruder from their brains."

Ethan focused on the individual injuries, saw Krychek was correct. People hadn't only gouged at their own eyes; they'd pulled out chunks of their hair and, in one gruesome case, shoved a sharp implement through one ear. "Have you checked the PsyNet?"

"Nothing, no indication of infection."

A kind of itch at the back of his brain, Ethan looked around until he saw a familiar face. *Abbot,* he telepathed, *which area of the PsyNet correlates to this location?* He didn't recognize the buildings, and the people around him were a mix of ethnicities, nothing in their features or clothing to nudge him toward a particular zone.

We're in Hamburg, the other man responded, his blue eyes vivid even from this distance. *Sector 17. I'll 'path you a map—but there's nothing to see there.*

Despite that confirmation of Krychek's cold statement,

Ethan waited only until he had the map to enter the area of the PsyNet that corresponded to this location. What he saw had him scrambling: *Aden, Krychek, the PsyNet here is crawling with parasites.* How had the two missed this?

Two brilliant minds appeared beside his.

"I see nothing," Aden said. "What do you see?"

"I'll send you an image." Ethan telepathed what he saw to both men, realizing too late that maybe there *was* nothing to see, and he was imagining the tiny glowing creatures with multiple feet that crawled all over the minds in this area. The power surges hadn't stopped. It was possible the Scarab power was free and he was hallucinating.

His stomach clenched as he waited for the two others to tell him his telepathed image was blank of anything relevant. But Krychek's midnight voice said, "That is disturbing. Can you safely capture one of the parasites?"

Exhaling, Ethan quickly wove together a tiny psychic vault. Such vaults were usually used for private conversations, but there was no reason it couldn't be used to contain one of the creatures. Though what they were, he couldn't comprehend—the PsyNet was a place of minds and data, nothing else.

He placed the small trap near an infested mind, and one of the creatures all but tumbled into it. Locking it, he left the vault in place.

"I wonder if an empath will be able to see what you do," Krychek mused. "I'll ask one nearby."

The E responded quickly, confusion in her mental voice when she said, "I see minds in the PsyNet. Am I missing something?"

Ethan waited until the E had left to say, "Ask Memory Aven-Rose." She wasn't like other Es and her mind had connected with his in a way he didn't understand; the impact of that contact continued to fracture his shields.

Either Krychek or Aden must've had a direct telepathic contact for her, because she appeared in the PsyNet moments later. "What are THOSE?" Her shudder was in her words, a fact Ethan wouldn't have believed if he hadn't heard it. As it was, he was simply glad someone else could see the creatures. For all he knew, it was possible to take a telepathic snapshot of a hallucination.

"You see them?" he asked, to be certain.

"The creepy crawlies munching on people's minds? How can anyone miss them?"

"We'll discuss that later," Kaleb said. "For now, are you able to clean the Net of them?"

A long pause before Memory shuddered again—or that was what it felt like to Ethan when she spoke. "As long as I don't have to touch them. Let me get my brush."

He didn't understand the reference, but he saw the PsyNet ripple with a midnight rainbow not long afterward, and when the rainbow passed some time later, the area was clean of the parasites.

"What about the one we trapped?" Ethan pointed out the miniature psychic vault. "It's still alive." He could feel it, a tiny itch at the back of his head.

"Yes, it is." Memory sounded tired. "You want me to—"

"No," Krychek said. "We'll keep it as a test to confirm who can see such parasites and who can't."

"Make sure you contain it," was Memory's order before she dropped from the Net.

Kaleb's obsidian power encased the vault.

Inside Ethan, the mating bond pulsed with a wolf's growl, his mate sensing his disquiet. Pride at being hers spread through his veins, and he went to drop out of the PsyNet so he could return home . . . but then all hell broke loose. Krychek's mind disappeared, only for his voice to blast into Ethan's skull a second later: *We have a second site. PsyNet coordinates as follows. Check for parasites.*

Ethan raced to the location beside Aden, their minds riding the slipstreams of the PsyNet in a way he couldn't explain except to say it was like riding the wind. He came to a screeching halt a short time later, slamming a blade of light across Aden's path to stop him, too. Their minds weren't anchored in this area and thus probably safe from the contagion, but there was no point in taking an unnecessary risk.

Aden stayed back. "Parasites present?"

"A massive number." Crawling on minds like ants on an

anthill . . . and all at once, he saw the shape of them, understood the truth. "They're shaped like scarab beetles."

Aden was silent, likely receiving data from multiple sources.

"What's the situation on the ground?" Ethan asked the leader of the squad.

"Three self-inflicted fatalities before Kaleb was able to get there, and the chaos is increasing despite our efforts."

"I'll—"

"No, Ethan," Aden said. "I can tell your power is fading and I need you to attempt something else before you stop to recover. Memory's already close to flameout and we can't have her totally out of commission—so as you're the only other person who can currently spot the parasites, I want you to see if you can affect them."

Ethan had nothing against making the attempt, but they had a practical problem. "My ability only works with light."

"There is light here."

Looking at the night sky of the PsyNet, Ethan saw it anew. The soft golden glow of the Honeycomb. The burn of all those living minds. Even the flickering pulse of the parasites. Accessing the part of his mind that created the light that stunned without doing harm, he imagined sweeping it across the psychic plane.

Only at the last minute did he think to warn Aden to close his psychic eye.

Light blazed against the black of the PsyNet and he had a moment to think, *I can create beauty,* before the flash faded into nothingness.

The parasites had stopped moving—stunned, as his targets would be in the physical plane. So stunned that they fell off their unwitting hosts, stopped burrowing through shields, and just lay in the fabric of the PsyNet.

Ethan, his own power close to redlining, used a fine blade of light calibrated to kill to sweep across a section of the creatures. The bugs died, not disappearing as they had with Memory, but burning up to nothingness. Tiny flashes along his light blade, the Net clean in the aftermath.

Mind aching though the surges had finally stopped, he used the last vestiges of his power to eliminate the rest of the creatures. It took pinprick strikes for the final few, but he made sure to sanitize the entire area. "I need to get back to Selenka." His body was close to shutting down.

Krychek was waiting for him when he dropped out of the PsyNet and, after one look at his face, teleported him directly to Selenka. She was in the middle of a huge stand of trees, had a clawed hand slicing toward Kaleb before she spotted Ethan. The telekinetic 'ported out even as she halted her strike.

And Ethan's vision faded.

"Ethan!" His mate's voice was the last thing he heard before his body hit the leaf fall on the forest floor.

Chapter 31

Ethan's flamed out. Initiate safeguards.
> —Aden Kai to the Arrow Squad

SELENKA'S WOLF WAS still snarling from Krychek's sudden appearance when Ethan went down and she didn't fucking care about anything else. She'd been a fraction too far to catch him and now he lay unmoving on the carpet of leaves, the early evening sunlight casting dappled shadows on him through the canopy.

She'd hooked into the news networks after Ethan teleported out with Kaleb and figured out where he must've gone. It had been obvious he wouldn't return quickly. So she'd spoken with Memory about getting in touch again the instant Ethan was back, then returned to den territory—quite aside from the hit apparently out on all her lieutenants, Emanuel's death was an open wound, and her pack needed her close.

And her mate was an Arrow. She'd known he'd find her. She just hadn't expected him to hitch a ride with the most dangerous telekinetic in the world. She and Valentin were both well aware the cardinal could lock onto faces as well as places, but Krychek was a smart political operator and had never before used that ability to violate their territories.

In this case, however, Selenka would forgive any trespass.

Crashing to her knees beside where Ethan had fallen onto his side, she caught the scent of wet iron, but it wasn't his nose that was bleeding. A crimson tear had beaded at the corner of one eye, while the bead from the eye closest to the forest floor was already trailing down his face.

Wolf shoving at her skin, she checked his pulse, found it thready but steady. Her mate had suffered a psychic wound, one with which she couldn't help. But . . . Ethan could've asked to be taken anywhere. Kaleb had brought him here because Ethan had wanted to come home. To his mate.

Overwhelmed by a piercing tenderness, she bent down to press a kiss to his temple, then used the end of her T-shirt to wipe the blood from his face. It did something to her to know he trusted her to see him at his most vulnerable. She realized then that she'd make the same choice in the same circumstances—Ethan would watch over her and never see weakness in her vulnerability. As she saw the deadly Arrow even now.

"I'm here, Ethan." Throat thick, she checked his pulse again, then sat down next to him so some part of her body was always touching his as she took out her phone and made a call—she needed foundational information before she contacted the squad.

"Selenka, what can I do for you?" Silver said in that crisp, clear voice of hers.

"I think Ethan's fried his brain helping with the recent outbreaks. What do I need to do to help him heal?"

"Is your mate unconscious?"

Selenka didn't bother prevaricating; Silver was the mate of an ally and an ally in her own right—she wouldn't give Selenka bad information. "Yes. Bloody tears in both his eyes."

"That may not be as bad as it appears." Silver's cool practicality was calming. "It sounds to me like he's flamed out—that's when we push our minds so far that we flatline on the psychic plane. He may have burst blood vessels in his eyes depending on the pressure involved."

Selenka had a feeling the tears had to do with another type of pressure altogether. "Is he vulnerable on the PsyNet?"

"Flameout does leave us vulnerable to psychic intrusion, but as he's an Arrow, I'm certain he must be safe. Give me a moment." She was gone for several seconds. "I've spoken to my Arrow contact for EmNet. He was not cooperative in the least until I stated I was asking on your behalf. You'll be receiving a direct call soon."

Selenka's phone indicated a second incoming call—from the official call code the squad used for Trinity. "I've got it. *Spasibo*, Silver." Hanging up, she took the call.

"My name is Axl," the male voice stated. "I and our squadmates have surrounded Ethan's mind on the PsyNet. No one will get through our shields."

Selenka's tight chest didn't ease up. She hated being unable to protect him herself. But Axl wasn't done. "There is an unusual shield immediately around Ethan's mind that doesn't appear to be Psy and is sending very aggressive 'come closer and you'll die' signals."

A smile curved Selenka's lips. Her wolf was standing guard over her mate. "Is there anything I can do to make this easier for him?"

"Keep his body safe and ensure you give him plenty of nutrient fluids and bars when he wakes. He'll be extremely enervated. It may take up to forty-eight hours for him to recover his psychic strength. He should, however, wake well before that."

Selenka had wiped away the bloody tears but she kept on scenting her mate's blood, kept on seeing his hurt. *"Spasibo."*

"I am happy to be able to assist." Perhaps it was her imagination, but Axl's voice seemed a touch rougher. "Contact me if you need any further data, or should you need a Psy medic. I'll message you my direct call code after we hang up."

Nodding though the Arrow couldn't see her, Selenka ended the conversation, then wiped away the new tear of blood that marred Ethan's face. "How, lover mine, am I going to get you into the den?" He wouldn't want people seeing him this way, but she wanted him safe and warm inside the stone walls of their home.

Axl would no doubt provide teleport assistance should she ask, but that would involve giving an Arrow teleporter visual coordinates inside her den. Not happening. She knew Ethan would agree with her call. Which left her with one option.

She took out her phone again.

Oleg appeared almost forty-five minutes later. She'd spent that entire time watching Ethan breathe, the jagged cold of his presence a relief inside her.

"What's happened?" Quickly putting down all the supplies he'd brought for her, the healer hurried over.

"A psychic flatline." Regardless, she moved aside so Oleg could run his hands over Ethan to check for any physical injuries.

"I smell blood, Selya."

When she told him about the bleed, he lifted Ethan's eyelids to check. "This is not helpful. His eyes have gone black." Sighing, the healer bent closer. "But I don't scent any fresh blood, so he's not continuing to bleed." A glance at her. "He should be in the infirmary."

"*Oleg.*"

The older wolf smiled. "Yes, yes. Your mate shouldn't be seen this way."

"It's not because he's my mate. It's because he's Ethan." Private, contained, wary of sharing himself; she wouldn't take that choice from him. "Did you bring everything?"

"Yes, the pop-up tent, the bedding, food and drink. I've left one set a little ways away, had to do two trips from the den so as not to draw attention."

"I'll get it." Selenka pressed another kiss to Ethan's cheek. "Look after him, Oleg. He's important to me."

After returning, she set up the tent colored to blend into their surroundings and cushioned the floor with piles of soft leaves before opening out the bedding over it. Everything in place, she went to Ethan and pulled his right arm around her shoulders, while sliding her other arm around his back.

Oleg did the same from Ethan's left side.

Since the healer had seen even Selenka laid flat, she felt no sense of conflict or guilt in allowing him to help her get Ethan inside the tent. Once they had Ethan on the bedding, she pillowed his head with an extra rolled-up blanket.

"Selya." Oleg's voice was gentle, his hand even more so against her shoulder. "Vadem's wolf is dangerously angry. Artem is with him to ensure he doesn't do anything stupid, but the man needs his alpha."

Selenka knew Emanuel's brother wouldn't be the only one suffering a delayed reaction. BlackEdge remained heartbroken and lost. "How can I leave my mate?" she said roughly.

"What would he say?" Oleg asked, wise and kind.

Selenka brushed Ethan's hair back from his face. "That a queen shouldn't attend her knight. That it's the knight's job to back his queen." She growled deep in her chest. "He's the most stubborn person I've ever met."

"A perfect mate for an alpha." Oleg patted her shoulder. "He'll sleep for many hours. I'll watch him while you're in the den."

When she didn't move, Oleg said, "This Ethan of yours, he does not seek to make you smaller. He seeks to be your support as you grow ever stronger and more powerful in yourself. I see this in him and it gives me such joy."

She turned toward Oleg to see that his gaze held old sadness, the memory of a small girl with scratched knees who'd climbed trees higher and higher and higher in an effort to see the people who'd walked away from her, leaving her behind like unwanted baggage. "Your Ethan, he knows how to keep his promises to his queen."

Selenka swallowed the knot in her throat. "He's not a mate I ever imagined. And now I can't imagine anyone else by my side." Needing time alone with him, she asked Oleg to leave the tent.

Then she removed Ethan's boots and socks, undid the fastenings on his uniform jacket and managed to haul him up enough to strip off the jacket. It left him dressed in the white T-shirt that hugged his biceps, and the jeans he'd put on this morning. She slid his belt from his jeans but went no further. Ethan wouldn't want to wake any less dressed in an unfamiliar situation.

"I'll be back soon." She left him with a kiss.

It caused a physical wrench inside her. She rubbed her hand over her chest as she ran. Such a short time she'd known him, and already, he'd broken through the wall that abandoned little girl had built. That he might leave her yet remained a blade hanging over them—but it wouldn't be a leaving made by choice. That mattered.

Zhanna's small face was the first one she saw when she entered the clearing in front of the den. The little girl was peeking out from around the door, her eyes searching and her face downcast. Lighting up at seeing Selenka, she made a happy sound and ran out toward her . . . shifting into wolf-pup form as she ran.

Selenka crouched down to gather her warm, wriggling form in her arms and nuzzled a kiss into her fur. Nipping happily at her, Zhanna rubbed her head against Selenka's neck, making small sounds of excited joy that triggered every protective instinct in Selenka's body.

Vadem was snarling when she tracked him down all the way on the other side of the den, but one look at Zhanna had the dominant slapping himself back into line. Handing the pup over to Artem, Selenka took Vadem into the trees, into privacy. Aggression pumped off him, his claws slicing out.

Sometimes, a hurting packmate required a hug. Other times . . .

Selenka swiped out at him with her claws. He reacted instinctively with all the pent-up rage inside him, coming at her no holds barred. Selenka met him blow for blow, kick for kick, though she did have to pull back on her speed at times— Vadem was a strong wolf, but he was a senior soldier and she was alpha. He could never physically beat her. Which was why he could be free to unload on her in such a violent way.

Physical aggression was part of why her grandfather had made the decision to step down. It wasn't because of any aggression directed at him, however, for older wolves *could* be alpha. In that situation, it was younger lieutenants who handled matters such as this. But not only had many of Yevgeni Durev's lieutenants been his compatriots, he'd known Selenka was ready.

"Either I step down," he'd said to her, "or I watch you leave to start your own pack. And I am no longer able to hold my packmates as they need—not when it comes down to teeth and claws."

"Deda, no," she'd argued, "I'll always be ready to serve at your side as your lieutenant, to take those tasks." As with the rest of the pack, she had the deepest respect for her grandfather.

He'd waved his hand. "I'm not so foolish as to use your loyalty to prop up my ego, my strong Selenushka. Being a good alpha includes knowing when to step aside for the future." An embrace that enfolded her in warmth and affection. "It's time."

Now she winced as Vadem's fist caught her cheek in a glancing blow, but swung out with a kick that had him folding over. But the angry, grieving male wasn't done yet. He came at her in a silent rage. Instead of dancing away from him, she stayed put for a furious exchange of blows, allowing Vadem to release his pain.

It was long minutes later before he finally collapsed onto his knees, his face bleeding from a cut above the cheek and his left eye already puffing up into a bruise. Dropping down at his side, Selenka just waited. He gave out a roar of pain before turning to burrow into her arms.

Her knuckles bruised and cut, but the rest of her in good condition, Selenka held Vadem as he cried until he had no tears left in him. Then she nuzzled him and whispered, "We will find them. There will be no mercy." It was a deadly promise from an alpha.

Chapter 32

Even alphas make mistakes, Selenushka. Always remember that.

Before you were born, I trusted a packmate to do work on behalf of the pack, and he betrayed BlackEdge by stealing. Such a mistake would've crushed me had I thought myself perfect and held myself up to some great standard of alphahood. Instead, I accepted that I can't see into the heart of every wolf, and I did all I could to fix the resulting damage.

You will make mistakes, too. You will never be the perfect alpha. Such a thing is a figment of the imagination. What you can be is the alpha who is ready to stand for and with her pack, the wolf willing to take the hardest blows, and the wolf who will learn and continue on, gaining in wisdom and strength and courage.

—Yevgeni Durev to Selenka Durev on his last and her first day as alpha of BlackEdge

IT WAS DARK by the time she emerged from the trees, with Vadem by her side. He winced, rubbing at his jaw. "Ma is going to kill me."

Selenka patted him on the shoulder. "You just survived a bout with your alpha. You should only be a little bloodied and broken after she gets through with you."

A sudden smile, a hint of the man behind the grief. "I know you went easy on me." But he looked proud anyway. "I got you a couple of times." A pause. "*Govno*, your mate is going to kill me, too."

Need clawing at her veins, Selenka nonetheless forced a grin. "Your mother will protect you," she said as they parted near the entrance to the den—where Loyal was sitting, waiting for Ethan.

Selenka petted him. "We'll go see him together," she promised the dog before she ducked into the infirmary so Ivina could check her back.

"Healing well in progress," the other woman said, before putting a clean dressing on it. "You shouldn't need this after today." She took a critical look at Selenka's face. "You might end up with a slight bruise on one cheek, but you don't need any work there."

Leaving the infirmary with Loyal by her side before the healer could see her knuckles and fuss, Selenka ran into Alia, who directed her to a group of trainee soldiers. "Pups are hurting," her lieutenant said.

As she sat with the young of her pack, aware her wolf would reassure them with no specific words being spoken, Selenka felt an enormous pride stretch her alpha's heart. Angry and sad they might be right now, but beneath that was a core of courage and love.

"They're clueless," one girl muttered when the conversation drifted to Zivko and the other wolves in the group of intruders. "Zero discipline over their wolves. One actually tried to hit on me and put his hand on my arm." She curled her lip. "I dumped him on his ass and shredded his face for good measure." A quick glance at Selenka. "Sorry—I know we're not supposed to physically hurt them."

Selenka raised an eyebrow. "You're not sorry." She chuckled when the girl ducked her head. "And he assumed skin privileges with a wolf female. If he's so clueless he doesn't know that's an invitation for being shredded, he deserved it." *No one* put hands on anyone else in this pack without permission. Often, that permission was implied by nonverbal wolfish communication, but it always existed.

"Still," she said, "I'll have Margo chat with them, make those rules clear." Youthful arrogance could be forgiven if the intruders were willing to learn—and she'd do this for Emanuel, who'd wanted so much to help those lost changelings.

"They can't have had very good alphas if they don't know

basic stuff." Ilarion frowned. "I kind of almost feel sorry for them. I mean, we have you." A blush. "Total advantage."

Selenka patted his cheek with an affectionate smile—the boy had a sweet crush on her, but he'd grow out of it, as she'd grown out of her crush on one of her grandfather's lieutenants. "Let's see if we can whip them into shape."

"Even though they tried to hurt us?"

"Depends on the choices they make now," Selenka said bluntly. "We see what they do with the chance they've been given."

The conversation continued, drifting to other matters.

"Your mate is handsome." A cheeky comment from dimpled Katina.

Grins spread around the circle. "Even better," Ilarion murmured, "he's lethal."

Chest tight, Selenka kept up an unbroken front till the conversation ended. She then went to see Emanuel's beloved Dia. The gentle submissive was at her parents' quarters, curled up in bed with her best friends on either side of her, all of them in wolf form.

Whimpering when her alpha entered the room, she waited only until Selenka was on the bed to put her head in Selenka's lap. Selenka petted her as Dia's best friends shifted to have contact with their alpha, too. The one mercy in all of this was that Dia's relationship with Emanuel had just begun.

The heartbroken wolf would recover, though it would take a lot of time.

Selenka would recover, too, but she'd forever carry a hole in her heart. That was what it meant to be alpha. To carry your whole pack in your heart . . . even the lost ones.

It was late by the time she left Dia, but she touched base with Margo before she headed out. Her security specialist had no news for her—the Arrows were sharing all data on the person who'd admitted to murdering Emanuel, but so far, that individual remained a ghost.

"Something Cray said about his conversation with the assassin has me looking at the Disciples," Margo told her, blue eyes hard. "But Ivo's dug deep into their finances and history, and we don't have a smoking gun. I don't want to blind myself by focusing only on them, but they're in my cross-hairs."

Selenka didn't rage at the lack of progress; her wolves were relentless hunters and so were the Arrows. The murderer would be found—and punishment would be harsh. "I need to talk to Blaise regardless," she said. "I'll see if I can shake anything loose there."

"Be careful—he has that kind, polite front, but no one forms what might as well be a cult without having delusions of godhood."

"If Blaise had anything to do with harming Emanuel," Selenka said on a growl, "he'll beg for death before it comes." Cold determination in her heart, she slipped away from the den at last.

Loyal padded alongside her.

The stars were brilliant overhead as she hit the night air, and she knew the closest sentries would clock her exit, but no one would begrudge her a run. And run she did, through the cool dark and in the shadow of trees that had stood for generations before her and would stand for generations to come.

Despite her need to get to Ethan, she took care to keep her pace at one his rescued pet could maintain.

Oleg was sitting just outside the tent when she arrived. He rose with a theatrical groan, as Loyal yipped joyfully and ran over to nose his way into the tent, his tail wagging rapidly. "Oh, these bones aren't meant for ground sitting."

As she'd seen Oleg racing over rocks the other day, Selenka didn't take that seriously. She embraced him, was embraced in turn. "I'll stay for the next five hours, head back in at dawn."

The healer left without further words, well aware of the wrenching pull of the mating bond. Crawling inside the tent the instant she was alone with Ethan but for Loyal, who sat attentively at his master's feet, Selenka rolled up all the sides. The night was clear and not too cold, and this way she could be with Ethan and still react quickly to a threat.

Stripping off her socks and boots, she also tugged off her second-favorite jacket. She was a wolf, could sleep in the forest naked with no ill effects, but she'd save the naked sleeping for when her mate was awake. It was a jolt of pleasure to see Ethan's eyes drink her up, feel his hands stroke over her body in that way of his, as if she were a great work of art that he'd been given permission to touch and he couldn't believe it.

"Sleep," she told Loyal, petting his head to reassure him.

Then, lying down beside her mate as she'd hungered to do for so many hours, she put her hand on his chest, closed her eyes, and listened to him breathe. She fell asleep to that sound and to the beat of his heart under her palm, at peace even in her worry and pain because she was with him.

SELENKA took Gregori with her to the meeting with Blaise the next morning. It was a deliberate choice on her part to invite him—the church leader had reacted aggressively to Gregori from the first. Oh, Blaise had hidden it behind a slick smile and pretty manners, but Selenka wasn't alpha because she was stupid.

"How are our prisoners doing?" she asked as she drove them out of den territory.

"Toeing the line." Her senior lieutenant settled into the passenger seat. "Probably because they're under constant watch from growling wolves."

"Good." Things would get worse for those perpetrators before they would get better. "We pick up any other details of their plans?"

"Just confirmation we don't have the mastermind—the humans and Psy in the group have no real appreciation of the strength of our hearing and keep whispering to each other, asking who came up with the idea of fire—the stupidity of that's gotten through and they're pissed, but no one has any idea." He grunted as she took a corner too fast. "Tell me again how you got your license to drive?"

"Scaredy-cat."

"Safety conscious." He tugged together the sides of his nonexistent jacket. "As for Zivko, the boy's realized he was manipulated—I can see a colder, harder anger growing inside him."

That could be either good or bad for the young wolf's development; it all depended on what he did with the anger. "You keeping an eye on him?"

"Yes, and when I'm not there, one of the other senior dominants. It'd be a shame to lose him, lose any of them, changeling or not." He clenched his hands on his knees. "Emanuel was so invested in them."

Heat burned Selenka's eyes.

Swallowing back the emotion, she said, "We'll try our damnedest to open their eyes." She was too pragmatic not to accept that some wouldn't want to see any truth but the one they'd already bought into—Blaise had a certain charisma and an ability to speak to a person as if they truly mattered. What Selenka considered a well-practiced act inspired incredible devotion in his flock.

A number of that flock were out front when Selenka arrived at the church gate. More than one shot her a hostile look, but every single individual dropped their gaze the instant she made eye contact—and the gate slid open without problem.

"Did you notice that?" she murmured to Gregori after they'd driven through.

"The upgraded security?" Her lieutenant tapped his finger on the open ledge of his window, his tattoos brilliant in the sunshine and eyes intent on their surroundings. "Pricey. But Blaise does have a nice fat bank account."

Ivo had managed to track the money trail to inheritances and other wealth brought in by the congregation—including a massive chunk left to the church by a parishioner who'd died without warning two years earlier, long before Haven's Disciples came to Moscow. It had been ruled a natural death, but Selenka had wondered at the efficacy of the investigation. Because the parishioner's death had left Blaise in total control of her millions.

"There he is," she said, spotting Blaise coming out of not the church, but a small home to the left. A slender—and *young*—woman stood in the doorway, her long blonde hair like silk and her dewy, pink-lipped face awash in awe.

Gregori whistled. "She's legal—I recognize her from Margo's spy files, but kid's only nineteen."

While Blaise was forty-three. A well-maintained and

handsome forty-three . . . and a man who didn't believe in moral lines. Because Selenka only had to take a single breath after exiting the vehicle to confirm the two had just engaged in sexual intercourse. Not skin privileges—she wouldn't give that name to this act. And it had nothing to do with the age difference, or even the simple fact that Blaise was the leader of this group.

Alphas often found comfort or love with a packmate.

No, Selenka's disgust stemmed from the fact that the woman obviously worshipped Blaise as her spiritual leader. The power imbalance was staggering, the ethical breach repulsive. It would be akin to Selenka choosing fresh-faced and in-awe-of-her Ilarion for a lover. Her wolf curled its lip in a snarl.

"Selenka." Blaise's strikingly handsome features were set in calm lines, his green eyes placid—the gate watchers had obviously alerted him to their presence. "Shall we go speak in the church?"

"I'd rather stay outside." She folded her arms, set her feet apart. "Certain scents are difficult to ignore inside an enclosed space."

Blaise's skin tightened over his cheekbones—and there it was, the truth he hid behind his serene mask. He didn't like Selenka calling him to account, and it wasn't the first time she'd clocked that reaction. She hadn't yet confirmed if it was because she was a woman, or because she was so clearly the more dominant wolf.

"Of course." He waved a hand. "Shall we walk?"

Selenka fell in beside him for the simple reason that she wanted the young woman out of earshot—Blaise was not the type to be kind to anyone who heard him getting dressed down by another party, much less a wolf alpha.

Gregori trailed them a short distance away.

"Your people have breached our hospitality," she said, keeping her tone civil even though she wanted to tear off his fucking head. This wasn't about anger—it was about pinpointing the person who'd sought to hurt her pack, possibly the same individual who'd murdered Emanuel. "BlackEdge has every right to kick you out."

Blaise's face grew pinched, his muscles bunching, but he

managed to keep his voice even as he said, "I beg leniency. This is our home now, and we shouldn't all be punished for the mistakes of a few misguided youth."

"Brother Blaise." A limber woman who moved with the stride of the martially trained, her black hair tied back in a long tail, raised a hand in hello from the other side of the drive. "Are you well?" She had a hand on her thigh, the weapon not visible, but Selenka could smell the oil used to clean projectile guns. As Nomani was the sixth—and final—wolf in the congregation, she had to know Selenka would scent it.

The threat was conscious.

"Yes, Noma." Blaise's smile was beatific. "Alpha Durev and I are discussing the Disciples' future in Moscow."

Emotion, hot and dark, flashed in the woman's eyes, but she inclined her head. "I will leave you to your conversation."

That conversation didn't take long—after what she'd seen and sensed today, Selenka knew without a doubt that Blaise was up to his neck in whatever was going on. But she needed more information before she rained hell down on his head. To make sure he wouldn't suspect anything, she kept her tone pitiless as she ended the conversation. "Another 'mistake' of *any* kind by *any* of your people and I come for you."

She could feel him staring after her as she strode back to the vehicle. She and Gregori didn't speak again until they were out the gates and on their way back to the pack.

"That never came up in the background check," Gregori murmured. "The brother-sister relationship, I mean."

Selenka had caught that, too—there was a familial thread to Blaise's and Nomani's scents, the kind of thread formed by blood. "It's interesting that he hides the relationship." The two had been careful till now not to be seen together around BlackEdge wolves. "Might be another way to track his past."

"I'll pass on the details to Ivo and Margo. I also want a constant patrol out here until we decide to move on them—I have a feeling they're stockpiling things we don't want them stockpiling."

"I'll alert Valentin and Krychek." Her fellow alphas needed to know of the possible threat in their region.

She made the notification as soon as she was back in the den. Both agreed to let BlackEdge handle it, and pledged assistance should the pack need it. Meanwhile, Gregori went off to liaise with Ivo to see what information they could unearth about Blaise now that they knew Nomani was his sibling.

Selenka did what an alpha needed to do—which included a visit to look over their captives—and she did it while fighting a keening need to go to her mate.

The Architect

To be a true architect, one must accept that sometimes, the foundations have to be demolished. Anything built on a shaky footing will fail. So raze it to the earth, and begin anew.

—Renowned architect Vance Oum (d. 2017)

THE ARCHITECT'S MIND flexed and stretched, growing ever stronger. Even though she'd discarded the Scarab alert, she'd kept an eye on her expanding powers, watching for signs of madness or a critical lack of control. She didn't find them. Perhaps it had to do with her decades of discipline—because she *did* spot such signs of instability in another mind to which her own was drawn.

It was easy enough to find his name: Ezra Ree.

It was equally easy to unearth where he lived, his work status, and personal details. What interested her the most, however, were the lightning bolts she could see in his mind. She saw the same bolts in her own mind.

Signs of a glorious awakening.

In contrast to her, however, Ezra didn't appear to be coping well with his new gifts—he'd called in sick two days in a row, though she could find no evidence of his having consulted a medical professional. After examining his mind one more time, she decided to take a risk. If she failed, well, he'd be far from the first threat she'd eliminated.

Calling in one of her private teleport-capable Tks, she had the male transport her to Dunedin, New Zealand, but had him drop her off a number of blocks from her destination. She had no cause to doubt the Tk's loyalty, but better not to take risks—teleport-capable Tks weren't exactly simple to source. "Wait for me here."

"Yes, ma'am."

Even as she walked, spiderwebs of power spilled over from her mind to spread throughout the Net. The Architect watched it happen with what the emotional would've called happiness. She saw it as her birthright.

She was the new coming of Psy, the next wave of power.

Chapter 33

Your grandmother was the shyest wolf in the den when I
began courting her. How I figured out she reciprocated my
interest was when she began to bake small treats for my
lunch. Just one. Just for me.
                              —Yevgeni Durev to Selenka Durev (14)

AN ENTIRE DAY passed with Selenka spending two hours
with Ethan and the rest on pack business, including the hunt
for the assassin. Oleg, too, was needed in the den. So she
made the call to bring in one more person. Gregori and
Ethan had formed a connection, and she didn't think her
mate would mind the other man holding the watch.

And because Ethan's physical status affected her on a deep
level, she also told Margo and her other lieutenants what had
happened, calling it a "psychic flatline"—but she asked them
to give her and Ethan privacy. "I know I can trust all of you,"
she said on a surge of fierce love for her men and women, "but
Ethan isn't used to being part of a pack yet. He won't be comfortable with being surrounded by wolves while he's down."

Kostya had spoken for all the lieutenants when he said,
"A mate knows a mate best." His tone held the knowledge of
a wolf who'd mated two years earlier, to a woman he'd
known since childhood. "You do what Ethan needs, Selya.
We'll take care of the rest."

As for Gregori, he'd stepped in without hesitation. "Knew
something was up," he'd rumbled. "Ethan's not the kind of
mate to disappear on you that way."

No, Ethan was the kind of mate who stuck.

Her grandmother found her soon after she returned to the
den. "Selenushka," Lada Durev said with a soft hug, the

scent of spring flowers lingering in her hair. "My sweet girl."
Cupping her face, she drew Selenka down to press a kiss to
her cheek. "Where is your mate?"

"He was injured." Never would she lie to her grandmother. "He'll be fine, but he's resting right now. I'll bring
him to your table when he's up and moving." Her babushka
most often showed her love with food.

Her grandfather's stories of his careful, so careful courting of her always made Selenka smile. She'd never quite
understood how her loud, blustery grandfather and her quiet,
shy grandmother could live together in harmony, but they
did. It was a life Selenka had been afraid to hope for, for
herself. Now she had a quiet, intense mate who trusted no
one but had given himself over to her.

"Ah," her grandmother said and gave her another hug.
"Your mate will understand that you must still be alpha, especially in such times." Her smile was luminous. "As long as
he knows he is first in your heart, as I have always known
with Yevgeni."

Selenka couldn't face that depth of vulnerability, couldn't
stare full frontal at the reality of what was growing between
her and Ethan. The mating bond was a primal connection,
but love . . . that required the participation of the human
heart, a heart that had been kicked hard in childhood and
carried the bruises to this day.

"Babusya!"

They both looked down to see Zhanna tugging at Lada's
skirt, her face bright. Selenka's grandmother smiled and
crouched down to cuddle the little girl. "And you, my darling
Zhannochka of the big ears and cheetah feet, what mischief
are you causing?"

Giggling, the pup threw her arms around Lada. "Party!
It's Tzi's birthday party! Come!"

And for a while, the Warren was a place of innocent joy,
the pups excited about cake and games and the adults delighted by them. Selenka wouldn't admit it even on pain of
torture, but her pack had learned to celebrate so openly from
the bears. The bears threw a party for everything. New packmate? Party! A clever juvenile getting into a top learning
institution? Party! A beautiful spring day? Picnic party!

Selenka's wolves didn't take it to that extreme, but after spotting how much fun the bears had with impromptu events, they'd been known to throw the odd party and picnic here and there. Which she would never, ever tell Valentin. The bear would laugh and then invite himself. Because he was a bear. As if she'd conjured him up by thinking about him, her phone rang as she entered her office a while later, his name on the display.

"Problem?" she asked.

"No. My Starlight told me your mate is psychically hurt."

Selenka had expected the information to flow from Silver to Valentin. Mates didn't keep secrets from one another. "He'll be fine."

"I know, but I called to drink beer with you over the line. The aggravation of not being able to protect our mates on the psychic plane is enough to drive an alpha to the brink."

Selenka had never thought she'd be so in sympathy with a bear, but she nodded. "I want to wrap him up in cotton wool and put him somewhere safe, but doing that would destroy him."

"My Silver thinks nothing of making herself a target by being the face of EmNet. I have to channel my bear through the mating bond to scare off everyone in the PsyNet."

Selenka was interested. "Does it work?"

"She says our bond sends out a 'go away if you don't want to die' signal," Valentin responded proudly.

Selenka's wolf immediately began channeling more "touch my mate and I will eviscerate you" thoughts down the mating bond. "Arrows say that even with Ethan flamed out, he has an inexplicable non-Psy shield around him."

"Hah!" Valentin's laugh was a boom. "As if we'd leave our mates vulnerable."

"As if," Selenka agreed.

Then she and Valentin had a ten-minute-long session groaning about how difficult it was to keep their Psy mates safe, especially as they insisted on doing dangerous things. At one point, Valentin invited Selenka to have a beer sometime, and she agreed. It wasn't until after she'd hung up that she realized what she'd done.

"*Govno.* I just agreed to have a beer with Valentin," she

told Margo when the lieutenant walked in as Selenka hung up.

Her best friend snorted coffee out of her nose. After wiping it up and getting back her breath, she said, "I'll bail you out of jail."

"Some friend," Selenka muttered. "He's a changeling alpha with a Psy mate. We have things in common."

Her phone buzzed. She still had it in her hand from her talk with Valentin, so raised it to glance at the name on the screen. "It's Aden," she said to Margo, who gestured for her to take the call and mouthed, *We'll talk later.* The lieutenant pulled the door shut behind her.

"How is Ethan?" Aden's voice was impossible to read, but that he'd called told Selenka everything she needed to know.

"Still unconscious." Her hand tightened on the phone. "My healer says his vitals are steady, and there's no need for any other intervention."

"He's correct." Aden's confirmation had her inhaling silently. She trusted Oleg with her life and her pack, but Ethan was Psy, and Oleg himself had told her that Psy bodies didn't always read the same as human or changeling.

"If he hasn't shifted from unconsciousness to a more natural sleep by tonight, however, contact me," Aden said. "I can do a telepathic scan to ensure he's healing as he should."

Selenka didn't agree—to do so felt like tempting fate. "How's he looking on the PsyNet?"

"No signs of instability. The shield-like construct around his mind has become stronger and stronger in the interim— a nearby E is of the opinion that it has 'claws.'"

Selenka smiled grimly. She'd share that with Valentin and with any other changeling she knew who was mated to a Psy who remained in the Net. Looked like they *could* protect their mates to a certain extent. "I'll call you when he wakes." She wouldn't make another alpha wait for news of one of his people. Because while Ethan might be hers now, he was also Aden's, and her mate needed those bonds of brotherhood he was just coming to accept and embrace.

"Selenka." Aden's voice stopped her when she would've hung up. "I'm glad for Ethan that he has you. Of all my men, he was the one I most feared I'd lose. You've held him to the world long enough for him to find his way out of the darkness."

Selenka frowned after she hung up, wondering if that was why her wolf had lunged so precipitously at Ethan. Because it knew its mate was hanging on an edge and needed to be hauled in before he fell.

It crushed Selenka's chest to imagine a world where she'd been too late and Ethan had fallen. She'd never have known him, never have felt this terrifying emotion inside her. She would've never known what it was to belong to a man who meant it when he said he was hers.

A pulse along the mating bond, the jagged shards shifting and resettling.

Shoving back her chair, she headed out, unable to any longer fight the need to see him.

She ran into Artem near the doorway. The lieutenant had his party dress–wearing but barefoot daughter riding his shoulders—you'd never know from seeing him now that, three years ago, he'd been a grumpy loner who'd eaten submissives for breakfast.

"Blaise's been trying to reach you," he said, canines flashing in the fine lines of a face that wouldn't look out of place in an aristocratic portrait. "I rerouted everything to me."

"Good."

"Senk! Senk!"

She smiled at the tiny girl on his shoulders, knowing that had been the baby's attempt at saying her name. When she blew Inja a kiss, the pup blew one back with both hands and Selenka's chest didn't hurt as much.

"Go take care of your mate, Selya," Artem said, his voice gentle. "We'll watch over the pack."

Selenka left with a brush of her hand over Artem's, her wolf taking over as she ran surefooted across the forest.

Gregori had rolled up the sides of the tent as she'd done and was sitting with his back against a tree from where he could monitor Ethan. He was listening to music playing softly from the watch he preferred to wear over carrying a phone, but his head was angled toward her even before she stepped from the trees. "Ethan's breathing changed not long ago. I think he's in a natural sleep."

Selenka knelt beside her mate, saw his color was better, his chest rising and falling in the deep breaths of heavy sleep. When she brushed his hair off his forehead, he turned into her touch. "You're right." It came out rough, tight.

Loyal leaned into her, the dog's tail wagging.

"Did you feed him?" she asked, allowing Ethan's pet to take comfort from her.

"Yes." Walking over to her, Gregori placed a hand on her shoulder. "Your mate's a tough bastard."

Reaching up with one hand, she squeezed Gregori's. "Thanks for doing this."

"Anytime. What I feel between you two, it's important. It's real."

Selenka turned to reply, but Gregori was already moving away, his shoulders big and his stride silent. Older than her by just over a year, he'd never come close to finding a permanent lover or a mate—and he wasn't a wolf who was happy with uncomplicated skin privileges. As alpha, she had to watch him, ensure he got enough contact to keep his wolf from getting edgy.

Edgy dominants ended up in fights and their irritability incited others.

"You worry about him."

Jerking back her head at that murmur, she looked down to see Ethan's pale eyes open. "Hey, you." Her hand trembled as she pressed it against his cheek. "I thought you were going to be out forever."

Even as Loyal barked excitedly, Ethan watched her in that way he had, with unwavering intensity, while inside her, the mating bond pulsed like a beating heart. "My psychic ability remains compromised." His gaze faded for a second before coming back into sharp focus. "My mind is surrounded by a dual layer of protection—one that comes from you . . . and the rest from members of my squad."

She thought of the man she'd first mated, distant and disconnected. "They are your brothers-in-arms."

"Yes," he said without hesitation, even as he lifted one hand to pet his ecstatic dog. "As you're my mate."

Selenka nodded, her throat thick. She couldn't talk about

who he was to her yet, so she said, "How do you know I worry about Gregori?"

"What?"

"Your first words when you woke were that I worry about Gregori."

"I don't recall that." The slightest impression of a frown. "Perhaps I was dreaming? Though I don't remember that, either."

Selenka didn't think so—her mate had picked up a subtle emotional cue while on the edge between sleep and waking but was no longer aware of it now that he was awake. "You okay to sit up?" She stroked wriggling, excited Loyal on the back and said, "Down."

The dog obeyed at once.

Ethan pushed up into a sitting position at the same time, so quickly that she would've fallen back if he hadn't gripped her with one arm around her body.

"The injury was psychic. My physical body is fine." His breath brushed her skin.

It was only a matter of a small movement to touch her lips to his, weave her fingers into his hair. But despite the violent craving that clawed at her, she pulled away after a bare taste and grabbed a bottle of nutrient drink from the food she'd stashed in one corner of the tent. "This first."

Ethan obeyed the order without argument. To be cared for as Selenka was caring for him . . . he'd do anything she wanted. "The fuel will help with my recovery," he said after drinking half the bottle, "but for the time being, I am akin to a device with zero charge." For a psychic being to lose such an integral aspect of his nature, it was worse than losing a limb. "Everything is dull, seen through a thick haze. Everything but you."

Her voice, her scent, her presence, it was a brilliant light in the dark.

As was her kiss when she put aside the empty nutrient bottle and touched her lips to his. An invitation to play from a wolf.

Chapter 34

Touch is our cornerstone
Cure for the heart
Medicine for the soul

—Anonymous changeling poet

ETHAN WRAPPED HIS arms around Selenka's body . . . and only then did he sense the faint trembling that shook her frame. "Selenka?"

"It was as if you were in a coma." Rasped-out words. "And your eyes bled."

Burying his face against the side of her neck, he held her tight as she held him. And though the world was heavy and dull right now, his senses in a fog, the import of her words hit him like a hammer. Selenka had worried about him until she trembled from her relief. Ethan had never mattered that much to anyone.

Pressing his lips to the skin of her throat was instinct and need. Such deep *need.* He wanted to gather in all that she felt for him, wanted to surround himself with it until he wouldn't ever forget. Until the power stretching his mind couldn't steal it away.

She arched her neck for him, her claws slicing out to prick him through his T-shirt.

But when he slid his hand under her jacket and tee, fingers splayed against the smooth warmth of the skin of her lower back, she gripped his wrist. "I want Oleg to take a look at you first." Breath shallow and pulse rapid, her fingers clenching on his wrist. "I need to know for sure that you're healthy and safe."

"I am," Ethan vowed. "Trust me."

Wolf-gold eyes examined him with a potent intensity. He held his breath, suddenly realizing how much it meant to him that she do that: trust him.

Releasing his wrist in silence, she leaned into him . . . an alpha wolf who trusted him with herself. Chest aching in a way that was a large rock on his rib cage, he said, "Your back?"

"All but healed." Clawed fingers scraping gently down his jaw. "Do what you will, Ethan. I'm a wolf." A soft growl. "I won't break."

Accepting her at her word because his mate *was* a wolf, a powerful one, he shifted to take her to the bedding on which he'd been lying, turning them so that the line of his body pressed up against hers as she lay below.

He needed to cover her this way, protect her, even knowing she was lethal and well capable of protecting herself. But the madness inside him was insistent that even alpha wolves needed tenderness when wounded and scared. His *Selenka* needed the tenderness.

He touched her with reverence, still not quite believing that she was his, that he had this right. But to care for her was his right and his privilege. Ethan would not guarantee the well-being of anyone who got between him and his mate.

When he went to remove her jacket, she lifted up enough that he could tug it off. Her body was sleek and strong under his, her hands possessive as they shaped his shoulders, and her mouth wet and hot. He drank it all in, each kiss, each caress, each instant with her filling a deep, empty well inside him.

He wanted to fall into her, devour her.

When she pushed up his T-shirt, he tore it off over his head and dropped it to the side. She learned him with her hands, her pleasure in his body doing things inside him he couldn't explain. Ming's henchmen hadn't been gentle about the physical punishments they'd meted out.

Selenka brushed her fingers over one of the ridged scars. "I want to kill them." Soft words, a predator's growl. "Rip their limbs from their bodies and their heads from their necks."

"They're already dead."

"Good." She tugged down his head for a kiss tangled and wet and possessive. Her chest rumbled with her wolf's voice, her fingers clawed against his scalp.

Ethan didn't fight the primal possession; he fell into it. Into her. Into a woman as wildly alive and vibrant as the summer storm he'd once seen when Ming forced him to commit murder. When he kissed her with voracious hunger, she responded with moans in the back of her throat and the pricking of claws at his nape before she slid her hands over his back.

Claws scraped his skin, but lightly, playfully. His mate was pleased with him, wanted him. "I'm so glad you're mine, Ethan Night. Strong, stubborn"—a nip of his jaw—"dangerous, beautiful, and tender. I'm keeping you."

The soul Ethan wasn't sure he possessed drank in the words, and even recovering from a flameout, the power of her claiming was a punch through his system. Breathless, hungry, *needing*, he kissed his way over her jaw and to her throat, and when he pushed up her T-shirt, she took it off to drop it beside his.

Loyal got up and wandered off.

A soft laugh from Selenka. "I think we're shocking your dog."

"He'll get used to it." Because Ethan intended to do this with Selenka as often as possible.

His mate's bra was black lace with each strap formed of two thin but strong ribbons, with a small bow at the end where it joined the cup. "I—" Pushing up on his arms, he looked down at how her breasts plumped pale against the cup of lace. "This isn't like your other item of underwear."

"Like it, do you?" A laugh that held a kind of power he'd never before faced, and he'd been around plenty of powerful Arrow women. "I'm partial to lace and satin at times." She ran a finger over one breast, drawing his attention to the soft, plump mound.

He pressed down on his hands to put his lips against her delicate skin.

Groaning, she said, "Ethan, you are ridiculously hot when you show off all that muscle." Her words trembled as she gripped his taut biceps. As if he did to her what she did to him. As if he had sensual power of his own. The warmth inside him grew and took on a tone of . . . satisfaction. Settling more firmly against her, he kissed and licked and stroked her breasts before cupping one and squeezing.

She clamped her thighs around him, her body arching in a sinuous curve as she ran her nails up his back in a caress that had the tiny hairs on his body standing up. Tugging down the lace of her bra cup, he closed his hand over her bare flesh, her nipple a pebbled hardness against his palm. He kept his gaze on her face as he squeezed this time, saw her eyes flutter almost all the way shut—but for the slitted gold gaze that watched him with predatory focus.

Soft lips curved. "Come here, Ethan."

He could and would deny her nothing.

His reward for surrendering was a kiss slow and languid that melted things in his body that shouldn't have melted. Even as it did so, he began to feel flickers of awakening power. Soon, he'd be dealing not just with his telekinetic abilities, but with the rogue power that was a thing of chaos and madness.

Wanting as much skin contact as possible before that happened, he stripped off his remaining clothes at furious speed. Selenka smiled, powerful and sensual, when he returned to her and put his hands on the waistband of her pants. She cooperated by lifting her hips off the ground, and he soon had his mate naked but for the lace of her bra.

Lifting her arms, she invited him close.

He went, sinking into her kiss, letting go in a way he wouldn't be able to do when the power surged. As if sensing his utter capitulation, Selenka flipped them so he lay on his back with her astride him, a powerful alpha wolf who liked the taste of Ethan Night, broken Arrow and devoted mate.

Her hair was a tumble of black, purple, and pink, and where many of his race would've seen that as a symbol of a lack of discipline, he saw a woman so confident that she didn't need the trappings of what passed as control.

"You are so beautiful." It was wrenched out of him, all his shields down and his heart laid bare. "You own me."

Smile slow, Selenka reached back and unhooked her bra,

sliding it down her arms to drop it on their other discarded clothes. His heart kicked, the reaction visceral and uncontrollable. His hands were on her hips before he was aware of it, and when she leaned forward into him, he felt caged by her powerful femininity—and it was the only cage he'd never wanted to escape.

"Those eyes, the way they look at me . . ." Selenka nipped him on the jaw. "Have a care, *zaichik*, or I'll eat you up."

"Anything you want. Anything you wish."

Wolf-gold eyes glowed in the semidarkness beneath the forest canopy before her kiss consumed him. He stroked the sweet slope of her back, filled his hands with her breasts, tried to kiss every inch of her. When he got her on her back again and went down her body kiss by kiss, she gripped his hair with one hand but didn't stop him.

Ethan licked her between the thighs.

Her moan created a haze in his brain, the taste of her a drug. Sinking into position, he kissed her as he would her mouth, the slick heat of her driving him on until his penis felt like stone and his skin was afire. Thighs quivering, she pulled at his hair until he looked up and began to crawl his way back up her body.

He wasn't truly thinking at this point, every cell in his body focused on her and her pleasure. The kiss they shared was erotic with the taste of her, and he wanted more. Dropping his head to her throat, he sucked. She growled and changed their positions again, so he was the one on the bottom—with a magnificent woman astride him.

The wet heat of her brushed his erection.

Neck rigid, he gripped her hips and aligned their bodies. *"Selenka."*

Wolf-gold eyes watching him, she sank down on his rigid length, enclosing him in scalding softness. His power stirred further to the surface. Gritting his teeth, he thrust up into her, wanting to reach the crescendo before he once more had to spend a massive part of his energy on controlling the rogue power.

Selenka's claws dug into his skin, her hair falling silkily on his chest as she moved with him. Ethan needed . . . something but didn't know what, or how to ask for it. Then

Selenka kissed him with ferocious affection and that was it, the caress throwing him over the edge of the abyss.

His body blazed with pleasure as his mind blazed to full power, and for a stunning instant that hung in time, he was all he would ever be, without walls or chains or shields.

Chapter 35

Operative Cray has been compromised. If you have ever had any contact with him, erase all data threads that could lead back to you.

—The Architect to the Consortium's upper-echelon membership

EZRA REACHED OUT gratefully to his new friend, the one who'd knocked on his door while he was at his lowest, then shown him that he wasn't broken at all. She'd been so kind, had taken his psychic hand and shown him how his mind was growing and becoming *more*.

Just like her own.

He wasn't a freak, wasn't going insane. He was one of a gifted new variant, part of a new *people*.

His friend had spoken of lightning bolts, but he couldn't see them. Yet he believed her. Far more powerful and connected than Ezra, she had no reason to lie to him. No, she was a good person, one who'd shown him the truth—including the horrible fact that ordinary Psy were attempting to wipe out their kind.

He'd read the alerts she'd forwarded, seen how "Scarabs" were being pinpointed. Given the fugues he'd experienced, he'd hesitantly suggested that perhaps this Dr. Ndiaye might be able to help. But, shaking her head, she'd told him how those ID'd as Scarabs disappeared after turning themselves in. Their kind was too strong and a threat to those in power—so they were being exterminated.

He didn't want to believe that of Kaleb Krychek, whose actions had released him from the shackles of Silence, but the truth was unavoidable. He saw it in all its ugliness, especially after his new friend worked on his mind to stabilize it. It was all so clear. As was the fact that *she* was the only one who cared for their kind, who wanted them to thrive.

So when she called on him to help her fight back against the annihilation of their species, he didn't even think about resisting.

Chapter 36

I'm so sorry, my heart.

—Varra Durev to Selenka Durev (2059)

SELENKA LAY CURLED up on Ethan, lazy and languid and not in the mood to move. Especially since her mate had his hand on her back and was petting her with small strokes. The tenderness made woman and wolf both smile and wallow in the delight of having a mate who saw her strength but didn't forget her heart.

"I'm going to have to add a chapter on outdoor recreation to the Arrow skin privileges manual that Abbot passed on to me."

Selenka laughed and drew circles on his chest. "Can I see it? The manual?"

A pause. "No, it's a secret. To give us some small advantage against experts."

Smile even deeper, Selenka said, "Fair enough." Her mind drifted, her guard low enough that she drifted all the way to the beginning. "I was conceived after a frolic in the forest."

"Your parents told you this?"

His startled reaction was so Psy that it eased the stab of pain that accompanied the memories. "My mother used to laugh about it with my father, about how he'd lured her out for a picnic and now she had a naughty pup. I guess I had big ears, and filed it away, understood it later." She drew another shape on the tensile warmth of his skin.

"Will your mother like me?" Ethan asked, an unexpected hesitancy to him.

Selenka considered his question. "Varra likely won't know what to make of you." She rubbed her head against him, and he immediately moved his touch to her nape, massaging gently.

Her heart hurt at the care he took with her, and she knew she could trust him with this, too, her greatest hurt. "My mother chose to leave my father and the pack when I was eight."

Ethan wrapped his other arm around her, her strangely intuitive Arrow mate holding her safe against the fractures of the past.

"My parents had been in a stable relationship for five years before I was born, long enough that she was able to conceive, but with my father getting increasingly bitter over the years . . . well, it poisoned what they once had."

"Why didn't she take you?"

The question was a blade thrust between her ribs.

Ethan's arms tightened. "I hurt you. I'm sorry. You don't have to answer."

"No." She pressed a kiss to his chest. "It only hurts because I asked the same question as a little girl." Abandonment like that didn't happen in a pack, even when a relationship ended.

"My mother is human." Her face lingered in front of Selenka's mind. "I was already showing indications of powerful dominance and she didn't think I'd do well outside of a pack. She took care to remain in contact with me—but it was nearly all over the comm. After she left BlackEdge, she chose to return to her home in Tajikistan."

"Is that where you get the shape of your eyes?"

"Yes. Most people never guess that I'm part Tajik, but the paleness of my skin, the shape of my eyes, it comes from her. Varra was born in the Pamir Mountains, and she carried those mountains in her bones and in her heart. As an adult, I don't begrudge her leaving Moscow for the place and the people she always thought of as home, but as a child . . . I needed her."

Ethan's heart beat strong and steady under her cheek. "Your father would not have been a good guardian."

"No." She thought of his bitter rages, his increasing dislike of a child who was outpacing him in power, and still couldn't understand how a father could be that way toward his own pup. "He didn't fight to hold on to me when my grandparents stepped in."

"That was a great hurt." Such simple words for such a profound understanding.

"Yes," she said to this man who saw so deep. "I think if one of my parents had fought for me . . ." She exhaled, pressed another kiss to Ethan's chest.

"I will fight *always* for you. Until my breath stops, I'll fight."

She accepted that to the core, and so she could tell him the rest. "I spent two summers in Tajikistan after I was older and no longer so angry at the world, got to know my mother and meet my half sisters Nodira and Maviya."

Her lips curved at the thought of the two delightful girls. "Both have visited the Warren and are pestering me for another visit soon." Selenka loved her sisters, but she couldn't bring them to Moscow until the threat against the pack was neutralized.

"You feel no resentment toward them?"

"No, my anger was never directed at them." To her wolf, they were pups to protect. "I also saw what nursing bitterness did to my father and I chose another path." It hadn't eased the hurt, but it had shoved it from the forefront to the past where it belonged. "My mother and I, we have a loving but not close relationship."

Ethan brushed his lips over her hair. "She was missing for too many critical milestones of your life."

"Yes, and I think even though the human part of me forgives her, the wolf doesn't understand how she could move so far away from me, to a place I couldn't go to see her when I needed my mother.

"I accept that she couldn't raise such a dominant wolf pup outside of a pack, but she could've stayed in the pack. She didn't have to leave the pack just because she left my father."

Selenka had thrown the cold question at her mother when she was twelve, maybe thirteen, and at the height of her anger.

Varra's lovely face with its soft lines and lush lips had crumpled, tears rolling down her cheeks. "I'm not like you, Selenushka. I was never so strong. I needed the comfort of my mountains. I needed the embrace of my own parents, needed to hear my own language."

"Looking back," Selenka said, "I can see that she never quite embraced pack life, was always a little distant." The memory had her sitting up with a frown. "What do you think of pack life?" Such a life would be even more alien to Ethan than it had been to her mother.

"I'm your mate, Selenka. My home is at your side."

The answer didn't satisfy her. An alpha's mate played a strong role in the pack, dependent on his or her personality and skills. Lada Durev was the kind of mate to whom packmates had often gone when they weren't confident enough to directly approach their alpha. She was also the kind of mate who had comforted packmates in distress.

Ethan was too strong, too deadly, to be in the background. The pack would expect him to step up and be a senior packmate with all the attendant responsibilities.

Would he be able to fulfill that role?

Her mind filled with the image of Ethan handling the intruders, Gregori in full agreement with him, followed it up with one of him with Zhanna in his arms. What the hell was she worrying about? Her mate was doing just fine—and he was doing it his way.

Rising to her feet on that thought, she pushed back her hair with one hand, and faced reality. "We have to head back, sort out the meeting with Sascha Duncan." The flameout had given them an unexpected window of freedom, but she could already feel the surges gaining in strength, the storm along the mating bond turbulent.

"What does our bond look like on your PsyNet?" she asked curiously as they dressed.

Ethan stilled. "It's invisible. On the PsyNet, I appear unconnected to anyone."

Selenka chewed that over—her wolf had stood guard over

Ethan on the psychic plane when he flamed out, so it wasn't a case of a Psy-changeling disconnect.

Ethan touched her hair. "It's the damage inside me."

"Say that about yourself one more time and I'll bite you," Selenka threatened, because filled with jagged shards and echoing with static it might be, but their bond filled the empty spaces inside her. The places not even her loving grandparents had been able to reach.

Her wolf might've lunged at Ethan without warning to save him from falling over the precipice, but he'd saved her from a life lived on the edges when it came to this most intimate of bonds between lovers.

She closed her hand over his nape. "You know how to give yourself to your person, Ethan Night. As your mate, I need nothing more." The kiss she laid on him had his eyes bleeding to black, his chest heaving.

ETHAN processed what Selenka had told him about Operative C as they walked, thought back over all his interactions with the man. "He wasn't very good at subterfuge, but the second Moscow operative was one secret he managed to keep." If Ethan had maintained contact for longer, it was possible he could've unearthed that second name.

"If you're worrying whether you should've stayed in touch with him longer," Selenka said, "don't. Latest note"— she held up her phone—"says he was planning your execution sooner rather than later. Too hard to control." A glint in her eye. "You have a wolf's heart, *zaichik*."

Veins pumping with pure pride, Ethan nonetheless focused on the problems at hand. "Any update on Haven's Disciples?"

"Nothing definite yet." Her tone turned grim. "Only good news is that Zivko and the other young wolves have started to think for themselves now that they're away from Blaise."

They reached the den moments later, and Ethan walked in to a sense of lightness in the air. That wasn't to say the sorrow was gone, but it was clear the pack had made the decision to move on and live in the present rather than being held captive to the agony of the past.

Margo was one of the first people he saw. The security specialist's face was set in tense lines, her shoulders tight, but she said, "Good to see you up, Ethan. I sent you a few more back issues of *Wild Woman*."

A touch overwhelmed by the overt welcome, Ethan said, "*Spasibo*, Margo. I haven't yet watched *Hourglass Lives*, but I intend to as soon as things are calmer."

Margo's expression shifted to one of pure joy for a second, the hazy blue of her eyes sparkling. "We'll do it together," she said. "So I can provide commentary. You *have* to catch up so we can dish about Ridge and Chantelle."

In front of them, Selenka was already surrounded by a large group of youths who all seemed to want to make contact with her as they told her what felt like a hundred different things. Loyal stuck close to her leg, giving everyone else a suspicious look. Ethan's dog was as gone over her as Ethan.

"How does she give so much of herself?" he found himself asking Margo.

"That's a big part of being alpha—that huge heart." Emotion in Margo's voice, intense and rich and woven with loyalty. "To her, it's not a drain. Her wolf is built for this."

A familiar mind touched Ethan's. *Ethan, your shields appear fully reinstated. Are you conscious?*

Yes, he told Aden. *You wish to discuss the incident?* He'd never forget the infestation of psychic bugs, their glowing carapaces and scrambling legs.

Yes. Comm conference. I'll send you the code.

After receiving it, Ethan turned to Margo. "Is there a comm I can use for a private meeting?"

"Sure. Follow me."

Ethan did so after a glance at Selenka. She met his gaze and when he mouthed, *Comm,* gave him a nod. Loyal stuck with her.

Alone in the small room set up with a large screen at one end, Ethan input the comm code. It took him through to a conference that held three familiar faces: Aden, Kaleb Krychek, and Memory Aven-Rose.

It was Memory, her presence still so strangely familiar, who said, "You're okay." A big smile that reached her eyes.

"That was creepy as all get-out. I'm going to be seeing nightmare bugs in my dreams for a while." She shuddered.

Ethan agreed. "I've never seen such an infestation." He picked up a small piece of memo paper and began to fold it out of sight of the cameras.

"From the psychic images you've both shared," Krychek said, "neither have I." His physically perfect face gave nothing away, his cardinal eyes impassive. "I'm also getting no answers from the NetMind or DarkMind, but they've devolved to such a point that communication is all but impossible."

Ethan hadn't known Krychek could communicate with the neosentience that was the heart of the PsyNet—and he knew nothing of a DarkMind. But those questions could wait. "Have you located any other Es who can see the bugs?" After a thought, he made another precision fold.

"No." Aden's sharp cheekbones and slick-straight black hair caught the light as he angled his head. "Once Memory recovered and was able to keep track of it, we used the trapped bug to test its visibility to a whole range of Psy from telepaths and empaths all the way to psychometrics. So far, you and Memory alone can see them."

"Could be because we're both a little nuts," Memory said, then looked off-camera and grinned. "It's a joke, Mr. Growly Wolf."

Ethan wasn't so sure about his own mental stability—but the chance of two near-strangers sharing a hallucination was unlikely. Especially as Memory had seen the bugs right after she entered the PsyNet, well before he'd had any time to—even inadvertently—cue her to their presence. "There must be something different about our brains," he said at last.

Memory's pursed lips were painted a vibrant autumn orange. "Can you do anything else related to Scarab Syndrome sufferers?"

"As far as I'm aware, no." He placed the completed origami animal on the table and began to fold another piece of memo paper. "You're the only one who appears to be able to help those with the Syndrome."

The empath made a face. "Only a limited percentage of those found so far."

"The most dangerous percentage," Krychek clarified. "The strongest of those suffering from the Syndrome."

"Not all sufferers are strong?" Ethan'd had the impression that Scarab affected only high-Gradient Psy.

It was Aden who answered. "It appears to be a case of degrees. A jump from Gradient 2 to Gradient 6 is a major shift, as is the shift from 5 to 8."

Memory's face lost its luster. "It doesn't look good. There doesn't seem to be any way to rewind the clock for those people. A couple of the worst affected have already made their end-of-life decisions known. They don't want to die with no awareness of who they are or what they've become."

Ethan had once made the same choice . . . but now his entire life had changed. He'd been given an alternate choice—but if Memory was wrong and he *was* a Scarab, it could mean annihilation for hundreds.

"Will you give us permission to compare your brains?" Aden asked. "Memory, you can have your scans done by whomever you trust."

"I'll think about it," the empath said with a scowl.

"DNA?" Ethan suggested, because it was less of an intrusion. "I'm curious about what links us."

Memory pondered it before giving a small nod. "But I want yours. My and Alexei's pack can run the tests."

"Aden, please forward my sample from the squad archives to Memory." Every Arrow had samples on file at Arrow HQ; Arrows who died in the field sometimes couldn't be identified any other way.

Krychek broke in before Aden could reply. "I requested another person join this meeting."

The comm screen split into four on the heels of his words, the face that appeared in the fourth quarter of a woman with blue-black hair cut in a blunt wedge, her skin like porcelain. Ethan had never before met her, but he'd heard at some point that her mother'd had Japanese ancestry, and that genetic history showed in the shape of her eyes and the angles of her face.

None of that was as important as the sense of power and lethal patience that clung to her. This was a woman who would take her time, eliminate her enemies with such vicious stealth that no one would be able to prove it—and she'd never lose her cool, never betray a single weakness.

He was face-to-face with Nikita Duncan, former Psy Councilor, mother of Sascha Duncan, and current member of the Psy Ruling Coalition.

And a woman with hands drenched in blood.

Chapter 37

Touch my child or grandchild and you make an enemy of me.
That will not be advantageous to your continued good
health. I am not my daughter, to concern myself with ethical
lines—the PsyNet is littered with the voiceless ghosts of
those who once thought to stand against me.
                    —Quote attributed to Nikita Duncan (unverified)

"NIKITA," KRYCHEK SAID in a voice so potent with power it
was midnight, "we need you to talk about your ability to
seed mental viruses."

To Ethan's surprise, Nikita didn't pretend not to have the
ability. "What do you wish to know?" she asked, her tone
cool to the point of coldness.

"Do you see creatures like these when you seed a virus?"

It was clear from the slight pause that followed that Krychek was telepathing her the mental images Ethan and
Memory had forwarded. That he was doing so without any
signs of strain when he was in Moscow and Nikita was most
likely in San Francisco spoke to a vast telepathic reach.

Nikita's eyes flared slightly at the corners. "What is this?"

Krychek explained. "We have one live sample." A pause.
"Do you wish to see it?"

His phrasing was interesting, Ethan thought. Clearly, the
cardinal didn't want to bias Nikita against *not* seeing the
creature.

"Yes," she said.

During the three minutes the two were on the PsyNet and
not paying full attention to their screens, Memory widened
her eyes at Ethan in a silent question.

He shook his head just slightly. *Not here.*

Memory scowled.

Ethan stared back.

And Aden's mind touched his. *What's going on?*

Once, Ethan would've ignored that question. Once he wouldn't have sensed the deep concern in the squad leader's face when he looked at Ethan. *Memory's of the opinion that I don't have the Syndrome. She wants me to lower my shields to see what power emerges.*

That seems risky in the extreme.

At least Aden got it, understood why Ethan was hesitating. *She believes Sascha Duncan can create shields that will help me maintain but I won't do it unless someone powerful is on standby to shut down my mind should my abilities go haywire.* It was a silent request, Ethan unused to asking for help.

Just tell me the time and place and I'll be there, Aden said without hesitation.

"That is a highly disturbing creature." Nikita's voice sliced the air and, despite her words, carried no sense of disgust or horror. "You say there were hundreds of them?"

Memory's mouth fell open. "*You* saw it?"

Nikita Duncan gave her a look so frigid it was glacial. "My visual cortex hasn't imploded in the last few seconds, so yes."

Unfazed, Memory threw up her hands, her curls bouncing. "I have no idea how you're Sascha's mom."

"It involves an egg and sperm."

Krychek broke into the chilly conversation to explain the issue to Nikita. At which point, she sat back in her seat and said, "I see." A good half minute passed before she added, "To answer your initial question, no, this isn't what I see— this is a macrocosm of what I see. Viruses magnified to a size visible to the naked eye."

Ethan saw it then, what Krychek was thinking. "A Scarab with your ability magnified to cardinal status," he said, knowing he was describing a thing of absolute horror.

Nikita went motionless. "My ability is a minor one for a reason. It's incredibly destructive even when applied with pinprick precision. Survival is impossible."

"We have survivors," Aden responded. "Three in critical

care, with severe brain inflammation, but the normal medications appear to be working. Two more are already stable, with no signs of long-term damage."

"Your doing, I assume?" Nikita said to Memory.

"Feel free to assume what you like," Memory said cheerfully, offering no further information.

Protecting Ethan.

He was starting to see why Selenka sometimes said *"Empaths"* in that tone of voice.

"But," Memory added, "if you can see them, you can probably zap them."

"I've never tried." Nikita shrugged, and Ethan knew it was apt to be a calculated gesture meant to appear natural. "When I release the virus," she said, her gaze locked on Memory, "I intend for the target to die."

Memory stared back, her arms folded across her chest.

"If you are able to affect them, your résumé will now include the title of rescuer." Krychek looked between Nikita and Memory but didn't comment on the silent standoff. "If this is a Scarab ability as all signs seem to indicate, we'll have another attack soon. Memory can't handle them all alone."

"I'll assist." Nikita's immediate agreement was unexpected. Then she added, "A rampant virus will decimate the Net. That is not good for any of us, and if this spreader of infection were sane, they'd be aware of that."

Even with his limited knowledge of Psy politics and power players, Ethan knew Nikita was a financial powerhouse—and that the PsyNet was her home ground. He had zero doubts that she'd survive should it suffer a total and catastrophic failure, but a shredded Net would crash the stock market, devastating her power base.

"So," Krychek said, "at this point, with the available information, it appears we have a major Scarab-linked threat. Without further details, all we can do is watch and respond. Ethan, your job is to watch for and attempt to track back *any* indication of virus activity. That is your priority."

Ethan glanced at Aden and got the squad leader's nod. Because while he was still coming to terms with being part of this brotherhood, he belonged more to them than he did to

Krychek. "Understood," he said, aware that if he could track down the individual behind the macrovirus, he'd save infinitely more lives than if he simply assisted to clean off the infection.

Yet . . . It was a choice to abandon some for the good of the many, and that felt intrinsically wrong to him. Maybe it was because of his bond with Selenka and how she valued each and every person. Including Ethan.

A mind touched his, her voice weaker than Aden's but not "soft" in the way he'd have expected of an empath. *I won't abandon them,* Memory promised when he accepted the communication. *Looks like Nikita won't, either. You don't have to worry.*

A surge began to build at the back of his mind. *Thank you,* he said. *Break off. Contact with you is exacerbating the rogue power.*

Ethan, you have to run the test soon. Your mind is under too much pressure, Memory said quickly before she closed the telepathic link.

Ethan caught a hint of wet iron at that moment, just as his head began to pound like a drum, and said, "I have to go." Disconnecting from the comm call before the bleed showed on his face, he rebuffed Aden's attempt at telepathic contact.

Pain wracked him, so hard that he bent over with his hands on his knees. It felt as if his brain were trying to push its way out past his skull. His blood was fire, the wolf inside him a clawing beast.

"Ethan!"

He heard Selenka's voice from a distance, sensed the force with which she'd slammed open the door, and knew he couldn't fall. He was the mate of an alpha wolf. He was Selenka Durev's mate. And he would stand by her side strong and dangerous. He would be her knight.

Rising to his full height after wiping away the blood, he met a golden gaze. He knew his own eyes had gone black, but he was upright, the pain gritted back behind an expressionless facade.

The origami wolf pack he'd been in the midst of creating lay tumbled on the floor.

"Enough." Selenka sliced out a hand. "I am not going to

stand around and watch you die piece by piece." Striding over, she gripped his jaw with one hand. "Contact Sascha Duncan or I'll do it for you."

"Not here." Ethan wasn't about to budge on this. "I won't bring strangers into your den, won't expose your vulnerable."

Selenka's eyes flashed, but she softened her grip. "Fine. We'll drive to the HQ. Can you arrange for her to meet us there?"

"Yes."

Ethan used Memory's telepathic imprint to send her a message then and there, keeping it as short as possible. *Can Sascha see me soon?*

A pause before she very quickly said, *Thirty minutes. Arrange teleport pickup,* and ended contact.

Ethan told Selenka the time period, and they both ran for the Warren's vehicle bay, Loyal pacing them. It'd be a hard drive to reach the city HQ within that period, but it was doable. At the same time, Ethan switched telepathic "channels" to link with Aden. *I need a teleport assist. DarkRiver territory to BlackEdge's city HQ in thirty minutes.*

Request status?

Urgent.

Wait. That wait period lasted less than ten seconds, during which time they reached an all-wheel-drive vehicle and jumped in, with Selenka in the driver's seat. *Vasic will do the pickup and drop-off. He'll need a visual.*

Sascha Duncan is the pickup. As a cardinal empath, she had to know Vasic's mate, Ivy Jane Zen. Vasic could well already have the necessary visual to anchor a teleport.

His theory was borne out when Aden said, *Vasic will contact Sascha to arrange pickup.*

Thank you. Then he thought of the silent request he'd made and that Aden had promised to fulfill. *I'll need you there when it's time to do the test.*

Aden was quiet for a moment. *Build your shields and do the test, Ethan. I won't lose one of my Arrows without cause—and this is a new world. We don't know all its secrets and we can't predict what our brains will do freed of the shackles of Silence. I'll be there. Should I bring Memory?*

As they drove out into the orange-red of the setting sun,

Loyal panting in the backseat, Ethan thought of how his rogue power reacted to Memory, the ferocity of it. Control would be meaningless unless truly tested. *Yes.*

Dropping out of the telepathic connection, he turned to look at Selenka. Her jaw was clenched, her cheeks flushed, and her hands tight on the steering wheel. "It's all set up. First the shields, then the test."

Her claws erupted from the tips of her fingers. "All the way, Ethan. We test this all the fucking way. I am *not* losing my mate."

Her growl was a vibration in his bones by the time they pulled up at the HQ with five minutes to spare—thanks to Selenka's reflexes. She could drive at lethal speed without error. Entering, they strode toward the back—but Ivo popped out his head from a room before they reached the courtyard.

"Cake?" The slender male, dark circles under his eyes but black jeans and aqua blue shirt sharply pressed, held out a saucer with a large red wedge iced in white. "Chaos"—a glance at Ethan—"that's the bears' head chef, dropped a giant cake off in thanks for me sourcing a rare spice for him a couple of weeks back."

Grabbing the saucer, Selenka took a huge bite, mumbling around it. It sounded something like: "Ghreet, nowam eatin bear cak."

Ethan waved off the offer of a slice, while Loyal walked over to peer out the back door into the courtyard. "Are you a cook, too?"

"No, I'm an eating specialist who has a vested interest in making friends with chefs." Ivo bit into the slice he'd offered Ethan. "And I need the sugar to keep me going. Disciples come off clean as fucking snow, but I don't buy it. *Somebody* in that group is brilliant with sleight-of-hand financial tricks, and my money is on Blaise."

"No shady paper trails?" Selenka asked after demolishing her cake.

Licking off frosting from his upper lip, Ivo shook his head.

"Any indication Blaise—or Nomani—have advanced financial training?"

"No, but that doesn't mean anything. I learned most of

my superskills"—he wiggled the fingers of one hand—"out of interest and obsessive determination."

"Ivo can hack into most Psy databases with one hand tied behind his back," Selenka told Ethan. "Don't give him access to your devices unless you want him knowing your bank account details."

"Hey!" Ivo threw up his hands. "Just because I look doesn't mean I'd ever *use* the information. I have principles!"

Snorting, Selenka jerked her head toward the courtyard.

It was softly lit against the night sky with strings of warm gold-hued lights that crisscrossed the area at roof level. He hadn't noticed them at all in the daytime, but, then again, he hadn't exactly been in the best frame of mind.

Today, his eyes went to the woman who now stood in the center of the courtyard, arms folded and feet set apart. Undaunted by her stance, he crossed the distance to her—and he touched her, because his mate was a wolf . . . and because he needed the contact. Though she didn't pull away when he cupped her cheek, she didn't soften.

He brushed his lips over hers.

When she still didn't soften, he repeated the action over and over while stroking his thumb over her jaw. It took an eon for her to part her lips, even longer for her to put her hands at his waist. Her eyes were slits of gold when he lifted his head.

"Fast learner," she said, her voice husky. "But I will *still* kick your ass if you allow the fear Ming put in you to win."

"You can't," he said, going with instinct. "I'm an Arrow."

A taut moment before she threw back her head and laughed.

Ethan was drinking in that sound, long-buried parts of him stretching and reaching for it, when he felt a prickling at the back of his neck. He turned to find Ivo escorting out Vasic, a heavily muscled male, and a woman with cardinal eyes.

The teleporter, his left uniform sleeve pinned neatly back to the stump where his arm had been removed, spoke to Ethan. "Sascha has my contact details for when she needs to leave. Memory and Aden are both in the city, within a fast drive of this location." He teleported out before Ethan could thank him.

Sascha Duncan looked nothing like her mother. She was tall, her skin honey brown, and her hair a soft ebony. She wore it in a single braid and was dressed in slimline tailored pants in black. The pants had tiny pink flowers on them, the color picked up by her silky long-sleeved top that was cuffed at the wrists and had a floppy bow at the neck.

On her wrist was a bracelet made up of small, colorful blocks that spelled out her name. It fit with nothing else in her outfit, but Ethan knew what it was—a gift from a child. Zaira had a similar bracelet, created for her by two of the children in the Valley, the sunlit place that was the new home of the Arrow Squad.

Then those eyes of cardinal starlight landed on Ethan.

The Architect

Three Consortium power players tracked using Cray's intel.
Two are in custody. The third was killed when she decided to
respond with weapons drawn.

—Abbot Storm, Strike Team Epsilon, to Aden Kai

FINDING EZRA HAD been a revelation. It had shown the
Architect how to unearth more of her kind. More of the new
breed of Psy. Ezra had also given her another gift—he'd
shown her what she could do if given access to other Scarab
minds. Ezra had been cooperative, even thankful for her intervention; he'd been full of terror, clutched at the safety
rope she offered. It had made things so much easier.

Now she had a thread that linked her to him, him to her.
As the empathic Honeycomb was meant to link all the minds
in the PsyNet, creating a strong foundation for their race.

A Honeycomb link was said to stave off madness, but the
Architect had seen the truth with the lens of her new power:
it had always been a mechanism of control and surveillance,
all of them constantly monitored by those who thought
themselves rulers of the Psy. She'd broken the connection
during a period of chaos; no one had noticed. The empath
linked to her probably believed she'd linked to another E in
the aftermath.

But the Architect wasn't about to be a puppet.

No, *she* would be the puppet master, the spider with a
network of powerful minds willing and ready to serve her.
Enslaved in a way that made it seem a joy to serve. Ezra had
been the first. Tonight, she'd found a fourth and he was full
of lightning bolts that spoke of immense power.

Releasing a single virus that she'd delicately and patiently worked so it wouldn't kill, but simply . . . encourage the other mind to be receptive to her own, she didn't immediately target the mind with the virus. Perhaps it would be better to do what she'd done with Ezra and ask for entry.

It was a pity the virus didn't work so neatly with normal minds. She'd tested it on five subjects after first becoming aware of her ability. All five had gone mad and died by their own hand. Oh well, they were beneath her anyway. As were the panicked questions coming in from the stupid in the Consortium who'd permitted themselves to make connections with Cray. She had far more important things to occupy her mind.

There was a miracle taking place among the Psy.

The growth of a new people.

A better people.

The PsyNet belonged to the Architect and her brethren . . . her children.

Chapter 38

It's time. Prepare.

—The Architect

SASCHA DUNCAN WAS far from the first cardinal Ethan had ever met, but the sight of her eyes still had a visceral impact. Cardinal eyes were the most extraordinary eyes in the world. A sweep of obsidian dotted with white "stars," their eyes were pieces of captured night sky. Each set was said to be unique; however, Ethan had never spent enough time with different cardinals side by side to compare. But that Sascha was a power was indisputable.

Her psychic energy pulsed in the air in the same way as Selenka's alpha strength. But where Selenka's power was aggressive, a thing of claws and teeth and dominance, Sascha's was water that just moved around all obstacles in its path.

Selenka half laughed, half groaned right then. "Healer."

Sascha's lips curved. "Alpha." A gently affectionate reply. "I live with one—claws and growls don't work on me, I'm afraid."

"Your mate is a cat," Selenka rumbled. "Wolves are very different."

"That's what Lucas keeps telling me," Sascha said with a light in her eyes that said she wasn't buying it. "This is Clay." She indicated the green-eyed male at her side.

His hair was black against dark skin, as were the cargo

pants he wore with a plain gray T-shirt. That he was a dominant predator wasn't in question, but he wasn't a wolf. No, there was something intrinsically feline about his movements.

Selenka and the leopard shook hands, two predators sizing each other up.

Leaving them to it, Sascha directed her next words at Ethan. "We should speak alone so we can concentrate."

"Clay and I will wait in the HQ," Selenka said, before she hauled Ethan down for a kiss, the wet heat a branding. "Everything, Ethan. You deserve everything. *Fight for it.*"

Her touch, her words, lingered long after she strode into the building. Clay's shadow didn't budge after the male stepped inside the doorway.

"Clay's stubborn," Sascha murmured, catching Ethan's look. "I told him you wouldn't hurt me, and he gave me the 'look' dominants reserve for healers and empaths."

"It's a wise precaution in unfamiliar territory."

"See?" came a growling rumble from inside the doorway. "The Arrow agrees with me."

Lips twitching, Sascha said, "We'll go sit in those outdoor chairs at the far end, where big cat ears can't hear us."

Once seated, Ethan said, "You'll need to look inside my mind?"

Sascha's expression turned solemn, no humor in her now. "That's really why I wanted to speak to you alone—allowing someone inside your mind is a thing that requires great trust, and you don't know me." Leaning forward, she braced her forearms on her thighs. "I'm willing to answer any questions you have, tell you what you need to feel that trust."

"It's not necessary." Ethan didn't budge. "I've decided."

Sascha looked at him for a long moment. "And once you decide, that's it," she said, and it wasn't a question. "Right, then let's get down to it." She sat back up, suddenly a cardinal blazing with power where before she'd been an empath, gentle and kind. "First things first—risk factors?"

Ethan told her about his ability to utilize light as a weapon. "There is a minor chance it'll go wild during the shield-building process while I'm between shields."

"We'll build the new ones first," Sascha clarified. "They'll be up before you lower the old ones." The cardinal shook out her shoulders. "Ready?"

"Yes."

The mental knock against his mind was soft.

It took incredible effort to force himself to lower his public shields, the ones that kept his mind private from the world. *No one* had been inside his mind since the day he broke free of Ming. But Sascha's psychic presence had nothing in common with the former Councilor's. She was also scrupulous in sticking to a path that led only and directly to his inner shields.

It took her time to investigate those shields, but when she finished, it was with a frown even darker than Memory's. "I do sense a massive power behind your shields, but your mind doesn't have the feel of one that's disintegrating."

"There's no other explanation for such a violent power rising to the surface after a lifetime of dormancy." Ming would've certainly taken advantage of any power of Ethan's, especially as he'd been a child when he went into the squad, without the ability to hide anything. "My mind sublimated it for a reason."

Sascha parted her lips before shaking her head. "We'll argue about the what and the why later. First, the shields." She began to throw telepathic instructions at him after requesting access to his mind once more. Ten minutes into it, he realized she was designing his shields from scratch. Her myriad instructions were intended to expose both his strengths and his weaknesses in the area.

Ethan had thought Ming a master shield builder, and there was no question the former Councilor was brilliant at caging minds, but this delicacy of construction was on another level. "Does Aden know you can do this?" he asked halfway through.

"Hmm?" Frowning, she shot him another instruction. "We've never talked specifically on the topic."

"Can I report to him about what you're building for me?" He had a deep need to give back to the squad that had embraced him when he couldn't even embrace himself. "I think you could build better shields for some of the squad."

"Sure." Sascha's attention was obviously on his mind. "I like shield mechanics and we always have Arrows around at the empathic training compound." The instructions came again, so hard and fast that he had to narrow his focus to a tight beam to keep up.

He was sweating by the time she called things to a halt, his heart pounding.

He felt no surprise when his mate walked out with nutrient drinks. Taking one, while Sascha accepted the other, he leaned his head against Selenka's thigh as she stood by his side.

"Ethan," Sascha said after finishing her drink, "I saw a lot while I was inside your mind." No threat or boast in her tone. "I'm not talking about secrets or memories. I'm talking about what you call the rogue power—whatever it is that you have corralled behind those shields is devastatingly powerful. But it feels familiar."

"Scarab abilities are ordinary abilities supercharged," Ethan pointed out.

Sascha nodded in reluctant agreement. "I need to be there when you drop your shield. If not me, then another E you trust. You also need a Psy who's had enough contact with a large range of psychic abilities—including unusual ones—that they're capable of recognizing what it is that exists behind your shields."

"I can—" Ethan began.

"No." The cardinal's tone was unexpectedly hard. "You're deeply biased. You've been conditioned to see it as a threat."

"I've asked Aden to be there, too," Ethan said, realizing he hadn't mentioned that to Selenka. "As a protective measure."

Selenka narrowed her eyes at him but nodded. "As long as he doesn't try to override your mate." She played with his hair while she tapped her foot. "With non-pack players involved, we can't do the experiment at the main den like I originally suggested. But I've got an idea of another place that—"

A scream of agony speared through Ethan's skull. It was so strong, so loud, that it took him a split second to realize it came from the PsyNet. Opening his eyes on the psychic plane, he saw a tidal wave of lightning bolts. Crash after crash, all of it pounding at a section of the Net already in danger of fatal collapse.

A single look and he knew the area was home to tens of thousands.

He got in the way of that power but didn't have the strength to hold it back for longer than a second or two. Then a dark midnight power joined his. "I have it," said a voice as dark, the power behind it so vast that Ethan knew who it was at once: Kaleb Krychek, cardinal telekinetic. But seeing the depth of his power in action, Ethan knew without a doubt that Kaleb was more. Perhaps one of the mythical dual cardinals.

"The PsyNet is buckling here," the other man said.

"It's not buckling," Ethan responded. "It's under attack by waves of power from a focused source." And if Kaleb couldn't see it, it had to be connected with Scarab.

"Follow it," Krychek said at once. "Find the source."

Ethan was already moving before Kaleb spoke, driven by the need to protect tens of thousands of people who didn't deserve to die just because someone had decided to push a PsyNet breach into a catastrophic failure.

Ethan would not sit aside and be a witness to wholesale murder.

Ahead of him, the lightning flashes began to flicker and lose shape, but he could still see the faint afterglow they left in the Net. He caught the last glimpse just before the energy disappeared into a particular mind. *I have it,* he telepathed to Krychek. *Coordinates as follows.*

Aden is on the way to intercept. I must seal this breach. Watch for another strike and send out a warning to us both.

On the physical plane, Ethan was aware of Selenka standing with her hand in his hair, while Sascha rose and said her good-byes. His mate knew he wasn't fully present, but she didn't push for him to return . . . and he understood. She might be furious with him for inadvertently delaying the experiment, but she would not supersede his decisions—because she wasn't his alpha. She was his mate.

It wasn't until some time later that Aden confirmed the target had been acquired, and Ethan dropped out of the Net.

He woke to Ivo sitting in the chair opposite, the otherwise empty courtyard surrounded by night and lit by the soft glow of the strings of lights he'd noticed earlier. "How long?" he asked after taking the nutrient drink the other man held out.

"Ninety minutes." Dropping the large tablet he'd been working on into his lap, the lieutenant ran a hand over his smooth-shaven scalp, revealing the titanium of a bracelet Ethan had seen on him each time they met. "Selenka had to return to the den—a juvenile managed to injure himself pretty badly doing a stupid stunt. As alpha, Selenka can share pack energy with the healers and the wounded."

Ethan thought of how Selenka had known of Emanuel's death, understood she was bonded to her pack by blood. "Will the juvenile be all right?" BlackEdge couldn't take another loss, another hurt.

"Dinara's the one who responded first after the accident— she messaged me just before you woke to say he's out of the woods. Except for having to face the maternals after he's up and running." Ivo whistled. "Would *not* want to be him. They're so nice and make things all homey—until you cross them. Then—" He drew a finger blade across his throat.

Ethan guessed that "maternals" were part of the wolf hierarchy, but it was a question he shelved in favor of another. "Where's Loyal?" When Ivo looked blank, he said, "My dog."

"Oh, the skinny guy. I got him a treat; then Selya took him back with her. She thought he might get distressed with you unresponsive."

Shoulders easing, Ethan took in the other man again. "Why are you here?"

A raised eyebrow. "You were out of it, Ethan. Selenka wasn't about to leave you helpless—and neither would any of us." His next words held an intensity that was a wolf's fur against Ethan's skin. "She's our heart and you're hers."

The words hit him hard—as did the realization of his vulnerability. Always before while on the psychic plane, he'd continued to be fully aware of the physical plane. It looked like following the lightning strikes, however, caused a full physical detachment. "Did she say anything about the location for an experiment I intend to run?"

Ivo nodded, but the comm on Ethan's gauntlet went off before he could speak.

"Take that." The lieutenant rose, and in that move was evidence of the fluid muscle Ethan had seen the night Ivo helped move the body of his murdered friend. "I have to use the head anyway."

Ethan was unsurprised to find Aden's face on the screen built into the gauntlet. "How," the squad leader said, "did you find the source of the power surge?"

"I tracked its signature. You can't see it?" he asked, to confirm what he'd realized after Kaleb entered the Net.

"Nobody can see it. We've been assuming the Net is fracturing because of the underlying disintegration. We had no reason to believe the damage was being exacerbated by violent surges of power."

"Earlier collapses may have been simpler. Kaleb did see a ripple in the Net today."

"It's becoming increasingly difficult to hold the Net together—this type of concentrated attack could make it impossible." Aden's face was tired. "Are you available for teleport pickup?"

Ethan looked up to see Ivo walking back to him. "A moment." Muting his end of the call, he spoke to the man who was now his packmate.

"Coming with you." Ivo's expression was resolute. "Your eyes aren't quite all there yet."

Ethan understood brotherhood now—both among the squad and in the pack. So he simply nodded, then confirmed the pickup with Aden. "Out in front of BlackEdge's city HQ," he said, he and Ivo walking out together.

Vasic arrived moments later. The teleporter was now wearing a metal prosthetic that had colored lines of electronics and what appeared to be veins. Not a man who spoke often, Vasic just met their gazes in greeting before completing the 'port.

And Ethan found himself in a screamingly white corridor broken up only by hard plas chairs of dull gray that were bolted to the wall—and an unnaturally green plant that proved to be fake.

The walls threatened to close in on him.

Chapter 39

Create fail-safe switch in servant minds in case of capture.
Difficulty level apt to be very high. Begin work on it at once.
—Note to self from the Architect

"WHERE ARE WE?" Ethan asked, fighting his revulsion; the place reminded him strongly of the infirmary where he'd been taken after his physical punishments.

"PsyMed SF Echo," said the woman of medium height who stood with Aden, her English holding a lilting accent and her curvy body clad in a tailored black jumpsuit around the neck of which hung a plain old stethoscope—a device that had survived all the ages of modernity.

"I'm Dr. Maia Ndiaye." Her eyes were large, the shade a dark brown flecked with amber, her skin blue-black, and her hair obscured by a vivid green scarf that she wore wrapped around her hair in a complicated pattern.

From his research, Dr. Ndiaye was a forty-one-year-old M-Psy with a specialization in neurology who hit 9.3 on the Gradient, but her face had no lines of age, and her presence didn't pulse with power. She'd grown up in Silence, he realized, likely had intense control over what she projected.

"The target you pinpointed." Aden nodded toward a door not far from them.

When Ethan looked through the window at the top of that door, it was to see a thin blond woman sitting in a high-tech hospital bed. Dressed in pale blue pajama pants and a matching top, she was staring straight ahead at the wall in front of her, her lips moving.

Ethan's muscles locked.

"We found her in this state," Aden said quietly. "She hasn't come out of it."

"It could be a deep fugue state." Dr. Ndiaye's voice didn't alter in pitch or tone, but Ethan sensed a type of concern that had him reassessing his initial view of her as entombed in Silence. "Her mind displays the classic symptoms of Scarab—per all the confirmed cases to date."

A flicker to the right, Memory Aven-Rose and her mate appearing with Kaleb Krychek. The empath flinched as if hit hard by a painful object, her head jerking toward the room that held the patient.

"Scarab," she said. "Definitely." A deep inhale, an embrace with her mate, then she walked through the door.

As Ethan watched, she touched her hand to the patient's hand and held it there. The woman blinked not long afterward, shook her head, and focused on Memory. *"Qui es-tu?"* she asked. *"Où suis-je?"*

Ethan didn't know French, but Dr. Ndiaye did and translated: "Who are you? Where am I?"

While Memory murmured to the woman, and Dr. Ndiaye slipped in to join them, Aden spoke to Ethan. "It looks like you can track sufferers of Scarab Syndrome when they begin to lose control and surrender to the urge to free their powers." He glanced in the direction of the patient room. "We don't know why she decided to attack the integrity of the PsyNet, but I need you to maintain a watch for any others like her."

Ethan thought about the lightning echoes, the ghosts he saw constantly. "Aden, there are a lot. I can't track them until they go active and use their power, but their signature is all over the PsyNet."

Aden's dark eyes evidenced no surprise. He'd expected it, Ethan realized, was braced for it. Braced for anarchy. "Rest," the leader of the squad said, thrusting one hand through the short strands of his hair. "We're going to need you in the battles to come."

Ethan didn't step away. "What about you? I can see exhaustion in every inch of you."

Aden's responding glance held rueful acknowledgment.

"Zaira's threatened to tie me to our bed if I'm not back in an hour and ready to rest." A frown. "When is the experiment? Zaira knows I have to be present for that."

The power surges inside Ethan had grown to a point where intervention was urgent, but he was nearly swaying on his feet. Surrendering to the inevitable, he said, "I'll need to get some downtime before I can continue. I'll contact Zaira when I need you."

Then he asked Vasic to take him and Ivo back to the pickup point.

Once there, the wolf lieutenant nodded toward a vehicle parked nearby, the street night-quiet. "Better if you're in den territory if you're going to crash."

Ethan's head felt heavy as he took the passenger seat, his eyes threatening to close. As he struggled to keep them open, Ivo started up the engine. "Take a nap. You're wiped."

Ethan wasn't used to just shutting down and leaving his well-being in another's hands, but this man had already kept watch while Ethan wasn't mentally present. "One day, I'll return the favor," he managed to get out before his eyes shut.

"Next time I decide to lose my mind and have a beer or five with a bear, I'll expect you to be my wingman."

Ethan didn't understand the reference, but he was too tired to follow it up. Relaxing into the seat, he permitted his mind to slip into sleep. A curtain fell over his thoughts, the last thing he felt a kiss along the mating bond.

"ETHAN, wake up."

He came awake at once at the urgency of Ivo's tone, but opened his lashes a bare fraction, using the caution of a man who'd often woken in an unfriendly situation. Their vehicle was stationary on a quiet road Ethan recognized as being about ten minutes from den territory.

In front of them was a fallen tree that blocked the path forward, a small dark-colored truck crumpled half-under it.

Ethan lifted his lashes, scanned the area. "I sense two changeling minds."

Leaning on the steering wheel, his eyes nightglow, Ivo said, "That's an old tree, could've come down on its own . . .

but I don't like it. Nice and convenient to have it happen while someone's trying to kill Selenka's lieutenants." His voice held none of its customary lightness, his tone hard. "Are the two minds in the truck?"

"One is either inside or very close to it. The other is in the trees." Ethan couldn't get much more than that without attempting a psychic breach.

Ivo opened his door after a careful scan of the area. "I can't hear anything and I won't scent anything until I'm closer. My gut doesn't like it, but I have to check in case two of our people had an accident. That truck looks like some in our fleet, and one person could've been thrown out."

Ethan went to open his door but Ivo shook his head. "Stay back. Moon's out, but it's still pretty dark. I usually drive home alone—if it *is* an ambush, you can be a nice unwelcome surprise."

"Understood." With the moon providing enough light to fuel him even without the assistance of light sources such as his phone, Ethan could assist from a distance, so it made sense for Ivo to make the initial reconnaissance, while Ethan watched his back. "Call it in before you go."

Ivo did that in silence by sending a message via his phone, then left quietly, without latching his door. Ethan watched him with unrelenting focus . . . and just barely glimpsed the shadow rising from in front of the crumpled truck, its arm lifted in a firing stance.

Ethan shot a bolt of light through the glass of the windscreen. As it shattered around him, he was aware of two things—first, his blow hadn't hit the target but the vehicle, and second, the other mind he'd sensed had used his distraction to move closer. Close enough to point a weapon at Ethan's temple.

His response was the result of years of Arrow training—and a grim fury that anyone would dare hurt Selenka in such a way. He dropped sideways into the seat while unclipping the seat belt. The laser fire cut over his head, close enough to singe, but he was already kicking the door open—right into the would-be assassin's body. He was outside the door a split second later. The shooter was in the midst of attempting to swing the weapon back in his direction.

A burst of light and the assailant was down.

He looked up to find Ivo standing unmoving over his assailant's body, his claws dripping and his formerly pristine shirt flecked with wet shadows. From the thrust of her breasts as she lay on her back, he could tell the second assailant had been female. Her mind no longer existed on the psychic plane.

She was dead. And Ivo wasn't moving.

After using ties from his pocket to immobilize the male who'd attacked him, Ethan walked over to Ivo, driven by an instinct he couldn't understand—one that told him the lieutenant needed him. But he didn't touch Ivo. Instead, he crouched down beside the woman's bloody body, her abdomen torn out by wolf claws.

Death spasms meant she still clutched her weapon.

"Set to kill." He indicated the clearly visible setting. "At that range, it would've liquefied your brains. One of you had to die."

The lieutenant took a long breath, exhaled harshly. "It's Blaise's sister, Nomani." A look over at where Ethan's assailant lay next to their vehicle. "Blaise is alive?"

"Yes." Ethan had recognized him from the images he'd downloaded of the church leader after the intrusion onto BlackEdge land.

"Good." Ivo's bunched shoulders eased up a fraction. "Selenka's going to want to question him."

With Ivo still emotionally unstable, Ethan was the one who called Selenka, and he felt the fury of her rage along the mating bond, her wolf ready to tear down the world. But she said, "Look out for Ivo."

Once he'd hung up, Ethan went to their vehicle and found a bottle of water in the back, which he took back to the wolf. "To wash your hands." Ivo hadn't yet retracted his claws, and Ethan could tell the blood bothered him.

The other man didn't say a word as they stepped away from the scene, but took care to wash his hands with attention to detail, while Ethan poured the water in a steady stream. Only once his claws were free of blood did he retract them. He then washed his palms off. And when Ethan shrugged off his uniform jacket and said, "You're more slender than I am. It'll fit," Ivo didn't refuse the gesture.

He took off his blood-splattered shirt, used a clean edge to wipe off any blood on his skin, then pulled on the jacket over a bare chest. *"Spasibo."* A rough word, a short nod, Ivo's eyes not quite meeting his.

The bloody shirt and empty water bottle in hand, Ethan said, "I hate being shut up in rooms without light. The walls crush me until I can't breathe."

Ivo froze . . . then met Ethan's eyes again, his own night-glow with the wolf. He nodded slowly. "We're all a little fucked up." A slight smile, a deep release of the tension in his muscles. "Thanks for that warning shot. She was just out of sight, the angle I was walking. If you hadn't turned the night ablaze, I might be lying there with liquefied brains."

Features grim but no longer distraught in that quiet, withdrawn way, Ivo glanced at the body before the two of them began to walk back to their vehicle. "This is technically still our territory," Ivo told Ethan as he put the bloody shirt and empty bottle in back. "The only vehicles that use this road are those coming in and out from BlackEdge."

"Does this attack seem strange to you? It's after ten at night, for one."

"That's not so strange." Ivo shrugged. "The HQ has a five percent better data link. I've been known to work till all hours there, then drive home." Despite his words, he was scowling. "But I crash in the HQ just as often, so it's a lot of trouble to go to, on the off chance they'd get me. Unless the fuckers were happy to settle for any BlackEdge wolf."

Ethan shook his head. "There's too much risk in this—they had to hit a high-ranking target for it to pay off."

Ivo parted his lips, then paused, head angled. "Jetcycle coming in from the city."

Ethan didn't pick up the sound for another half a minute. When the jetcycle came to a stop beside their vehicle not long afterward, the man who took off his helmet proved to be Selenka's father. He took in the scene, his pupils flaring. *"Bozhe moi,"* what have you done?"

Ethan went motionless. "You aren't surprised to see these two here." It was a sense inside him that he couldn't explain.

Mouth tightening, Selenka's father snarled, "I don't have to explain myself to some Psy interloper."

As Ivo growled deep in his chest, Ethan lifted a hand limned with light. "I can burn out your irises and leave you blind, or, if you prefer, I can amputate your arms and legs. Or you can answer my questions."

Kiev Durev's cheeks went hot with color. "You wouldn't dare."

Ethan sliced horizontal stripes across the other man's arms, each line flawless. The smell of burned flesh hit the air as Kiev screamed.

"I have no loyalty to you," Ethan said, "and I have no desire to protect you. If you are a threat to Selenka, I will end you right now."

Whimpering, Kiev stared at Ivo. "Do something!"

Ivo folded his arms.

Kiev snarled before turning back to Ethan, his face red. "She'll hate you for hurting me."

That might well be true, but Ethan would still protect her. "Are you prepared to answer or shall I perform the first amputation?" He lifted a hand licked by shadowlight.

Flinching, Kiev began talking. "Blaise wanted me to help smooth things over with the pack, with Selenka, that's all."

"His people would've burned our territory." Ivo's voice trembled, the words hard to understand, they were so rough.

"It was only youths being stupid," Kiev argued. "At least he was respectful when he called me—he understood he had to go through the pack's elders. Now look what you've done!" A pointed glance at the bloody body by the fallen tree. "The world already thinks changelings uncivilized monsters; you've proven them right."

"What was your task here tonight?" Ethan had an idea and it was turning his blood to black ice; he wanted to end Kiev Durev then and there.

Kiev tried to slide around the question. "Blaise wanted to do it late at night because he thought Selenka would be more relaxed then, in a receptive frame of mind."

Ethan's hand glowed.

"Fine!" The older man threw his helmet on the ground. "I was to go to the den, get Selenka out here so they could meet in privacy." He swallowed hard. "But I'm twenty minutes late and it's all ruined now!"

Ethan wondered if the other man really was that stupid, or if he truly didn't care that the people he wanted to assist had set his daughter up to die. The answer didn't matter to Ethan. All he wanted to do was end this threat to his mate.

Ivo closed his hand over Ethan's forearm. "Selenka's call." A whisper so quiet it would reach only Ethan.

Knight, Ethan reminded himself, *I'm her knight. She is the queen.* And this wasn't an exigent circumstance.

As if giving Ethan time to regain control, Ivo bared his teeth. "How did Blaise and Nomani get out of their compound without being tracked? Gregori has the place under full watch."

Ducking his head, Kiev mumbled something too low for Ethan to hear, but Ivo's chest rumbled. "One of Blaise's congregation deliberately got into an argument with a sentry as a distraction so the two could slip out."

"You didn't find that strange?" Ethan managed to say through his cold need to kill. "That they'd use subterfuge to get out instead of simply requesting a meeting?"

"Blaise couldn't even get through to Selenka! Artem blocked him!" Kiev's eyes weren't human anymore . . . and they were gold rather than the more prevalent shades of amber.

Father and daughter.

But genetics was where the bond ended. Because as Ethan considered everything that had happened to date, the pieces clicked into place one by one. "You planned to meet with Blaise once before, didn't you?" He spread out his palm, fingers glowing. "On the day of Emanuel's murder."

Chapter 40

Endless masks
A cupboard of faces
Betrayal painted in glitter
— "Duplicity" by Adina Mercant, poet (b. 1832, d. 1901)

ANOTHER JETCYCLE SOUNDED from the direction of den territory before Kiev Durev could respond. Exchanging a glance with Ivo, Ethan stopped the questioning. It was two jetcycles that emerged, not from the road, but from the trees. Parking their sleek black vehicles side by side, Margo and Selenka strode over.

Ethan's mate took in both him and Ivo. "No injuries?"

Even as they confirmed they were unharmed, her father jumped off his own jetcycle. "I'm the fucking injured one! Look what your pet Psy did!"

Selenka's look was as hard as stone. "If you can't handle a couple of small bites, you don't deserve to call yourself a wolf." Her voice was pitiless. "What're you doing here, Father?" This time, Ethan heard the "push" in her voice, the tone of an alpha who wanted an answer. *Now.*

Kiev Durev sweated and looked away before mumbling out the same explanation he'd given Ethan. Pain raked its claws across Selenka's features, but she was stone-faced again by the time her father looked up. "Is this the first time you've collaborated with Blaise?"

"It wasn't collaboration! The Disciples can help us be more a part of the future, civilized and intelligent!" His voice was breathy and his eyes kept flicking away. "Look at the respect Blaise commands from his flock without any show of brawn."

"Did you intend to meet him the day Emanuel was killed?" Selenka's voice was colder than Ethan had ever heard it, colder than he'd imagined she could ever sound—yet it wasn't a Psy cold. No, this cold was a flame so hot it had turned blue.

When Kiev didn't reply, she said, *"Did you intend to meet him on the day of Emanuel's murder?"* The threat in her voice was a knife thudding into bone, claws ripping flesh off the body.

"Yes." Kiev spoke as if the word was torn out of him, his Adam's apple bobbing. "But he got spooked at being caught in our territory without a guide and took off before I arrived. He was long gone by the time Emanuel was murdered!"

To Ethan, it appeared that Kiev actually believed that. Or he'd told himself that so many times that he'd turned a hope into a truth.

"Did you disable the cameras at our border?" Selenka's voice had no give in it, no forgiveness.

"What? No." A flicker of confusion. "I don't do technology."

"But you know it well enough to call in a false alert about a lost child using an ID stolen from an elder."

Kiev Durev paled. "I didn't permit Blaise anywhere close to the den," he said, as if that excused anything. "The area in our territory was just a good private meeting spot."

That made no logical sense. If Kiev had wanted to meet Blaise away from prying eyes, all he had to do was go to Blaise's church. To bring an outsider into pack territory without his alpha's permission and knowledge? It reeked of arrogance that said Kiev Durev was more important than anyone else—more important than the safety of his pack.

Selenka's face mirrored Ethan's thoughts, the bleak pain Ethan felt emanating along the mating bond shuttered behind a stony facade. "Your punishment will depend on what Blaise says when he wakes up, but, Father?" She waited until Kiev met her gaze. "We're done. There is no longer any father-daughter relationship between us. I am your alpha and you *will* obey my commands or you will die at my claws."

Kiev's face went white. He, too, had heard the finality in Selenka's voice, heard the lack of give.

Leaving the older male standing helplessly next to his jetcycle, she strode over to join Ethan and Ivo while Margo continued to crouch by Nomani's body, a phone to her ear. The first thing Selenka did was cup Ethan's jaw and look into his eyes. Apparently satisfied by what she saw, she dropped her hand and turned to Ivo. He got the same intense scrutiny before she said, "Tell me what happened."

Ivo did the talking and it didn't take long. The lieutenant ended with, "Her weapon was set to kill. I had to take her out." There was no guilt in those words, and his body didn't tense up.

"Blaise's weapon was also set to kill." Ethan showed Selenka where the weapon had fallen. "I believe we were a target of opportunity. You were the intended one." Even saying the words made shards of light ricochet inside him, body and mind both ready to eliminate the threat.

His mate stepped in to tug him down for a kiss.

When she broke it, he had moved away from the murderous precipice.

"There's also a slight chance they intended to kill your father." Ivo folded his arms across the jacket he'd never zipped up.

"No. Blaise wouldn't eliminate his source of intelligence about BlackEdge." The wolf lived in Selenka's eyes. "Ivo, you go brief Margo. Tell her I want a team at the church to round up the congregation. Sit tight on them until I decide what comes next."

A groan, Blaise stirring. But the cult leader wasn't yet awake.

Selenka looked at Ethan after Ivo was out of earshot. "You say something to Ivo about the weapon being set to kill?"

"It was," Ethan replied. "He had no choice."

"The woman attacked a predator. She asked for death," Selenka said on a growl. "But Ivo, he has scars not so different from yours." Fingers caressing his jaw. "You took care of one of ours, Ethan, and because you did, Ivo will probably sleep tonight instead of waking with nightmares."

Blaise groaned again, his eyelids fluttering. Hauling the male up so his back was against the side of the car, his arms tied behind him and his ankles lashed in front, Ethan then stood watch, ready to take him down the instant he became a threat.

Selenka didn't crouch down to speak to him. Feet set apart, she stared down at Blaise as he focused on her with eyes boiling with rage. "I'll have you prosecuted for this!" were the first words out of his mouth. "You animals can't go around attacking innocent civilians."

"Since you seem to have forgotten, Blaise," Selenka drawled, "you're an animal, too. So was your sister. Now she's just cold, decomposing flesh."

Blaise's face chilled. "You're lying. Nomi! Nomi!" When it was silence alone that greeted his cries, he screamed. "Murderers!"

Selenka leaned down and slapped him. Just once. Very hard. With claws scraping lines across his cheek.

The noise cut off, but the rage continued to boil.

"You attempted to kill my mate and one of my lieutenants," she said. "Why?"

"You're going to take the word of a Psy assassin over one of your own kind?" Blaise spit on the ground. "No wonder your father is ashamed to have you as a daughter."

"Make up your mind, Blaise. Either you're one of us or we're filthy animals." Selenka raised an eyebrow. "And yes, I'll take my mate's word over that of a man who murdered one of mine."

The flicker of satisfaction was fast, there one second and gone the next, but Selenka caught it. Snarling, she struck out with a clawed hand . . . only to bring her claws to a stop a bare millimeter from the wet ball of Blaise's left eye. Perspiration scented the air, his fear acrid. It gave her no satisfaction. Emanuel was still dead, and for what?

"You don't get to die easy," she whispered silkily. "I'm going to give you to Emanuel's parents and brother." Taking vengeance for their son and brother was the only thing she could give them to assuage their pain—maybe humans would find it barbaric, but she wasn't human and neither were they.

"Bitch."

Selenka held up a hand when she felt Ethan stir. "Yes, I am. A deadly bitch who is going to raze Haven's Disciples down to the foundations and wipe your name from history." She smiled as he jerked toward her, as if wanting to headbutt her. "It's pathetic, really, how small and weak you truly are—so weak that you had to kill with a weapon instead of your claws, and had to manipulate *children* to do your dirty work."

Blaise snapped. "You think you're so wonderful. Selenka Durev, granddaughter of Yevgeni Durev. Such an honorable lineage. Do you ever ask your grandfather about the friend he shoved out into the cold to cover his own ass? Do you ever wonder where your grandfather gets the money for all these trips he takes with his mate?"

Selenka stared at Blaise. "Andriy Golyas," she said slowly. "I see it now, in the shape of your face, the color of your eyes. I saw a photo of your father a long time ago." It had been after her grandfather stepped down, when he took her through the pack's history.

She could still remember the dual lines of anger and pain on his face as he told her the full story of the packmate of his who'd been a highly qualified accountant, the perfect person to help Yevgeni and his lieutenants maneuver a growing pack's finances. Andriy Golyas was guilty of many crimes—including fracturing a part of Yevgeni Durev's generous and loyal heart.

Yet because the crimes had all been financial, with Andriy not taking enough to affect the physical health of his packmates, her grandfather had followed unwritten pack law and imposed a sentence of expulsion instead of execution. BlackEdge wolves rarely demanded blood for nonphysical crimes.

"Andriy didn't have a son when he was exiled from the pack," Selenka murmured. "He didn't have any children."

"He met my mother after he was kicked out of the pack." Blaise's face was red, his words like bullets. "We had to scrape by alone because no pack would take us. Your grandfather badmouthed him all over the world."

"My grandfather simply answered questions when asked. As I would if another pack asked me if an exile was safe to have in the pack." Selenka couldn't imagine spending an entire life nursing hate, and yet this was what Blaise and Nomani had done. "Your father not only embezzled from his own people after being given a position of great trust, he betrayed his alpha over and over again."

"Lies!" Blaise wrenched against his bonds. "Lies! Your grandfather took the money and put the blame on him!"

"Blaise, I don't know what Andriy told you, what poison he fed you, but the pack brought in a neutral human auditing team to do the accounts in the aftermath." Yevgeni had given them full access to all records and then left them alone to do their job. "Your father blew tens of thousands of pack funds on high-class escorts."

"My father was a good man! A blessed man! A man of God!"

Selenka twisted her mouth. "There are plenty of wolves still alive who know the truth and will give it to you—but I don't think you're interested in the truth. I just want to know one thing: why did you kill Emanuel?"

Having obviously decided that he had nothing to lose, Blaise bared his teeth. "BlackEdge took everything my father loved. Why should you be happy?" A harsh laugh. "At least your father despises you. That'll delight me for the rest of my life."

Ethan's light power burned, wanting out, wanting to eliminate the threat of Blaise. He held it back with sheer force of will. He was the knight, he repeated to himself. Selenka was the queen. A queen who had made her decision. Taking out her phone, she walked away into the trees—after stopping by Margo for a short discussion.

When Blaise tried to taunt Ethan into a conversation, Ethan burned an *X* onto his cheek. It was a deliberate choice on his part—Blaise was a man well aware of his looks and proud of them.

Eyes red with fury, Blaise nonetheless got the message and shut up.

Selenka said nothing about the new mark when she returned. "Emanuel's parents and brother have accepted the vengeance due to them." Her tone was merciless. "They've asked to hunt you to the death. You will know fear and pain and helplessness before you leave this earth. It will never be enough to make up for the murder of a wolf worth a hundred of you, but it will be justice."

Blaise hissed at her . . . and the area around his body began to shimmer.

A glance from his mate and Ethan hit the male with his light. Blaise slumped, the shift stopping before it began. Selenka looked impassively at the cult leader. "What did he think? That he'd escape me in wolf form?"

"The man has delusions of power."

Selenka's expression didn't change. "I have to drop him off at a particular spot. I'll see you afterward."

"I'll find you." The mating bond was bruised with her pain, but she needed to be alpha right now, and he needed to back her up. But he'd hold her before this night was out, and he'd remind her that trust wasn't always betrayed, and people didn't always let you down.

Instead of leaving right then, Selenka turned to Kiev Durev, who was sitting on the ground in a fog of shock. "You were disloyal to your pack and your alpha," she said flatly. "Those actions led to the presence of an enemy in our lands and to the death of one of our own. At which point, you sought to hide your disloyalty instead of helping the pack find the killer."

Kiev Durev's hands shook as he rubbed his face. "I didn't know. I swear it."

"Your vows are meaningless." The words were cut from glass, each one a razor-sharp shard. "Emanuel's family doesn't want your head—they're more merciful than I would be in their place and I think they do this for their alpha, even though I made it clear execution was on the table."

Because, Ethan understood, her packmates loved her and not even for their own vengeance would they put her in the position of having to execute her father. That she'd been willing to do it would be enough for them . . . and was crushing for Kiev Durev. For the first time, the man looked broken.

"But," Selenka continued, "they never want to see your face again and neither do I. You may remain a member of

BlackEdge, but you are banished from den territory. Your actions will be made known to the pack and your possessions delivered to your office. Should you attempt to enter den territory, you will be executed on sight."

Kiev's face was a white sheet. "I'll be an outcast. Selen—"

"You do not *ever* address me as anything but Alpha Durev."

Swallowing, Kiev said, "What will I do? I'm a wolf. How can I live without pack?"

"At least you get to live. Be thankful for that." A hunting wolf in her voice. "Grandfather showed mercy in allowing Andriy to live and it ended in blood—and will cause him pain he does not deserve. I have the veto of an alpha, can end you now regardless of anyone else's wishes, but Grandfather and Grandmother will mourn you even if you are not worth a single tear—and so I will bow to the wishes of Emanuel's family and allow you to continue breathing."

With that, she turned on her heel and didn't look back, a queen who had made a brutal judgment and would not flounder . . . not even when Ethan could feel the blood dripping from the grievous wounds on her heart.

Chapter 41

Changeling justice is brutal in its honesty. We humans love to call it barbaric, but is it not more barbaric for a proven murderer to walk free because of a legal loophole?
—Editorial by Oceane Vargas for *The San Francisco Gazette* (January 2082)

SELENKA FELT NO pity for Blaise when she dropped his semiconscious body in a small forest clearing, only a hot, primal satisfaction. Emanuel's parents and Vadem weren't stupid and had no intention of allowing Blaise to escape—she could scent them on the air, knew they were in the trees already.

This was also deep in the pack's territory. The chance he'd slip out was close to nil, but Emanuel's friends had weighted things in his family's favor even further by ringing the entire area. Most of those friends were powerful dominants—including Gregori and Artem.

Blaise would not survive this night.

As she cut the ties at his wrists and ankles, Blaise came awake enough to say, "Barbaric animal."

"I'm at peace with who I am." She wasn't her father, to want to be something other—Selenka Durev was a changeling wolf and would go to her grave proud to be a changeling wolf. "You could've come to this pack and been accepted as one of our own. Did your father tell you that?"

Blaise's eyes held too much hate to accept anything she said, but she told him the truth that had been erased by another man full of bitterness. "We don't blame the child for the crimes of the father. He could've raised you to know you could always come home to BlackEdge. Instead, he chose to raise you in hate."

"I'm not the only one raised in hate," Blaise growled back, his wolf coming into his eyes and his claws slicing out. "Your father can't stand you."

"That's the thing, Blaise—I wasn't raised by my father. And that is a gift for which I'm thankful each and every day." Stepping back, she said, "I hope you die with courage, finding honor in this at least."

She disappeared into the trees as he entered the shift, but she didn't go far. As she'd expected, he lunged in her direction the instant he was in wolf form . . . only to come face-to-face with two gray wolves who had no pity for the killer of their child. A third, more deadly wolf stood farther back.

Vadem, giving his grief-stricken parents the opportunity to strike the first blow.

Seeing they had the situation under control, Selenka left in truth. When a large wolf with fur of reddish brown stepped in her path, she crouched down to hug him around the neck, rubbing her cheek against his fur. "Watch over them, Gregori. Make sure they get the vengeance that may allow them some peace."

She left to the sound of his answering growl.

Though she'd driven up with Blaise, she ran home, needing to burn up her rage and grief. It was halfway to the den that she felt a shift in the jagged bond that tied her to Ethan and knew her mate was close. She didn't know if all mating bonds worked this way, but she hoped theirs would always be like this.

Always.

Teeth gritted at the reminder that her mate was in a critical state, she ran in the direction from which she'd sensed him and realized he was coming at her from the site she'd found for the shield experiment.

Ivo must've shown it to him, after Margo's team arrived to clean up the location of the ambush. Nomani, as an enemy of the pack, would not be given a burial. Selenka had made that call at the site. But, because Nomani could've been a child of BlackEdge if she hadn't been twisted by her father, Selenka had ordered that she be taken to the city's bio-cremation facility and her ashes left there to be collected should she have any family who claimed her.

Unclaimed ashes were returned to the earth.

The pack would do the same for Blaise if there were enough pieces left of him by the time this night was over. The only reason Selenka had made that decision was because she'd seen what bitterness and envy and hate could do to a person—and she'd experienced how it could affect a child. Who would she be today if her grandparents hadn't taken over the raising of her?

She wanted to believe she'd have found her way, been a good adult, but no one could say that for certain. And because she'd been loved and taught the right path, she could take this small mercy on the children of Andriy Golyas. Mercy she would never show to her father—Kiev had been raised in Yevgeni's and Lada's love, too, yet he'd *chosen* a path that led him to betray the pack.

Growling low in her throat, she exploded out of the trees and saw Ethan looking directly at her. Ivo was nowhere in sight. Coming straight to her, he slid his arms around her waist before bending his head and burying his face against her neck.

Undone by the sudden bolt of affection, of her formerly remote Arrow asking for affection, she forgot her simmering anger and wove the fingers of one hand into his hair, her other hand on his nape. "Hey." She nuzzled at him, nipping lightly at his throat as she did so.

He held her even tighter, stroking her back and dropping small kisses on her skin. Until Selenka was the one who had her face buried against his neck, and he was the one murmuring to her. She didn't cry, *couldn't* cry. Not yet. "I never truly had a father, so it's not a loss." It was a hard thing to accept, but it helped in a way. "But making that final cut, releasing the hope I didn't even know I'd been carrying around . . . yeah, it hurts. Bad."

"You are loved." Ethan's voice was rough, his words firm. "Your grandfather, your pack. I don't know if my concept of love is the right one, but I know I would lay down my life for you. I know that when I'm with you, I feel . . . unbroken."

Selenka's claws sliced out, her wolf rising. "You're mine, Ethan." Jagged pieces and cold and all.

When he kissed her, she went to pull away, tell him they

had to take care of what was happening in his brain, but then he said, "Please, Selenka. I need you," and she crumbled.

Her Ethan wasn't a man who ever asked for anything. For him to ask for skin privileges so openly, it wasn't a request she could ever deny. Opening her mouth under his, she sank into the kiss, sank into him.

His breath was fast, his pulse staccato when she dropped her head to kiss his throat. He shifted back only so he could pull off his T-shirt, then closed the distance between them once more, his body all hard lines and ridges.

Grabbing her hands, he put them on the hot silk of his bare skin . . . and shivered. "Beautiful man," she whispered huskily, petting him with a possessiveness that was only growing as the days passed. "I want to eat you up, Ethan Night."

About to drop her head to kiss his chest, she found herself being spun around, her jacket pulled off her arms.

A pulse between her thighs, her breasts swelling against the lace cups of her bra.

Jacket off, she raised her arms and Ethan pulled up her tank top to throw it aside without care before he hugged her from the back, his face buried in the curve of her neck. Skin to skin, chest to back, lips to throat.

And yet, he remembered not to put too much pressure on her healing skin, her Arrow who had a vein of protectiveness as wide as the Moskva River. Then he pushed up the lace of her bra to release one breast, and cupped his hand over it with open possession, squeezing and molding.

Moaning, Selenka reached back to scrape her nails over his nape before she turned in his arms, desperate to claim his lips. He met her lick for lick, one hand cupped around the side of her neck, while he tugged at her bra in frustration with his other. Nipping at his lower lip, she reached back to unhook the bra and drop it to the forest floor. His eyes zeroed in on her bare breasts, his erection shoving at the fastening of his pants.

Dropping her hands to her waistband, she flicked open the button . . . then smiled with wolfish intent. "Catch me."

She kept her speed down because this was play, but he moved far faster than she'd expected. Hooking one foot around her ankle before she'd even exited the clearing, he tripped her—only to catch her so that she fell against his body.

"Caught." It was a satisfied statement.

"That'll teach me to underestimate an Arrow," she said with a soft laugh, delighted by him and this unexpected moment of joy. Claws out, she scratched lightly at his nape as he kissed her again with open-mouthed demand, her breasts pressed to the taut muscle of his chest. There was a layer of hair there, the curls crisp against her nipples.

She rubbed up against him.

Body rigid, he released her only so he could tear at her pants. Aroused by his need, her own body slick, she helped him undress her, and then, somehow, she had her legs around his hips and her back was pressed to a tree trunk—with Ethan's forearm a barrier between her skin and the rough bark—and he was kissing her as if she was the tastiest dish he'd ever sampled and he'd never get enough.

"This is an advanced position, *zaichik*," she said with a smile against his mouth.

"I can learn," he said with that intense concentration that undid her.

Groaning, she gripped his hair and held on to him with her thighs as he dropped his free hand to his waistband to release his cock from the prison of his pants.

A second later and both his hands were back on her and he was nudging at her with the blunt tip of his rigid flesh. Sensation quaking through her, she gripped his shoulders and held on, sure her Arrow would figure this out.

He did.

It took a couple of tries, but he was a man who paid attention, *and* he was a telekinetic. He knew how to move. Today, he thrust deep into her, making her snarl and rake his back with her nails.

The slightest pause, his eyes on her own. Checking she was with him. She licked his lower lip in answer. Muscles bunched to beautiful tautness, he began to move.

And Selenka danced with her mate, a hard, fast dance that thrust pleasure through them both and left them shaking in the aftermath. She held him close, her Arrow who wasn't sure he understood love, and yet who held her with such sweet tenderness, his devotion to her a thing written in stone.

"The rogue power," he rasped at last, "it's violent."

Selenka's fingers dug into his skin, her wolf no longer lazy and lethargic. "Are the new shields holding?"

"Yes, but my mind . . ." Raising his head from her neck, he lifted his lashes.

Selenka sucked in a breath.

Multiple bloody pinpricks dotted the whites of his eyes.

The shields were working . . . but they were also serving to increase the pressure inside his brain.

Chapter 42

Sir, the construct is beginning to fray at the edges. You will have to reinforce it periodically to guarantee continued containment.
　　　—Dr. Rebekah Patel to Councilor Ming LeBon (2080)

SELENKA'S GUT LURCHED, her wolf feeling terror as it had never before done. "That's it," she said, gripping his chin. "No more delaying the experiment."

Blood-specked eyes fading into pure black. "I'll contact Aden, get the people we need."

Even with Psy abilities, Selenka knew that would take a little time. Enough for her to wrap her arms around Ethan and just hold him. "You won't be alone in that room without light, Ethan," she murmured. "You'll never be alone again."

Shuddering, he fell into her and they stayed locked like that until Aden telepathed to say everyone would be at the entrance to den territory in ten minutes. Only then did they break apart and dress. Selenka alerted her team to expect visitors, asking Kostya to escort them to the location she'd chosen for the experiment.

She and Ethan made it to the spot below a small hill with several minutes to spare.

Reaching underneath a fall of vines, she twisted the old-fashioned doorknob. The door opened in smooth silence. "This is a small den created by a pack that was here long before us. We don't know who they were or when they lived here, but our specialists say it dates to at least four hundred years ago."

Once inside, Ethan touched his hand to the inner wall, the

surface smooth under his palm—as if thousands of hands had touched it before his. "I wonder what a psychometric would read if they placed their hand here." It felt as if this place was full of untold stories.

Selenka gave him a bemused look. "I've never thought of allowing one here, but some are qualified archeologists and historians, aren't they? Maybe I should think about it—after all, I have my own personal Arrow to ensure they don't do anything underhanded."

"The chance to examine an old wolf den would be far too unique for them to risk it," he said as Selenka picked up a flashlight from a box close to the door. "You'd have the best of the best Ps-Psy fighting to be chosen."

"You're selling me on the idea," she said, switching on the flashlight. A powerful beam of light pierced the dark. "This den's built similarly to ours, with stone walls and internal rooms without windows. Unlike us, however, they didn't have artificial light systems."

In other words, turn off the flashlight and this became a cocoon of pure darkness.

Ethan didn't say anything until Selenka showed him to the closest internal room. "It's perfect." A place that made his breath quicken and his skin grow hot, it was so near the claustrophobia of his old cell.

His mate's hand closing over his, the scent of her in his lungs. He gulped in air, reminding himself that he wasn't in a cage, would never again be in one. "I'm in charge of the light," she said, her fingers tight on his. "And on whether the door stays open or shut."

She slammed a hand over his mouth when he would've argued. "We are not negotiating on this. I *will not* allow you to torture yourself without reason."

Ethan looked at his fierce, deadly mate, this woman who fought for him. A woman he'd promised to court and only gotten as far as a single paper wolf. Nowhere near what he wanted and planned. *After this,* he thought on a roar of determination and pressed a kiss to her palm.

Vow sealed.

Narrowed eyes from his mate before she angled her head to the door. "They're here."

Aden had gathered together a team that included Memory and her mate, as well as Sascha Duncan. The person who accompanied the cardinal this time was a green-eyed man with black hair and what appeared to be claw marks on one side of his face. Lucas Hunter, alpha of DarkRiver and Sascha's mate.

Memory's right cheek was indented with sleep wrinkles, her curls wild around her head, but her eyes bright with determination. Her mate was a predator on full alert, his gaze taking in everything around them.

Aden stayed with the others, but his mind touched Ethan's. *I'll keep constant watch.*

I know, Ethan said, because Aden Kai was a leader who kept his word.

As for Kostya, the lieutenant had a private update for Selenka. "Blaise's people are contained, church secured." His square-jawed face held the echoes of fury. "Ivo's onsite with Dinara."

Selenka's mouth tightened, her eyes turning partially wolf, but she just nodded before leading everyone into the historical den.

Kostya stayed outside, on guard.

Ethan was partway down the entrance corridor when he realized Memory had balked at the doorway. Her mate was arguing with the empath, his growls low and deep, and Ethan knew Alexei didn't want her to do this.

I was kept captive by a psychopath in an underground cell, my mind caged, for fifteen years.

Setting her jaw as Ethan was about to tell her it was all right, she didn't have to come, Memory stepped into the den—with her hand locked to bone-white tightness on Alexei's. The wolf followed, his temper flashing in his eyes . . . but the kiss he pressed to her temple was tender, his body angled so hers was nestled into it.

"She has courage." Selenka's voice, low and quiet.

"Yes." Ethan took his own mate's hand. "She shows me the life I could have, the life I *want*." He stepped forward.

It was time to fight the madness that would steal his future.

Once inside the chosen room, he released his mate's hand

and went into the farthest corner, his path lit by the beam of
Selenka's flashlight. Sealed against the external world, the
space was clean except for a musty scent to the air and a bit
of dust. His head ready to explode from the pressure of the
rogue power, Ethan took one last look at his mate, then
turned his back to the doorway and pressed his palms to the
wall.

*You have permission to enter my mind to watch the re-
sults,* he telepathed to Sascha, Memory, and Aden.

Sascha and Aden responded with a simple acknowledgment, while Memory remained silent. She understood by
now how her mind affected his. But he knew she'd heard
and would do as asked; they had to find the answer . . .
whether good or bad. Ethan had to know the enemy he
faced.

He stared at the wall against which he'd braced his
hands.

Should his ability go rogue, the position would minimize
the amount of light to which he had access. Shards of stone
would ricochet into his face, but that was a small price to pay
to keep from becoming an accidental murderer. Closing his
eyes, he looked inside his mind. His telekinetic shields were
holding with no sign of strain.

However, the far stronger shields he'd constructed against
the rogue power bulged outward with every beat of his heart,
the surges violent smashes. Yet they didn't fracture—
because unlike with his previous shields, Sascha had designed these to flex.

Swallowing hard against the fear of madness that was his
nightmare, he went to begin the experiment . . . and felt
strong feminine arms sliding around his body from behind.
His back muscles stiffened. "It's not safe."

Selenka pressed a kiss to his back. "I'm not letting you do
this alone." Another kiss. "We walk into the darkness together."

Eyes hot and heart cracking into pieces, he closed one
hand over her own . . . and dropped the shields against the
rogue power.

Chaos slammed his mind, but it was oddly distant. Overwhelmed by a ferocious wave of protectiveness and concern

and an emotion tender and potent and with claws that curved around him in a defensive wall. *Love.* Even as the winds of chaos howled, he held on to that fierce, beautiful emotion as he looked inward.

His telekinetic shields were holding strong. He would not be a murderer today.

Ethan, re-engage shields.

Aden's voice came through the chaos crackled with static. But Ethan heard. Pulling up the flexing shields Sascha had designed, he began to corral the rogue power. It didn't work. The power was too violent, waves of radiant light behind his eyes. Gradient 9 or higher.

Sweat dripping down his brow, he pressed both hands to the wall once more.

Selenka pushed her hand under his clothing to press it flat against his abdomen, the skin-to-skin contact a shock that cut through the nightmare of fighting a battle he could feel himself losing. "Lock onto me," she ordered. "Sense only me."

It was easy to find her wolf in the insanity. Easy to anchor himself to that wild, beautiful emotion that stole his breath. Gripping on to her, on to their bond, he began to rebuild his shield, piece by piece by piece. Until his muscles quivered and his head throbbed, and the rogue power shoved furiously against the flexing shields.

He had it contained, but it had taken almost all he had.

It was the worst possible time for him to get an urgent telepathic call from Krychek: *Major new surge in the Net. High chance of total failure. Fifty thousand affected. Check for a Scarab trail!*

Ethan's muscles were shaky, and his head ached, but he couldn't turn away from this, couldn't abandon all those innocent lives. "PsyNet emergency," he managed to say before he entered the PsyNet. Not having the energy to maintain his body on the physical plane, he felt it collapse . . . but he knew his mate wouldn't let him fall.

Once on the Net, he went to ask Krychek for directions, then realized he could see flickers of lightning in the distance. So *many* flickers. A cascade. Racing to that area, he discovered the lightning was already fading, the damage done catastrophic. A large section of the PsyNet was badly buckled and cracked, an inch away from critical failure.

He saw two huge minds working on it, knew both Kaleb and Aden had been pulled into this repair. Other strong minds joined them one after the other, all the high Gradients who could pouring their power into the repair.

Bypassing them, Ethan continued to follow the trail. It split without warning. He went for the strongest of the three, and had just barely pinpointed the source mind before the trail blinked out.

Conscious Aden was busy, he reached telepathically for another senior Arrow mind. Vasic wasn't within reach. Neither was Axl. But he found Nerida. *I have the location of one of the Scarabs.* He sent through the PsyNet coordinates. *I'm unable to maintain a watch. There were three, and—*

His mind went blank, his consciousness blinking out.

SELENKA caught Ethan as he slumped, and though she was strong, he was a man made up mostly of muscle and bone. It took serious effort on her part not to let him fall—but she growled when Alexei made a move to enter the room. "I have him." She would *not* allow anyone else near her mate when he was so helpless.

Lucas Hunter's voice was quiet, and obviously directed at Sascha Duncan, but Selenka heard it. "You do not get between an alpha and their mate, kitten. You know that better than anyone."

"We'll wait outside," Alexei said to Selenka at almost the same instant, so she missed Sascha's reply. "Aden was teleported out by Vasic ten seconds ago."

A beam entering the room, a flashlight being placed on the floor so she and Ethan wouldn't be in darkness.

She heard a protest, was about to snarl again, when she realized it was Memory. Of course it'd be an empath who wouldn't want to leave when someone was down. Healers were like that. The only reason Sascha had probably listened to Lucas was because she was more experienced and able to control her instincts.

"He's fine," she said, trying not to growl too much—not that Memory struck her as particularly fragile. "On the PsyNet assisting with an emergency. We'll be out when he's up."

She heard Alexei grumble, "You want Selenka to claw your face off, lioness? Time to move."

Memory's responding growl as she finally left almost made Selenka grin.

Using every muscle she had, she held her mate against her as she lowered them both to the floor. He ended up seated in a leaning position against her shoulder, his head tilted slightly to the side. Pressing a kiss to his throat, she made sure he was comfortable, then just held him, stroking his hair in that way that always made him lean into her, and drinking in his scent.

He might not be conscious, but affection carried through the mating bond, and she hoped it'd carry through to whatever battle Ethan was currently fighting. At least she knew he was alive and well—not only could she see the rise and fall of his chest, hear the beat of his heart; she could feel him along the mating bond.

Dark as night and cold as frost, but with a new depth that fascinated . . . and less bloody sharpness to the jagged edges. The static that had disappeared during the experiment was back, but it was muted, less in the way of their bond.

None of it surprised her.

Selenka was no Psy, but she was dead certain she'd ID'd what lived inside Ethan. The impact had reverberated loud and clear through their bond the instant he lowered his shields, but her mind struggled against the impossibility of it. *Bozhe*, that he was sane was a miracle—and a testament to his incredible mental strength.

"I'm here, *zaichik*." She kissed his jaw. "I really will claw off the face of anyone who tries to get to you. You're mine, and I'm a possessive wolf."

She didn't know how long the two of them sat there, but the dust disturbed by their earlier movements had long since settled when he stirred at last. His lashes fluttered . . . and he froze.

"It's me." Wolf puppyishly happy he was awake, she kissed his jaw, nipped excitedly at his throat. "Wake up, sleepyhead."

"You're here." Dazed words.

Nipping at his shoulder, she said, "Don't sound so surprised or I'll really bite you."

"I felt you in the darkness, a wild golden glow that lit up the dark. But I thought it was an illusion."

"I'm no illusion, Ethan, and never will be." She pressed her lips to his nape, her own heart starting to beat in a proper rhythm at last. "Tough one?"

Sitting up to face her, all pale eyes and devotion. "Tracking those with Scarab Syndrome—they appear to be attacking the Net." He pushed sweat-damp hair from his forehead, looked around. "The others?"

"I kicked them out—they might still be outside." Rising to her feet, she held out a hand.

It did something to her when her deadly Arrow took her hand without hesitation and allowed her to pull him up to his feet. No smile, because Ethan never smiled, but she felt a whisper of warmth against her wolf's fur, a caress that came through loud and clear.

Smiling, she leaned into him. "You'll have to pet my wolf in reality soon. She's getting impatient." The wolf lived in her every second of every day even when she wore her human skin, but it needed direct physical contact with its mate.

"I'd be honored to pet your wolf, *zolotse moyo*." Ethan nuzzled at her throat as he called her his "gold," and she knew he wasn't talking about the precious metal but the light she was to him.

Selenka melted. Her wolf wanted to grip at his throat with its teeth and tumble him playfully to the ground.

But play would have to wait.

For now . . . Reaching into a side pocket of her pants, she pulled out a nutrient bar.

Food was a thing with meaning among wolves, and Selenka watched in satisfied pleasure as Ethan all but inhaled the bar . . . though with a distinctly dubious look on his face. "Not to your taste?"

"It isn't what I'm used to." Smoothing out the wrapper, he read the label aloud. "Strawberry yogurt." A squaring of his shoulders. "Sometimes, the old ways are the best."

Chuckling, Selenka patted his cheek, his bristly jaw beloved and familiar. "You never know, you might decide you like hazelnut crunch, or mint cream." The look he gave her had her wolf throwing back its head in a howl of laughter.

Chapter 43

Every frog praises his own pond, Selenushka.
But, Deda, isn't it sandpipers and their swamp?
Would you rather jump into a pond or a swamp?
Um, a pond?
So why would you send the poor frog to the swamp?
                    —Conversation between Yevgeni Durev and
                                        Selenka Durev (8)

ETHAN AND SELENKA emerged into the crisp air and the smudged charcoal of very early dawn. Sascha and Memory stood together, speaking, while Lucas Hunter had a watchful—and slightly amused—air about him.

Kostya, meanwhile, was scowling at Alexei. "I am not cousin to a pretty California boy with yellow hair."

"Check your family tree." Alexei's scowl was as dark. "It's unfortunate but true. And at least this California wolf tans. What do you call that color? Curdled milk?"

Growls were exchanged, and it was odd, but Ethan was near certain the two were enjoying the exchange. "Are they playing?" he muttered to Selenka.

"Wolves have strange senses of humor," she said, her lips twitching.

Memory and Sascha were the ones to approach them, the other three keeping their distance, no doubt sensing Ethan's mate's bristling protectiveness. Selenka, Ethan knew, wasn't in the right frame of mind to allow anyone but submissives and healers near him. *Him.* Ethan. An Arrow perfectly able to defend himself.

Ethan felt that warmth inside that he thought might be a happy smile.

"You're okay." Memory's smile was wide, her hug unexpected but not unwelcome. Despite how she aggravated the rogue power with her mere presence, she continued to feel familiar on the deepest level.

He hugged her back, feeling protective of her in a way he couldn't explain.

After they drew apart, he said, "Did you sense the chaos I hear when I drop my shields? It is anarchy in its purest form."

Memory exchanged a glance with Sascha, seemed to silently pass the baton to the more experienced E. Eyes pure black, Sascha said, "It *would* be a howl of chaos for you. When you drop your shields, you have no secondary shields to help filter and moderate the input."

Ethan looked from one to the other, then to Selenka, who stood beside him, her arms folded and her body close enough that she was a line of heat along one side of him. But before he could voice his questions, Sascha said, "Where was the first place you dropped your shields? The first place you felt the howls?"

"While I was in Moscow for an early security meeting. I had a couple of hours open and decided to see what would happen if I permitted the power free." Looking back, it had been a distinctly stupid thing to do while alone in a Moscow park, but to the man he'd been at the time, his mind distant from the world, it had made perfect sense. "I didn't realize how clouded my thinking had become."

"You did that in central *Moscow*?" Memory's mouth fell open. "Ethan, it's a wonder the influx didn't blow your circuits."

"I wasn't that careless," he clarified. "I only lowered my shields a fraction and slammed them back up the instant I realized what was happening." Even then, his head had rung, screaming agony inside his skull.

"Was it less intense today?" Sascha's tone gave nothing away, her eyes filled with stars once more. "Even though you totally lowered your shields?"

"Yes. By a significant margin." His mate's primal heat wrapped around him, a wolf's comfort. "Is it because of the mating bond? Is it leaching off a percentage of the pressure?"

"It's possible, but the main factor is the number of unshielded, untrained minds in your vicinity." Thrusting her hands into the pockets of her light coat, Sascha took a moment before she began to speak. "All humans and changelings leak a low level of emotion. Psy are beginning to be the same now that those of our race no longer face punishment for feeling."

"Why are you speaking to me about emotions?" Ethan could see no correlation between his situation and the fall of Silence.

Memory stepped forward, her face luminous. "Because you're one of us, Ethan. That power inside you? It's empathic."

"Very close to cardinal level." Sascha's words were a blur in the buzz of his mind. "If I had to guess I'd say 9.5 or higher on the Gradient."

Unable to process what they were saying, Ethan looked at his mate. Her eyes were wolf, her gaze holding a scalding anger. Cupping his face in her hands, his mate kissed him with a raw emotion that was an anchor in the chaos. "You're an empath, Ethan," she said in the aftermath. "A fucking powerful empath."

He couldn't get enough air into his lungs. This—it was too huge a thing to digest. "I can't be an empath." The words fell out of his mouth. "I'm a killer."

Selenka would've eviscerated Ming LeBon with her claws, then spit in his dying face had the former Councilor been anywhere near her vicinity. He'd taken a traumatized young boy and instead of helping him, had used that trauma to his own ends, reinforcing all of Ethan's terrible views about himself.

But Selenka didn't give voice to her fury; her mate needed something else from her at this instant. "So am I," she said, extending her claws so they touched the sides of his face, pricking in just a little.

"I've executed threats to my pack without a second thought," she said, "and I have no guilt at all over Blaise's death." She'd heard the faint howls of triumph not long ago, knew the cult leader was dead. "If a telepath came at me and tried to break open my mind, you'd better fucking believe that I'd rip out their throat."

Ethan's hands were clamped over her wrists and he was listening. *Actively* listening. So she kept talking, trying to smash through this seemingly immovable barrier in his mind. Maybe one day, he'd be ready to talk to someone else about this, but right now, she had the best chance of ending his belief that he was a killer and only a killer.

"The first time you killed," she said, conscious everyone else had shifted out of earshot, "you did so in self-defense. We train our pups not to use their claws or teeth—*unless* someone is hurting them and they need to get away. Then they're taught to fight. You *fought*, Ethan, and you had a right to fight."

He parted his lips, but she spoke before he could. "Your adult kills? How many did you do voluntarily? Without Ming's mind controlling yours?"

Silence was her answer.

Hands still clawed, she brushed her lips gently against his. "If someone chained up a changeling as a child and beat and abused them until the changeling had no choice but to kill on command, it's not the changeling who would be the monster."

Those clear eyes darkened on a sweep of black. "I wanted to kill the intruders and Blaise. I still do."

"You have a violent protective drive—they came to hurt people under your care."

"It's not a very empathic way to act."

"*You're* an empath—your reality is an empathic reality."

Emotions swelled the mating bond: torment, pain, guilt, a fierce devotion . . . and hope.

Selenka kissed him again. "You are not the monster."

Her words were still reverberating in Ethan's mind when he heard her say, "I thank you for your assistance, but I need you to leave now. Kostya will show you to the entrance and we'll provide hotel rooms in the city if you have to wait for a teleport pickup."

This time, Memory didn't argue, but Sascha said, "Until Ethan has a chance to build the appropriate filters, he needs to create a pressure release valve in his shields." Her voice was unbending. "I can give him the instructions now if he allows a telepathic send, but he has to follow those instructions within the hour if he isn't going to risk further bruising to his brain."

Ethan found the mental space to say, "Send. I'll do it." No fucking way was he not doing anything that would give him a lifetime with Selenka.

Sascha was as good as her word, transmitting the instructions at once. Then she and the others all left. Ethan shuddered, his forehead pressed to Selenka's. He knew he would have questions, so many of them, in the days to come, but right now, he just needed to be with his mate.

Once alone, he went to kiss her in an effort to find his feet again . . . and inside him stirred a sensation akin to a wolf's fur. He halted, another hunger overwhelming the first. "Can I see your wolf?"

Her eyes shifted from human to wolf before she stepped back and began to strip. She did so with changeling practicality and still he watched her like a slave. She was sleek and strong and beautiful. And *his*.

"Am I too possessive?" he asked, the vague thought dawning in the part of his brain that wasn't awash in emotion.

She padded to him naked and proud. "We are as possessive as each other, *zaichik*."

Ethan could feel her teeth at his throat, was more than happy with that. Hand at her waist, he looked into her eyes and saw the wolf take control a heartbeat before she broke into shatters of light, and where had stood a woman powerful and dangerous now stood a sleek wolf with dark gray fur at the back that faded gradually into pale dawn gray by the time it reached her stomach.

Her pricked ears were dark at the base, pale at the tips, as was her tail.

Everything about her was beautiful.

Crouching down on a wave of wonder as she shook herself to settle her fur, he ran his hand reverently over her back. She nuzzled at his throat, bit playfully. He felt no fear. This was his mate. "Lovely and deadly," he murmured. "And mine."

His alpha mate didn't argue with his claim, but it wasn't enough for Ethan. What they had wasn't enough. "There's something wrong with our bond, isn't there?" Static continued to crackle between them. "It's me. It's because of my damage."

He felt the wolf's primal answer deep inside him: a clawing possessiveness that said it didn't matter, that he was perfect to her. It was echoed by a rumbling growl and the closing of powerful jaws over his shoulder.

But Ethan shook his head. "I want it all. I won't let Ming steal this from us." A dark heat rose in him, a thing with claws that didn't feel wolf. "Will you have me?"

The look the wolf gave him was very Selenka.

He found the dark embers morphing into a softer, warmer sensation. Rubbing his face against the side of the wolf's, he said, "I know how to fix it. I know what to do." It was a crystalline realization inside his mind, born in the wildness of emotion soaking into his senses.

He released the shield Sascha had created, the one that contained his empathy. He released it *all the way*, and he didn't put it back up even when the first faint howls growled into his brain. For the first time in his life, he opened his soul . . . and in ran a wolf, the contact so hard and powerful and potent that his mind screamed in ecstasy.

He had told her he was keeping her.

ON the PsyNet, a new bond shimmered into life, a golden rope prickly with claws and entwined with oil-slick black shimmers that were almost impossible to see. That bond snarled at people to keep their distance and it emerged from a martial mind that was all but invisible.

Then the bond was gone as quickly as it had appeared,

and the martial mind faded into the Net. Those who'd seen the bond's split-second appearance were left with dazzled afterimages but could find no trace of either the mind or the bond in the moments that followed. It was as if the two had never existed.

Chapter 44

I do not wish to sacrifice any of my newborn children of power, but war and loss are entwined. To win the world, we must be ready to bleed.

—The Architect

ETHAN OPENED HIS eyes to find himself sprawled on the forest floor, facing Selenka. In human form once more, she had her eyes open and was breathing harshly. He could feel her inside him . . . and the static was gone, the channel between them clear of jagged shards. "I told you you were mine."

A breathy laugh. "Stubborn Arrow." A hard kiss. "Boom." Falling onto her back, she smiled as he came over her. She was naked and he wanted to kiss every inch of her, but he also didn't want to look away from her smile, so he satisfied himself with petting her with one hand while he braced himself on his elbow and looked into her eyes.

"How did you—" Her eyes narrowed. "You dropped all your shields, didn't you? Sascha said you need proper filters."

"Yes," Ethan admitted reluctantly. "I'll have to reinitialize my shields as soon as we leave this isolated area." Or the emotions of the world would pour into him in screaming, howling chaos.

Selenka nipped at his chin. "Don't be a grump. Now we know any static will be temporary—it'll disappear once you're no longer trying to suppress your abilities."

Forcing himself to accept the logic of that, he checked the PsyNet—a place rife with lightning shadows. Fading imprints too weak to follow. "My Arrow shields have reinitialized, leaving me hidden in plain sight. Those shields are also protecting our bond."

"I want everyone to see it." Selenka scowled and gripped at his hair. "Make it visible."

He nipped her on the chin, got a growl in response. "It's a defensive skill. No one can find me on the PsyNet this way."

Selenka considered that, seemed to decide it was acceptable. "I heard empaths give out sparks of color on the Net. How do you hide that?"

He looked, saw black shimmers that slipped secretively into the Net. "I'm not a normal empath," he said, and for the first time, the word "normal" didn't hold a terrible weight. "I think . . . I'm okay with being abnormal."

"You know another word for that?" Selenka's eyes dazzled, her wolf prowling at the surface. "'Unique.' You, Ethan Night, are unique. One of a kind."

Unique.

Still heavy in the head and in the bones, he nuzzled his mate.

Wrapping an arm around his shoulders, Selenka tugged him down until he lay half on her, half off. When she pulled at his T-shirt, he got the message and took it off. She sighed at the skin-to-skin contact, and he felt the warmth inside him grow and grow and grow.

"I'm happy." They were the last words he remembered saying before he fell into a sleep contented and at peace, his mate's body soft beneath his and her fingers caressing his hair.

TWENTY-EIGHT hours later, Aden asked Ethan to join him as they attempted to speak to the man whose mind he'd pinpointed during the last attack on the Net. Their aim was to find out why those with Scarab Syndrome were turning on the Net.

"His name is Ezra Ree, and he's not in a good state," Aden told Ethan when he arrived. "But we can't wait any longer—the continual surges in the PsyNet have destabilized sections to the extent that it's become impossible to stitch them back together."

"Why me?" Ethan was no interrogator.

"We can't get a response from him—since you have some type of affinity to Scarab sufferers, I'm hoping he'll react to you out of instinct."

Nodding, Ethan stepped into the secure hospital room. A man with brown hair and white skin flushed with pink, his body formed of large bones, sat on the bed. His expression was vacant as he rocked slowly back and forth.

A cessation of movement, Ezra's eyes focused on Ethan. "I know you. I felt you chasing me. You're a bloodhound and you chased me until I couldn't breathe."

Ethan took advantage of the middle-aged male's moment of lucidity. "Why were you cooperating with others to cause power fluctuations in the Net that strain its integrity?"

"The spider." Arms wrapped around himself, Ezra began to rock again.

Ethan grabbed his shoulder. "What is the spider?"

"Spider is friend," Ezra mumbled. "Spider says what to do. 'Ezra, push energy into the Net. It will give us power.'"

"How can a broken PsyNet give you power?"

Ezra blinked at him.

Ethan tried again. "Who is the spider?"

"Spider is spider." The rocking began again, faster this time. "Eensy, weensy spider . . ." The faint words faded. "Eensy, weensy spider . . ." Ezra tried again and again.

From that point on, however, he wouldn't react or respond to either Ethan or anyone else—including Memory. That night, he suffered a severe seizure with no apparent medical cause and entered a coma from which he never woke.

"I hope you're not feeling guilty," Selenka said when the news came through, the two of them alone in their quarters.

Wearing only black boxer briefs, Ethan took her wrist, touched the pad of his finger to the pulse below. "No. Ezra was lost the instant Scarab took hold of him." Patient Zero had apparently had enough awareness to seek assistance, but according to Memory, Patient Zero was a powerful telepath trained in critical thinking.

Not everyone had that advantage.

"But I still mourn a life lost." Ethan felt the beat of her pulse inside him, as strong as her wolf's presence. "It's important to me, to mark these losses. Ezra Ree didn't choose the Syndrome, didn't choose to lose himself to it—by all accounts, he was a good man just finding his feet in the post-Silence world."

Face softening, Selenka nipped at his jaw. "Empath." Affection flowed through the bond, and because she lived inside him—was welcome inside him—he let that affection bathe him in a growly kind of softness. Because his lover was a wolf and her love had teeth. *"Zolotse moyo,"* he said. "You are my light, the star I can always follow to find my way home."

"Good—or I'd have to track you down and haul you home," said his alpha mate, before she pulled him down into a kiss. "I love you, Ethan Night, and I'm never letting you go."

Ethan gloried in the chains of her claim.

Never again would he be alone in the dark.

The Architect

THE ARCHITECT SAW it now, saw what she was—a creature of boundless power.

A Scarab.

Taking a computronic pen, she drew a large red cross across the latest Scarab information sheet. The weak would no doubt turn themselves in like sheep, but the strong would become her army, her people. As for the Consortium, it was something to consider later, when her mind wasn't stretching this strongly.

Her biggest problem was going to be the memory loss that seemed entwined with this new power. It was possible she could create a telepathic tracker, one she could rewind to capture glimpses of what she did while in her most powerful state. If this was the cost of power without limits, it was one she was more than willing to pay.

Krychek and the others would not, could not win.

Opening her hand, she looked at one of the tiny glowing creatures she'd seeded on the PsyNet. It didn't register that she was viewing it on the physical plane, a construct that couldn't exist outside the psychic space. Her mind said it was there, and so it was.

This was it. How the future would begin.

With extermination.

Vanguard

Lioness: I have our DNA profiles! It looks like we're related! A couple of generations back maybe? Or could be a different branch of the same original tree. We can find out the specifics later, but we're family!

EN: That explains why our two empathic specialties dovetail, while being dissimilar to all others in the Net. And also probably why your presence kept setting off my ability before I had the proper filters and shields.

Lioness: Yes, we're oddities from the same Odd Tree. It's nice. Right?

EN: Yes. Though I appear to be the most bloodthirsty E of all. Ivy Jane says my designation on the squad's rolls should be changed to E-Arrow even though that's a nonexistent subdesignation.

Lioness: Who cares! You're an E and you're an Arrow. As for the bloodthirsty, I have a little of that, too. If I'd had Arrow training, maybe I would be even more like you. But you know what Sascha says—Es aren't a monolith. Our entire designation was buried over a century ago, and even before that, no one much studied us because we were meant to be nicey-nice. So maybe we oddballs have always been around.

EN: Or maybe we were created by the NetMind when it became clear the PsyNet was going to face a catastrophic Scarab threat. It is, after all, the guardian of the Net, and even if it's not sentient in the same way as you and I, it did—before its current disintegration—have a certain level of thought. Instinct alone could've led it to manipulate strands of psychic energy to create certain outcomes in receptive unformed minds. We could be but the vanguard of a wave of unexpected abilities.

—Messages exchanged between Memory
Aven-Rose and Ethan Night

ETHAN PUT DOWN his phone after sending that last message to Memory and considered the idea of having family. It was no longer so alien—not when he had an entire pack as well as a squad of Arrows on whom he could rely. And a mate who'd claimed him down to the bone. It was a state with which he was utterly content.

As for being family with Memory, it would be no hardship. According to Selenka, he already treated the empath like a sibling—and Memory apparently responded to him the same way.

"Ready?" Margo, dressed in yellow fleece shorts and a matching sweatshirt with a giant glittery rainbow on the front, her feet clad in nothing but fluffy pink socks, dropped down onto the sofa next to him. "Did you make the popcorn?"

"I've got it." Selenka exited the break room's kitchenette with a huge bowl, which Margo immediately claimed.

Loyal, his coat shiny and his ribs no longer showing, had jumped to his feet the instant Selenka appeared and was now nosing around her legs, as devoted to her as Ethan. She bent to pet him, giving him a scratch behind his left ear that sent him melting to the floor in a puddle of joy.

"I can't believe you've hooked my mate on a soap opera," Selenka said to Margo after a final pat of Loyal's head. "It's like sugar for the brain."

"It's educational," Ethan argued, setting aside his phone. He'd share Memory's data with Selenka tonight, while they were alone and naked. The latter was very important. Ethan was now addicted to tactile contact with his mate.

Coming down onto the sofa on his other side, she allowed him to put his arm around her shoulders as she settled into the crook of his arm. She, too, was dressed casually— but in jeans and a simple vee-necked gray tee that followed the shape of her body. Unlike Margo, Selenka had to head out of the den in an hour. She was meeting Valentin Nikolaev for a "no mates allowed" beer.

"Oh wait, before I start this." Margo turned to him. "Ivo was all smug about something he got you. He wouldn't tell me what." Wolf eyes stared at him.

When he didn't break, she bounced in place. "Pleeeeease tell me. I can't not know! It'll drive me insane."

As Selenka laughed, Ethan said, "Turn off the lights and I'll show you."

Margo did it with alacrity, but the room wasn't pitch black—he could see a blade of light from under the doorway, the dot of blue that indicated the power status of the entertainment comm, even the faint glow from where Margo had dropped her phone when she jumped up.

But it was dark enough for this demonstration.

Using the ring finger of his right hand, he reached across his palm to the subdermal implant Oleg had put in place yesterday. The healer had sealed up the small cut, and the remaining tenderness was minor. So it caused him no pain to press on the implant. A glow suffused his palm under his skin.

"*Blin!*" Margo came closer, leaning down to peer intently at it, Loyal wriggling in at her side. "You'll always have a light source, no matter where you are!"

So you'll never again be locked in the dark.

That was what Ivo had said to him when he handed Ethan the device he'd created. It ran on a tiny battery and would need to be replaced every year, but a five-minute visit to the infirmary once a year was no price at all for the gift of light. One day, Ethan hoped he could give a gift of such value to Ivo, something that helped him fight his own demons.

In the interim, he spent time with the other lieutenant in a way he'd never before done with anyone but Abbot. They were becoming friends, two men who understood each other's scars. "You can examine it more later," he said, switching it off. "We have to catch up on the latest three episodes."

"Oooh yeah!"

They soon had the comm going, Ridge and Chantelle's story playing out onscreen in glorious color. "You two realize a billionaire alpha wolf is an oxymoron?" Selenka muttered, rolling her eyes. "Alphas are about pack, not—"

"Shh," Ethan and Margo both said, with Margo adding, "He's about to break down the door of the castle and rescue Chantelle from that awful Ruslan Barnett."

Making a "hrrump" sound, Selenka settled down. It lasted three minutes. "She is an idiot!" Selenka cried. "Poor Ridge! Tied to this brainless embarrassment of a wolf who gets herself kidnapped every five seconds and is soooooo 'terrified' of her champagne-and-caviar-offering captor that she can't even walk out when the door is fucking open!"

"That's it." Features set in severe lines, Margo pointed a finger at Selenka. "We're going to kick you out of our viewing club if you can't zip it."

"Grr." Arms folded across her chest, Selenka managed to stay silent until it was time for her to leave—though Ethan thought she'd explode from the pressure of keeping her opinions to herself.

Rising after the first episode, she bent down to kiss Ethan. "Do not, ever, in any circumstances, pick me up and throw me over your shoulder as a grand gesture. I will leave bite marks on your gorgeous butt so deep they'll turn into tattoos."

Ethan nipped at her lower lip. "I know my mate."

Mollified, she left at last, but he and Margo waited until they got a message from Kostya telling them Selenka had exited the den before they sprang into action. The comm went off, Ethan stood, Alia entered the room with a full tuxedo in a garment bag, and Margo made the call to the kitchen.

The two women then stepped out, taking an excited Loyal with them, so Ethan could change at the speed of light, and by the time he exited in a perfectly fitted tuxedo—thanks to Alia's skills—Manuil was standing there with a carry bag that should hold ice-cold craft beer, dark chocolate, black cherries that Abbot had teleported for him just because Ethan asked, and a nonalcoholic cocktail since Psy didn't do too well with alcohol.

Margo whistled at seeing him, as did Ivo, who was standing with his forearm braced on Margo's shoulder. "He does scrub up pretty," Margo said. "Though I'm not sure about the clean-shaven look."

"It'll grow back." Ethan had said the same thing to Selenka this morning, after he shaved. She'd scowled, but she'd also petted his smooth face with curious hands, testing whether she liked it or not; since he'd ended up backed up against the counter while his mate had her way with him, he was pretty sure the verdict was positive. "Have I forgotten anything?"

Gregori paused in eating the bowl of ice cream with which he'd wandered over, a square bandage on the side of his neck over the site of a new tattoo. "Music?"

"I have it loaded onto my phone." He also had a backup in a small device he'd borrowed from Ivo. "Call Valentin."

Margo put the phone to her ear. "It's time. Call off the meet." She listened for a moment, then made a face. "Yeah, yeah, we owe you one. And I know damn well you won't forget." She hung up. *"Bears."*

"I've alerted Dinara." Alia held up her own phone. "She'll redirect Selenka in the direction you want her to go once our alpha turns back into den territory."

"Did she come up with a rational reason for the redirect?" Ethan asked, since Dinara had said, "I'll think of something," when he'd requested the assist.

"A love-struck date happening a small way away between two submissives who might get shy if they knew a dominant was around." Alia's soft lips curved as Ethan bent to rub Loyal's head. "Our tough Dinara is a romantic."

"You'll take care of him?" he said to Margo; Loyal was used to going where Ethan went, but Ethan couldn't take him today.

"Loyal and I will finish our *Hourglass Lives* marathon." Margo patted the side of her thigh, and Loyal wandered over. Margo crouched down to put an arm around his back, so he wouldn't follow Ethan when Ethan left.

"Oh, and my love has set up your table and chairs," Alia said with a smile. "Tyoma also wants you to know you're making him look bad."

Carrier bag slung over his shoulder, Ethan said, *"Spasibo,"* to the group and made sure to touch Manuil's shoulder before he headed out.

The boy's face lit up like a small sun. "Good luck, Ethan."

Ethan hoped he wouldn't need luck, that it would all go according to plan. When he reached the den's vehicle bay, Kostya was waiting for him by the jetcycle Ethan had already ridden more than once. "Selya's just back in den territory." He handed over a helmet. "Probably in a bad temper and muttering about bears. You have seven minutes."

Pulling on the helmet, Ethan thanked the lieutenant, then roared out of the vehicle bay and onto the path that'd lead him to the small table and two chairs Artem had set up. He'd done this exact trail three times this week, to ensure he was aware of all possible hurdles that might come up.

But the ride was smooth today, the moon a silver spotlight on the world.

Reaching the small clearing surrounded by huge trees that created a kind of amphitheater, he parked the jetcycle and hung his helmet on one of the handlebars. Then he quickly arranged the table with the items he carried; the one thing none of the others knew about was the bunch of paper flowers he'd brought in his pocket.

Selenka delighted in the origami he left for her to find.

Table set, he got a beep on his phone that proved to be Dinara giving him the one-minute countdown. Taking a deep breath, he slipped out through the trees to stand at the side of the dirt track Selenka was driving. Her headlights appeared around the corner not long afterward—and Ethan stuck out his thumb as if hitching a ride.

Switching off the lights the instant she spotted him, so he wouldn't be blinded, she brought the car to a stop and jumped out. Hands on her hips, she stared at him with a stern expression, but delight bubbled along the mating bond. Because this was a game, and wolves loved to play.

"Ethan Night, if you tell me Valentin was in on this, I really truly *will* bite you," she threatened.

"He was only peripherally involved," Ethan said and held out a hand. "No details. But you can still bite me. I like it."

Shoulders shaking, she took his hand. "What are we doing, *zaichik*?"

"Having dessert in the moonlight." Tenderness filled him at the emotions he sensed in her, the simple pleasure and happiness that suffused her.

She sighed when she spotted the white-draped table, the bowl of cherries, the chocolate he'd found for her after she'd mentioned it once in passing. "Oh, Ethan." Taking the seat he pulled out, she propped her chin on her hands and looked up at him. "Is this in the manual?"

It had been a joke between mates, but Ethan solemnly shook his head. "I thought of this myself using a little inspiration from *Wild Woman*." He wasn't an expert yet, after all.

Primal delight in her. "Aren't you going to sit?" she asked after he poured her the beer she liked. "How am I supposed to straddle your lap and kiss you stupid if you aren't seated?"

His cock reacted as it always did to any flirtatiousness from his mate. But Ethan had more to do this night. "I learned something. I want to show you."

A tilt of her head.

Taking out his phone, he started the quiet background music, then inhaled, exhaled . . . and began to sing to his mate who loved his voice. In front of him, Selenka ignored her drink, ignored the cherries and the chocolate, her eyes closing as she *listened* with every cell in her body. Her pleasure was a song of its own through his blood.

She shuddered when he stopped, her eyes pure gold when she opened them. "Your voice, Ethan . . . You could captivate my entire pack with it."

"No, it's only for you." For his queen.

"The things you say, Ethan Night . . ." Rising from her

chair, Selenka took a cherry and bit into it. She kissed him with lips stained cherry red before she fed him the other half and threw away the pip. "You're not the only one with secrets."

She took a step back with another lush kiss, then reached into the vee of her T-shirt to pull out the pendant she wore on a chain. He'd noticed the chain, but the ring-shaped pendant was new to him.

"I planned to do this later tonight, but . . ." A deep smile as she undid the chain and dropped the ring into her hand. A thick band with a simple design that made it appear like beaten metal, it had the letters *E* and *S* entwined in the central section.

"Our mating," she said, "was a thing of instinct. But it's become so much more. We've become who mates should be to one another—lovers, friends, swords, and shields." She held up the ring. "I want you to wear this so you never doubt who you are to me. My mate, my love, and my Ethan."

Chest crushingly tight, he stood frozen as she slid the ring onto his finger; then he curled his fingers inward into a fist, holding the gift close. "How did you know?" he rasped. That he still sometimes worried she wouldn't have chosen him if her wolf hadn't pushed her into it.

"I'm your mate." A chiding glance, but her kiss was tender. "You're my always, Ethan, and I wouldn't have it any other way."

Wrapping her up in his arms, Ethan lifted her off the ground . . . then he spun her around as his heart spun, his blood turning to dazzling light. Throwing back her head, his mate sent up a howl that was a song more beautiful than any he could ever sing—because in that howl was untrammeled happiness.

He was her always and that made her happy.

It was a joy the broken, trapped boy he'd once been could've never imagined, but the shadow of that boy danced in the light today, no shackles on his mind or on his heart. A heart that belonged to an alpha wolf.

AS Ethan and Selenka spun under the moonlight, Kaleb Krychek looked at the fault lines in the PsyNet, the weak spots created by multiple recent hits, and turned to Aden. "We no longer have a choice."

The leader of the Arrow Squad showed no emotion, but his eyes were obsidian when he looked at Kaleb. "No, we don't."

They were agreed: it was time to break the PsyNet into pieces . . . and hope it survived.

ACKNOWLEDGMENTS

While writing this book, I had questions relating to the Russian language and Russian naming conventions. My thanks to Tetiana Matsypura, Karen Lamming, and Vladimir Samozvanov for generously answering those questions.

In cases where the transliteration from Cyrillic included different spellings, I've chosen one and gone with it.

Any errors are mine, and I hope you'll forgive them.
Spasibo!

Read on for an excerpt of

Quiet in Her Bones

The new thriller by Nalini Singh

Chapter 1

MY MOTHER VANISHED without a trace ten years ago.

So did a quarter of a million dollars in cash from my father's safe.

The police came.

The neighbors whispered that she was a thief.

My father called her a bitch.

"She'll turn up, and when she does, I'll have her in handcuffs!"

That's what he said. That's what he screamed.

He was right.

It took ten years, but she has turned up.

The police found her car in the dense bush of the Waitākere Ranges regional park four hours ago. She was inside. Well, her bones were, anyway. Those bones were clothed in the remnants of the red silk shirt she was wearing that night.

The night I heard her scream.

Chapter 2

I'D JUST SPENT two hours staring at my unfinished manuscript when the police came to the door of my father's subtly upscale residence of glass and polished wood. Designer enough to make it clear he was no ordinary man, but understated enough to blend into the dark green landscape that surrounded it.

I'd come "home" to live after my hospital discharge a month ago. Doctors' orders.

"You can't be on your own," Dr. Binchy had said, hazel eyes unblinking behind square black spectacle frames. "Not yet."

I don't know why I hadn't just hired a nurse instead of returning to this unhappy place, thick with ugly memories. Before adding then deleting a thousand pointless words in my next book, I'd started to look up nursing agencies. Then the police came. The middle-aged man in plain clothes, the twenty-something woman in full uniform, cap included.

Recognition flashed in her eyes when I opened the door.

The man, solid and stolid with a square jaw and watery blue eyes, flashed his ID. "We'd like to speak to Mr. Ishaan Rai."

"Sure." Turning on my crutches, I saw that my father was already coming down the hall, a well-dressed CEO on top of the world, his graying black hair perfectly styled and his shirt a crisp blue.

He wasn't a tall man, nor was he short. Average height, with average features. He should've looked ordinary, even bland, but my father has a presence, a dignity to him that I've always found a grand irony.

"What's this about?" he demanded, because that's what Ishaan Rai does. Demand. It's served him well, except for his son, who is his disappointment.

"Mr. Rai," the man began, raising his ID. "If we could speak in private."

"Oh for god's sake, just spit it out. What complaint is it now? The plant is built to the highest specifications—it isn't breaching any environmental restrictions." He's so used to ordering people about that it doesn't seem to occur to him that a senior officer wouldn't knock on his door at eight in the morning for a complaint about emissions or discarded chemicals.

The male officer's expression stilled, and right then, I saw an intelligence I hadn't previously spotted. Solid and stolid could also mean dogged and relentless. "I'm Detective Senior Sergeant Oliver Regan, and this is my colleague Constable Sefina Neri. We regret to inform you that the body of a deceased female was discovered early this morning in the Waitākere Ranges regional park.

"Her identity has yet to be officially verified, and normally, we wouldn't inform you at this stage—but, given the likely publicity and attendant conjecture, the decision was made to alert you. She had her driver's license and credit cards with her. All in the name of Nina Rai."

Time stopped, filled with the sound of a sharp, pained scream.

Even my father seemed stunned into silence, but that never lasts long with him. "Where's she been all this time?" he barked. "Living it up on my money, I'm guessing."

Constable Neri's eyes were a deep, intense brown, and she locked them, unblinking, on my father, but let her senior officer do the talking. Her job, I understood, was to watch and make note of any and all reactions.

The intensity of her—it reminded me of Paige.

"Indications are that the deceased has been in place for a significant period," Regan responded, the pale skin of his

face pockmarked with old acne scars. "Full forensic exami-
nations will take some time, of course, but we have reason to
believe that she's been there since the night she was last seen
alive—our people have discovered remnants of the clothing
you described her wearing in your theft complaint."

Red silk, a top that had left her arms bare and slipped
neatly into the high waist of her wide-legged and tailored
black pants. Her heels had been black, too, her lips a pop of
red that matched her top.

Around me hung silence.

Heavy. Cold. Cutting.

Like the silence my father had utilized as a weapon
against my mother. She, in turn, hadn't been much for silence. My mother preferred smashing things, preferred
screaming.

But not like that final scream.

"Could it be someone else?" I asked, because my father
was just staring at them—and because I didn't want their
words to be true. "Someone could've stolen her wallet and
you could be wrong about the clothes. It's been a long time."

Regan's expression didn't soften as he said, "The body
was discovered in a vehicle registered to Nina Parvati Rai."

My hand tightened on the edge of the door. I had no more
straws left to clutch.

At the same time, deep, aching stabs of pain in my left leg
transmitted from the bones in my foot and ankle, knitting
themselves back together cell by cell.

"If you have something of Mrs. Rai's that might hold her
DNA," Detective Regan said, "that'll speed up the process.
But we realize that may be impossible after all this time—a
familial DNA match will be our next option."

My mouth opened. "I might have something." I had no
intention of elaborating further in front of my father—what
normal son went into his mother's room and carefully picked
up and bagged her favorite hairbrush? What normal son kept
it all these years?

A son who'd heard a scream.

"In the interim, do either of you recognize this?" Regan
removed a transparent plastic bag from his pocket, sealed
with police tape.

Diamonds glinted within, big and showy.

"I bought her that ring," my father said, his voice gritty. "For our tenth wedding anniversary. Aarav was only seven then."

The same age as the little girl who played in another part of the house. Born three years after the last time I saw my mother alive.

"Happier times," my father added, his head dropping for a moment. "Happier times."

Taking the plastic bag, I touched the ring through it. "She lost a diamond two days before she disappeared." I pointed out the empty spot, so tiny among all the glitter, all those carats. "She was angry because the ring was from an exclusive designer boutique that had guaranteed her the setting wouldn't fail."

She'd yelled at the jewelers on the phone, threatening to destroy them among her set if they didn't fix this "right now." She'd been pacing in our manicured backyard, phone to her ear, while I sat on the back balcony trying to eat a sandwich. In the end, I'd rolled my eyes and taken my meal to my room.

I still remembered how she'd looked, the marigold yellow of her dress silhouetted against the native bush that rose dark green and ancient beyond the flimsy barrier of our fence. As if the forest was watching. Waiting.

Retrieving the ring, the cop said, "We can offer you a liaison officer. There's likely to be intense media interest in this, given your standing in the city."

Regan's eyes were on my father, but Constable Neri's gaze flicked my way. She knew who and what the media would latch onto, what would give them the best headlines, the most clickbait links.

Words came out of my mouth before I was aware of thinking them. "Was it an accident?"

"Of course it was, boy," my father snapped, as if I were still sixteen and not twenty-six. "You know your mother liked to drink." He looked at Regan again. "That's what you're saying, aren't you? That Nina drove off the road into the forest?"

Into the chasm of green, where a car could remain lost for

decades. It had rained that night. So much rain, a torrential storm. Enough to hide the tracks of a car going off the road?

"We can't say either way right now," Regan responded, with no change in his expression as he tucked the evidence bag back inside his jacket. "We'll know more after we complete the forensic investigation."

"I'd like a liaison," I said, before my father could wave away the offer. "I want to know when you find things, before it ends up in the papers." That was why they were here, after all, before the official DNA identification. Someone high up had made the call that Ishaan Rai, CEO of an empire that employed thousands, and best friend to the mayor, should be warned about the sudden reappearance of his first wife.

A wife he'd divorced in her absence.

Regan nodded. "Of course. Constable Neri will be happy to be the liaison."

Neri spoke for the first time, her voice holding a low timbre that was likely put to good effect when soothing distraught relatives. "Here are my details." A card taken from a pants pocket, held out. "Call me anytime."

Taking the card, I slid it away. My father would eventually break out of his paralysis and ask for it, but I wouldn't volunteer it.

"We'll make sure to keep you updated," Regan said. "Please do remember that the investigation is in its very early stages. We're still working the scene."

"I'm coming with you." Hobbling over as fast as the orthopedic moon boot—aka a walking cast—strapped around my fractured bones would permit, I grabbed my outdoor jacket from the hallway closet while Regan was still objecting. "I won't cross the police tape or make a scene. I just want to know where my mother died." Where she'd effectively been buried for ten years.

Regan exchanged a look with Constable Neri before saying, "You can ride with us."

"No, I'll take my car." A rental sedan with an automatic transmission that I could drive with one functional leg. Having my own vehicle would also leave me free to go to other places, begin to dig other graves.

Considering the status of my injury, I grabbed the

crutches I'd propped to one side of the doorway when I went to get my jacket; the surgeon who'd worked on me had given me the go-ahead to start putting my full weight on my foot, but she hadn't told me to go hiking.

"Cautious, Aarav," Dr. Tawera had said after looking at the latest X-rays. "We don't want to negate all your progress to date."

No, *we* fucking didn't.

My father spoke at last. "I'm coming, too."

My chest tightened, my solar plexus crushing in on itself, the reaction one I'd thought I'd long ago conditioned out of myself. "We'll follow you," I said to the cops, then stepped out after them.

My father trailed silently at my back, not remembering his coat even after he stepped out into the chill winter air, the sky a dull gray that flattened the world. I didn't remind him as I headed to the sedan. A dull dark blue with nothing distinctive about it, it wasn't a car I'd have chosen at any other point in my life.

It was nothing like the gleaming black Porsche with its custom metallic paint job currently cooling its heels in the garage of my city apartment. Yeah, the Porsche was a piece of dick-waving assholery, but at least I knew it. I'd bought it when *Blood Sacrifice* turned into a blockbuster book that, in turn, became a blockbuster movie.

Murder and gore.

The world laps it up.

The discovery of my mother's body, even if her death proved to have been accidental—it'd be terrific publicity. My publishers would dance a quiet jig. And all it had cost was the death of a woman of only forty-one.

Chapter 3

MY HANDS TIGHTENED on the wheel as my father got into the passenger seat.

We didn't speak, my eyes on the unmarked police vehicle up ahead. Driven by Constable Neri, it led us out of the leafy gilded surrounds of The Cul-de-Sac and onto a long and winding road bordered by the dense forests of the Waitākere Ranges regional park, with only small hamlets of habitation along the way—and glimpses of breathtaking vistas where the foliage opened up.

Scenic Drive lived up to its name. But only if you weren't expecting pretty and safe.

All that rich green turned parts of the road claustrophobic. It was never searing hot here, not in the cool darkness of the shadows cast by the forest giants. This was a quiet place, a place that whispered that humanity was an intrusion that would be swiftly forgotten once we were gone.

An unexpected flash of white, a large sign at the entrance to a trail warning that the area was under a *rāhui* because of kauri dieback disease. No one was permitted to go on those trails, because the disease spread through the forest on the soles of human shoes, bringing a slow death to trees meant to grow far older than my mother would ever be.

I followed the police car, knowing that if it stopped anywhere on this road, it'd be a spot I'd driven past hundreds of times.

Passing my mother's grave over and over again.

The unmarked car slowed as it turned a corner, and when I followed, I saw flashing lights, road cones, and an orange-vested officer waiting to direct traffic through what had become a single narrow lane.

One of the darkest sections of the road and of the forest.

The land dropped off precipitously to my right, but not into emptiness. Into bush dense and thick and impenetrable to the human eye. Ancient kauri trees, nikau palms, huge tree ferns; this landscape was theirs.

Constable Neri brought the police vehicle to a stop behind a van, and I pulled in behind her. Everyone waited while I got the crutches from the backseat, no one speaking. Armpits snugged into the tops of the walking aids, I nodded, and the cops led us to a part of the road that had no safety barrier against the fall into the green. I couldn't remember if it ever had.

"The car was found at the foot of this incline," Regan told us. "Nose down."

That fit my father's theory of it sliding off the road and down the steep slope into the devouring forest. I wanted to dispute the idea of my mother driving off the road on a rainy night, such a neat and tidy end to everything, but she *had* drunk too much as long as I could remember, and she *could* be a reckless driver.

Of course, if I were the one writing this story, I'd use those very things to cover up a murder. Cover up a scream.

"Why did no one notice?" my father demanded, an edge to his voice that could've been either shock or fear. Maybe both. "There must've been a trail, broken trees, something!" He's using his "I am the CEO" tone.

That's what my mother used to call it.

"Yes, Mr. CEO-ji. No, Mr. CEO-ji."

That honorific "ji" at the end had been the icing on the sarcasm cake. Maybe it had begun in affection, but it had ended in mockery. In truth, I didn't really remember affection between them. Sometimes I remembered a softer voice, less aggressive encounters, but even then, it had been brittle and one fight away from splintering.

My father is a hard man to love. I've never been sure if he even wants love, or if all he wants or needs is obedience. As for returning any affection given, that's a non-event. To Ishaan Rai, his family is his possession. Most specifically his wife. I don't know if my mother was ever happy to be owned, if she began married life compliant and quiet, but the woman I remember hated it with a vengeance.

"At this stage," Regan said, "all I can tell you is that the vehicle is now so well hidden that no one might've seen it for years longer if a DOC survey team hadn't been looking around below. They were checking on the kauri."

The skin of my father's face mottled. He has fair skin, the kind that splotches with anger and is coveted by mothers of Indian brides everywhere. Call it what you will—internalized oppression, a long shadow cast by the British Raj, brutal classism—but my mother had been equally fair, two book-ends in what was meant to be a perfect marriage.

My father's second wife is as dark as teak.

"It rained the night she disappeared," I said before he could launch into one of his tirades. "The rain turned into a storm that crushed fences and trees all over the city." It would've washed away any tire tracks, the resulting citywide carnage making the sight of broken foliage nothing out of the ordinary.

And my mother's car had been a dark green Jaguar.

Such a stunning hue.

So easy to miss in among the deep greens of the forest.

But while I could imagine a single car being swallowed up by the forest, I also knew someone might've helped the forest along. It wouldn't have needed to be much. A few branches thrown over the Jaguar, some vines. Nature would've soon taken over. Especially after all that nourishing rain.

"You have a good memory." Hands in his pants pockets, Regan appeared only idly interested.

I wondered if I was a suspect. After all, sixteen isn't a child. "That was the day my mother vanished. Every minute detail of it is engraved on my memory, along with the days immediately following." Days when I'd still hoped and waited.

"Of course, of course." A glance at Neri.

I didn't care what they thought of me, what conclusions they'd drawn in the car on the way here. I was more interested in what lay below. Even knowing the Jaguar was down there, I couldn't see it.

When the two officers stepped aside to confer with another colleague, I said, "Why did she scream that night, Dad?"

The question lay between us, dark and taunting.

"Know your place, boy," he finally spit out before heading to the sedan.

The keys were still in the ignition, and he started the engine while giving me a challenging look through the windscreen. When I didn't run to heel as he expected, he backed up the vehicle and did a U-turn to return to The Cul-de-Sac.

Such a pretentious name. As if there's only one cul-de-sac in the world, nestled in this isolated and green tributary of Auckland. The name also conjures up images of street parties and block barbecues, when these days, The Cul-de-Sac is a frosty place where opinions are hidden beneath a gauzy layer of politeness, and neighbors keep to themselves.

In my mind, it all changed that night. As if my mother's disappearance took the life out of The Cul-de-Sac.

I'm still standing there staring at the forest long after the sound of the sedan's engine has faded, my mind on the wall of rain that night, how it had been hushed thunder across the world. It was her scream that had woken me, piercing the veil to jerk me to heart-pounding alertness. I hadn't been sure exactly what I'd heard, my pulse a drum in my ears as I waited for more.

I'd almost convinced myself I'd imagined hearing the bang of the front door.

Once. Twice.

Scrambling out of bed, I'd run to the sliding doors that led to my private balcony. But the door had stuck, as it always did when it rained. By the time I stepped out, naked, into the chilling rain, needles of water stabbing my skin, the Jaguar's distinctive taillights were already fading into the rain-blurred distance.